Orange Pulp

ORANGE PULP

Edited by Maurice J. O'Sullivan and Steve Glassman

Stories
of Mayhem,
Murder, and
Mystery

University Press of Florida
GAINESVILLE
TALLAHASSEE
TAMPA
BOCA RATON
PENSACOLA
ORLANDO
MIAMI
JACKSONVILLE
FT. MYERS

05 04 03 02 01 00 6 5 4 3 2

LIBRARY OF CONGRESS CATALOGING-IN-PUBLICATION DATA
Orange pulp: stories of mayhem, murder, and mystery / edited by
Maurice J. O'Sullivan and Steve Glassman.
p. cm.
ISBN 0-8130-1803-x (cloth: alk. paper)
1. Detective and mystery stories, American—Florida.
2. Florida—Fiction. I. O'Sullivan, Maurice. II. Glassman, Steve.
PS648.D4 O73 2000
813'.08720832759—dc21 00-032585

The University Press of Florida is the scholarly publishing
agency for the State University System of Florida, comprising
Florida A&M University, Florida Atlantic University, Florida
International University, Florida State University, University of
Central Florida, University of Florida, University of North
Florida, University of South Florida, University of West
Florida, and Florida Gulf Coast University.

University Press of Florida
15 Northwest 15th Street
Gainesville, FL 32611–2079
http://www.upf.com

Dedicated to the memory of Brendan Aren Micah O'Sullivan, 1977–1999

Contents

Preface

Orange Pulp celebrates murder. It also celebrates the heroes and villains who have shaped what is now the most lethal and successful community of mystery writers in the world. Florida has come a long way from an obscure frontier territory known only for oranges and alligators to the promised land for literary masters of mayhem and murder. Each month seems to bring a fresh series hero or a promising writer hailed as the new Travis McGee or the new Carl Hiaasen, while the old McGee and old Hiaasen continue to make booksellers smile.

As our introduction discusses, Florida's mystery industry did not develop overnight. From the 1930s through the 1960s, a remarkably diverse and talented collection of writers explored shadows in all corners of the sunshine state. Most of those authors learned to write in the pulp magazines, which taught them how to attract and keep audiences. Those who succeeded graduated to novels. As the pulps declined, newer writers got their start in the mass market series of paperback novels. We now regard John D. MacDonald as one of the state's literary icons with a journal and a biannual conference dedicated to his work. But MacDonald, who began his career just as the world of pulps was fading, published some sixty paperback originals before he started finding his works on the best-seller lists.

Even when these writers left the pulps, they carried the spirit of that tradition with its emphasis on tough private eyes, vivid language, and nonstop action into their work. *Orange Pulp* is a tribute to that spirit. From the blazing guns of Carroll John Daly's Race Williams and the unforgiving fists of Brett Halliday's Mike Shayne to the disillusioned ironies of Don Tracy's Francis MacWhalen Coombs and the frustrated idealism of John D. MacDonald's flawed heroes, all of these writers recognized, as Charles Dickens had a century earlier, that the heart of any good story is good storytelling. Even the odd woman out in this collection, Mary Roberts Rinehart, the queen of the "Had I But Known" gothics, learned her craft in the first years of this century by writing stories for popular magazines, including *Argosy*, the very first pulp magazine.

We offer these stories with only one regret, that we could not include a hundred more. And even though the pulp tradition has gained some critical and academic respect in recent years, we hasten to re-assure readers that this stuff is still fun. It should carry you back to a simpler, more appealing time when everybody knew what was right and wrong, when a person's word and integrity counted, and when people of character could solve problems with a little intelligence, a lot of effort, and the judicious use of force. Even if that time never existed in reality, it certainly did in the world of the pulps.

Because we are primarily interested in extracting the best work produced by these writers about Florida, the selections *Orange Pulp* offers take the term "pulp" very broadly. Some, such as Brett Halliday's *Dividend on Death*, Carroll John Daly's *The Hidden Hand*, and Jonathan Latimer's *The Dead Don't Care*, emerge directly from the pulps. Others, such as Stephen Ransome's *The Night, the Woman*, Don Tracy's *The Hated One*, and Charles Willeford's "The First Five in Line," show the possibilities of style and characterization that pulp writers occasionally matured into. And still others, including Ed Granberry's "A Trip to Czardis," Mary Roberts Rinehart's "Murder and the South Wind," and John D. MacDonald's *A Flash of Green*, reveal not only the influence of the pulps but also ways writers in Florida extended traditional forms during that era.

In addition to our appreciation to all of the writers into whose work we can escape from our everyday world of comma splices, vague theses, and split infinitives, we would like to express our thanks to those who have nurtured—or at least suffered—our love of popular culture: our parents, Eugene and Marguerite Glassman and Maurice and Agnes O'Sullivan; our siblings, Philip (Doogie), Mary, Martha, Maureen, and Michael; our families, Susan and Quinn; and our colleagues. We owe a continuing debt to our Florida *noir* collaborators—Julie Sloan Brannon, Sarah Fogle, Ed Hirschberg, Anna Lillios, Harold and Susan Nugent, Ellen Smith, and Lynne Phillips—and to the administrators of our respective colleges who made this project financially possible: Ira Jacobson, academic vice president of Embry-Riddle, and Steve Briggs, dean of the faculty at Rollins. Bill Brubaker's encyclopedic knowledge of Florida's early fiction and his fondness for Jonathan Latimer deserve special thanks. Finally, we thank the three people whose patience and skill helped us with all the physical labor of producing a manuscript: Christine Keenen, Karen Slater, and Jenevieve O'Neal.

Introduction

From the City of Angels to the Magic Kingdom

During the last third of the twentieth century, a curious cultural migration has occurred. The American detective story, centered mythically and literally for most of the century in California, especially in its City of Angels, Los Angeles, has shifted to South Florida, and its capital, Miami, the city *Time* magazine once called "America's Casablanca." From 1930 when Dashiell Hammett's Sam Spade first appeared in *The Maltese Falcon,* through the work of James M. Cain, Raymond Chandler, and Ross MacDonald, California writers dominated the archetypal American, hard-boiled school of detectives. Today, however, the popularity of writers like Carl Hiaasen, Elmore Leonard, James Hall, and Edna Buchanan reflects the cross-country shift. And when established northeastern urban novelists such as Ed McBain and Lawrence Sanders chose to develop new series, they looked south to Florida rather than west to California.

The four factors that seem to have had the most significant influence on this shift are the state's explosive post–World War II population growth, the appearance of John D. MacDonald's Travis McGee in 1964, the popularity of the *Miami Vice* television series from 1984 through 1989, and the slow but steady rise of a group of mystery writers in Florida during the middle third of the century. As the state's population soared from some two and a half million in 1950 to almost fifteen million today, a combination of the space program, the growing sophistication of Central Florida's tourist attractions, and South Florida's fascinating experiments in ethnicity made people notice a complex phenomenon occurring in the state. And as concerns about crime grew, fueled by startling statistics and political opportunism, Miami came to symbolize America's heart of darkness. With its fluid population, ethnic diversity, flexible morality, and subtropical setting, at the end of the American century Miami seemed a much more substantial site for vice than did a city nicknamed Tinseltown.

The least explored factor in the rise of a detective-mystery industry in Florida is the development of a broad base of mystery writers in the state, especially during the 1930s, 1940s, and 1950s. Although John D. MacDonald clearly catalyzed attention, his work built on a tradition that had been firmly established, primarily in pulp magazines, as he reinvented that tradition for a new, post-pulp audience. The astonishing growth of mysteries set in the state during the past thirty years is a tribute not only to him but to that heritage. Although pulps did not reach their prime until after World War I, their roots stretch back to the middle of the previous century. When the publisher Beadle and Adams began printing dime novels during the Civil War, it started a tradition of providing popular fiction for mass audiences. In 1889 its rival Street and Smith, which had offered inexpensive fiction since the 1850s, began its own dime novel series. These paper-covered accounts of the progress of the indomitable Horatio Alger, the western adventures of Deadwood Dick and Calamity Jane, and the urban exploits of detective Nick Carter feature formulaic action heroes rarely given to reflection or complexity. (Incidentally, Nick Carter, the master of disguises who first appeared in the September 18, 1886, issue of the *New York Weekly* and became one of the few heroes of dime fiction to survive as dime novels evolved through pulpwood magazines into paperback novel series, after more than one thousand adventures, finally visited the Sunshine State eighty years later as a fairly mature, James Bondish spy in *Danger Key*.)

When Frank A. Munsey changed his children's magazine *The Golden Argosy* into an adult magazine of mass fiction called *Argosy* around the turn of the new century, he began printing it on rough wood-pulp paper to save costs. Although this short-fibered, high-acid-content paper made from ground wood was cheap, it eventually proved fragile and difficult to preserve compared to the slick paper stock traditionally used for magazines. Critics quickly attached the same adjective to both the medium and the content, as Quentin Tarantino affectionately noted in his 1995 tribute, *Pulp Fiction*. After World War I, the pulps replaced dime novels so rapidly that the two dozen or so pulps in 1919 had become several hundred by the 1930s.

Although many of these new magazines focused on a single popular literary genre from romances and westerns to horror and science fiction, others included stories and serialized novels across a range of genres. The most famous of all, *Black Mask*, for example, was originally subtitled "An Illustrated Magazine of Detective, Mystery, Adventure, Romance, and Spiritualism," even though "Westerns" soon replaced "Spiritualism" in the title. Much of the most memorable writing appeared in mystery magazines with titles that advertised their affordability and sensational nature, titles including *Dime Detective, Ace-High Detective,* and *Rapid-Fire Detective Stories.*

Although prices rose throughout the 1920s when pulps developed a fairly standard format as 112- to 144-page, seven-by-ten-inch magazines with bright covers of more expensive coated stock, the Great Depression forced the price of many of them back to a dime. The enormous growth and popularity of the pulps created a need for writers to fill their pages and, in turn, provided those writers who could do so quickly, consistently, and entertainingly with large audiences and regular incomes. As writers such as Dashiell Hammett, Erle Stanley Gardner, and Raymond Chandler moved from stories to novels, they often continued to be seen as essentially pulp writers. Just as the pulps had replaced the Victorian dime novel, the pulps themselves began to disappear in the early 1950s with the rising popularity of paperbacks and television. When Pocket Books began expanding its paperback reprint series beyond the polite cozies of Agatha Christie and the elegantly plotted mazes of Dorothy Sayers to include novels by Gardner and Hammett, the pulp audience found the new format more convenient and only slightly more expensive.

Despite attempts to trace the mystery novel back to Hamlet searching for his father's murderer, Oedipus unraveling the mystery of Thebes, or even God questioning Adam and Eve's acts and motives in Eden, most readers and scholars date the detective story as we know it from the appearance of Edgar Allan Poe's "The Murders in the Rue Morgue" in the April 1841 issue of *Graham's Magazine.* Poe's elegantly ratiocinative creation, C. Auguste Dupin, established a model for the form by approaching those murders, as well as the subsequent "The Mystery of Marie Roget" and "The Purloined Letter," as intellectual and scientific problems rather than moral ones, relying primarily on a combination of intuition and logic, the ability to sort the significant from the superficial, and an unwavering confidence in his own abilities. As crime replaced sin and aesthetic and social concerns edged out moral and theological issues, the detective novel would be able to evolve through characters like Dickens's Inspector Bucket in *Bleak House* (1852) and Wilkie Collins's Sergeant Cuff in *The Moonstone* (1868) to Arthur Conan Doyle's brilliantly realized Sherlock Holmes, who permanently defined the model of the ideal detective with his first case, *A Study in Scarlet,* in 1887.

Doyle's successors, unable simply to resurrect the idiosyncratic consulting detective with his deerstalker cap, magnifying glass, and calabash pipe, began experimenting with equally eccentric figures (for example, G. K. Chesterton's Father Brown, Melville Davisson Post's Virginia squire Uncle Abner, and S. S. Van Dine's Philo Vance), an even greater emphasis on the logic of detection (for example, R. Austin Freeman's Dr. John Thorndyke and Jacques Futrelle's Thinking Machine, Professor S. F. X. Van Dusen), variations in style and plot (for example, Edmund Clerihew Bentley, Freeman Wills Crofts, and Gaston Leroux), or, in many cases, some combination of all of these (for example, Agatha Christie, Georges Simenon, and Dorothy Sayers). The enormous popularity of detective stories in England, France, and the United States encouraged a wide variety of writers to build more elaborate puzzles and search for more satisfying heroes and heroines.

One major innovation to the form would come from the emerging world of pulp magazines in the United States. When journalist H. L. Mencken and drama critic George Jean Nathan found their slick, sophisticated magazine *The Smart Set* in financial trouble after World War I, they decided to use popular culture, which they disdained, to subsidize their vision of higher culture. After experimenting with pulp magazines such as *Parisienne* and *Saucy Stories,* Mencken and Nathan started *Black Mask* on April 20, 1920. They soon sold it for a significant profit, and the new owners and editors began searching for a distinctive voice for the magazine with a logo featuring a masked Satan. In the May 15, 1923, issue, Carroll John Daly discovered that voice with "Three Gun Terry," a crisply written story about tough

Terry Mack surviving in a cold, unforgiving world. The following month Daly introduced Race Williams, a hard-boiled hero who would continue his adventures and become in 1927, with *The Snarl of the Beast*, the first of these new heroes to appear in a novel. Two years later, in his fifth novel, Williams would sail south to Miami to confront the Hidden Hand gang. Once Daly created a new, harder-edged hero, other writers began exploring the possibilities of this new Jazz Age style, most notably Dashiell Hammett, whose Continental Op first appeared in *Black Mask* in October 1923.

This new American detective clearly owed a deep debt to the pulps' fascination with adventure stories, especially westerns. As his urban landscape came to resemble more a lawless frontier than the comfortingly familiar London of Holmes, the detective needed to rely more on his own resources than on traditional social structures to establish some semblance of order and justice. And his language recreated the terse, colorful jargon of the city. In his essay "The Simple Art of Murder," Raymond Chandler, one of the form's most adept practitioners, described the limitations of traditional mysteries while paying homage to Dashiell Hammett's role in establishing a new model:

> Hammett wrote at first (and almost to the end) for people with a sharp, aggressive attitude to life. They were not afraid of the seamy side of things; they lived there. Violence did not dismay them; it was right down their street. Hammett gave murder back to the kind of people that commit it for reasons, not just to provide a corpse; and with the means at hand, not with hand-wrought dueling pistols, curare, and tropical fish. He put these people down on paper as they are, and he made them talk and think in the language they customarily used for these purposes. He had style, but his audience didn't know it, because it was in a language not supposed to be capable of such refinements. They thought they were getting a good meaty melodrama written in the kind of lingo they imagined they spoke themselves. It was, in a sense, but it was much more.
> . . . In his hands it had no overtones, left no echo, evoked no image beyond a distant hill.
> He is said to have lacked heart, yet the story he thought most of himself is the record of a man's devotion to a friend. He was spare,

frugal, hard-boiled, but he did over and over again what only the best writers can ever do at all. He wrote scenes that seemed never to have been written before. (pp. 14–15)

In ending his essay with a powerful, if slightly sentimentalized, description of the new detective, Chandler evoked an Emersonian hero as the new American Adam struggling for truth in a decidedly post-lapsarian Eden:

> In everything that can be called art there is a quality of redemption. It may be pure tragedy, if it is high tragedy, and it may be pity and irony, and it may be the raucous laughter of the strong man. But down these mean streets a man must go who is not himself mean, who is neither tarnished nor afraid. The detective in this story must be such a man. He is the hero, he is everything. He must be a complete man and a common man and yet an unusual man. He must be, to use a rather weathered phrase, a man of honor, by instinct, by inevitability, without thought of it, and certainly without saying it. He must be the best man in his world and a good enough man for any world. I do not care much about his private life; he is neither a eunuch nor a satyr; I think he might seduce a duchess and I am quite sure he would not spoil a virgin. If he is a man of honor in one thing, he is in all things.
>
> He is a relatively poor man, or he would not be a detective at all. He is a common man or he could not go among common people. He has a sense of character, or he would not know his job. He will take no man's money dishonestly and no man's insolence without a due and dispassionate revenge. He is a lonely man and his pride is that you will treat him as a proud man or be very sorry you ever saw him. He talks as the man of his age talks, that is, with rude wit, a lively sense of the grotesque, a disgust for sham, and a contempt for pettiness.
>
> The story is his adventure in search of a hidden truth, and it would be no adventure if it did not happen to a man fit for adventure. He has a range of awareness that startles you, but it belongs to him by right, because it belongs to the world he lives in. If there were enough like him, I think the world would be a very safe place to live in, and yet not too dull to be worth living in. (p. 18)

While various critics have tried to distinguish multiple forms of detective novels, the form essentially divides, as critics including John Cawelti and Howard Haycraft have pointed out, between those which emphasize the mystery, the puzzle, the detection and those which focus on a violent confrontation. The former generally envision a world that is essentially just and sane but temporarily out of kilter because of some act that has disrupted society. It is the job of the detective either to identify the person who has committed the act or to provide the evidence that will allow that person to be removed so that society can return to normal. Excessive violence would only challenge the very foundations of those societies. For the latter detectives, however, the pursuit must physically engage the hero and require some personal commitment. Because traditional forces of order in such books appear both corrupt and corrupting, the hero must establish a personal vision of justice and resolve the problem according to that vision. Since the appearance of the American hard-boiled heroes in the 1920s, writers have had to choose between the two branches or attempt some reconciliation of them.

Even though for many readers Florida's detective history begins with Travis McGee's birth in 1964, others push that date back a quarter century to the last year of the 1930s, when another South Florida detective, Mike Shayne, opened his Miami office. In fact, we can actually trace the lineage of these two detectives back to 1896, when U.S. Revenue detective Thomas Duff Mastic attempted to establish law and order among the notorious smugglers and wreckers of Key West. Mastic's exploits epitomize the ideal resourceful frontier hero popularized in Victorian America's dime novels.

Detective and mystery novels about America's southernmost contiguous state appeared slowly but regularly with the beginning of the twentieth century. English author Bessie Marchant's *The Secret of the Everglades* (1902) and Edward H. Hurst's *Mystery Island* (1907) offer mysteries barely more challenging than those Wilmer Ely has his adolescent adventurers encounter in *The Boy Chums Cruising Florida Waters* (1914). The Boy Chums resolve problems in much the same way as their spiritual heirs, the Hardy Boys, who themselves would visit Florida in 1980 to solve *The Mystery of the Smuggler's*

Cave. In 1914, the same year that the Boy Chums nonchalantly sailed Florida's waterways, Earl Derr Biggers offered a more sophisticated, satirical vision of fraud in *Love Insurance*. More than a decade before he began creating the six Hawaii-based Charlie Chan novels, Biggers reveals a similar fascination with the equally exotic and fluid culture of St. Augustine, which appears under the *nom de fortress* of San Marco.

The 1920s were framed by two action-oriented adventure stories, A. Stone's comprehensively titled *Fighting Byng: A Novel of Mystery, Intrigue, and Adventure* in 1919 and Carroll John Daly's account of Race Williams's trip to Miami to destroy the notorious Florida gang known as *The Hidden Hand* in 1929. In 1920, however, the same year that *Black Mask* first appeared, Florida gained its first series detective, Eric Levison's Dr. Edward Lester. This Jacksonville physician, modeled on Levison's friend Dr. Hermann H. Harris, uses his medical training and social connections in crisply and efficiently resolving three fairly conventional cases: *Hidden Eyes* (1920), *The Eye Witness* (1921), and *Ashes of Evidence* (1921). For the remainder of one of the state's most tumultuous decades, as its economy ballooned with enormous land speculation only to see the bubble burst in the deadly hurricane of 1926, mysteries followed the state's fortunes in ranging from tales of hidden treasure (for example, the twin 1922 novels Absalom Martin's *Kastle Krags* and Albert Payson Terhune's *Black Caesar's Clan*) and conspicuous consumption (Arthur Somers Roche's *The Pleasure Buyers* [1925]) to the melancholic romantic adventures of Lydia de Bechevet's *Mystery of the Twisted Man* (1927) and Josephine Chase's *The Mark of the Red Diamond* (1929).

While the early 1930s followed the pattern established in the 1920s, one notable novel appeared in 1933, Wesley Price's *Death Is a Stowaway*. Miami detective James Wick lives in the same unsentimental, brusque world as Dashiell Hammett's Continental Op. Four years later Ernest Hemingway incorporated a couple of previously published Florida stories into the only novel which he set in the continental United States, *To Have and Have Not*. Hemingway's account of the decaying fortunes and misadventures of fishing guide Harry Morgan in the waters off Key West captures both the tone and values of the hard-boiled school while, at the same time, showing its potential for tragedy as well as adventure.

But 1936 proved to be the seminal year for the Florida mystery novel. That year Dennis Wheatley produced the first of his four police dossiers, *Murder off Miami*, a work which provided all the evidence necessary to solve a crime, including photos, letters, personal statements, and bits of physical evidence. While this work may be the purest police procedural ever published, that same year two Florida series detectives appeared. Baynard Hardwick Kendrick, who had followed Eric Levison's lead two years earlier by using a physician-detective in a complex case of counterfeiting and murder among the state's citrus magnates in *Blood on Lake Louisa*, introduced Deputy Sheriff Stan Rice ("I'm Miles Standish Rice—the Hungry!") in *The Iron Spiders* and *The Eleven of Diamonds*. An innovator as the creator of the Duncan Maclain mysteries and one of the first mystery writers in the Dell paperback Mapbook series with their depictions of crime scenes on the back covers, capsule character descriptions in the introductions, and vivid teasers, Kendrick eventually promoted Stan Rice to an investigator for the state attorney's office in *Death beyond the Go-Thru* (1938).

Far better known than either Wheatley or Kendrick, Theodore Pratt, whose most famous novel, *The Barefoot Mailman* (1943), is the first book in his Palm Beach trilogy, assumed the pen name Timothy Brace that same year to create the millionaire sportsman Anthony Adams, an elegant, slightly idiosyncratic amateur in the tradition of Lord Peter Wimsey, Philo Vance, and the cinematic rather than fictional Nick and Nora Charles. With the help of his faithful manservant, Thurber, Adams solves three mysteries with characteristically Floridian settings: *Murder Goes Fishing* (1936), *Murder Goes in a Trailer* (1937), and *Murder Goes to the Dogs* (1938).

Florida's distinctive environment and culture play an even larger role in Jonathan Latimer's *The Dead Don't Care* (1938). When Latimer's William Crane takes an assignment in Miami and Key West, the Chicago P.I. finds himself in a frighteningly alien environment of menacing flamingos, tropical gardens, and exotic neighbors. In 1939, Canadian writer Rufus King, who had, like so many of his countrymen, relocated to Florida, moved his New York police detective Lieutenant Valcour south for *Murder Masks Miami*. The Valcour series, which began a decade earlier and was much admired by Ellery Queen, a contemporary whose first book also appeared in 1929, follows the puzzle mystery tradition with an emphasis on interviews and analysis rather than action and confrontation. Even more significant, 1939 also saw the emergence of Florida's first best-selling detective series when Davis Dresser, writing as Brett Halliday, opened the Miami office of Mike Shayne to investigate a *Dividend on Death*. In more than seventy novels the tough redhead, with one hand reaching for a bottle of cognac and the other beckoning to his compliant secretary, Lucy Hamilton, helped make South Florida a pulp heaven.

Maxwell Grant's The Shadow slipped into the state seven times to foil an ethnic mix of gangs from *The Yellow Band* (1937) to Nazis in the belated *Five Keys to Crime* (1945), while Leslie Charteris's debonair Simon Templar materialized in *The Saint in Miami* (1940). Some decades later, their spiritual descendant, Donald Hamilton's master spy, Matt Helm, would spend a decade in the state ranging the coast from Pensacola (*The Shadowers* [1964]) to the Bermuda Triangle (*The Intimidators* [1974]). Like Nick Carter, many of these pulp series are the products of teams of writers working from a master outline. The Shadow series, for example, includes some 326 novels, all but one published originally in *The Shadow* magazine by Street and Smith under the pen name Maxwell Grant. Although the series had a number of authors, the primary one was Walker Gibson, who wrote 282 of the stories, or about fifteen million words.

In the years after Mike Shayne arrived, three followers of the distinctively American tradition of Hammett and Chandler created a series of memorable works with tough heroes searching for truth in a rotten and rotting world. George Harmon Coxe's *Inland Passage* (1949) and *Never Bet Your Life* (1952) suggest perfect vehicles for Bogart and Cagney. Like many of the early *noir* writers, Frederick Clyde Davis honed his craft with a thousand stories in pulp magazines such as *Black Mask, Detective Tales,* and *Dime Mystery*. Although he used numerous pseudonyms, writing under the *nom de crime* Stephen Ransome he produced a series of Florida-based thrillers beginning with *I'll Die for You* in 1959. His most frequent character, Lee Barcello, a state's attorney investigator like Baynard Kendrick's Stan Rice, generally plays the foil in finding that even those who are not guilty are rarely innocent in novels with such classic *noir* titles as *The Night, the Woman* (1963), *Alias His Wife* (1965), and *Trap #6* (1971). Donald Tracy's harder-edged novels do not always rely on the kind of outwardly respectable characters who fill Ransome's books. From the alcoholic, cracker charter boat captain in *The Big Blackout* (1959) to the grizzled Greek sponge divers of *Bazzaris* (1965), Tracy shows a flair for punchy dialogue and convincing local color. His finest achievement, however, is *The Hated One* (1963), a hard-boiled deconstruction of *To Kill a Mockingbird* that replaces Harper Lee's idealized Atticus Finch with a disbarred attorney "presently part-time bill collector, part-time gas station attendant, fulltime ginhead."

In a more classical vein, Mignon Eberhart used Florida for three elegantly plotted books which reflect her strong sense of place (*Unidentified Woman* [1943], *The White Dress* [1945], and *Another Man's Murder* [1957]); Lee Thayer brought her series detective, Peter Clancy, to Florida's lake country to solve an academic murder in *Five Bullets* (1944); the revered queen of American mystery writers, Mary Roberts Rinehart, used her winter home on the exclusive Gulf Coast resort of Useppa Island as the setting for a story, "Murder and the South Wind," in *Good Housekeeping* in 1944; and Britain's prolific John Creasey, author of more than five hundred mysteries, sent his relentlessly bourgeois Chief Superintendent Richard West on a transatlantic case in *Murder, London-Miami* (1969). A very different kind of classic appeared in 1965 when Donn Pearce, a U.S. Merchant Marine officer, drew on his experience in a Florida prison to tell the grimly realistic story of Lloyd Douglas, an amiable drifter who cannot accept authority and wins the prison nickname Cool Hand Luke.

During the 1950s the paperback original came of age, and its acknowledged king was St. Petersburg–residing, Ocala-born Harry Whittington. Whittington quit his job as a mail carrier in 1948 to embark on the perilous career of a full-time writer. Fawcett's Gold Medal paperbacks and other markets such as Avon and Handicraft seemed to have an insatiable appetite for what he produced. For twenty years Whittington drove Cadillacs, doused himself with Canoe cologne, and sported Hickey-Freeman jackets. Suddenly, in the 1960s, after 140 novels, publishers quit buying his work and creditors clamored at his door. Today he is best remembered in France, whose *Magazine Littéraire* has called him "one of the masters of the *roman noir* in the second generation—after Hammett, Chandler, Cain of the first generation."

After getting his start in the pulps, John D. MacDonald experimented through the 1950s with a series of mysteries which combined brisk action and ironic environmental and social commentary. His early mysteries and thrillers, like *The Brass Cupcake* (1950), *Murder in the Wind* (1956), and *A Flash of Green* (1962), introduce themes of natural disaster and human corruption which would appear both in the Travis McGee series and in such best-sellers as *Condominium* (1977), his warning about the ecological and human risks involved in developing the barrier islands. In *The Deep Blue Goodbye* (1964), MacDonald unveiled Florida's most famous knight-errant, Travis McGee. Living just off the edge of his fading paradise, on an elaborate houseboat, the *Busted Flush,* moored at Slip F-18, Bahia Mar Marina, Fort Lauderdale, McGee operates an extralegal salvage business, collecting 50 percent of whatever he recovers to finance his frequently interrupted early retirement. In twenty-one colorfully titled mysteries from *Bright Orange for the Shroud* (1965) and *Darker Than Amber* (1966) to *The Dreadful Lemon Sky* (1974) and *The Lonely Silver Rain* (1985), the tough but vulnerable McGee mounts his electric-blue Rolls Royce pickup, *Miss Agnes,* to battle evil.

MacDonald reinvented the hard-boiled American mystery by allowing his hero to explore his own emotional relationships while investigating the environmental and social corruption of a potential paradise. Recognizing that to preserve his innocence the hero must avoid fully confronting maturity, MacDonald grafted an appealing protagonist onto well-crafted stories filled with compelling villains and a fascinating supporting cast. Unlike the worlds of Hammett and Chandler, where only their protagonists' unbending integrity anchors a world layered with betrayal and dissolution, McGee preserves some shreds of innocence on his boat moored just east of Eden and, under the tutelage of his guru, Meyer, holds out a slim promise of redemption and renewal.

Perhaps even more than his influence on the form, MacDonald's popularity inspired a broad range of writers to follow his lead in exploring the possibilities of crime fiction in the sunshine state. In 1978 Ed McBain, the pseudonym novelist Evan Hunter adopted to create a highly regarded series of carefully and realistically detailed police procedurals set in the 87th precinct of a fictional northeastern city startlingly similar to New York, began developing a series revolving around a lawyer, Matthew Hope, set in a fictional West Coast Florida community disturbingly similar to Sarasota. Recasting classic fairy tales and children's rhymes from *Goldilocks* (1978) to *There Was a Little Girl* (1994) as violently erotic and graphically realistic murder mysteries, McBain explores the ways such childhood memories symbolically reenact inevitable human and psychological conflicts. Although Charles Willeford, a former editor of the *Alfred Hitchcock Mystery Magazine* and author of more than a dozen and a half paperback originals, had published the fascinating *noir* character study of an amoral West Palm Beach art critic, *The Burnt Orange Heresy*, in 1971, it was not until the middle of the next decade that he began his blackly comic series about a balding, toothless Miami Police sergeant, Hoke Moseley, in the elegantly titled *Miami Blues* (1984). In the midst of his search for comfortable dentures, a reasonably priced place to live, and an inexpensive wardrobe to replace his leisure suits, Moseley confronts a parade of criminal sociopaths and bureaucratic psychopaths.

Equally adept at capturing the bizarrely dark comedy of South Florida have been two major best-selling novelists, Elmore Leonard and Carl Hiaasen. Working in the tradition of Damon Runyon, whose four stories about Florida's gamblers and juke joints appeared in *Runyon a la Carte* (1946), Elmore Leonard began moving his memorable dialogue and idiosyncratic rogues from his chilly native Detroit to South Florida's glittering warmth in his 1980 *Gold Coast*. In a world in which the boundaries of law seem as transient as the population, Leonard recognizes that *Rum Punch*'s bail bondsman Max Cherry might easily have far more integrity than the fire-and-brimstone judge *Maximum Bob*. Mixing a strong dose of Southern gothic into the same tradition, *Miami Herald* columnist Carl Hiaasen has written a series of novels detailing the dismantling of paradise. In *Tourist Sea-*

son (1986), a terrorist gang offers a lethal solution to the tourist problem; in *Skin Tight* (1989), plastic surgeons offer a cosmetic fountain of horrors; and in *Native Tongue* (1991), an ex-governor turned eco-terrorist decides to dismantle a new theme park.

A colleague of Hiaasen on the *Herald*, Edna Buchanan has drawn on her work as a Pulitzer Prize–winning crime reporter for more optimistic but equally vivid novels about her mildly neurotic alter ego, investigative crime reporter Britt Montero. An archetypal Miamian as the offspring of a WASP and a Cuban executed by Castro, Montero draws on her knowledge of the city's distinctive ethnic stew in novels such as *Contents under Pressure* (1992) and *Miami, It's Murder* (1994) to solve racial and sexual crimes while negotiating tricky gender issues both in the pressroom and on the street. The most prolific of the state's female mystery writers, T. J. MacGregor, who has also published under her maiden name, Trish Janeshutz, and the pseudonym Alison Drake, has also set her major series in Miami. With the occasional touches of New Age spiritualism (for example, *Blue Pearl* [1994]) that appear so often in her Alison Drake novels (for example, *Tango Key* [1988]), MacGregor's protagonists, private detectives Quin St. James and Michael (Mac) McCleary, find themselves unraveling both fairly traditional cases and a fairly untraditional personal relationship (for example, *Death Sweet* [1988]).

With its overlapping patchwork of sensuous and mobile cultures, Miami has continued to attract mystery writers through the 1990s. A former prosecutor, Barbara Parker, debuted her ex-debutante, current civil litigator, and sometime detective Gail Connor in *Suspicion of Innocence* (1994) and developed her through a series of personal and professional crises, while Carolina Garcia-Aguilera, a detective herself, created the intensely loyal Cuban-American female detective Lupe Solano in *Bloody Waters* (1996). Paul Levine and Les Standiford have also introduced Miami detectives fairly recently. Levine's flashy Miami Dolphin linebacker turned trial lawyer, Jake Lassiter, investigates cases with a distinctively Florida flavor, such as the windsurfing in *Slashback* (1995), unlike Standiford's low-key contractor John Deal, who reluctantly but effectively finds himself battling a range of voracious developers (for example, *Deal on Ice* [1997]).

If Miami appeals to an urban *noir* sensibility, its southern neighbor, the Keys, mixes psychology, comedy, and murder with coral reefs and bonefishing. Poet James Hall has had his prickly hero Thorn, a somewhat ambivalent loner, wander a darkly Freudian geography in search of his identity (*Tropical Freeze* [1989]) or an elusive personal justice (*Mean High Tide* [1994]). Former longshoreman W. R. Philbrick and Paul Leslie show their affection for the Keys in their detailed accounts of people and places, while Laurence Shames explores the cultural conflicts that arise when New York mobsters and wannabes decide to invade Key West in a series of comic novels beginning with the ironically titled *Florida Straits* (1992).

A fascination with the state's edges also marks the ecomysteries of Sanibel's Randy Wayne White. A fishing guide who developed a cult following while writing essays for *Outside* magazine, White uses his hero, Marion "Doc" Ford, an ex-NSA operative with a doctorate in marine biology, to collect marine specimens and expose a wide range of environmental and social threats to life in contemporary Florida. From his introductory *Sanibel Flats* (1990) to *The Man Who Invented Florida* (1993), a fascinating history of the state disguised as a bittersweet mystery, White offers a surprisingly hopeful survey of our fragile human and physical ecologies.

When best-seller Lawrence Sanders decided to write about Palm Beach, he abandoned the hard-edged, ironic heroes of his earlier works for the narcissistic, foppish playboy Archie McNally, whose speech, lifestyle, and affect owe more to Bertie Wooster than to Lord Peter Wimsey. Between cocktails at the club and dinner among the glitterati, Archie steals a few hours to help his father's law firm resolve crises among the affluent in his eponymous series (for example, *McNally's Caper* [1993], *McNally's Puzzle* [1996]). In contrast to Archie's casual elegance and freedom from physical injury, John Lutz and Kevin Robinson have created physically crippled heroes working a far darker world. Lutz's private detective Fred Carver, an Orlando detective sergeant who retires to the Atlantic Coast after his kneecap is shattered during a routine grocery store robbery, methodically solves the kinds of cases, such as the bombing of abortion clinics in *Lightning* (1996), that Disney would prefer not exist in a territory that stretches from Orlando's Magic Kingdom to Daytona's neon beaches. Robinson's Stick Foster, a wheelchair-bound *Orlando Sentinel* reporter, leads readers into worlds most people know little about, from the adolescent *Mall Rats* (1992) to Orlando's wheelchair basketball teams.

Completely outside Florida's urban sprawl are two panhandle writers, Mickey Friedman and Geoffrey Norman. Friedman's fairly unusual mysteries, from *Hurricane Season* (1983) to *Riptide* (1994), examine a Faulknerian South of moonshine stills and religious fanatics in which plot invariably takes second place to character. Norman, a prolific contributor to magazines ranging from *National Geographic* and *Forbes* to *Sports Illustrated* and *Playboy,* has reinvented Travis McGee as Morgan Hunt, a not always so good old boy living simply on a sluggish North Florida river with his coon dog and Cajun girlfriend. When he is not protecting his cracker Eden from a range of predators, Hunt occasionally leaves on missions like the one in *Blue Chipper* (1993) in which he helps a rising basketball star.

Amid the proliferation of series, South Florida has also had a rich tapestry of individual works that deal with some aspect of crime. Thomas McGuane sketches an existential duel between bonefish guides in *Ninety-Two in the Shade* (1973); Joy Williams portrays a young couple systematically stealing the homes and lives of families from the panhandle to the Keys in *Breaking and Entering* (1981); Pulitzer Prize–winner Alison Lurie brings a biographer to Key West's Old Town to uncover the mystery at the heart of her subject in *The Truth about Lorin Jones* (1988); Thomas Sanchez has his characters discover truths about a killer terrorizing Key West and themselves in the cemetery at the heart of America's southernmost city in *Mile Zero* (1989); and Peter Matthiessen reimagines an historical case of community justice in the Everglades in the highly acclaimed *Killing Mr. Watson* (1990).

While many of the novels of the 1970s, 1980s, and 1990s are widely available in paperback and libraries, Florida's earlier mysteries are much more difficult to obtain. Copies of those out-of-print works which still exist have suffered from the ravages of time and climate on their cheap paper stock. The few excellent examples which survive are generally locked away for preservation or as investments. *Orange Pulp* reintroduces classic examples of those works, novels and stories from the 1930s through the early 1970s that established the Florida mystery and prepared the way for the Leonards and Hiaasens, the McBains and Buchanans. Our title pays homage not only to our state but to those magazines in which most of these writers learned how to tell a story. Our goal in this anthology is not so much to be comprehensive as to give readers a good taste of the richness of this heritage. We hope this taste will encourage in readers an appetite for more of these writers and their works. We have included one complete novel, Don Tracy's extraordinary study of race and culture, *The Hated One*. To complement Tracy's work and suggest the range of Florida's early crime fiction, we have brought together the previously unpublished opening to a novel by Charles Willeford, Edwin Granberry's "A Trip to Czardis," winner of the O. Henry award, and Mary Roberts Rinehart's only Florida story, "Murder and the South Wind." And we have also included the first chapters of Brett Halliday's earliest Mike Shayne novel, *Dividend on Death*, and Stephen Ransome's *The Night, the Woman*, along with three fairly self-contained sections from novels that helped pulp writers focus on Florida: Carroll John Daly's *The Hidden Hand*, Jonathan Latimer's *The Dead Don't Care*, and John D. MacDonald's *A Flash of Green*. While there are dozens more authors we would love to include, we believe these works offer readers an excellent start to exploring the rich and diverse world of mystery literature in the sunshine state.

Note

While an earlier version of some of this material appeared in *The Book Lover's Guide to Florida*, edited by Kevin McCarthy (Pineapple Press, 1992), the editors are also indebted to their colleagues who contributed chapters to *Crime Fiction and Film in the Sunshine State: Florida Noir* (Popular Press, 1997).

Works Cited

Biggers, Earl Derr. *Love Insurance*. Indianapolis: Bobbs-Merrill, 1914.
Brace, Timothy. See Pratt, Theodore.
Buchanan, Edna. *Contents under Pressure*. New York: Hyperion, 1992.
———. *Miami, It's Murder*. New York: Hyperion, 1994.
Carter, Nick. *Danger Key*. New York: Universal-Award, 1966.

Cawelti, John. *Adventure, Mystery, and Romance: Formula Stories as Art and Popular Culture.* Chicago: University of Chicago Press, 1976.

Chandler, Raymond. "The Simple Art of Murder." In *The Simple Art of Murder.* New York: Houghton and Mifflin, 1950. Rpt. New York: Random House, 1988.

Charteris, Leslie. *The Saint in Miami.* Garden City: Doubleday, 1940.

Chase, Josephine. *The Mark of the Red Diamond.* Philadelphia: Penn, 1929.

Collins, William Wilkie. *The Moonstone.* London: Watts, 1868.

Coxe, George Harmon. *Inland Passage.* New York: Knopf, 1949.

———. *Never Bet Your Life.* New York: Knopf, 1952.

Creasey, John. *Murder, London-Miami.* New York: Scribner, 1969.

Daly, Carroll John. *The Hidden Hand.* New York: Clode, 1929.

———. *The Snarl of the Beast.* New York: Clode, 1927.

Davis, Frederick Clyde. See Ransome, Stephen.

de Bechevet, Lydia. *Mystery of the Twisted Man.* New York: Grafton, 1927.

Dickens, Charles. *Bleak House.* London: Bradbury and Evans, 1852.

Dixon, Franklin. *The Mystery of Smuggler's Cave.* New York: Wanderer/Simon and Schuster, 1980.

Doyle, Arthur Conan. *A Study in Scarlet. Beeton's Christmas Annual.* London: Ward, Lock, 1887.

Drake, Alison. See MacGregor, T. J.

Dresser, Davis. See Halliday, Brett.

Eberhart, Mignon. *Another Man's Murder.* Roslyn: Black, 1957.

———. *Unidentified Woman.* New York: Random, 1943.

———. *The White Dress.* New York: Random, 1945.

Ely, Wilmer. *The Boy Chums Cruising Florida Waters.* New York: Burt, 1914.

Friedman, Mickey. *Hurricane Season.* New York: Dutton, 1983.

———. *Riptide.* New York: Saint Martin's, 1994.

Garcia-Aguilera, Carolina. *Bloody Waters.* New York: Putnam, 1996.

Glassman, Steve, and Maurice O'Sullivan. *Crime Fiction and Film in the Sunshine State: Florida Noir.* Bowling Green, Ohio: Popular Press, 1997.

Grant, Maxwell. *Five Keys to Crime.* New York: Street and Smith, 1945.

———. *The Yellow Band.* New York: Street and Smith, 1937.

Gunter, Archibald Clavering. *Don Blasco of Key West.* New York: Home, 1896.

Hall, James. *Mean High Tide.* New York: Delacorte, 1994.

———. *Tropical Freeze.* New York: Warner, 1989.

Halliday, Brett [pseud. of Davis Dresser]. *Dividend on Death.* New York: Holt, 1939.

Hamilton, Donald. *The Intimidators.* Greenwich: Fawcett, 1974.

———. *The Shadowers.* Greenwich: Fawcett, 1964.

Hammett, Dashiell. *The Maltese Falcon.* New York: Knopf, 1930.

Haycraft, Howard. *Murder for Pleasure.* New York: Appleton- Century, 1941.

Hemingway, Ernest. *To Have and Have Not.* New York: Scribner, 1937.

Hiaasen, Carl. *Native Tongue.* New York: Warner, 1991.

―――. *Skin Tight.* New York: Warner, 1989.

―――. *Tourist Season.* New York: Warner, 1986.

Hurst, Edward H. *Mystery Island.* Boston: Page, 1907.

Kendrick, Baynard Hardwick. *Blood on Lake Louisa.* New York: Greenburg, 1934.

―――. *The Eleven of Diamonds.* New York: Greenburg, 1936.

―――. *The Iron Spiders.* New York: Greenburg, 1936.

King, Rufus. *Murder Masks Miami.* Garden City: Doubleday, Doran, 1939.

Latimer, Jonathan. *The Dead Don't Care.* New York: Doubleday, Doran, 1937.

Lee, Harper. *To Kill a Mockingbird.* Philadelphia: Lippincott, 1960.

Leonard, Elmore. *Gold Coast.* New York: Arbor, 1980.

―――. *Maximum Bob.* New York: Delacorte, 1991.

―――. *Rum Punch.* New York: Delacorte, 1992.

Levine, Paul. *Slashback.* New York: Morrow, 1995.

Levison, Eric. *Ashes of Evidence.* Indianapolis: Bobbs-Merrill, 1921.

―――. *The Eye Witness.* Indianapolis: Bobbs-Merrill, 1921.

―――. *Hidden Eyes.* Indianapolis: Bobbs-Merrill, 1920.

Lurie, Alison. *The Truth about Lorin Jones.* New York: Avon, 1988.

Lutz, John. *Lightning.* New York: Henry Holt, 1996.

MacDonald, John D. *The Brass Cupcake.* New York: Fawcett, 1950.

―――. *Bright Orange for the Shroud.* Greenwich: Fawcett, 1965.

―――. *Condominium.* Philadelphia: Lippincott, 1977.

―――. *Darker Than Amber.* New York: Fawcett, 1966.

―――. *The Deep Blue Goodbye.* New York: Fawcett, 1964.

―――. *The Dreadful Lemon Sky.* Philadelphia: Lippincott, 1974.

―――. *A Flash of Green.* New York: Simon and Schuster, 1962.

―――. *The Lonely Silver Rain.* New York: Knopf, 1985.

―――. *Murder in the Wind.* New York: Dell, 1956.

MacGregor, T[rish] J[aneshutz]. *Blue Pearl.* New York: Hyperion, 1994.

―――. *Death Sweet.* New York: Ballantine, 1988.

―――[as Alison Drake]. *Tango Key.* New York: Ballantine, 1988.

Marchant, Bessie. *The Secret of the Everglades.* London: Blackie, 1902.

Martin, Absalom. *Kastle Krags.* New York: Duffield, 1922.

Matthiessen, Peter. *Killing Mr. Watson.* New York: Random, 1990.

McBain, Ed. *Goldilocks.* New York: Arbor, 1978.

―――. *There Was a Little Girl.* New York: Warner, 1994.

McCarthy, Kevin. *The Book Lover's Guide to Florida.* Sarasota: Pineapple Press, 1992.

McGuane, Thomas. *Ninety-Two in the Shade.* New York: Farrar, 1973.

Norman, Geoffrey. *Blue Chipper.* New York: Williams, 1993.

Parker, Barbara. *Suspicion of Innocence.* New York: Dutton, 1994.

Pearce, Donn. *Cool Hand Luke.* New York: Scribner, 1965.

Pratt, Theodore. *The Barefoot Mailman.* New York: Hawthorn, 1943.

———[as Timothy Brace]. *Murder Goes Fishing.* New York: Dutton, 1936.

———[as Timothy Brace]. *Murder Goes in a Trailer.* New York: Dutton, 1937.

———[as Timothy Brace]. *Murder Goes to the Dogs.* New York: Dutton, 1938.

Price, Wesley. *Death Is a Stowaway.* New York: Godwin, 1933.

Ransome, Stephen [pseud. of Frederick Clyde Davis]. *Alias His Wife.* New York: Dodd, 1965.

———. *I'll Die for You.* New York: Doubleday, 1959.

———. *The Night, the Woman.* New York: Dodd, Mead, 1963.

———. *Trap #6.* New York: Doubleday, 1971.

Robinson, Kevin. *Mall Rats.* New York: Walker, 1992.

Roche, Arthur Somers. *The Pleasure Buyers.* New York: Macmillan, 1925.

Runyon, Damon. *Runyon a la Carte.* New York: Pocket, 1946.

Sanchez, Thomas. *Mile Zero.* New York: Knopf, 1989.

Sanders, Lawrence. *McNally's Caper.* New York: Putnam, 1993.

———. *McNally's Puzzle.* New York: Putnam, 1996.

Shames, Laurence. *Florida Straits.* New York: Simon and Schuster, 1992.

Standiford, Les. *Deal on Ice.* New York: HarperCollins, 1997.

Stone, A. *Fighting Byng: A Novel of Mystery, Intrigue, and Adventure.* New York: Britton, 1919.

Terhune, Albert Payson. *Black Caesar's Clan.* New York: Doran, 1922.

Thayer, Lee. *Five Bullets.* New York: Dodd, 1944.

Tracy, Donald. *Bazzaris.* New York: Ravenna, 1965.

———. *The Big Blackout.* Roslyn, N.Y.: Black, 1959.

———. *The Hated One.* New York: Simon and Schuster, 1963.

Wheatley, Dennis. *Murder off Miami.* London: Hutchinson, 1936.

White, Randy Wayne. *The Man Who Invented Florida.* New York: St. Martin's, 1993.

———. *Sanibel Flats.* New York: St. Martin's, 1990.

Willeford, Charles. *The Burnt Orange Heresy.* New York: Vintage/Random, 1971.

———. *Miami Blues.* New York: St. Martin's, 1984.

Williams, Joy. *Breaking and Entering.* New York: Vintage, 1981.

Carroll John Daly

1889–1958

The most popular of the *Black Mask* stable of writers, Carroll John Daly created the hard-boiled hero with Three Gun Terry Mack. As Mack metamorphosed into Race Williams, the hard-living, hard-fighting hero of the first hard-boiled novels, Daly developed a clearly defined vision of Williams: 30 years old, 5' 11 1/2", 183 pounds, with black eyes and dark brown hair. Unlike Mike Shayne, who always preferred fists to guns, Race Williams, perhaps best known for his remarkable accuracy with his pistols, often fired both his guns at once as he dispatched entire gangs in a single chapter. Like many of the pulp heroes who would follow him, Williams not only served as a detective but as judge and executioner as well. Far better traveled than most of his peers, Williams wandered the United States from New York to Chicago and California, and even a mythical foreign country, to earn his fees and help his clients: "I ain't afraid of nothing providing there's enough jack in it." Never one to make subtle moral distinctions, Daly emphasized uncomplicated plots, truly nasty villains, gritty language, and high body counts.

Daly's feel for popular taste and sense of the dramatic may have stemmed from his background. A graduate of the American Academy of Dramatic Arts, he spent his early life as a projectionist, actor, and theater owner, eventually opening the first movie theater on Atlantic City's boardwalk. With a comfortable income from the theaters he had owned, he began writing in 1922. As he became even more successful, he moved his family to White Plains, New York, where he gained a reputation as a recluse, rumored never to set foot outside his home during winter. In addition to the Race Williams books, Daly developed other popular series centered on figures like the wonderfully named Satan Hall and the delicate-looking but deadly Vee (Vivian) Brown, who divides his time between solving crimes and writing popular music.

During his travels Race Williams visited Miami in the fifth novel of his series, *The Hidden Hand* (1929), and there destroyed a conspiracy controlling the city and state. In the following section from the book, this original tough guy detective finds himself confronting one of the bizarre killers who typically stalk him. Williams's narrative, with its staccato prose, mild paranoia, fascination with interiors, and absolute sense of self-righteousness, reflects the simple but pulsing style which came to epitomize the pulps, attracted enormous audiences to their authors, and helped transform both the detective novel and American taste.

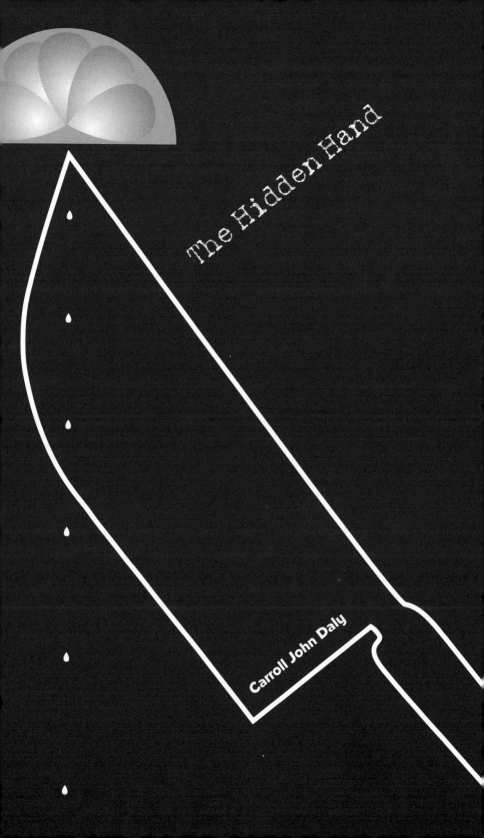

Chapter 8: Creeping Death

One hour—two—passed. No chills ran up and down my spine. There was little of a thrill about the thing. That had worn off years before. A man had sent some one to kill me; a man perhaps tried to kill me; a man had arranged to trap me here on the boat, with the girl as a decoy. Now—I stretched off comfortably and waited. Was that man, Jack McCleary, deserving of and needing one good killing, coming to murder me? Maybe I'd have to kill him—maybe I wouldn't. But if I did, I was already planning my story for the Captain of the ship; the court of law—wondering if there was any way of horning Gregory Ford in on the show. His agency had a nation-wide reputation, he had the backing of the State—his shoulders were broad enough to carry this killing. And—

The first card was dealt in the game. At my window a blurred whiteness hovered for a minute before the glass. Maybe it was one of those flying fish we hear about, in the Florida waters. But I had more than a sneaking suspicion that the white blur was a face. Fine! I clutched my guns the tighter—and the face was gone. I don't know if I saw it after that. If I did, it was more distant and indistinct—maybe just the wavering of the clouds, or—

I sat the straighter in my bunk. The knob of the door had turned—hardly a noticeable click, maybe—partly lost in the throb of the engine—but I knew that it had turned just the same. After my first jar erect I pulled the sheet over me and fell back slightly. Surely this bird might, or would, take a look-see over the transom before he entered the room. Maybe he'd just shove down an electric flash and fire, without coming in. But that was his party—not mine. Anything he decided was all right by me.

I lay still and watched the transom above the door. The face that would appear there would be discernible even in the semi-darkness—maybe not enough to recognize it in the dimness of the corridor light at that time of the morning, but discernible enough to pick out a nice spot to shoot at, if the occasion warranted it.

Again I cast a look toward the window. And again I thought that I saw the white face—distant, like the clouds. I wondered if one watched by the window while another entered by the door. But any way it suited McCleary suited me—I'm not particular.

Silence in the hall without! The knob of the door did not turn again, or if it did, it turned in tune with the throb of the engine and made no sound. But no face appeared at the open transom. There came a hand—a hairy wrist—an arm; and I strangled the impulse to put a bullet through that arm. Those fingers opened and something flashed for a moment in the dim light above the transom, then was lost in the darkness of the cabin. But I heard it strike the wall, back of my berth just above my feet and where my head should have been. I sucked in my breath.

There was a tinkle of metal—or was it metal? Didn't it seem more like falling glass? And the hairy arm again—thick, searching, groping fingers—a sudden jar—and the transom was slammed shut. Now, what was that for? Certainly—and I drew in another deep breath. A sweet, peculiar sort of breath—a breath that made me suck quickly again—once more. And then I breathed no more.

I didn't want to breathe. I couldn't breathe. I didn't dare breathe. And my eyes were burning like my throat—a dry heat set into my head, parched my lips and coated my tongue. I put up a hand—a hand that was meant for my face and didn't reach it. Chloroform—gas—ether—something deadly. And I knew the truth!

I knew what had come over the transom; a package—a can—a glass jar—a tube—some damnable thing of—of death. I wasn't dizzy. I wasn't wheedle-headed. I was like a man in a dream—a horrible nightmare. The thing gripped at my body, tightened upon my muscles, brought a sudden sweat through the heat. There was no pain—no sense of something gripping and clutching at my throat, like there had been at first—just a dull listless feeling—a tired, worn-out sort of indifference—but above all, the nightmare grip. Keen senses—a fairly good vision, if a blurred and distant one, and the lack of power to control the movements of my limbs—no coordination between mind and body—no response of the muscles to the sharp quick orders of the brain. Some place in my body the nerve energy had stopped—and I knew what the dead youth had meant when he spoke of the "Gas Man."

My left hand lay upon the sheet where it had dropped from my face. My right hand still clutched a gun—a gun that it could not lift. A finger encircled a trigger—a trigger which it could not press. And through it all was no special fear—just an indifference yet a knowledge of what had happened, and a terrible straining effort to hold my breath.

It was all clear enough, but distant—like looking through the wrong end of a telescope. And he came—the door opened—broad shoulders—the hairy arm—and a hand with a flash of steel in it. My eyes bulged, popped wide, and the sweat poured down my forehead. There was a sense of fear—a sense of horror that I don't think I ever experienced before. It was new to me—yet it couldn't be true—for the man who opened the door and was advancing from that great distance upon me, had—had no head.

I tried to close my eyes to shut out the thing that stood in the doorway. I had been poisoned, gassed, chloroformed—but was I going mad? I couldn't even shut my eyes—then came a breath of air from the open door. Like ice it felt, across my hot face—and I think I breathed it in, choked with it, too—coughed, maybe, but I'm not certain. The door closed again, shutting out the apparition—or at least the clearness of it in the distance. Now, just a blurred something, it came toward me. It passed the light from the transom and I saw it again—the headless thing. And I knew.

There was no white face and no hairy head—but there was a head. The man wore a gas mask. Somehow, that gave me relief, and, somehow, my mind cleared—but my body was paralyzed. Still that soft, sweet-smelling death engulfed me. God! how I longed for the door to open again—for another breath that might—that would break the grip upon my muscles. For there I lay with my hand upon a gun, and powerless to use it. Just one more suck of air and—

The man was close to the berth now but at the wrong end of it. I could see the thing in his hand—see it flash up, and knew that it was of steel. Silent death, then, this was to be—with a knife. McCleary had beaten me—and I was tempted to open my mouth and swallow in the sweet, paralyzing stuff, and sleep; go out without knowing it. Not from fear, you understand—not from the horror of watching myself die, as if from another world—but from a certain sense of shame that I had let myself be taken in like this.

Gas man! Gas man! Gas man! I repeated the words over and over to myself. They helped me hold my breath—the thing that was almost driving me to bursting. I wondered if a man ever did burst—and I thought that I might, for I'd die before ever I sucked in any more of the deadly sweetness—and I'd die, too, if I did suck it in. And—

A hand was on my foot. I saw the whiteness of it rather than felt it. The man was feeling for my face, as I should have been lying the other way in the bunk. Slowly the hand ran up my leg, paused at the knee and held it a moment. He turned then—eyes glared at me through misty windows. Eyes that bent forward; eyes that through the gas mask saw the whiteness of my face.

Slowly that hand crept up the length of my body. It seemed a long distance and a great while, though it couldn't have been more than a few seconds. Still I held my breath. A hand was on my face now, and the knife was raised. What a way to go out! Frantically I tried to raise that gun—just an inch—just a fraction of an inch—not at all. If my fingers could only move—if one finger could only close upon the trigger.

The knife started down—and stopped. The man was careful—a thorough man. A light flashed for a moment—shone full upon my face and into my eyes, yet they did not blink—just stared and stared at the light and the raised hand, and the knife in it—the knife that had started slowly down again, like a slow-motion moving picture.

There was a crash—the breaking of glass. And the knife held, the weird face turned to the window. I, too, was looking toward that window, and saw the white blur fade from the glass—the glass—but there was no glass. There was a rush of cold, crisp air from the sea—my mouth opened and my lungs sucked it in.

The figure hesitated between the window and me. Then turned again, raised the knife—and I lifted my gun and pressed the trigger. A stab of yellow, a roar that sounded above the throb of the engine, a falling thing in the moonlight, the thud of a body—and quiet and blackness. Then again, the throb of the engine, the swish of the sea—and I sat up on the edge of the berth, the gun dangling in my hand, a yawn on my lips and my eyes fastened on the window. This time when the face came I knew it was a woman's face—then it was gone, and I heard the beating of feet across the deck.

In a dazed way I knew that the window had been crashed in—that the girl had done it, and had saved my life. Peculiar that—and the door burst open and I swung around, half raising my gun. Gregory Ford rushed into the room. He was talking.

"I was keeping an eye on your cabin and I saw the girl by your window. Then—I heard the glass crash and the single shot. You're all right, Race?" and there was real concern in his voice. "I've come in time?" And stepping forward he tumbled over the body. "Good God! What's this—and what's the damn smell?"

In a moment the door was closed and the lights were on. Gregory Ford jerked the gas mask off the lad on the floor. There was a hole where one of his eyes had been. But I knew him. It was Jack McCleary.

"No polish to your work." Ford rolled the man over on his back. "Think this is McCleary? But he's dead enough." He flopped back one of his arms. Then looked at me suspiciously. "Well—there's your corpse. I ain't even in on the picnic."

"You can have him," I said wearily. And then warming to my idea I leaned toward Gregory Ford and gave him what was on my chest. "You take the blame and you can have the glory. You see, there's others—and I don't want them to know I'm on the lot."

"You're generous with your stiffs." He eyed me a moment. "But I'll take him. No squawking afterwards—understand. I've got a pretty free hand with the State. I won't have to explain much—if he's the right bird." He compared the face on the floor with a worn picture he took from his pocket. "That's him—that's McCleary." He nodded.

I didn't listen to Gregory Ford's story of the killing that he'd feed the captain and the authorities. Certainly, it wouldn't be noised about the boat. As for the glory—the very doubtful glory—well, he could have it. It didn't interest me. I wanted to sleep—take it any way you looked at it, I got five thousand. McCleary was dead and—damn it all—I'd of been a mess if some one hadn't crashed in that window. The girl had saved my life. But why? She had tried to take it—trapped me. But then she hadn't known or suspected that McCleary had killed the youth. Yep—it looked like that boy who died in my arms was her husband.

I just staggered down the hall to Gregory Ford's room, found the door open and flopped onto the bunk. I needed sleep—and when I thought of my closeness to death, I hit the hay with an easy conscience. I don't think any one would put up a squawk that Jack McCleary didn't need doing in. But who was the man behind him—the Big Gun—this directing genius who terrorized all Florida and whom the girl had called "The Hidden Hand"?

Edwin Granberry

1897-1988

Born in Meridian, Mississippi, Ed Granberry migrated to Lake City before beginning college at the University of Florida. During World War I he left to join the marines, finished an A.B. at Columbia University, and began a career as a professor of Romance languages at Miami University in Ohio. When he found that his teaching responsibilities interfered with his writing, he resigned and joined George Pierce Baker's famous 47 Workshop at Harvard, a seminar which included students like Thomas Wolfe. Over the next decade he wrote a series of plays, stories, and three novels: *The Ancient Hunger* (1927), *Strangers and Lovers* (1928), and *The Erl King* (1930).

In 1932 Granberry published his most famous story, "A Trip to Czardis," in *Forum Magazine*. This darkly realistic, poignant story of a cracker family from Florida's scrub pine country brought him immediate recognition, along with the O. Henry Memorial Prize for best story of the year. Reprinted often—in 1954 it appeared in *Ellery Queen's Mystery Magazine*—the story was adapted for radio by the Columbia Workshop and for television as one of the first videotaped films in a widely praised CBS production in 1960. After reading the story, Rollins College president Hamilton Holt was so impressed that he invited Granberry to join his faculty in Winter Park, promising him lots of free time to write.

As Irving Bacheller Professor of Creative Writing, Granberry supported young and established writers, translated French novels, continued to write plays, co-authored the Buz Sawyer comic strip, and transformed "A Trip to Czardis" into a novel with the same name in 1966. In this tale of a mother bringing her sons to a last visit with their father, Granberry evokes the simple dignity of average people confronting an extraordinary event. While the story's surface precisely captures the details of their trip and the elder son's growing realization of its meaning, Granberry's language and imagery reveal the dark truths underlying their journey. Even the name of their destination, Czardis, which at first represents a great exotic adventure for the boys, comes to reflect its tart, bitter, harsh, sour reality.

A Trip to Czardis

Edwin Granberry

IT WAS STILL DARK in the pine woods when the two brothers awoke. But it was plain that day had come, and in a little while there would be no more stars. Day itself would be in the sky and they would be going along the road. Jim waked first, coming quickly out of sleep and sitting up in bed to take fresh hold of the things in his head, starting them up again out of the corners of his mind where sleep had tucked them. Then he waked Daniel and they sat up together in the bed. Jim put his arm around his young brother, for the night had been dewy and cool with the swamp wind. Daniel shivered a little and whimpered, it being dark in the room and his baby concerns still on him somewhat, making sleep heavy on his mind and slow to give understanding its way.

"Hit's the day, Dan'l. This day that's right here now, we are goen. You'll recollect it all in a minute."

"I recollect. We are goen in the wagon to see Papa—"

"Then hush and don't whine."

"I were dreamen, Jim."

"What dreamen did you have?"

"I can't tell. But it were fearful what I dreamt."

"All the way we are goen this time. We won't stop at any places, but we will go all the way to Czardis to see Papa. I never see such a place as Czardis."

"I recollect the water tower—"

"Not in your own right, Dan'l. Hit's by my tellen it you see it in your mind."

"And lemonade with ice in it I saw—"

"That too I seen and told to you."

"Then I never seen it at all?"

"Hit's me were there, Dan'l. I let you play like, but hit's me who went to Czardis. Yet I never till this day told half how much I see. There's sights I never told."

They stopped talking, listening for their mother's stir in the kitchen. But the night stillness was unlifted. Daniel began to shiver again.

"Hit's dark," he said.

"Hit's your eyes stuck," Jim said. "Would you want me to drip a little water on your eyes?"

"Oh!" cried the young one, pressing his face into his brother's side, "don't douse me, Jim, no more. The cold aches me."

The other soothed him, holding him around the body.

"You won't have e're chill or malarie ache to-day, Dan'l. Hit's a fair day—"

"I won't be cold?"

"Hit's a bright day. I hear mournen doves starten a'ready. The sun will bake you warm. . . .

Uncle Holly might buy us somethen new to eat in Czardis."

"What would it be?"

"Hit ain't decided yet . . . He hasn't spoke. Hit might be somethen sweet. Maybe a candy ball fixed onto a rubber string."

"A candy ball!" Daniel showed a stir of happiness. "Oh, Jim!" But it was a deceit of the imagination, making his eyes shine wistfully; the grain of his flesh was against it. He settled into stillness by himself.

"My stomach would retch it up, Jim . . . I guess I couldn't eat it."

"You might could keep a little down."

"No . . . I would bring it home and keep it . . ."

Their mother when they went to bed had laid a clean pair of pants and a waist for each on the chair. Jim crept out of bed and put on his clothes, then aided his brother on with his. They could not hear any noise in the kitchen, but hickory firewood burning in the kitchen stove worked a smell through the house, and in the forest guinea fowls were sailing down from the trees and poking their way along the half-dark ground toward the kitchen steps, making it known the door was open and that within someone was stirring about at the getting of food.

Jim led his brother by the hand down the dark way of yellow-pine stairs that went narrowly and without banisters to the rooms below. The young brother went huddling in his clothes, aguelike, knowing warmth was near, hungering for his place by the stove, to sit in peace on the bricks in the floor by the stove's side and watch the eating, it being his nature to have a sickness against food.

They came in silence to the kitchen, Jim leading and holding his brother by the hand. The floor was lately strewn with fresh bright sand, and that would sparkle when the daybreak got above the forest, though now it lay dull as hoarfrost and cold to the unshod feet of the brothers. The door to the firebox of the stove was open, and in front of it their mother sat in a chair, speaking low as they entered, muttering under her breath. The two boys went near and stood still, thinking she was blessing the food, there being mush dipped up a steaming in two bowls. And they stood cast down until she lifted her eyes to them and spoke.

"Your clothes on already," she said. "You look right neat." She did not rise, but kept her chair, looking cold and stiff, with the cloth of her black dress sagging between her knees. The sons stood in front of her, and she laid her hand on first one head and then the other and spoke a little about the day, charging them to be sober and of few words, as she had raised them.

Jim sat on the bench by the table and began to eat, mixing dark molasses sugar through his bowl of mush. But a nausea began in Daniel's stomach at sight of the sweet, and he lagged by the stove, gazing at the food as it passed into his brother's mouth.

Suddenly a shadow filled the back doorway and Holly, their uncle, stood there looking in. He was lean and big and dark from wind and weather, working in the timber as their father had done. He had no wife and children and would roam far off with the timber gangs in the Everglades. This latter year he did not go far, but stayed near them. Their mother stopped and looked at the man, and he looked at her in silence. Then he looked at Jim and Daniel.

"You're goen to take them after all?"

She waited a minute, seeming to get the words straight in her mind before bringing them out, making them say what was set there.

"He asked to see them. Nobody but God Almighty ought to tell a soul hit can or can't have."

Having delivered her mind, she went out into the yard with the man, and they spoke more words in an undertone, pausing in their speech.

In the silence of the kitchen Daniel began to speak out and name what thing among his possessions he would take to Czardis to give his father. But the older boy belittled this and that and everything that was called up, saying one thing was of too little consequence for a man, and that another was of no account because it was food. But when the older boy had abolished the idea and silence had regained, he worked back to the thought, coming to it roundabout and making it new and his own, letting it be decided that each of them would take their father a pomegranate from the tree in the yard.

They went to the kitchen door. The swamp fog had risen suddenly. They saw their mother standing in the lot while their uncle hitched the horse to the wagon. Leaving the steps, Jim climbed to the first crotch of the pomegranate tree. The reddest fruits were on the top branches. He worked his way up higher. The fog was now curling up out of the swamp, making gray mountains and rivers in the air and strange ghost shapes. Landmarks disappeared in the billows, or half seen, they bewildered the sight and an eye could so little mark the known or strange that a befuddlement took hold of the mind, like the visitations sailors beheld in the fogs of Okeechobee. Jim could not find the ground. He seemed to have climbed into the mountains. The light was unnatural and dark, and the pines were blue and dark over the mountains.

A voice cried out of the fog:

"Are worms gnawen you that you skin up a pomegranate tree at this hour? Don't I feed you enough?"

The boy worked his way down. At the foot of the tree he met his mother. She squatted and put her arm around him, her voice tight and quivering, and he felt tears on her face.

"We ain't come to the shame yet of you and Dan'l hunten your food off trees and grass. People seein' you gnawen on the road will say Jim Cameron's sons are starved, foragen like cattle of the field."

"I were getten the pomegranates for Papa," said the boy, resigned to his mother's concern. She stood up when he said this, holding him in front of her skirts. In a while she said:

"I guess we won't take any, Jim. . . . But I'm proud it come to you to take your papa somethen."

And after a silence, the boy said:

"Hit were Dan'l it come to, Mamma."

Then she took his hand, not looking down, and in her throat, as if in her bosom, she repeated:

"Hit were a fine thought and I'm right proud . . . though today we won't take anything . . ."

"I guess there's better pomegranates in Czardis where we are goen—"

"There's no better pomegranates in Czardis than right here over your head," she said grimly. "If pomegranates were needed, we would take him his own. . . . You are older'n Dan'l, Jim. When we get to the place we are goen, you won't know your papa after so long. He will be pale and he won't be as bright as you recollect. So don't labor him with questions . . . but speak when it behooves you and let him see you are upright."

When the horse was harnessed and all was ready for the departure, the sons were seated on a shallow bed of hay in the back of the wagon and the mother took the driver's seat alone. The uncle had argued for having the top up over the seat, but she refused the shelter, remarking that she had always driven under the sky and would do it still today. He gave in silently and got upon the seat of his own wagon, which took the road first, their wagon following. This was strange, and the sons asked:

"Why don't we all ride in Uncle Holly's wagon?"

But their mother made no reply.

For several miles they traveled in silence through their own part of the woods, meeting no one. The boys whispered a little to themselves, but their mother and their uncle sat without speaking, nor did they turn their heads to look back. At last the narrow road they were following left the woods and came out to the highway, and it was seen that other wagons besides their own were going to Czardis. And as they got farther along, they began to meet many other people going to the town, and the boys asked their mother what day it was. It was Wednesday. And then they asked her why so many wagons were going along the road if it wasn't Saturday and a market day. When she told them to be quiet, they settled down to watching people go by. Some of them were faces that were strange, and some were neighbors who lived in other parts of the woods. Some who passed them stared in silence, and some went by looking straight to the front. But there were none of them who spoke, for their mother turned her eyes neither right nor left, but drove the horse on like a woman in her sleep. All was silent as the wagons passed, except the squeaking of the wheels and the thud of the horses' hoofs on the dry, packed sand.

At the edge of the town the crowds increased, and their wagon got lost in the press of people. All were moving in one direction.

Finally they were going along by a high brick wall on top of which ran a barbed-wire fence. Farther along the way in the middle of the wall was a tall, stone building with many people in front. There were trees along the outside of the wall, and in the branches of one of the trees Daniel saw a man. He was looking over the brick wall down into the courtyard. All the wagons were stopping here and hitching through the grove in front of the building. But their Uncle Holly's wagon and their own drove on, making way slowly as through a crowd at a fair, for under the trees knots of men were gathered, talking in undertone. Daniel pulled at his mother's skirts and whispered:

"What made that man climb up that tree?"

Again she told him to be quiet.

"We're not to talk today," said Jim. "Papa is sick and we're not to make him worse." But his high, thin voice made his mother turn cold. She looked back and saw he had grown pale and still, staring at the iron-barred windows of the building. When he caught her gaze, his chin began to quiver, and she turned back front to dodge the knowledge in his eyes.

For the two wagons had stopped now and the uncle gotten down and left them sitting alone while he went to the door of the building and talked with a man standing there. The crowd fell silent, staring at their mother.

"See, Jim, all the men up in the trees!" Daniel whispered once more, leaning close in to his brother's side.

"Hush, Dan'l. Be still."

The young boy obeyed this time, falling into a bewildered stare at all the things about him he did not understand, for in all the trees along the brick wall men began to appear perched high in the branches, and on the roof of a building across the way stood other men, all gaping at something in the yard back of the wall.

Their uncle returned and hitched his horse to a ring in one of the trees. Then he hitched their mother's horse, and all of them got out and stood on the ground in a huddle. The wall of the building rose before them. Strange faces at the barred windows laughed aloud and called down curses at the men below.

Now they were moving, with a wall of faces on either side of them, their uncle going first, followed by their mother who held each of them by a hand. They went up the steps of the building. The door opened, and their uncle stepped inside. He came back in a moment, and all of them went in and followed a man down a corridor and into a bare room with two chairs and a wooden bench. A man in a black robe sat on one of the chairs, and in front of him on the bench, leaning forward, looking down between his arms, sat their father. His face was lean and gray, which made him look very tall. But his hair was black, and his eyes were blue and mild and strange as he stood up and held the two sons against his body while he stooped his head to kiss their mother. The man in black left the room and walked up and down outside in the corridor. A second stranger stood in the doorway with his back to the room. The father picked up one of the sons and then the other in his arms and looked at them and leaned their faces on his own. Then he sat down on the bench and held them against him. Their mother sat down by them and they were all together.

A few low words were spoken, and then a silence fell over them all. And in a while the parents spoke a little more and touched one another. But the bare stone floor and the stone walls and the unaccustomed arms of their father hushed the sons with the new and strange. And when the time had passed, the father took his watch from his pocket:

"I'm goen to give you my watch, Jim. You are the oldest. I want you to keep it till you are a grown man. . . . And I want you to always do what Mamma tells you. . . . I'm goen to give you the chain, Dan'l. . . ."

The young brother took the chain, slipped out of his father's arms, and went to his mother with it. He spread it out on her knee and began to talk to her in a whisper. She bent over him, and again all of them in the room grew silent.

A sudden sound of marching was heard in the corridor. The man rose up and took his sons in his arms, holding them abruptly. But their uncle, who had been standing with the man in the doorway, came suddenly and took them and went out and down through the big doorway by which they had entered the building. As the doors opened to let them pass, the crowd gathered around the steps pressed forward to look inside. The older boy cringed in his uncle's arms. His uncle turned and stood with his back to the crowd. Their mother came through the doors. The crowd fell back. Again through a passageway of gazing eyes, they reached the wagons. This time they sat on the seat beside their mother. Leaving their uncle and his wagon behind, they started off on the road that led out of town.

"Is Papa coming home with Uncle Holly?" Jim asked in a still voice. His mother nodded her head.

Reaching the woods once more and the silence he knew, Daniel whispered to his brother:

"We got a watch and chain instead, Jim."

But Jim neither answered nor turned his eyes.

Jonathan Wyatt Latimer

1906-1983

The year after Dashiell Hammett introduced a comic strain into the hard-boiled tradition with the witty repartee of Nick and Nora Charles in *The Thin Man* (1934), a young writer, Jonathan Latimer, merged screwball humor, hard-boiled prose, random violence, complicated plots, and social critiques into a grotesquely effective series. The five William Crane novels published between 1935 and 1939 take their sophisticated, alcoholic, cerebral hero around the country to help the wealthy in their quest for security and safety. With his vast capacity for mixed drinks, his fascination with the netherworld, and his deep loyalty both to his boss, the urbane and avuncular Colonel Black, and to the Black Detective Agency, Bill Crane negotiates through an alcoholic and social maze to resolve the kind of complex puzzles more often found in classical mysteries.

Named to honor a great-great-grandfather who served on George Washington's staff during the Revolutionary War, Jonathan Latimer became a reporter for the *Chicago Herald-Examiner* and *Chicago Tribune* and a ghostwriter for retired secretary of the interior Harold Ickes before eventually settling in Hollywood as a writer for film and television. Among his many projects were screenplays for classic *noir* films including Hammett's *The Glass Key* (1942), Kenneth Fearing's *The Big Clock* (1947), and Cornell Woolrich's *The Night Has a Thousand Eyes* (1948), as well as scripts for the Perry Mason television series.

The following excerpt from *The Dead Don't Care* (1937) reflects the odd mixture of urbane wit, hard-boiled sensibility, social satire, and hard drinking that characterizes Latimer's five Bill Crane novels. When Colonel Black sends Crane and an assistant, O'Malley, to Miami to protect the wealthy young Penn and Camelia Essex, Crane finds the city's tropical streets so alien that he must search for comfort in the security of the New York Bar, where he can instruct O'Malley in the linguistic niceties of class etiquette, demonstrate his quick wit, exchange information with Doc Williams, and show his reluctance to wander too far away from a bottle of Scotch.

The Dead Don't Care

Jonathan Latimer

Chapter 3

Miami's sidewalks dazzlingly reflected sunlight on south and west sides of streets, bore crowds of deliberate shirt-sleeved tourists on shady north and east sides. The convertible passed a yellow building with a sign, FIVE COURSE DINNER—25¢, and swung into a parking lot. "Back after lunch," Crane told the Negro attendant.

They walked over to Flagler Street, elbowing their way through the crowds, and turned right toward the bay. Two blondes in halters and white shorts, sauntering arm in arm, smiled at O'Malley, but Crane said, "Hey! None of that." He looked over his shoulder. "Besides, we can do better."

They passed a stand selling orange juice, a stand selling pineapple juice, a drugstore, a clothing store bearing a banner marked, END OF SEASON SALE—FIFTY OFF, a stand selling a mixture of coconut milk and pineapple juice. A policeman warned them not to jaywalk. From a loud-speaker over a leather goods store came a sticky Wayne King waltz. They both began to sweat.

"The town's lousy with dames," observed O'Malley.

"Probably recruiting for Gertie, over on the Bay Front," said Crane.

They turned into a bookstore and Crane asked the elderly lady clerk for a Bartlett's Familiar Quotations.

Behind tortoise-shell glasses her eyes seemed about to shed tears. "The only one we have is secondhand." Her face was thin.

"That's all right. How much?"

He gave her two dollar bills and a fifty-cent piece, said, "You needn't wrap it," and handed the heavy book to O'Malley. "That's for you."

"What do I want with it?" asked O'Malley, surprised.

Crane was looking from one side of the street to the other, up and down side streets as they walked. "I'll tell you soon as I find some beer."

A block to the left they found the New York Bar. It was cool inside and there was a lovely odor of scotch whiskey, limes, Cuban rum and beer in the air. They sank into leather chairs on opposite sides of a black composition table.

"Two Bass ale," Crane told the waiter.

O'Malley pretended astonishment. "What'll the major say?"

"Wait!" Crane called to the waiter. "Cancel the order. Two triple scotch and sodas instead."

"Make 'em *double* triple scotches," said O'Malley.

His expression dazed, the waiter hurried away to consult with the bartender.

Crane felt all right about disregarding the major's orders. He belonged to the pleasure school of crime detection, anyway. He never found that a little relaxation hindered him in his work. His best ideas came while he was relaxed. However, it was hard to make a client see this. Clients were often stupid. That's why they had to hire detectives.

"Give me a jit," he said to O'Malley. "I'll make that phone call we came in for."

When he returned he was smiling. "Doc Williams and Eddie Burns are in town."

O'Malley looked up from his half-finished drink. "So that phony plate of spaghetti did get here after all?"

"Yeah, the count's over at the Roney Plaza. Burns is with him on the beach and Doc's coming right over." Crane raised his glass above his head. "Here's to the major."

They drank and ordered another, and O'Malley said, "What about this book?"

"Oh yeah," said Crane. "That's culture. That's what you need, a little culture."

"What is it, a book on etiquette?"

"No. Look. You look all right; you dress all right; most of the time you act all right."

"Hell, I act all right all the time."

"O.K., you act all right all the time. But sometimes you don't say the right thing." Crane took a long drink. "That's good. A good bar. But here's how the book'll help you."

"How?"

"You're a strong, silent guy at the Essex house, see? Most of the time you don't say anything but yes and no and thank you. But every once in a while, to show you got culture, you spout one of the quotations in this book; whatever'll fit the occasion."

"You mean I gotta learn everything in this whole book?"

"No. Just a half-dozen or so quotations. Look up the ones on women and liquor and love; those'll fit in easiest."

O'Malley thumbed through the book. He halted somewhere in the center. "You mean like this?" He read: *"I'd be a butterfly born in a bower, Where roses and lilies and violets meet."*

Crane said, "Why *Mister* O'Malley!"

"Well, Goddam it," said O'Malley. "That's in here."

"You have to use judgment," said Crane. "Or some big strong man will elope with you."

Ice clinked against the bottom of O'Malley's glass as he set it down. "O.K. I'll drip culture all over the place. Now what about another drink?"

"I think we ought to have a sandwich."

"What! No drink? No toast to the major?"

"Oh sure. But I think we ought to have a sandwich. Waiter, two double triple scotches and two roast beef sandwiches."

"Two triple roast beef sandwiches," said O'Malley.

"That reminds me," said Crane. "The word 'trun.' You do not use 'trun.'"

"No."

"No. You do not use 'trun.' We are going to be 'trun' to the alligators."

"You're tellin' me?"

"If you have to use 'trun,' use it in this way: he fell like a trun of bicks."

"You mean a trun of bricks."

"Or a one-trun tuck."

[44]

"You seemed to be confused," said O'Malley. "Perhaps a sip of this harmless beverage . . . ?"

Doc Williams found them very gay. "I might have known it," he said sadly; "I might have known it." He was a dapper man with a waxed mustache and pouches under his eyes. His black eyes were bright; there was a streak of perfectly white hair over his left temple; he was wearing a green gabardine suit with a sport back, a tan silk shirt, a maroon necktie. Chorus girls always thought he looked "distinguished."

Crane said, "Have a drink. Have one of our new drinks."

"Well, I hardly . . ."

"Waiter, a double triple scotch."

"Kay-riste!" Williams shuddered. "Where'd you get that drink?" He peered at the beverage list. "Scotch and soda, fifty cents. Doubled is a dollar. Tripled—" His voice went up the scale. "My God! That's three dollars a drink."

"It's economy in the long run," explained Crane. "You don't drink as many as you do of the cheaper kind."

Eyes raised to the cream-colored ceiling, Williams said, "Why can't I work just once with sensible men?"

"We are sensible men," said O'Malley. "And besides, we got culture." He added: "'Learning is ever in the freshness of its youth, even for the old.'"

Williams shoved back his chair, stood up. "I think I musta made a mistake," he mumbled.

They prevailed upon him to sit down again, to try his drink. "Tell us about the count," urged Crane. "How did he get down here?"

"On a plane." Williams said he had picked up the count as soon as the Union Trust had given Colonel Black the Essex case. "The colonel's got an idea Di Gregario's back of those notes." Crane nodded and he went on, "Last night he takes the Florida plane at Newark and Eddie and I go along. He goes right to the Roney from the plane, gets a room and meets with a lot of other dagos. They are plannin' something, but Eddie and me can't get near enough to hear. Now he and Eddie are sunning on the beach."

"You don't think the dagos are just friends of his?"

"They may be friends, but they're up to something, y'bet. They're like cats—that nervous. And most of 'em are packing rods."

Crane shook his head sadly. "Do they know there's a law against carrying weapons?"

"I'm not plannin' on breaking the news to them."

O'Malley said, "That gives us two guys to investigate: the count and Tortoni."

Crane told Williams of their experiences, of The Eye and Major Eastcomb. "That's why we're drinking," he explained. "We can't let the major bluff us."

Williams grinned. "Of course, you wouldn't think of drinking otherwise?"

"Oh no," said O'Malley. "Certainly not."

"Who do you think's dropping those notes around?" asked Williams.

"Must be somebody planted in the house," said Crane.

"Any tough-looking mugs in the house?"

O'Malley said, "They're all tough looking."

"I know Tortoni," said Williams. "He used to work for Luciano in the slave racket. Runs a joint called the Red Castle out on Long Island. Gambling and women."

"A torpedo?"

"Naw. Yellow as a banana. He's shifty, though."

"Well, we'll be seeing him ourselves tonight," said Crane. "We're going to give his joint a whirl."

Williams said, "You better lay off these drinks or you'll be in a whirl yourselves."

Crane said, "Waiter, three more of the same."

Brett Halliday (Davis Dresser)

1904–1977

Davis Dresser always claimed that he had based his rangy, raw-boned, redheaded hero, Mike Shayne, on a man he met briefly in the Mexican oil fields and later in a New Orleans bar. But Shayne's existence owes as much to Dresser's persistence and a publisher's suggestion as to any chance encounters. After receiving his twenty-second letter of rejection for the manuscript of *Dividend on Death*, Dresser set it aside, finished a second mystery (*Mum's the Word for Murder*), and finally found a publisher for that book on his eighteenth try. When a Henry Holt salesman praised *Mum's the Word*, Dresser told him he had an even better story available. Editors at Henry Holt, one of the few publishers which had not rejected either of his books, liked *Dividend on Death* so much they suggested that he make it the first of a series.

That series, begun in 1939, would eventually include some seventy novels, with more than three hundred additional novellas printed in the *Mike Shayne Mystery Magazine*. While Dresser completed many of the novels himself, eventually he and his publishers developed a guide, "Mike Shayne of Miami," for the ghostwriters who would take over after 1958. *Dividend on Death* introduces the tough hero who would rather use his brains and fists than his guns. It also introduces Phyllis Brighton, who, despite Mike's cavalier treatment of her in the book, would later become his wife. When Dresser discovered that the Hollywood studios had lost interest in his novels because of his hero's growing domesticity, he killed Phyllis off and never again threatened his hero with a purely romantic relationship. Instead, Mike met Lucy Hamilton in New Orleans and brought her to Miami where they developed an ambiguous relationship in which, among other roles, she became his secretary and confidante. As the series progressed, Mike also developed a close friendship with reporter Tim Rourke to complement his solid working relationship with Miami police chief Will Gentry and his abiding disdain for most "John Laws," especially Miami Beach chief of detectives Peter Painter.

As these opening two chapters from *Dividend on Death* suggest, Dresser moves between the hard-boiled tradition with its edgy dialogue, physical confrontations—most of which Mike loses—and violent conclusion, and the classical tradition with its complex plots, emphasis on deduction, and conventions like gloomy mansions, locked rooms, hidden chests, and lengthy interviews in the library. Despite his apparently casual approach to cognac and sex, Mike clearly draws some lines according to his own highly idiosyncratic code of morality. And while he has no qualms about destroying awkward or confusing evidence, he is meticulously practical in ensuring and calculating his own profit.

In the introduction to her *Great Short Stories of Detection, Mystery, and Horror* (London, 1928), Dorothy Sayers pointed out that James Fenimore Cooper's frontier novels had inspired in mid- and late-nineteenth-century writers the fascination with tracking and hunting that led so many into the detective novel. Dresser's childhood suggests that the frontier tradition also shaped both him and his hero. Born in Chicago, Dresser grew up in Texas, ran away from home at fourteen to join the army, and spent time with Pershing chasing Pancho Villa. When the army learned his true age two years later, he was discharged and pursued a variety of manual-labor jobs before becoming an engineer and surveyor. Those experiences appear to have nurtured the confidence, pragmatism, and resourcefulness of his heroes. They also influenced a series of engineering adventures he wrote for *Ellery Queen's Mystery Magazine*, the westerns he produced under his own name, and the dozens of other books he wrote under such pen names as Asa Baker, Don Davis, Anthony Scott, Kathryn Culver, Matthew Blood (with Ryerson Johnson), and Hal Debrett (with his wife, Kathleen Rollins). Despite his prolific career, Dresser's fame will always rest on his work as Brett Halliday in creating Florida's first major detective, Mike Shayne of Miami.

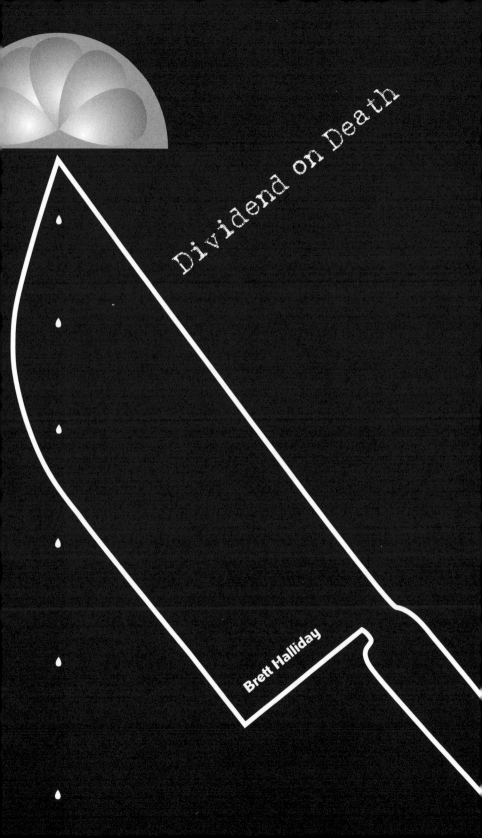

Dividend on Death

Brett Halliday

Chapter 1

The girl who faced Michael Shayne in his downtown Miami apartment was beautiful, but too unblemished to interest Shayne particularly. She was young, certainly not more than twenty, with a slender niceness of figure that was curiously rigid as she sat in a chair leaning toward him. Her lips were too heavily rouged and her cheeks were too pale.

She said: "I am Phyllis Brighton," as though her name explained everything.

It didn't. It didn't mean a thing to him. He said, "Yes?" wondering why there should be that expression of self-loathing in her eyes; she was too young and too beautiful to have that look. The pupils of her eyes were contracted and cloudy beneath heavy black lashes, and they stared into his face with a fixed intensity that wasn't quite sane. "We're on the beach," the girl told him as though that should convey a great deal. She drew herself stiffly erect in the deep chair, gloveless fingers weaving together in her lap.

Shayne said, "I see," without seeing at all. He stopped looking into her eyes and leaned back, loose-jointed and relaxed. "You don't use the phrase in its slang meaning, I suppose?"

"What?" The girl was beginning to loosen up a trifle in response to Shayne's easy manner.

"You don't mean you're down on your luck . . . a beachcomber?"

A nervous smile hovered on her tight lips. Shayne had an idea there would be a dimple in her left cheek if she relaxed and really smiled. "Oh, no," she explained, "We're at our Miami Beach estate for the season. My . . . father is Rufus Brighton."

Things began clicking in Shayne's mind. She was *that* Brighton. He crossed inordinately long legs and clasped his hands about one bony knee. "Your stepfather, I believe?"

"Yes." Phyllis Brighton's words came with a rush. "He had a stroke in New York four months ago . . . only a month after he and mother married while I was in Europe. They were sending him down here away from the cold when I arrived so I came down with him and the doctor and his son."

"Brighton's son?" Shayne asked. "Or, the doctor's?"

"Mr. Brighton's son by his first marriage. Clarence. Mother stayed in New York to attend to some business matters and she is arriving this afternoon." Her voice grew shaky on the final words.

Shayne waited for her to go on. There was no hurry or impatience in his mind. It was quiet and comfortably cool in the apartment above the Miami River, and he had nothing urgent on hand.

Phyllis sucked her breath in sharply and faltered: "I . . . don't know how to say it."

Shayne lit a cigarette and didn't help her out. She had something inside her that she would have to get rid of her own way.

"I mean . . . well . . . you're a private detective, aren't you?"

Shayne rumpled his coarse red hair with his left hand and looked at her with a fleeting grin. "That's a nice way of saying it. I've frequently been called worse . . . with emphasis."

She looked away from him, wet her lips. Her next question came with a rush:

"Did you ever hear of someone killing a person they loved devotedly?"

Shayne shook his head slowly. "I'm thirty-five, Miss Brighton, and I'm never sure that I know what a person means when he speaks of love. Suppose you tell me what's on your mind."

Tears came into Phyllis' eyes. She flung out her hands toward him. "Oh, I have to! I just have to tell someone or I'll go mad!"

Shayne nodded, repressing an impulse to suggest it wouldn't be a long journey. He looked directly into her eyes and asked: "Who are you thinking about killing . . . and why?"

She jerked back involuntarily and her breath came out between clenched teeth. "It's . . . mother."

Shayne said, "U-m-m," and looked away from her, taking a deep drag on his cigarette. The girl's answer had startled him for a moment, accustomed as Michael Shayne was to surprising revelations from clients.

"You think I'm crazy, don't you?" The girl's voice was almost out of control.

"We're all slightly haywire at times."

"I don't mean that way. I mean really crazy. Oh, I know I am. I can feel it. It gets worse every day."

Shayne nodded agreement, and mashed out his cigarette in a tray on the small table between them. "Haven't you come to the wrong place? Sounds to me as though you need an alienist instead of a detective."

"No, no!" She placed the palms of her hands flat on the table and leaned sharply forward. Full red lips were drawn away from white teeth and her eyes were clouded with fear.

"*They* tell me I'm going crazy. Sometimes I think they're trying to drive me crazy. *They* say I may try to kill mother. They're making me believe it. I won't let myself believe it but then I do. With mother coming this afternoon . . . " Her voice trailed off to silence.

Shayne lit another cigarette·and pushed his pack toward her. She didn't see it. She was staring upward into his face.

"You've got to help me. You've *got* to."

"All right," agreed Shayne soothingly. "I'll help you. But I'm no good at guessing games."

She said: "It's . . . it's . . . I can't bear to talk about it. It's too awful. I just can't."

Michael Shayne slowly unlimbered himself and stood up. He had a tall angular body that concealed a lot of solid weight, and his freckled cheeks were thin to gauntness. His rumpled hair was violently red, giving him a little-boy look curiously in contrast with the harshness of his features. When he smiled, the harshness went out of his face and he didn't look at all like a hardboiled private detective who had come to the top the tough way.

He smiled down at Phyllis Brighton, turned away from her, and crossed the living room of his apartment to an open east window which let in the afternoon breeze from Biscayne Bay. Better, he figured, to give her a chance to spill the whole thing. It didn't look like a real case, but he wanted to give her a chance.

"Take it easy." His voice was unruffled, steadying. "You've got things bottled up inside of you that you need to get out into the open. I don't think you need an alienist after all. I think you need someone to talk to. Go ahead. I'm listening."

"Thanks." The word was a faint whisper which barely carried to him across the stillness. "If you only knew . . ."

Shayne did know, sort of. He remembered reading the papers, and he could guess at other things that hadn't been in print.

He said: "You're not going crazy, of course. Count that off your list. You wouldn't realize it if you were." He paused. "About your mother . . ."

"She's coming this afternoon. From New York."

"You told me that."

"I hear them talking about me when they think I'm not listening. I heard them last night . . . talking about having me watched when mother arrives." She shuddered. "That's what gave me the idea of coming to you . . . myself . . ."

"You've said 'they' several times. Who are 'they'?"

"Dr. Pedique and Monty. Mr. Montrose. He's Mr. Brighton's private secretary."

Shayne turned and lounged against the window, elbows hooked on the sill.

"What basis is there for their fear? What's it all about? Do you hate your mother?"

"No! I love her . . . That's . . . what they say is the matter."

A rush of blood crimsoned Phyllis' cheeks beneath Shayne's steady gaze. She lowered her eyes.

This seemed to him to be getting them nowhere. "Suppose you tell me just what they do say." Shayne's voice was gently impersonal. "Don't make any excuses or explanations. Let me sort things out for myself first."

Phyllis Brighton clasped her hands together and began to speak in a glib, curiously sickening patter, as though the words had been committed to memory and she was delivering them without letting herself consider their meaning. "They say I've got an Electra complex and it's driving me insane with jealousy because mother married Mr. Brighton and I'll kill her before I let him have her."

"Is it true?" Shayne threw the question at her before she had time to catch her breath.

She raised her opaque eyes to his and cried out a "No!" then dropped them and added as if it might strangle her, "I don't know."

Shayne said dryly, "You'd better make up your mind, if she's due this afternoon."

"It's too horrible to be true. It isn't. It can't be. But I . . . everything's mixed up. I can't think any more. I'm afraid to let myself think. There's something horrible inside of me. I can feel it growing. I can't escape it. They say I can't."

"Isn't that something you'd better decide for yourself rather than let *them* decide for you?"

"But I . . . can't think straight any more. It's all like a nightmare and I have . . . spells . . . "

She was so damned young. Michael Shayne studied her morosely from across the room. Too young to be having spells and to have lost her ability to think straight. Still, he wasn't a nursemaid. He shook his head irritably, went to a wall liquor cabinet and took down a bottle of cognac. Facing her, he held it up and raised bushy red eyebrows.

"Have a drink?"

"No." She was looking down at the carpet. While he poured himself one she began talking with dreary hopelessness:

"I suppose it was silly of me to come . . . to *you*. No one can help me. I'm in a lonely place, Mr. Shayne. And I can't face it alone any more. Perhaps they're right." Her voice sank to an awed whisper. "I do hate him. I can't help it. I don't see how mother could have done it. We were so happy together. Now, it's all spoiled. What's the use of . . . going on?" Her lips scarcely moved.

Shayne let the drink trickle down his throat. The girl was talking to herself, not to him. She seemed to have forgotten him in fact, and was staring at the window with remote, glazed eyes. After a while she stood up slowly, her face twitching, and took one slow step toward the window. Abruptly she flung herself at it in one desperately swift motion.

Shayne lunged in front of her.

Then she was clawing at him, her breath coming in short gasps.

Shayne's face hardened; he smashed one big hand down on her shoulder, and shook her with an almost savage violence.

When she went limp he slipped his arm about her waist to keep her from sliding to the floor; she hung there with her head back and eyes closed, her breasts taut against the thin knit jacket of her sports outfit.

Shayne's face lost its impersonal fierceness. He looked down into her face moodily, remarking how her lips were parted and her breath was coming unevenly. It was a hell of a note. She was just a kid, but old enough to know better than to act like one.

Abruptly, he realized he didn't believe that stuff she had hinted about herself and her mother. He would have felt an instinctive repulsion if it was true, and she was not repellent. Far from it. He had to shake her again roughly to keep himself from kissing her.

She opened her eyes and swayed back when he shook her. "That'll be enough of that," he said with self-annoyance in his tone.

She sank back into a chair and regarded him gravely, catching her lower lip between sharp teeth. Her eyes were clearer. "I'm all right . . . now."

Shayne stood before her with his hands on his hips. It hadn't been an act, that hysteria of hers. None of it was an act. But it didn't make sense. Still, he told himself, he liked things that didn't make sense. Hadn't he started passing up routine stuff a long time ago? That's why he had no downtown office and no regular staff. That sort of phony front he left to the punks with whom Miami is infested during the season. Mike Shayne didn't touch a case unless it interested him. Or unless he was dead broke. . . . This case—if it was a case and not a case history—interested him. There was the feel of beneath-the-surface stuff that set his nerves tingling in a way that hadn't happened to him for a long time.

He sat down in front of Phyllis Brighton and said: "What you need more than anything else right now is someone to believe in you. All right. You've got that. But you'll have to start trying to believe in yourself a little bit. Is it a bargain?"

Phyllis' eyes blinked with tears, like a small girl's. "You're wonderful," she said finally. "I don't know how I can ever pay you . . ."

"That is an angle," Shayne admitted. "Haven't you any money?"

"No. That is . . . not enough, I'm afraid. But . . . would these do?"
She lifted a beautifully matched string of pearls from a bead bag
and held them toward him with a hesitation that was either genuine
timidity or a wonderful imitation.

Shayne let the pearls dribble into his hand without change of expression. "They'll do very nicely." He opened a drawer of the center
table and dropped them in carelessly. His manner became brisk and
reassuring:

"Let's get this straight, now, without hysterics. Your mother is coming from New York and you're suffering from a morbid inward fear
that you may go out of your head and do her some harm. I don't
believe there's any danger, but we'll let that pass. The important thing
is to see that nothing of the sort *can* happen. When is your mother
expected?"

"On the six o'clock train."

Shayne nodded. "Everything will be taken care of. You probably
won't see me, but you have to remember that it's part of a detective's
job not to be seen. The important thing for you to keep in mind is that
I'm making myself responsible for you. The matter is out of your
hands and in mine. If you feel you can trust me . . ."

"Oh, I do!"

"That's swell then." Shayne patted her hand and stood up. "I'll be
seeing you," he promised her casually.

She got up and moved close to him impulsively. "I can't tell you
how you've made me feel. Everything is different. I'm glad I came."

Shayne went to the door with her and took her hand briefly. "Keep
your chin up."

"I will." She smiled uncertainly and went down the corridor.

Shayne stood for a moment looking after her and rubbing his chin.
Then he closed the door, went back to the center table and lifted out
the string of pearls to study them with narrowed eyes. He wasn't an
expert but they certainly didn't look phony. He dropped them back into
the drawer, shaking his head. There were a lot of possible angles . . .

Ten minutes later, when he left his apartment, he was whistling
tunelessly. At the desk downstairs he told the clerk he'd be gone half

an hour—he never forgot to do that at the start of a case—and went down the street to a newspaper office, carefully read all the dope he could find on the Brightons, and went back to the hotel. This time he entered by the side door and climbed the service stairway to his second-floor apartment. His phone was ringing. It was the clerk:

"Mr. Shayne, there's a Dr. Joel Pedique here to see you."

Shayne frowned at the telephone and told the clerk to send Dr. Pedique up. Even after he had hung up and given the room a swift, characteristically speculative look, he was still frowning. From what Phyllis Brighton had told him, he had an instinctive feeling that he wasn't going to like Dr. Pedique.

He didn't. Dr. Joel Pedique was a man whom Shayne, surveying him at the doorway, would have instantly disliked if he had met him with no previous knowledge of him at all. He was small-boned and dark-skinned. His black hair was too long and it glistened with oil, combed straight back from a V where it grew low on his forehead. His lips were full and unpleasantly red. His eyes were beady and nervous, and his nostrils flared as he breathed. The rest of his appearance pleased Shayne equally little. The man's double-breasted blue coat clung snugly to his sloping shoulders and sunken chest, and immaculate white flannels were tight about plump hips. Brown spats above patent leather shoes completed the ensemble.

Shayne stood aside with his hand on the door-knob and said, "Come in, doctor."

Dr. Pedique held out his hand: "Mr. Shayne?"

Shayne nodded, closed the door, and walked back to sit down without taking the doctor's hand.

Dr. Pedique followed him mincingly and sat down.

"You have been recommended to me, Mr. Shayne, as an efficient and discreet private detective." Shayne nodded and waited. The doctor folded his hands in his lap and leaned forward. They were effeminate hands, soft and recently manicured. "I have an exceedingly delicate mission for you," he went on in a voice like thin silk, his sharp white teeth flashing behind full lips. "I am the physician attending Mr. Rufus Brighton, of whom you must have heard." He paused as though for effect.

Shayne blinked and looked at his cigarette. He said, "Yes," non-committally.

"An exceedingly curious and difficult situation has arisen." Dr. Pedique seemed to choose his words carefully. "You are perhaps not aware that Mr. Brighton has lately married and his stepdaughter has accompanied him here." He paused again.

Shayne kept on looking at his cigarette and didn't tell him whether or not he was aware of the fact.

The doctor purred on. "The unfortunate child is subject to certain . . . ah . . . hallucinations, I may call them in non-technical terms, stimulated by a violent sexual oestrus and marked by unmistakable symptoms of an Electra complex. In her depressed moods she sometimes becomes violent and I fear the poor child might do harm to her mother if such a mood were to come upon her."

"Why the hell," Shayne asked irritatedly, "don't you put her in an asylum?"

"But that would be too terrible," Dr. Joel Pedique exclaimed, spreading his hands out, rounded palms upward. "I have every hope of effecting an ultimate cure if I can keep her mind at ease. The shock of being incarcerated in an asylum would completely unhinge her reason."

Shayne asked: "Where do I come in?"

"Her mother arrives from the north this afternoon. I should like to arrange for some sort of a superficial guard to be kept over the mother or child during the first few days of her stay. During that period, I shall keep the child under close observation and determine definitely whether she can be cured or if she is doomed to enter a psychopathic ward."

"I see." Shayne nodded slowly. "You want me to arrange to keep the crazy girl from murdering her mother while you observe her?"

"Bluntly, yes." Dr. Joel Pedique nodded his small head with a bird-like motion.

"Do you want her tailed from the moment of the mother's arrival?" Shayne became very brisk and businesslike.

"I hardly think that will be necessary." The doctor smiled, thinly. "I feel that a rather informal watch will be sufficient. It is a matter which must be handled with discretion and the utmost privacy. I . . . wondered if you might undertake it yourself instead of sending an operative."

"I might," Shayne told him casually. "It will cost you more."

"That's perfectly splendid." Dr. Pedique stood up enthusiastically, slipped his right hand inside his coat and drew out a fat wallet. "I suggest that you drop over tonight after dinner and meet Mrs. Brighton and the girl. Everything could be arranged quietly."

Shayne stood up. "I'll be there," he promised, "about eight-thirty."

Dr. Pedique nodded and fiddled with his wallet.

"Two hundred for a retainer," Shayne told him.

Dr. Pedique's eyebrows shot up. Shayne stared at him coldly. The doctor reluctantly drew out two one-hundred-dollar bills. Shayne crumpled them in his hand and led the doctor to the corridor door.

"Eight-thirty," he said as he let the doctor out. Dr. Pedique bowed stiffly and went down the corridor. Shayne closed the door and walked back to the table, smoothing the bills out between his fingers. He opened the drawer, took the pearls out, rolled them up in the bills and stuck the wad in his coat pocket.

Then he grinned and muttered: "Now, if the old lady would come around and hire me as her bodyguard, the set-up would be perfect."

Chapter 2

Seven-thirty, Shayne came up a side street from Flagler to the service entrance of his apartment hotel. Down concrete steps and through a door into a square vestibule, then up two flights and to the right.

In his apartment, he crossed to the table, took the wadded pearls and bills from his pocket, unrolled the pearls and let them lie shimmering on the table while his eyes brooded over them. After a minute, and leaving the bills on the table, he carried the pearls into the kitchen, opened the refrigerator and took out the hydrator, which held a head of lettuce. He put the pearls in the bottom, scattered lettuce leaves over them, and replaced the pan.

When he returned to the living room, he was carrying a glass and a pitcher of crushed ice cubes and water. He set these things down on the table and brought out a bottle of Martel five-star cognac and a wine glass from a cupboard. Shayne's actions were apparently almost unconscious; the precise somnambulism of habit was in every motion, an automatic smoothness that lasted while he sat down, poured a drink and lit a cigarette. There was nothing in his face to show what he was thinking.

For the next half hour he sat silently, alternately sipping from the wine glass and the water glass, lighting one cigarette from another. Finally he stood up, turned out the lights and went out. His expression had not altered but there was purposefulness in his walk.

The elevator deposited him in a large and ornately furnished lobby. Shayne thrust his way across it toward the desk, caught the clerk's eye and received a negative shake of his head. Without stopping he went on, out through the side front entrance and across to a row of garages, where he unlocked the padlock on one door, and folded himself into the driver's seat of a middle-aged roadster. Once the car was backed out, Shayne drove a winding course to Southeast Second Street, thence east to Biscayne Boulevard and north on the right-hand drive. He paid no attention to his route, and very little to the other cars on the road.

At Thirteenth Street he turned to the right at the traffic circle and sped over the causeway across the Bay. When he reached the peninsula, he drove as far east as the ocean would allow, then turned north. His watch told him it was eight-twenty; the place could hardly be more than a few minutes ahead of him. Shayne relaxed imperceptibly at the wheel; he began to look around him. There was little traffic on the wide street, and few strolling figures in Lummus Park. He checked the house numbers as he drove along, and a short distance beyond the Roney Plaza, slowed and turned into a winding concrete drive between granite gateposts.

The general look of the place was luxurious but conventional to the point of dullness. There was a carefully tended terraced lawn on the left and a wide landscaped area of tropical shrubbery. The dark bulk of a huge mansion showed as he followed the drive to a porte-cochere, bougainvillea-draped in front. Lights shone from the lower windows.

An elderly woman in a maid's uniform opened the door. He told her his name and she said he was expected in the library, and would he follow her?

Shayne did, down a dimly-lit vaulted hallway, past a balustraded stairway. A woman was descending the stairway, and she reached the bottom just as Shayne passed. She wore the white uniform of a nurse and carried a napkin-covered tray. She was a full-bodied blonde of about thirty, with predatory eyes.

Shayne glanced at her as he passed and caught a fleeting, almost animal look on her face. Her lips were pouted as though in assent, though he had not spoken to her.

The maid led him on to the end of the hall and turned down a narrower one until she stopped outside a wide opening hung with brocade portières and said, "They're expecting you inside." He hardly noticed her noiseless, gliding retreat. It took plenty of money, he reflected, to get that kind of service . . .

Light streamed through a narrow opening between the curtains, and there was the low hum of voices. Shayne bent his head and listened but could distinguish no words. He parted the curtains a little more and looked in.

There was the sound of slithering feet on the carpet behind him. Sharp fingers dug into his arm. He let go the curtain and turned to look into the white face of Phyllis Brighton. She looked ghastly in the dim light. The lashes were drawn back from her eyeballs as though by some mechanical device, and the pupils were so contracted that the entire eyeball seemed to consist only of smoky iris. Shayne saw that she was wearing a flimsy chiffon nightgown and that her feet were bare. Streaks of blood showed darkly red down the front of her nightgown.

He stared at her face, and at the crimson stains, his mouth thin and hard. When he saw her lips begin to move, he thrust her back away from the doorway.

She spoke in a flat, low monotone: "I've done it. You're too late. I've already done it."

Without replying, Shayne pushed her back farther from the portières and held her out at arm's length to study her. Her eyes stared back but he felt that they didn't really see him. She stood stiffly erect with her gown hanging slackly from shoulders and breasts. Her lips continued to move but no articulate words came forth. There was only a low moan each time she exhaled. When she lifted one of her hands, he saw that the inside of the palm was smeared with blood. He caught her wrist as she started to grasp his arm. The abruptness of his motion had some effect on her; she drew back from him, her eyes still staring and sightless, and then turned and led him down the hall. Shayne followed, holding tightly to her wrist. Her bare feet glided soundlessly on the carpet and her breath wheezed in and out between set teeth. There was a back stairway at the end of the hall. Shayne put his left arm about her shoulders as they climbed the stairs side by side. Her flesh was cold under the thin gown. At the top of the stairs she turned to the right and stopped in front of a closed door. Her head moved jerkily, and her face was contorted with grief or remorse.

"*She's* in there."

Shayne opened the door and fumbled for a wall switch, keeping his arm tightly about Phyllis' shoulders.

The switch lighted a shaded floor lamp standing near the foot of a bed. Shayne moved inside and the girl moved with him. He closed the door softly with his heel and gazed down somberly at the body of a murdered woman lying outstretched on the bed. One white hand trailed down limply toward the floor and there was the slow drip of blood into a thickening pool on the carpet.

Shayne's arm tightened about the girl's shoulders as a shudder traversed her body. He roughly turned her away while he stepped near the bed and looked down silently at the woman whom he had promised to protect from harm. She wore, he noticed, a gray tailored traveling suit, with gray stockings and slippers to match, and she appeared not to have struggled against death. Blood was clotted on the white pillow and continued to seep from a gaping wound in her throat.

Shayne turned away from the bed, his left arm crushing Phyllis to him. Three traveling bags stood in partially unpacked disarray near the door. A fitted overnight bag lay open on the brocaded bench before the vanity, and there were toilet articles scattered out in front of the mirror. Half-carrying the girl, Shayne moved to the vanity. There was an open hammered silver jewel case holding a miscellany of personal jewelry. An elaborately-tooled handbag of gray leather lay beside the jewel case.

Shayne opened it with his free hand and dumped its contents out. There was a lipstick and compact, a wad of bills and a neatly folded cablegram, a small leather key-tainer. He smoothed the cablegram out and read it with a frown:

HAVE VERIFIED AUTHENTICITY AND WILL RETURN IMMEDIATELY
USUAL ROUTE CABLE WHETHER NEW YORK OR MIAMI
HENDERSON

It had been sent from London a week before, to Mrs. Rufus Brighton in New York. Penciled on the bottom were the words: *"Will meet you in Miami."*

Shayne stuffed the cablegram in his pocket. Phyllis Brighton stirred inside the circle of his arm and began moaning. He led her to the door, put both of his hands on her shoulders and shook her. Her eyes came open and she stopped moaning.

"Where is your room?" Shayne formed each word distinctly.

She shook her head as though too dazed to understand, but reached falteringly for the door knob. Shayne switched off the light and closed the door. Phyllis moved stiffly ahead of him down the hall to another door which stood partly ajar and which she entered.

A bed lamp burned at the head of a bed which he saw had lately been occupied. On the rug beside the bed lay a large wooden-handled butcher knife. The blade was stained red and the grip was smeared with blood.

Shayne pushed Phyllis down on the bed and stared at the knife. Then he looked at her and asked: "Is that what you did it with?" His face and voice were expressionless.

She shuddered and did not look at the knife. "I just woke up and . . . and there it was. I . . . don't know. I guess . . . it must be."

Shayne said: "Stand up."

She obeyed like a docile child.

"Look at me."

She looked at him. The pupils of her eyes had expanded to normal size but they were still glassy and unfocused. He asked: "How do you know you did it?"

"I just woke up . . . and *knew.*"

"Did you remember doing it?"

"Yes. As soon as I saw the knife I remembered."

Shayne shook his head. Her voice was dull, as if the words were unimportant to her. Something stunk about the entire set-up. He didn't know just what. There wasn't time to dig into it now.

He said: "Take off your nightgown. It's got blood on it."

Still staring into his eyes, Phyllis' hands went stiffly downward, gathered up the bottom hem of her gown and lifted it over her head.

Shayne turned his eyes away and held out his hand for it. Beads of sweat stood on his corrugated forehead. This was a hell of a time to be thinking about . . . anything except earning that string of pearls Phyllis had given him. Keeping his gaze averted, he said: "Give me the nightgown."

She put it in his hand and waited further orders.

He balled the soft material up in his fingers and said: "Now go in the bathroom and wash your hands and dry them. Get another night-gown and put it on."

His eyes followed her across the room to the bathroom door. When she went inside he shook his head, then bent and picked up the knife by the blade. He wrapped the bloody nightgown around the handle and transferred his hold there. Then he unbuttoned his coat and slipped the knife, blade downward, into the inside pocket; forcing the point through the lining until the handle rested against the bottom of the pocket. He then stuffed the rest of the nightgown inside the pocket and buttoned his coat.

Phyllis Brighton came out of the bathroom, took a clean night-gown from a hanger in the closet, and slipped it on.

Shayne stood beside the bed and watched her. She came back and stood before him numbly, as though she had no will of her own, but waited for him to instruct her.

"Get into bed," he said. "Cover up and turn out the light and go to sleep or pretend to sleep. Forget about everything. *Everything*, do you understand?"

"I understand," she said in a flat, weary voice.

"You'd damn well better." He watched her get in bed and waited until she turned out the light. Then he went out in the hall and closed the door. He hesitated a moment as he observed the key in the outside lock. With a scowl almost of uncertainty, he turned the key, left it in the door, and strode down the hall toward the stairs.

He met no one as he padded back to the curtained doorway. The entire incident had not delayed him more than ten minutes. This time he did not hesitate before the curtains.

Four men were seated in the library when he went in. Dr. Joel Pedique, who had visited him that afternoon; Dr. Hilliard, a tall ascetic man with eyeglasses fastened to a wide black ribbon, whom he knew; and two others whom he guessed were Mr. Montrose and Clarence Brighton.

"The maid told me I was expected," Shayne said as he stepped through the curtains.

Dr. Pedique rose and bowed from the hips. "We have been waiting for you, Mr. Shayne."

Shayne smiled and said: "Hello, Hilliard."

"Good evening, Shayne." Dr. Hilliard didn't get up, but smiled courteously.

"Mr. Montrose, Mr. Shayne," said Dr. Pedique.

Mr. Montrose was a wispy little man, bald and clean-shaven. His clothes seemed too large for him and his face was a pasty-white. He stood up and bowed, and Shayne nodded curtly.

"And this is Clarence Brighton," Dr. Pedique went on, his voice becoming more effusive.

The youth crossed his ankles in front of him, looked at Shayne in low-lidded indifference, and muttered something.

Shayne looked the boy over carefully as he took the chair Dr. Pedique offered him. About twenty, with a slender, well-knit body, slack mouth and furtive hazel eyes. His hands were small and the two first fingers of the left hand were heavily stained with nicotine. All in all, there was an obvious but ill-defined air of defiance about him.

Shayne said, "Well?" and let his gaze slide to Dr. Pedique as the latter resumed his seat.

"We were discussing you and some of your exploits," Dr. Pedique told him. "Dr. Hilliard has been kind enough to tell us something about your work."

Shayne lit a cigarette and grinned amiably at Dr. Hilliard. "Hope you didn't tell them anything they shouldn't know, doc. These people are my clients."

"I assured them that you generally get results," he answered seriously. Dr. Hilliard was one of the most respected members of his profession in Miami, an officer of the local Medical Association, and prominent in civic affairs.

"That's all right. So long as you didn't tell them how I go about getting results." Shayne then turned to Pedique. "I'm here on business. Everything's all right so far, I judge," he said casually.

"Oh, yes. Yes, indeed. Mrs. Brighton went to her room immediately after dinner and is resting from the trip. She asked me to bring you to meet her before you go away. The . . . ah . . . patient is resting quietly, also."

"That's great," said Shayne. "Now, have you worked out any definite plan of action?"

"That, I should think, would be for you to decide." Dr. Pedique cocked his head, nodded with pursed lips. "With all the facts in hand, you may proceed as you see fit."

Shayne nodded and turned again to Dr. Hilliard. "How about it, doc? Is Pedique having a pipe dream or is there any danger of the girl harming her mother? How do you see the set-up?"

Dr. Hilliard brought the tips of his fingers together in front of his chest. "I can't venture a prediction, having no more intimate knowledge of the case than a somewhat cursory observation had given me. I do approve, however, of taking all possible precautions."

"Christ!" Shayne complained, "it's as hard to get a definite opinion out of one of you birds as a lawyer."

Dr. Hilliard smiled suavely. "Mental cases require careful study and observation over a long period," he told Shayne. "I haven't," he added, "been consulted on Miss Brighton's case."

Shayne shot a look at Dr. Pedique. "You've kept her to yourself, huh?"

Dr. Pedique smiled thinly. "I felt perfectly capable of coping with her case. With Mr. Brighton I did consider that a consultant was necessary."

"See here," Shayne said abruptly, "how does the girl's name come to be Brighton? I understood she wasn't his daughter."

"He adopted her at the time of his marriage," Mr. Montrose explained. "It was his desire that she be legally regarded as his daughter."

Shayne watched Clarence as Mr. Montrose ended. The boy's lips poked out sulkily. He uncrossed and recrossed his ankles.

"You'd better let me have a talk with Mrs. Brighton and see if I can arrange a sensible method of going about this," Shayne said. He stood up and Dr. Pedique arose hurriedly. "By the way," Shayne added, "how does *she* take this? Mrs. Brighton, I mean."

"She was much relieved when I outlined the arrangement," Dr. Pedique said. "She is greatly concerned about the girl, of course, but she admitted to me that she had felt cause for alarm on previous occasions." He slid through the portières and held them apart for Shayne who passed through with a nod of his head toward the three men remaining in the library.

"This way." Dr. Pedique led him down the hall in the direction the maid had brought him, and on to the wide stairway. They went up the stairs silently, and at the top were met by the blond nurse whom Shayne had seen before. She carried a folded towel on her arm and was about to pass them when Dr. Pedique held out his hand and said:

"Ah, Charlotte, how is the patient?"

"He's resting, doctor." Her voice was low and huskily vibrant. Her eyes slipped past the doctor's face and rested with approval on the towering figure of the detective.

"That's fine," said Dr. Pedique. The nurse went on down the hall, followed by Shayne's speculative gaze.

"This way." Dr. Pedique led him to the same door which Phyllis had taken him to. The room was dark. Dr. Pedique knocked softly. There was no response. He knocked louder and listened, then said, "I wonder . . . " and tried the knob. The door swung inward and he called softly: "Mrs. Brighton."

When there was no response, he switched on the light. Shayne stood directly behind him and watched his body soften as he looked toward the bed. He crossed the room swiftly and bent over her. Shayne strode in after him, hard-eyed and watchful.

The face which Dr. Pedique raised to Shayne was contorted with horror . . . and with some other emotion which it was impossible to diagnose at the moment. He shuddered and averted his eyes from the chalk-white face of the woman on the bed. His face was greenish-pale even in the warm light from the floor lamp.

"Looks as if you won't be needing me now," Shayne said.

The dapper little physician rocked back and forth on the balls of his feet. "This is terrible, terrible," he groaned.

"It's not nice," Shayne admitted.

Dr. Pedique risked a second glance at the body and said, more firmly, "It's . . . that girl! We thought she had gone to bed. She must have slipped in here and . . . God! I've been a fool. I should have had a nurse watching her every minute." His suave, dapper manner deserted him completely and he covered his face with his hands.

The spectacle began to irk Shayne. "Looks like a case for the police. For Christ's sake, pull yourself together."

Dr. Pedique made an effort to recapture his professional manner. "I feel wholly responsible," he said. "Had I used better judgment, I should have sent the girl to an asylum instead of exposing her mother to this danger."

"Afterthoughts aren't worth a damn," observed Shayne. "Let's call the police and the others, and then get hold of the girl before she bumps somebody else off."

"It is the strictest necessity," Dr. Pedique readily agreed. He slid past Shayne and ran to the top of the stairs to call the news down-stairs and ask that the police be notified. Then he came back to Shayne, his mouth twitching.

"The girl's room. We'll see if she's there."

"We'll wait for some of the others to come up," Shayne protested. "Dr. Hilliard should be here. A crazy woman with a knife is likely to be a tough proposition."

Dr. Pedique agreed, his breath coming nervously and noisily. Clarence and Dr. Hilliard raced up the stairs; Shayne could hear the tension in Montrose's voice, below, as he telephoned the police.

Shayne took the newcomers to the open door of the death chamber and they both looked in. Dr. Hilliard fiddled with his eyeglasses and shook his head drearily. The boy, Clarence, drew back after one hasty glance during which his face went white and drawn.

"Where's the girl's room?" Shayne asked Dr. Pedique.

"This way." They followed him down the hall. Arriving at what Shayne knew to be Phyllis' door, Dr. Pedique stood back and moistened his lips, waiting for someone else to take the initiative.

Shayne stepped to the door and knocked authoritatively. There was no response. Then, he tried the knob. The door would not open. "Hell," he muttered, "it's locked." Making certain that Dr. Hilliard observed his every move, Shayne turned the key in the lock and opened the door.

The others crowded in the doorway behind him. The room was dark. He groped for a switch, found it quickly, and pressed it. As the light came on, Phyllis Brighton sat up in bed with a little scream of fright. She gasped, "What is it?" and stared at them with distended eyes.

Shayne stepped aside so the others could see her, and muttered: "Hell, she doesn't look like a murderess."

"What is it?" she screamed again, half-rising from her bed. The front of her nightgown showed stainless and clean.

"Hold everything, sister," Shayne said as he would have soothed a small child, "your mother has had an accident."

"Oh!" Her knuckles went to her mouth where she bit at them

frantically as if to hold back a scream. Her slender body crouched away from the men as she would have drawn back from wild animals ready to attack her.

"Keep as calm as you can," Shayne told her. "You didn't do it. Your door was locked on the outside and you couldn't have got out if you'd tried."

"Oh! Where is she? I must see her," the girl cried. She threw the covers back and started to get out of bed.

Shayne stepped forward and put his hand on her shoulder and gently forced her back. "Take it easy. You're not in any shape to see her now."

She sank back obediently. Shayne turned to Hilliard and said, "Better look after her, doc. Get her calmed down before the police come."

Dr. Hilliard stepped forward with professional calm and Shayne said to the others, "We'll get out. Whoever did the killing must have locked the girl in her room first. It's a cinch she didn't do it and then lock herself in."

Dr. Pedique took a white silk handkerchief from his pocket and mopped his face. "I don't understand," he said as they went down the hallway.

Shayne grinned at his back. "I don't either," he said, "but I guess my job's finished, I'll be running along."

"Wait!" sputtered Dr. Pedique. "The murderer. The police will be here!"

"Let them worry about the murderer," said Shayne. "That's their job, not mine. I'm breezing before they start pestering me with idiotic questions." He went down the front stairs while the doctor and Clarence stared after him, bewildered.

Shayne lost no time in getting his roadster out of the drive. Two blocks south a racing automobile passed him with screaming siren. He grinned at the police car and drove leisurely back to his apartment hotel in Miami. This time, he went in the front way and up the elevator. A grin accompanied an involuntary sigh when he closed the door of his apartment and walked over to the center table. He took off his coat and gingerly took the butcher knife and nightgown from his pocket and laid them on the table beside the bottle of cognac. The look of being withdrawn from what he was doing began to come over his face once again. It meant that Michael Shayne was beginning to add up the score. So, when his eye lit on the two hundred-dollar bills, which were lying where he had left them, he merely picked them up and stuck them in his pocket without any indication of whether he was surprised to find them still there or not. Then he went to the bedroom and undressed, slipped his gaunt length into tan pajamas and pulled on a dressing robe. With felt bedroom slippers on his feet, he padded out to the other room, took the tall glass to the kitchen where he crushed new ice cubes and made another glass of ice water.

Returning, he set the glass carefully on the table, poured a wine-glass of cognac, and set cigarettes and matches on the small stand near by. Next he lowered himself into the deep chair, lit a cigarette, and proceeded to gaze through the blue smoke at the chiffon-wrapped butcher knife before him.

It was a few minutes after ten when he sat down. Two hours later the ash-tray was filled with half-smoked butts; the level of the liquid in the brandy bottle was considerably lower, the small amount of water remaining in the glass was warm, but he had reached no con-clusion. Carefully he poured another glass of cognac and debated whether he should get more ice. Deciding it was too much trouble, he lifted the glass to his lips.

He held it there, but his eyes shifted toward the door as a soft tapping sounded on the panel. After one reflective sip, he set the glass down carefully and stood erect. The tapping sounded again. Shayne's arm shot out and opened the table drawer. The other arm swept the knife and nightgown in it. He closed the drawer soundlessly and pad-ded to the door.

When he opened it and looked out, he said: "I've been expecting you," and stood aside to let Phyllis Brighton enter.

Mary Roberts Rinehart

1876-1958

Founder of the "Had I But Known" mystery, a twentieth-century
variation on the classic gothic novel, Mary Roberts Rinehart
became the first important woman mystery writer with the
publication of *The Circular Staircase* in 1908. Adding romance,
terror, and occasionally humor in a distinctively American setting
to the traditional mystery, she would go on to become the
highest-paid American author and a national figure for her vivid
reporting from the Allied lines during World War I. Although
reporters were banned from the front, Rinehart used the Red
Cross credentials she had earned as a nurse to talk her way there.
Always an individualist unafraid to express her opinions, Rinehart
took time off from reporting on the political conventions of 1916
to join a suffragette march. In 1947 she became the first woman
to discuss her mastectomy publicly, and her article in the *Ladies
Home Journal* detailing her experiences with breast cancer and
advising women to have periodic breast examinations brought the
largest reader response to date in that magazine's history.

An Allegheny, Pennsylvania, native, Mary Roberts moved to
Pittsburgh to become a nurse, married Dr. Stanley Marshall
Rinehart, and quickly had three children. In 1903 she began sub-
mitting stories to help support her family. Selling forty-five stories
that first year for a total of $1,842.50, she found herself increas-
ingly popular with editors and audiences. After experimenting
with serial murder mysteries, she began publishing those serials
as novels. Most of her work involves a woman in a large, often
decaying house or isolated community confronted with a crime.
As the woman begins to investigate, she generally finds herself
working with—and often competing against—professional detectives, encountering romance, and uncovering hidden family or
community secrets. While the professionals investigate physical
clues, Rinehart's heroines, like her principal series character
Nurse Hilda Adams (nicknamed "Miss Pinkerton"), explore emotional ones. Despite their intelligence and talents, Rinehart's
heroines invariably fail to absorb critical information, leading

them inevitably to announce, "Had I but known then what I know now. . . ." Rinehart also published a popular series of comic, quasi-detective stories about Letitia (Tish) Carberry.

During the early 1930s, at the suggestion of Herbert Hoover, the Rineharts began wintering on Useppa Island, a Gulf Coast resort frequented by the Vanderbilts, Rockefellers, Rothschilds, and such celebrities as Hoover, Teddy Roosevelt, Zane Grey, Gene Tunney, Shirley Temple, and Gloria Swanson. (Rinehart's daughter-in-law, Gracia, bought nearby Palmetto Key for $2,500 in 1937 and renamed it Cabbage Key.) Of her many novels and stories, the only one located in Florida is "Murder and the South Wind," published in *Good Housekeeping* in 1945. Set in an affluent, civilized Gulf Coast community like Useppa Island, the story weaves into a fairly typical Rinehart mystery both the tarpon fishing, bridge, and golf that she enjoyed and a suggestion of the world outside as fighters practice shooting targets in the Gulf while dirigibles hover above observing both the military and civilian communities.

Murder and
the South Wind

Mary Roberts Rinehart

THE TROUBLE WAS that no one knew just when the bridge game started that afternoon. That left none of us with an alibi—not even Mother—and at least two of us had a possible motive.

It was frightfully hot in Florida last winter. There had been a south wind for weeks, which meant mosquitoes, no fishing, and everybody's nerves in poor shape. I had coaxed Tom, my husband, down for a month's vacation from the Washington madhouse, but with no fishing he risked sunstroke by playing golf every day. Thank God, he was on the course that afternoon. At least he had an alibi.

Anyhow, there we were, the four of us, and the fifth who wasn't there in body was certainly there in spirit. He was Captain Hugh Gardiner, on a ten-day furlough, and he was there in spirit because one of our players, Fanny Raeburn, had divorced him and taken her maiden name, and because Pat Wilson was supposed to be going to marry him.

They had wandered in separately in search of a cool place, but even our patio was hot that day. Fanny was already there when Pat came in. Pat looked as though she was going to back out, but Fanny gave a queer little laugh.

"Come on, Pat," she said. "I hope we're civilized enough to behave ourselves. How about some bridge?"

Pat came in. She looked lovely in spite of the heat and I saw Fanny staring at her. But Pat didn't look well. There were circles around her eyes, and Fanny leaned toward me as she put up her bicycle. We all used bicycles on the island. No gas.

"She and Hugh had a fight last night," she said. "Something about a girl at the hotel."

"How on earth do you know?"

"Our Mary Pearl," she said smugly. "The Negroes know everything that goes on. It gives me the creeps."

"Where's Roy?" I said, to change the subject. Roy was the brother she was visiting.

"Where do you think?"

Well, of course, I knew. Roy Raeburn was out after seashells. It was more than a mania with him. It was a science. He was an authority on shells of all sorts, and every beach on the island knew his stooped, near-sighted body and the collector's box he carried. Which, of course, put him in the picture later.

We played in the patio, but the game wasn't a success. For one thing, Pat played terribly. And there were five or six fighter planes out over the Gulf of Mexico shooting at a towed target and making a lot of noise. I remember Mother tucking away the two dollars she had won when it was over and looking up at them.

"I hope it's cool for those boys out there," she said. "When I think of what's ahead of them—"

Pat stared at the sky.

"I don't think it's safe," she said. "Those bullets travel a long way. If anyone is out there in a boat—"

Fanny grinned.

"Worried about Hugh?" she inquired, rather nastily. Pat flushed.

"Hugh?" I said, astonished. "Don't tell me he's fishing?"

"He heard the tarpon were in," Pat said defensively.

"That's ridiculous," I said. "With this wind? There isn't a tarpon within a hundred miles."

"They may be in, but they're not showing," Mother said idly.

I kept quiet. There is an old argument about the tarpon. One school of thought maintains that they are in the Pass all the year round but simply not interested. The other insists that they go somewhere back to spawn in the spring. Friendships have crashed over this. But this is only incidentally a tarpon story. Actually it is about a murder.

I remember that Fanny had gone into the house to get her sun hat when one of the guides came through the gate in the hedge. He seemed embarrassed when he saw us, and took off his cap.

"Could I speak to you, Mrs. Hull?" he said to Mother.

"Why, of course, Joe," Mother said. "What is it?"

I think now that he was pale, under his leathery tan. And just then a four-engined bomber came over the treetops and nobody could speak for a minute or so. Joe simply waited. I noticed that he had not looked at Pat.

"If you don't mind, I'd rather see you alone, ma'am," he said doggedly when the noise had subsided. "It's sort of a private matter."

Mother looked surprised. She got up, however, and took him into the house. Only Pat and I were left, and Pat had lost all her color under her make-up.

"Something's happened, Peg," she said. "Did you see Joe's face?"

"Probably just a row about something," I said.

She stood still, looking rather odd. A Navy dirigible had come sailing overhead, and as it was low the engines made a lot of noise. But Mother was still in the house and I was puzzled.

"Joe wouldn't look at me," she said, her lips stiff. "I think it's about Hugh."

"Don't be an idiot," I said sharply. "He's safe enough. Who's guiding him?"

She said it was Bill Smith, and I said Bill was a good guide and to stop worrying. Then Fanny came out of the house, with her hat on one side of her head and her eyes wide.

"Why on earth is your mother calling the sheriff?" she demanded. "What's wrong?"

"Didn't you hear?"

She let that pass. She was not above listening to things that didn't concern her, but now she was excited.

"Only the call," she said. "After that she shut the door."

I grinned. Then I saw Pat's face. "It's probably nothing," I said. "The whole village comes to Mother. Sit down, Pat. Fanny, your hat's crooked. What's all the excitement anyhow?"

But I knew something was wrong when Mother came out of the house, followed by Joe. She didn't look at Pat or Fanny. She glanced at me.

"I'm going down to the guide dock, Peggy," she said. "Joe's got his car here. You'd better come with me."

I got up, and so did Pat. She stared at Mother.

"It's Hugh, isn't it, Mrs. Hull?"

I think Mother had meant to lie, but there was something in Pat's face that warned her.

"There's been an accident," she said. "I wouldn't worry too much, Pat dear. Wait until we know."

"What sort of accident?" Pat's voice was frozen.

"Bill Smith says it was a bullet from one of the planes."

"Is he badly hurt?"

"I don't know yet. Better go home, Pat. I'll let you know at once."

But Pat was not going home nor, as it turned out, was Fanny. I suppose you can divorce a man and even hate him, but it must come as a shock to know that something has happened to him. Anyhow we all got into Joe's ancient open car and headed for the guide dock. None of us said anything, but over our heads the dirigible had turned suddenly and headed for the Pass which leads between the islands to the Gulf, and from down at the mouth of the bayou I could hear a Coast Guard boat moving out. That's nothing unusual, of course. The guides have a conviction that the Coast Guard puts out merely to go fishing. But they were not going fishing that day.

At the guide house Bill Smith was sitting on the dilapidated steps, with his head in his hands and three or four guides around him, not talking. Just standing. Pat was the first out of the car.

"Where is he?" she said. "Maybe he's not—Why haven't you got a doctor, or somebody?"

Bill looked up. His face was agonized when he saw who it was.

"He ain't here, Miss Wilson," he said. "He went overboard and he never came up. I've been an hour in the Pass, looking."

It was Fanny who spoke then, her voice incredulous.

"You're crazy, Bill," she said. "He can swim like a fish."

"He was shot first," said Bill, and put his head down in his horny fisherman's hands again.

Pat didn't faint. She just stood there, and she made no protest when one of the guides offered to take her home. She even got into the car herself, but she looked completely dazed. I wanted to go with her. I didn't like to think of her going back by herself, but she refused.

"Let me alone, Peg," she said. "I'm all right. It's just—"

She didn't finish. The car drove off, and after that Bill told his story.

"I been afraid of them planes right along," he said. "But Captain Gardiner was set to go." He got out a cigarette and tried to light it, but his hands shook too much. "I told him it was no good with this south wind, but you know how he was. And I was wrong at that. He struck a fish right off." He gulped. "Never anything like this happened to me before," he said dully. "If only I could have brought him in, but he was gone in a second. Must have caught in the line some way, and he never came up. I been looking for him like a crazy man for the last hour or more."

That was Bill's story, and the details did not change it. Hugh had struck a tarpon on the slack tide. It was a good one, a hundred pounds or more, Bill thought. It had been a fighter, and it had jumped seven times, trying to throw the hook. The boat had been all over the Pass, and it was near the lighthouse when it happened.

Hugh had been excited. He stood up when the fish stopped jumping, and began to pump it in.

"He's licked," he said. "Get ready, Bill."

Bill warned him to get in his chair again. There was a lot of fight still in the fish. "Those big boys don't know when they're whipped," he told him. However, Hugh only swore at him and kept on reeling. Then it happened. It looked as though something hit him in the head, for he put his hand there. Then he staggered, and the next minute he went overboard. He never came up.

"Only way I can figure it," Bill said, "is that the fish was towing him. He may be out in the Gulf by now."

"You think it was a spent bullet from a plane?" I asked.

"What else? There was a pelican with a broken wing out there yesterday. I had to shoot it."

"I thought you weren't allowed to carry guns now," I said.

"What's a fellow to do if somebody he's guiding gets a shark?" Bill asked defensively. "I didn't shoot the captain, if that's what you mean."

But of course, there it was. Bill didn't carry a watch, and he had no real idea when it happened. But he had had a gun in his boat, and Hugh was dead.

I got Mother home after that. She was looking shocked, for, if she hadn't liked Hugh Gardiner, she was fond of Bill. But she knew Bill's temper, too, and that Hugh was the cocksure type to rouse it. The one thing he wants in that part of the world is to bring in the year's first big tarpon. If Hugh had mishandled his fish, and the two men had quarreled—

But there was no body, and there was Bill's story about the pelican to account for the fact that his rifle had been recently fired. Anyhow, none of us was really thinking about murder then.

On my way home I stopped to see how Pat was. The house on the point at the Pass is Roy Raeburn's, and next to it the Wilsons'. Beyond that is the Drakes', who were not there this season, and then comes ours. The rest sprawl for a couple of miles along the beach, each fairly hidden in palms and tropical stuff, and with the village and the hotel behind them.

I walked in without ringing and went up the stairs. Pat's door was closed, but her mother's was open and she called to me from her bed. She had broken her hip the summer before and was still practically bedridden.

"Come in, Peggy," she said. "What's this about the Gardiner man? Lulie says he's dead. I can't get anything out of Pat. She's shut in her room."

Lulie was their colored maid, and as all our servants are Negroes our domestic grapevine just misses being the African drum sort of thing.

"I wonder how she heard about it," I said. "I'm afraid it's true, Mrs. Wilson. A spent bullet from a plane, probably."

I told her what I knew. In a way I felt sorry for her, cooped up as she was and all this drama going on around her. She was a little woman, and she looked pathetic lying there. She listened intently.

"I'm not pretending I'm grieving," she said. "I didn't like the fellow.

He treated Fanny like dirt, and I hear he's flirting with some girl or other at the hotel. I told Pat so, but it didn't do any good," she added dryly.

Lulie carried in her supper tray just then. She looked sulky, as well she might, with one maid in a house that needed four, although Pat helped her all she could. Mrs. Wilson was what locally was called close with her money. I left them and went across the hall. Pat didn't answer my knock, so I opened the door and looked in. She was standing at the window, staring out at the water, and when she didn't turn I closed the door and went away.

Nevertheless, I didn't like to leave her alone. Our colored servants all make a break for their homes after they finish dinner in the evening, and I was afraid Pat's unnatural calm would break. I bribed Lulie to stay until eleven, when I would take over for the night, and I told her to say nothing about it.

When I got home Tom was already back from his golf game. He was having a Scotch and soda listening to Mother, and I thought it was a pity to have his month's vacation from Washington disturbed. But when I said so he merely observed that when men were dying all over the world we couldn't expect not to have some troubles of our own. His detachment made me indignant.

"Don't tell me a spent bullet killed him," I said. "They're falling all over the island, and nobody's been hurt."

"He was standing in the boat. It could have knocked him out, and the fish did the rest."

"Bill said he was hit in the side of the head. Would a bullet from the air do that?"

"Possibly. How about some dinner?"

We ate in the patio, although the mosquitoes were pretty bad, and we had just reached the dessert when the sheriff appeared, having come by a boat from the mainland. He was a tall, gangling man with a battered soft hat and an equally soft voice. Mother knew him, of course, and he accepted a glass of iced coffee, putting his hat carefully on the tiles as he did so.

"Kind of a funny accident, Mrs. Hull," he said. "Don't know as I've ever heard of one like it before."

"I'm glad you realize it must have been an accident," Mother said. "I've known Bill Smith for thirty years. He's quite incapable of murder."

He sipped his coffee. "Don't know it's murder yet," he said dryly. "Trouble about Bill is his rifle's been fired lately."

"I understand he shot a wounded pelican."

"So he says. But until we find the body—Anybody else around here would want to shoot the captain? If he was shot, of course."

"Nobody," Mother said firmly. "His former wife is visiting her brother, but she is out of the question. For one thing, she was playing bridge here when it happened."

"Far as I can make out, nobody knows when it did happen," he drawled. "Anyhow, I guess divorce isn't a cause for murder any more. Time was when—" He let that go. "I've been to the hotel," he said. "Nothing in his room, except a lot of good-looking clothes. No letters, no anything." He put down his glass and got up. "Ate a hearty breakfast this morning, read the papers, went swimming and back to the hotel for lunch. Hotel says he was playing around with a Patricia Wilson. What about her?"

"She was engaged to him, or about to be," Mother said shortly. "Also she was here this afternoon. Why on earth do you think this is a murder anyhow? The way those bullets were falling—"

"They're falling over most of the state," he said, and picked up his hat. "Nobody's been killed yet."

Tom went out to the street with him, but he had nothing to say when he came back, except to protest violently when I said I was staying with Pat that night. He may not always know when I am around, but he certainly raises the roof when I am not. In the end I simply walked out on him at eleven o'clock. Owing to the blackout I had practically to feel my way, and the temperature was still a good ninety degrees. Not a leaf or branch was moving, and I was drying the back of my neck with a handkerchief when someone grabbed me by the arm.

I had just opened my mouth to yell when Fanny spoke in a whisper.

"I was on my way to see you," she said.

"What's the idea, scaring me to death?"

"I thought you were the sheriff, so I hid in the shrubbery. He thinks it's murder, doesn't he? That somebody shot Hugh from the beach?"

"How on earth did you get that?"

"How does anyone learn anything here?" she said dully. "Mary Pearl told me. She says he's looking for rifles, and I can't find Roy's."

"Doesn't Roy know where it is?"

"He's asleep. He was out shelling all day, and he went to bed early. Peg, I'm frightened. He and Hugh had a terrific row the other day. Hugh was behind in my alimony, and I'm about out of money. If anybody heard it—"

The idea of Roy shooting anybody because he hadn't paid his alimony made me smile. I reassured her as well as I could and went on to the Wilsons'. But I was rather startled to find the sheriff at their back door, talking to a frightened Lulie.

"Now listen," he said. "I don't want any lies out of you. People have been trying to lie to me for years. They don't get away with it."

"I'm not lying," Lulie said shrilly. "There's no gun in this house. I been here every winter for five years. I ain't never seen no old gun."

He let her go then, and she scurried off like a small black beetle. He looked at me.

"Never know where you are with these people," he said. "Do you know if they have a rifle here? Or any sort of gun?"

"I'm pretty sure they haven't," I told him. "They had one, years ago, when we had a rifle range. But after the golf course was extended Mrs. Wilson gave hers to Bill Smith. I suppose that's the one he had in his boat."

Lulie had left the door open, and when he had gone I went in. Upstairs everything was quiet. Mrs. Wilson was asleep and Pat's door was locked, so I turned out the lights and tried to find a breath of air on the porch. I couldn't see the Pass from where I sat, but out in the Gulf a number of boats were moving slowly about, their lights looked strange, since no boats had been allowed out after sunset since the war began. They were searching for the body, of course, and in spite of the heat I felt chilly.

I was still convinced, however, that Hugh's death had been an act of God, if not of Providence. Upstairs at one time I heard Pat moving about, but when I listened she was merely getting her mother a glass of water. I could hear Mrs. Wilson's querulous voice.

"You ought to thank heaven he's gone," she said. "He was no good. He never was any good."

"I'd rather not discuss it, Mother."

There was more, but I didn't listen. I was turning away when I had a surprise. Standing where I was I could see across to the Raeburn house, and someone was moving about in it and carrying a light. Not a flashlight—we couldn't buy any batteries for them, of course—but what seemed to be a candle. It was going from room to room on the lower floor, and at first I thought it was Fanny, still looking for Roy's rifle.

I walked across, determined to send her to bed, but when I reached the window I saw it was not Fanny. It was Roy, Roy in his pajamas and bedroom slippers, moving furtively from the living-room to the library, and peering about through his spectacles. As I watched he set the candle on a table and began feeling behind some books on the shelves. He fumbled for a minute or two. Then to my horror he took out a row of books and set them on the floor. And the next thing he did was to haul out his missing rifle.

I was stunned; steady mild old Roy, with his spectacles and his stoop, and his shells. It didn't make sense. It didn't make any more sense when I saw the light next in the basement and was certain he was down there cleaning the gun.

I went home at daylight, confused and in what is called a state. Tom was still asleep, and I didn't tell him. For there had been something fumbling about Roy as he found the rifle. As though he wasn't sure where it was. In that case, had Fanny killed Hugh? She loathed him, of course, and she might have done it before the bridge game. But in that event why tell me she couldn't find the gun? Why not have thrown it into the sea? Or have cleaned it herself? Or—and this kept me awake a long time— was she merely being clever and involving Roy? Fanny was nobody's fool. Only—her own brother!

I overslept that morning and was late for the Red Cross. But I was not surprised when Fanny came into the workroom where we were about to make new kitbags for the Army. I was still puzzling how to put the stuff together when I saw her getting off her bicycle at the curb outside. She came directly to me, and she was looking cheerful and perfectly calm.

"I'm sorry I made an idiot of myself last night, Peggy," she said. "I suppose I was excited."

"Does that mean you've found the gun?"

"Of course. It was in the hall closet. In Roy's golf bag. I didn't see it, that's all. It hasn't been fired for ages."

I let it go at that. After all, we still had no body and so no murder, and I had always felt sorry for Fanny.

They had not found the body by the third day, and the sheriff left that morning. Then at noon Peter Randolph arrived. He was not Peter Randolph to me at that time. He was merely a nice-looking young man, getting off the train across from the Red Cross room along with a lot of other visitors, and armed with an old suitcase and a brand-new rod trunk. But he looked rather lost. He was still there when the train pulled out. Then to my astonishment I saw my own Tom loping across the platform and shaking hands with him; Tom, who should have been on the golf course and who never met a train for anybody.

He says I have a suspicious nature. Perhaps I have, but the whole thing looked phony to me. I put down my work and went across the street, and I saw that my beloved husband was longing to strangle me. He pulled himself together, however.

"Well, Pete," he said, "here's the whole family to meet you. Peg, this is Peter Randolph, an old friend of mine. My wife, Pete."

I looked at them. I didn't believe they were old friends. I knew all Tom's friends, and there wasn't a Pete among them. I didn't believe they had ever seen each other before. I even had an idea that a wilted red carnation in Pete's buttonhole was for identification purposes. And I certainly wasn't going to let them pull anything over on me.

"How nice!" I said. "Any old friend of Tom's is mine, of course. We can't let you go to the hotel, can we, Tom? You'd probably have to sleep in a bathtub. Mother has loads of room. Where's the car, Tom? He'll want to clean up."

Tom looked furious and Pete slightly bewildered. But I won in the end. There wasn't much else they could do about it. I drove them both home in triumph, although Tom didn't speak to me until we reached the house. Then he caught me alone.

"I suppose you think you've pulled a fast one," he said sourly. "Why the hell bring him here?"

"Any old friend of yours, darling," I told him primly, "is welcome at my mother's house. And you're the one who's pulling a fast one, aren't you?"

Mother was faintly surprised but rather pleased when she discovered Pete at lunch and learned he was staying with her. And he must have been delighted with Mother. She told him about everybody, including Bill Smith and Hugh Gardiner's death. And when the meal was over and Ebenezer, the colored butler, had disappeared, she said something else which made him sit up rather sharply. She had been quiet for a minute or two, as though she was listening.

"I wonder what's wrong with the servants," she said. "They're too quiet."

"Maybe it's the heat," Tom said idly. Tom is, of course, an import. He doesn't know the Negroes as we do. But Mother shook her head.

"Usually the kitchen sounds like a Holy Roller meeting," she said. "Now, as Peggy would say, they've clammed up. That always means something."

As I say, Pete was watching her.

"What do you think it means?" he asked.

"It's a form of self-protection," Mother said. "They know something, and they don't intend to be mixed up in it. Of course, it may be only a knifing among themselves."

Pete lit a cigarette.

"How long has it been going on?" he inquired, conversationally.

"Just the last day or two," Mother said. "It isn't the heat. They like it. And it isn't only here. It's all over the island. Even my laundress acts as if she'd lost her tongue."

I saw he was interested, but he asked no more questions. He went fishing that afternoon, in an old pair of slacks and a sweater, and I was not surprised when I learned Bill Smith was taking him. I tried my best to get something out of Tom about him while he was gone. I even played a round of golf in the heat to do it. But, while Tom is the king of my particular world, the good old oyster has nothing on him when it comes to keeping his mouth shut, if that is what an oyster does.

"It's funny you never spoke about Peter Randolph before," I said. "When and how did you know him?"

"Oh, hither and yon," he said vaguely. "Look, don't try to drive over the bayou and talk at the same time. We're almost out of balls."

"Well, I ought to know something about him. After all, he's our guest."

"Only because you acted like an idiot," he said. Which made me so furious that I drove straight into the water. There was no use asking any more about Pete after that. We were hardly on speaking terms until dinner.

Pete was gone all afternoon. He came home with a violent sunburn and said he had caught a ladyfish, which Bill had thrown away, and hooked onto a mackerel shark, which towed them all over the Pass. He showed his blisters with pride, but I didn't believe for a moment that he had only been fishing.

And then, of course, he met Pat Wilson. Perhaps I haven't said enough about Pat, how gay she has always been, and how lovely to look at, and—in a way—how lonely she was that season, with so few other young people around and a querulous mother to care for. But Pete saw it in a minute. He had come down, looking very nice in flannels and a tweed jacket, and Tom was mixing cocktails when she ran in, pale and scared to death.

"It's Mother," she gasped. "She's had a heart attack. Telephone a doctor, somebody."

Of course, they had no telephone. It had been taken out, to send to Russia probably. But Mother had kept hers by threatening to sue the company for breaking and entering or something of the sort if they tried to get it. She went to it at once.

Tom grabbed a cocktail and offered it to Pat, but she shook her head. "I'm all right," she said. "I have to go back. It's Lulie's day out. Mother's alone."

She started out and Pete hurried after her. By the time I got to the house they were both upstairs, and he had broken an ammonia capsule under Mrs. Wilson's nose and was feeling her pulse and telling Pat everything was under control.

He came downstairs after the doctor arrived, and stood at a window looking out.

"Does that girl live with this old woman all the time?" he asked.

"She's her mother. What else can she do?"

"It must be the hell of a life," he said glumly. "She was engaged to Gardiner, wasn't she?"

"I think she was. She never said so."

"Anything to escape, eh?"

I had no time to speak. Pat herself came down, looking almost collapsed, and he put her on a sofa and offered to get Lulie for her. She only closed her eyes and nodded. I suppose he located Lulie—it was movie night on the island—and I heard him coming in very late.

We still had the south wind the next day. Mrs. Wilson was better, but I was nervous and irritable, and so was everybody else. They had stopped the search for Hugh's body, and in a way it was a relief. After all, death was all around us anyhow. Every now and then some poor lad would crash his plane into the Gulf and never be seen again. And it was time for the mackerel and kingfish to come in. All the boats were out loaded with visitors and with boxes and barrels for the catch, but the only people who got anything were the guides, who were being paid. We saw very little of Pete, although he turned up each night for dinner. He had hired a bicycle, but I didn't think he was using it for exercise, although he seemed to be all over the island.

Then, three days after his arrival, I decided to go out with Bill Smith to get a breeze, if nothing else, and that was when they found Hugh. I had just closed about four million pores when I saw Bill staring seaward with his sharp fisherman's eyes.

"Something going on out at that channel marker," he said. "Maybe we better run out and see."

It was a good thing we did. The people in the boat were guests from the hotel, and one woman had already fainted. There was something behind them in the water, and the guide was holding it with a gaff. We left him there, and took the others back to the guide dock in our boat. Then I telephoned Tom.

"You'd better come down," I said, "and bring Pete if you can. I think they've found Hugh."

I passed the two of them in the local taxi as I went home, but they didn't see me. And Tom had nothing to say when he came back, except that it was Hugh, all right, and that he was glad I hadn't seen him. Pete didn't turn up until the next morning, and then it was only to say grimly that Hugh had been shot in the head with a bullet from a rifle, and that they had the bullet.

"Not too hard a shot," he said. "Anybody on the beach near the Pass could have done it. Bill says they weren't far from the lighthouse when it happened."

Well, there we were. With all the tropical stuff around our houses, the beach was practically cut off, and as I said at the beginning none of us really had an alibi, except Tom. What with the shooting in the air and the bombers and even the blimp that were constantly overhead, the noise would never have been noticed. And the next day Fanny came in, looking like death and on the edge of hysteria.

Pete had taken Roy's rifle away.

She sat down as though her legs wouldn't hold her, and stared at me out of red-rimmed eyes.

"Maybe he did do it," she said. "I've tried not to believe it, but I lied to you before. That rifle wasn't in his golf bag. I looked. It wasn't there until the next morning." She tried to light a cigarette with shaking hands. "If you tell that, I'll deny it, but it's the truth."

"He couldn't have seen well enough to shoot anybody," I said. "His eyes are bad. I just don't believe it, Fanny."

But she only got up and put down her cigarette. "It had a telescopic sight," she said drearily, "and I'd like to bet Mary Pearl was out of the house the minute I left it that day."

She went back to the house, leaving me pretty thoughtful. It might be, I considered. Maybe that was what our colored servants knew, that Mary Pearl had been out, and that Roy's rifle had been missing that evening when Fanny looked for it. That wasn't all they knew, of course, but I didn't realize it then.

I didn't even realize it that same night when the Wilson garage was burned.

It was a terrific excitement. The fire siren got us all out of bed, and Pete was on his way before I was fully awake. The garage was dry and it burned with a tremendous noise and with sparks that flew all over the neighborhood. It was in full blast when I got there. The fire engine was useless, and for a while I thought the house would go, too. Even the palms were burning. Pete had carried Mrs. Wilson out and put her in a chair on the lawn, and Pat was standing beside her looking worried and bewildered.

"It's the car," she told Pete. "There was no time to get it out. Even if there had been, there was no gas in it."

She was pretty well shocked, and Pete wanted to get her a drink. She shook her head, however.

"It's queer," she said. "We haven't used the garage this year. I didn't even keep my bicycle there. What in the world set it on fire?"

Just then the roof crashed in, and the whole structure fell. I can still remember Pete's face as he stared at the ruins.

"Is there a cellar under it?" he asked.

"No. Why?"

"Because there's no car there," he said. "Not even the skeleton of one."

Well, anyone could see that. The onlookers seemed to realize it, too. They were muttering. As for Mrs. Wilson, she was not too feeble to be furious.

"Somebody took it out and wrecked it," she said shrilly. "That's why they burned the garage. To cover it up."

Nobody argued with her, even when she accused Pat of having done it herself. When it was all over, Pete and Tom carried her up to her bed, and we went home. Tom fixed some highballs and we sat around, but Pete seemed thoughtful. He spoke only once, and that was to say that Pat was an unusual sort of girl.

"Found her trying to carry the old lady downstairs herself," he said. "Me, I'd have let her burn!"

But before he went to bed he said something else.

"If I knew why and how that car got away I'd know the hell of a lot of things," was what he said.

It was still hotter than blazes the next morning. Pete stayed around the house. He seemed to be waiting for something, and it turned out finally to be a telephone call from the mainland. The next thing I knew he and Roy Raeburn were on their way to the dock. I felt a little sick, but if Tom knew anything he wasn't talking.

"Does that mean the bullet came from Roy's gun?" I asked anxiously.

"How do I know?" he said stiffly. "This is the hell of a vacation anyhow. Look at that thermometer!"

I didn't look at the thermometer. I didn't need to. And I tried to see Fanny that morning, but Mary Pearl said she was shut in her room with the door locked. She looked excited, as all our servants do when anything happens to any of us, but she looked secretive, too. And when I went to the Wilsons' their Lulie looked the same. I lost patience finally.

"See here, Lulie," I said, "if you know anything about Mr. Gardiner's death you'd better talk, and talk soon. They put people in jail for suppressing evidence."

"I don't know nothing," she said sullenly. "Me, I mind my business and let other people mind theirs."

Which was, I thought, a not too delicate hint.

Pat looked rather better that day, although she was still bewildered about the fire. I wondered if she had really been in love with Hugh, after all, or if Pete wasn't right and he had been an escape from the life she had been living, dragged around after her mother for years, and without much prospect of anything else. But there was a difference in her. She looked worried.

"I never thought of Roy," she said. "He doesn't seem the sort, does he? I suppose—well, Hugh must have treated Fanny pretty badly, for this to happen."

"She thinks he did," I said, rather dryly.

That was as far as we got, for at that minute one of the clerks from the general store drove up in a car and we stared at him in astonishment. For the car he brought was the Wilsons,' and he was grinning cheerfully as he got out.

"Found it up the island," he said. "Went up for some pinfish, and there it was, on a back road. Looks all right, too."

He eyed us both with interest. The village likes the winter visitors, but it is always curious about them.

"Not very far from the railroad trestle," he said. "Looks like somebody stole it and then set fire to your garage. Unless you left it there yourself," he added.

"I haven't used it this winter," Pat said, bewildered. "There wasn't even any gas in the tank."

"Well, there's some there now," he said. "Came back under its own steam."

So there was a new mystery. Not that it seemed very important at the time, although, of course, it was. The heat still obsessed us. The mosquitoes had come out of the mangrove swamps and hung around in clouds. The hotel porch was crowded with irritated fishermen who watched the flag on its pole still defiantly pointing north when it pointed at all. Tom was, I presumed, playing golf and using language unbefitting a gentleman. Fanny was still incommunicado. And late in the afternoon Mrs. Wilson had another heart attack, and the doctor got a nurse from the mainland to look after her.

I was in the patio when Tom came home. He drove up in the village taxi, and he looked as if he wanted to bite me when he saw me. He got his clubs out of the car and then lifted out what was obviously a heavy suitcase.

"What's that?" I inquired. "And what's in it? Bricks?"

"It belongs to Pete."

"Good heavens! Is he planning to stay forever?"

He didn't answer that. He carried the thing in carefully and took it upstairs, leaving me to get his golf clubs, and when I went up later to shower and cool off the door into Pete's room was not only closed. It was locked. I marched straight into Tom's room, where he was trying to pull a fresh shirt over his sticky body, and demanded to know what was going on. But the light of my life merely glared at me.

"You keep out of this," he growled. "And let that room alone."

"I'm no snooper," I said tartly. "I merely wondered. If that thing's full of explosives, I'd feel better if it was in a bathtub full of water."

"Explosives!" He laughed—he has a very nice laugh—and rather unexpectedly came over and kissed me. "Well, you can call it that, my wilted darling. Take a shower and forget it."

Pete came home after dinner. Roy was not with him, and he looked tired and worried. I wasn't surprised when he went to see Pat as soon as he had bathed and shaved, but he seemed depressed when he returned, although he said Mrs. Wilson was better. He was puzzled, too, about the car incident.

"It doesn't fit," he said morosely. "Nothing fits. Why the fire? Why steal the car and then leave it? Unless—"

He didn't finish that. He went up to bed, but hours later I heard him going out again, and I was not entirely surprised the next morning to see his door open and the suitcase gone from his room. He himself was at the breakfast table when I went downstairs, and he was looking as pleasant and innocent as though he had spent the night in gentle slumber. It was Mother who added to my bewilderment.

"Did you see Lindy?" she asked him.

"I saw her. Yes."

"Did she talk?"

"No. It's what she wouldn't say that matters."

Well, Lindy is our colored laundress, and all at once I was filled with fury.

"What goes on?" I inquired. "Is this a guessing game, and am I supposed to guess? Or am I merely a stupid fool, too dumb to be told anything?"

Mother opened her mouth to speak, but Pete gave her a warning look.

"I merely wanted to ask Lindy a question," he said mildly. "She wouldn't answer it, so that's that."

"And I suppose you took your washing to her in that suitcase," I said. "You should have emptied the bricks out of it. Lindy's particular about washing bricks."

Mother looked startled.

"What washing?" she inquired. "And what about bricks?" But the grapefruit came just then, and there was no more chance to talk.

The day passed somehow. Mother went to the club for bridge in the afternoon. The fighters were still shooting overhead, and the dirigible passed low over the treetops. Far out in the Gulf a few bombers were dropping practice bombs. They would peel off from the formation, dive, level off, and leave behind them what looked like small geysers in the sea. And Pete spent the afternoon simply loafing, if you can call it loafing when a man sits still for a minute and then jumps up and looks at his watch.

At five o'clock he got his bicycle and went to get some cigarettes, although the house was full of them, and at six he was back, looking as if he had lost all hope of heaven and pretending that the parcel he carried was tobacco. He went upstairs to where Tom had been taking a shower, and through the open window I heard him talking.

"What the hell am I to do?" he said. "There it is! Absolutely foolproof. Look at it."

Tom apparently looked. I couldn't hear what he said, but Pete was excited. I could hear him well enough.

"Look how it shoots up here. And here," he said. "You get it don't you? Only I wish to God I knew the exact time. When did that bridge game start? And how long was Bill Smith in the Pass searching for the body? It didn't take long, of course."

That was all I heard, for evidently my suspicious lord and master had noticed the open window. He slammed it shut, and left my particular world to chaos and to me.

Pat's mother died that night. She was already gone when Lulie ran over just after dinner, and we all went to the Wilson house. Pat was in the lower hall when we arrived. She looked dazed, but calm.

"She didn't suffer," she said. "She merely turned over in bed and— went. Perhaps it's better. She hated being helpless."

I said all the proper things, but I don't think she heard me. She said her mother had been all right that day, but that she was tired after the doctor left that afternoon. He had taken an electrocardiogram, and it had exhausted her.

She didn't really break until Tom and Pete came in. Then, as though it was the most natural thing in the world, she went to Pete, and he put his arms around her and held her. That was when I wandered into the living-room and saw Pete's suitcase. As I've said, I'm no snooper, but it wasn't locked, and what was inside it was not laundry.

Some time later Tom and I left them together and walked home. Tom was having one of his taciturn fits, but I didn't intend to be put off any longer.

"I suppose it's the best way out, isn't it?" I said casually. "It solves Pete's problem anyhow."

"What problem?"

"Pat. He's crazy about her."

"I don't know what you're talking about," Tom said, in his best War Administration manner.

"And the Negroes knew it all along, didn't they? That's why they burned the garage. To prove it."

"To prove what?"

"See here," I said, "I'm not deaf or dumb or blind. That electrocardiogram machine was a lie detector, wasn't it? The doctor put it on her and then asked the questions Pete gave him. That's right, isn't it? And the Negroes knew Mrs. Wilson could get around when she wanted to. That broken hip was healed long ago. Only they were afraid to talk, so I suppose they burned the garage to scare her into running out of the house and giving herself away. That's why they saved Pat's car."

"You're guessing, darling," Tom said, with masculine superiority. "You haven't an ounce of proof."

"Haven't I? What about Roy's gun?"

He stopped and looked down at me.

"What about Roy's gun?"

"She knew he had it. She sent Lulie off, and she fixed it so that Mary Pearl went with her. Then she went to Roy's house and shot Hugh from the porch. Only she didn't have time to put the gun back. She put it behind some books in the library."

Tom looked dazed.

"How on earth do you know all that?"

"Because I saw Roy find it that night. He thought at first that Fanny had done it, so he took the gun to the basement and cleaned it. Later on, I suppose, he suspected the truth. He probably knew Mrs. Wilson could walk. He knew a lot of things besides shells."

Tom stood gazing down at me. Maybe there was love and admiration in his eyes or maybe he was just a male, irritated that a female had put something over on him. I'll never know.

"I suppose," he said, still trying to be superior, "you know why she did it. Or has that escaped you?"

"Maybe it was this south wind," I said. "And, of course, she didn't like him. But anyhow she didn't want Pat to marry anybody. That's why she played helpless. She wanted Pat to stay with her. And, of course, there's the money, too."

"What money?"

"Pat gets half of it when she marries. Hugh knew it, of course."

That, I think, was when he gave up.

"Then, Pete—"

"Certainly. Pete, the old college chum! Pete with a red carnation in his buttonhole so you would know him! Pete will marry money, my beloved. Only he doesn't know it."

It was dark, but I think he had the grace to blush.

"Colonel Peter Randolph of the Military Intelligence, my dear," he said. "Gardiner knew a lot of stuff. When it looked as though he had been murdered, they sent Pete here. That's all."

"And who suggested that?" I asked sweetly.

He didn't answer. He stuck a finger in his mouth to wet it and held it up in the air.

"By God," he said, "I believe the wind is changing."

John Dann MacDonald

1916-1986

Before creating Travis McGee, Florida's knight-errant who subsidizes and justifies his early retirement on the *Busted Flush* by salvaging both cash and broken spirits, John D. MacDonald published thirty-five paperback originals, beginning with *The Brass Cupcake* in 1950. While some of these books rely on stereotypes, predictable plots, or repetitive dialogue, the best of them (for example, *A Flash of Green* and *Cape Fear*, originally published as *The Executioners*) reflect the fascination with human psychology, corporate corruption, and environmental pollution which the color-coded McGee novels would capture so effectively.

After receiving an M.B.A. from Harvard, MacDonald found only frustration in the business world, which may explain his consistency in portraying conglomerates and executives as villains. In 1940 he joined the army, eventually serving with the fabled OSS, the predecessor of the CIA, in China, Burma, and India. Because military censorship inhibited his correspondence, he began writing short stories to his wife, one of which, "Interlude in India," she sold to *Story Magazine*. Finding writing more appealing than business, MacDonald left the army and spent the rest of the 1940s writing for both the pulps and more establishment magazines such as *Cosmopolitan* and *Esquire*. In 1949 he moved to Florida, searching for new challenges.

In *A Flash of Green*, published only two years before Travis McGee appeared in *The Deep Blue Goodbye* (1964), MacDonald tells his archetypal tale, the story of a loss of innocence. Set on the state's southwest coast in the mythical Palm City, a community closely resembling Sarasota, the novel describes a battle between environmentalists and a group of businessmen trying to fill in the shallow Grassy Bay in order to construct waterfront homes. Near the beginning of the novel, Jimmy Wing experiences the tension between his lifestyle and the demands of tourists and developers. As the reporter finds himself more and more deeply enmeshed in the struggle over the bay's future, MacDonald explores the ways money and power corrupt both nature and people.

A Flash of Green

John D. MacDonald

HE DROVE BY the small area of commercial development on Sandy Key adjacent to the causeway, and when he was beyond it he looked south along the blue reach of Grassy Bay. The bay was narrowest near the causeway, widening out toward the south. As he crossed the causeway he saw a small white cruiser setting out from Hoyt's Marina, with a stocky brown woman on the bow, coiling a line. Further down the bay he saw a pattern of flashing white on the water and saw the birds circling and diving in agitation. Maybe mackerel, he thought, in from the Gulf. More likely a school of jacks chopping the bait fish. Two outboards were converging on the roiled area.

When he came off the causeway he was stopped by the traffic light at the intersection of Mangrove Road and Bay Highway. After the May and June hiatus, the summer tourist season was gathering a rather shabby momentum. In the winter months the biggest contingent came from the central states, and there were so many of them that at last, to the residents of Palm County, they seemed to become but one elderly couple, endlessly repeated, driving a bulbous blue car with Ohio plates (at wandering unpredictable speeds), the man in Bermudas, the woman with a big straw purse questing through all the towns of the shallow-water coast, bemused, slightly indignant, frequently bored, like people charged with some mission who had lost their sealed orders before they had a chance to open them.

As was so solemnly and frequently stated by all public officials and all Chamber of Commerce executives, the winter flow of this endlessly duplicated couple was the backbone of the economy, and it often seemed that the supply was inexhaustible, yet Jimmy Wing had noted among the businessmen of Palm City an anxious and almost superstitious attitude toward the continuity of the flow. They heartened themselves with every evidence of repeat business, no matter how questionable the source of the statistics. They fretted about the accessibility of the Caribbean islands. But at the heart of their unrest was the never-spoken conviction that there was really nothing to keep them coming down. It was a fine place to live, and a poor place to visit. They could not quite see how any sane reasonable person would willingly permit himself to be "processed" through that long junk strip of Tamiami, exchanging his vacation money for overpriced lodgings, indifferent food, admission to fish tanks, snake farms, and shell factories.

So secretly disturbed were these businessmen about the proliferating shoddiness of the coast that they were constantly taking random and somewhat contradictory action. The more the beach eroded away, or disappeared into private ownership, the more bravely the huge highway signs proclaimed the availability of miles of white-sand beaches. As the shallow-water fishing decreased geometrically under the attrition of dredging, filling, sewage and too many outboard motors, they paid to have the superb fishing advertised, and backed contests which would further decimate the dwindling fish population. As the quiet and primitive mystery of the broad tidal bays disappeared, as the mangroves and the rookeries and the oak hammocks were uprooted with such industriousness the morning sound of construction equipment became more familiar than the sound of the mockingbird, the businessmen substituted the delights of pageants, parades and beauty contests. (See the Grandmaw America Contest, with evening gown, talent and bathing suit eliminations.)

So quietly uneasy were the business interests that the few tourist attractions of any dignity or legitimacy whatsoever were pointed to with more pride than they merited. (Weeki Wachee, Bok Tower, Ringling Museums—and "The Last Supper" duplicated in genuine ceramic tile.)

One motel operator on Cable Key had expressed the hidden fear to Jimmy Wing one quiet September afternoon. "Some season we'll get all ready for them. We'll fix up all the signs and raise the rates and hire all the waitresses and piano players and pick the trash off the beaches and clean the swimming pools and stock up on all the picture postcards and sun glasses and straw slippers and cement pelicans like we always have, and we'll set back and wait, and they won't show up. Not a single damn one." He had peered at Jimmy in the air-conditioned gloom of the bar, and laughed with a quiet hysteria. "No one at all."

And this hidden fear, Jimmy realized, was one of the reasons—perhaps the most pertinent reason—for the Grassy Bay project. Once you had consistently eliminated most of the environmental features which had initially attracted a large tourist trade, the unalterable climate still made it a good place to live. New permanent residents would bolster the economy. And so, up and down the coast, the locals leaned over backward to make everything as easy and profitable as possible for the speculative land developers. Arvida went into Sarasota. General Development went into Port Charlotte. And a hundred other operators converged on the "sun coast," platting the swamps and sloughs, clearing the palmetto scrub lands, laying out and constructing the suburban slums of the future.

In the Palm City area it had not worked the way the downtown businessmen had hoped it would. Buck Flake had developed Palm Highlands, and Earl Ganson had set up Lakeview Village, and Pete Bender had made a good thing out of Lemon Ridge Estates, but just as fast as the population density in the newly developed areas warranted it, the big new shopping centers went in.

Grassy Bay would be an entirely different kind of scrub-land housing. The waterfront lots would be more expensive, the houses bigger, the future residents a little fatter in the purse than the retireds who bought their budget tract houses back in the piny flats where the cattle had once grazed.

Ahead of Jimmy Wing as he waited for the light was a typical summer tourist vehicle, an old green Hudson from Tennessee, the fenders rusting, the back seat full of kids, a luggage rack on top piled high and covered with a frayed tarp. A car in the traffic headed out onto Sandy Key honked and somebody called his name, but he did not turn quickly enough to see who it was. Two cars later he recognized Eloise Cable alone in her white Karmann Ghia with the top down. The yellow scarf tied around her black hair made her face and shoulders look exceptionally brown. She grasped the wheel high and held her chin high, looking arrogant, impatient and behind schedule.

When the light changed he turned left on Bay Boulevard and drove on into the middle of the city, turned left on Center Street and drove out over City Bridge onto Cable Key. He drove a mile and a half south, past all the motels and the beach shops, the bars and the concession stands, and turned right into the long narrow sand driveway that led to his rented cottage on the bay side of Cable Key.

It was an old frame cottage of cypress and hard pine, with one bedroom, a small screened porch facing the bay. The neighbors on either side were close, but he had let the brush grow up so thickly along the property line he could not see them.

The interior of the cottage was orderly, in a cheerless, barren way. Except for a shelf of books and a rack of records, it looked as if it had been put in order to be inspected by a prospective tenant, in a semi-furnished category. When the infrequent guest would comment on how it looked as if no one lived there, Jimmy Wing would be mildly surprised, but he would look around and see the justice of the accusation. When he had sold the house in town and moved out to the cottage on Cable Key two years ago, the habits he had established had been, perhaps, a reaction to the dirt, clutter and endless confusion and turmoil of those last few years of Gloria. But once he had satisfied his need for a severe order around him, the pattern had been fixed, and he had no particular reason to change it.

Breakfast was the only meal he ate at home. He was usually out of the house by ten in the morning. The four housekeeping cottages were owned by Joe Parmitter, who also owned the Princess Motel over on the Gulf side, across Ocean Road from the cottages. One of the motel maids, Loella, had a spare key to Jimmy's cottage, and every morning after finishing up the motel rooms, she would come over and clean the cottage and make the bed.

Jimmy Wing had been for several years a reporter on the Palm City *Record-Journal*, the morning newspaper Ben Killian had inherited. He covered the courthouse and the city hall, the police beat, special news breaks, and did feature stories of his own devising rather than on assignment. Nearly all his work was by-lined, and his copy was clean enough and safe enough to escape rewrite. He had a desk assigned to him in the newsroom, but he did not use it very often, preferring to hammer out his copy on the old standard Underwood on the table by a living room window in the cottage. The paper went to bed at midnight, and it was the only paper in town, so the pressure was seldom noticeable.

He had learned long ago that if he spent too much time in the newspaper offices in the old pseudo-Moorish building on Bayou Street, J. J. Borklund, Ben Killian's managing editor, would rope him into any kind of dog work available, from obits to Little League. Borklund had a double-entry approach to journalism. You squeeze every dime out of advertising and circulation, and you put the minimum back into wire services, syndicated features and operating staff. And you take an editorial stand in favor of the flag, motherhood, education, liberty and tourism, offending no one. And so the *Record-Journal,* on a county-wide circulation of 23,000 returned a pleasant and substantial profit each year.

Borklund had long since given up trying to make Jimmy Wing conform to his idea of proper diligence. He had given up after two disastrous weeks during which Jimmy, in order to prove his point, had reported to the newsroom every day at nine and quit at five, and had done exactly what Borklund had told him to do.

Jimmy Wing knew that the paper could not hope to acquire a man as perfectly suited to the job as he was. He had grown up in Palm City. He had an encyclopedic memory for past relationships and pertinent detail. He could transpose rough notes into solid and entertaining copy with a speed which dismayed the other reporters. When anything had to be ferreted out, he knew exactly whom to talk to. And he was able to report about 20 percent of what he had learned.

But, as Jimmy Wing knew, and Ben Killian knew, and presumably J. J. Borklund knew, it wasn't the way he had planned it. For a time it had gone according to plan. He had worked for the paper during the summers while he was at Gainesville. After graduation he went onto the paper full time, knowing he could use two or three years of that highly practical experience before moving along to a bigger city, a bigger paper. Gloria had agreed. And during those first two years he had begun to place minor articles with secondary magazines. That too, was part of the master plan.

In fact, he had actually resigned and had worked for seven weeks on the Atlanta *Journal* before Gloria had that first time of strangeness and the doctor in Atlanta had said she would be better off in a more familiar environment of Palm City. Ben Killian had been glad to get him back.

During the bad years he had resigned himself to this smaller and less demanding arena than the one he had trained himself for. When the necessity to stay had been ended, he had remained. The strain of the bad years had somehow leached away his eagerness for a greater challenge. Now he could adjust his effort to the extent that it filled his days, amiably enough, with enough mild pressure to keep him from thinking about anything which might make him feel uneasy.

Stephen Ransome
(Frederick Clyde Davis)

1902-1977

The name Frederick Clyde Davis might not spring immediately to mind in connection with North Florida detective fiction. Even substituting the nom de plume Stephen Ransome probably does not produce more recognition for most modern readers. Born in St. Joseph, Missouri, Davis, like so many early *noir* writers, perfected his craft by grinding out up to a thousand stories—a year—for pulps like *Black Mask, Detective Tales,* and *Dime Mystery.* Although he wrote dozens of novels under several pseudonyms, it was with Stephen Ransome's mostly Florida-based thrillers that he gained the most notoriety.

The fact that Davis earned his spurs in the pulps shows clearly in his work. Even though some of his crime novels were published under Dodd, Mead's famous Red Badge imprint, a hardbacked series that also featured Agatha Christie and G. K. Chesterton, the Ransome novels often require an extra measure of suspended disbelief. In *Without a Trace,* for instance, a vial of ink that can be used to alter checks is stolen from its inventor. The inventor, a college professor, abandons his tenured position and lams it to Florida to work as a yard man and support his nubile daughter, for no better reason, it would seem, than to service the plot. Many of Ransome's books show similar weaknesses in plot, characterization, and locale.

Despite those weaknesses, when Stephen Ransome is good he is very good indeed. As these opening chapters of *The Night, the Woman* show, the characteristic protagonist of a Ransome novel is a guiltless but perhaps not totally innocent man, trapped by a turn of events. Blake Carden is only trying to help his brother out of a jam when he finds himself accused of a murder it appeared his brother has committed. His altruism, however, is easily mistaken by Lee Barcello, the head investigator in the state's attorney's office, who seems more interested in gaining a conviction than ferreting out the truth. Barcello—Ransome's best stock character—is absolutely relentless in this riveting page-turner.

The Night, the Woman

Stephen Ransome

Chapter 1

The Westcoast Florida Bank building stood tall in the center of down-town Fernanda Beach, three stories of flamingo-pink stucco, bright in the midsummer sun-light. An electric sign on the marquee announced the time and the temperature, alternating once every sixty seconds. This afternoon it was *Temp* 94 . . . 2:57 . . . *Temp* 94 . . . 2:58 . . . *Temp* 94 . . . Blake Carden came around the corner from Gulf Boulevard just as 2:59 flashed on. He came with a quick, rangy stride until a new thought stopped him on the sidewalk facing the entrance.

He saw the bank's armed guard stationed inside the glass door, ready to lock it on the dot of the hour. He still had a fraction of a minute left and the decision was still his: he could walk right in or he could turn away. If he delayed he could say, later, "Got there a little too late—couldn't get in." It would be a lie, but a small one which would gain him an advantage: one night's time—time enough to try to dig out the real reason behind the demand for more money.

He stood thinking. Thirty-two, a salting of premature gray in his sandy hair, spare and trim in his charcoal slacks and white sports shirt, he looked cool despite *Temp* 94 and the wilting humidity. He gave others an impression of quick but unhurried decisiveness. His hesitancy now was unnatural, the effect of a vague sense of guilt—as if he were on the verge of conniving at a crime.

Come now, let's be reasonable. He was conniving at nothing. What he had set out to do was entirely legitimate. There could be nothing wrong in the simple act of withdrawing money from his own account; yet he knew it would arouse curiosity, and it might even start some suspicious gossip going around.

While hesitating, turning over in his mind the pros and cons, he raised his gaze to the front windows on the second floor of the building. With an ever-new lift of pride he saw his name neatly lettered on the panes above the designation *Attorney-at-Law*. It had been up there for three years and eight months now, following a fledgling's

beginning in a much smaller office. This street corner and its sur-
roundings had become as familiar to him as his right hand scribbling
case notes on foolscap. Two blocks to the west the beach stretched
past and the Gulf of Mexico lay a vast whitecapped gray after last
night's line squall. On the coast the compact downtown section of
Fernanda Beach was connected with St. Petersburg by a busy causeway across Boca Ciega Bay. This was a clean, progressive little community and he was solidly a part of it; he was reputably established in
his profession, and incidentally better known to the bank's employees
than most of their depositors. He was feeling this qualmish about it
without knowing why.

The unexpected phone call from his older brother Todd had
caught him at a moment when he was preoccupied with work. He had
had to cut Todd short in order to rush down here from his desk,
leaving an important client waiting. Todd's insistence still puzzled
him. "Can't wait until tomorrow; got to have it today"—as much as
he could raise. "No, dammit, not a check, kid, not a check; folding
money"—giving him too little time to consider.

He had had no reason to doubt the explanation given him when
Todd had asked for a loan the first time, two weeks ago, but now a
feeling of mistrust had begun nibbling at him. Since he couldn't account for it, he thought he ought to ignore it. He couldn't quite, but
at any rate he could clear up the whole matter later. Questions could
easily wait a few hours. When your only brother is in a tight box, and
counting on you for help, you can't let him down.

The sign on the marquee blinked again, closing its hot eyes on the
unvarying *Temp* 94 and opening them wide on 3:00.

The bank guard was holding the door open now, leaning out, looking at him.

"Coming in, Mr. Carden?"

Reasonable question. Competent, relevant and material. Why else
would he have come here with a passbook in his hand?

He hurried in and heard the bolt closing behind him with a steely
traplike click.

Less than ten minutes later he was back at the entrance and the
guard was unlocking it to let him out. In that short time the balance

in his savings account had nose-dived to $121.52. In the left-hand pocket of his slacks he had three thousand dollars in cash—thirty one-hundred-dollar bills.

He looked over his shoulder at the teller who had handled the transaction. The teller's name was Titus Osgood. With his pince-nez, his hard collar and his sleeve garters Osgood had the look of a rock-ribbed New England schoolmaster at the turn of the century. Two weeks ago Blake had found himself dealing with this same frosty character for the same unlikely purpose. Osgood had raised his eyebrows then; and he remembered. He was frowning after Blake with dark moral disapproval. He seemed to be thinking: *So much cash! Twice now. Why? An under-the-table deal? Blackmail? . . . He must be paying blackmail! . . .*

Chapter 2

The two floors of offices above the bank were reached by way of a separate entrance on Gulf Boulevard. Blake went into the small lobby and saw that the panel of the self-operating elevator was closed; the car was in use. Not waiting to call it down, he took the stairway, two steps at a time. With each swing of his left leg he was aware of the substance of the cash pressing against his thigh. Another man's trust-money having an ultimate destination not too clearly known to Blake.

Todd, four years Blake's senior, was in business in St. Petersburg: Carden & Hawes, Advertisers. Since forming the firm six years ago, the two partners had driven themselves hard to build it up to leadership in the city. Eighty per cent of its accounts were local; by Madison Avenue standards it was minor-league, but within its own scope it had achieved a showy success.

These had been good years for Todd, enjoyable and auspicious, until five months ago, when a calamity had crashed down without warning. In one black week two top clients, a wholesale baker and a brewery, both with state-wide distribution, had canceled. It had been a crippling setback, soon aggravated by the defection of two key staff men. Todd and Wally Hawes were scrambling for new accounts and had landed three, all too small to add up to much but promising growth that in time would make them worthwhile. Meanwhile an extravagant overhead had drained reserves dry. The partners had borrowed to the limit elsewhere before Todd had appealed to Blake with a promise to repay within a few months. Blake had not hesitated; the business was inherently sound, and he had every faith that it would stage a healthy comeback, given the good breaks which Todd and Wally were working toward.

"I've got a fat one biting now," Todd had told Blake at the time of the first loan—grinning, looking hopeful in spite of his anxiety. "Really big . . . but slippery. I'm playing him for all I'm worth, trying my damnedest to keep him from throwing the hook. In this insane business so much depends on keeping up a glittery front. But my God, kid, the cost!"

Blake knew something about that—a look of prosperity was an asset to a lawyer also—but in the past ten minutes he had begun asking himself whether Todd's problems were purely business. He shook his head over the question, unable to answer it, thinking that something more, something not mentioned, must be pulling Todd into deeper water—some added liability, some sort of sticky involvement. But if so, what was it?

Since Blake was willing to help his brother all he could, Todd's part in return was to tell him what new complications had developed. They had had too little time to go into it on the phone. Blake would hand over the money at home this evening, and Todd undoubtedly would open up to him then—in all fairness volunteer the information he was entitled to have. And that, he hoped, would exorcize the ghost of his uneasiness.

A short corridor led to the double door bearing Blake's name. His office, the choicest in town, remodeled and redecorated to his own design, had an unequaled three-way view: the Gulf on one side, the bay on the other, and southward down the length of the long, fish-shaped key. A narrow waiting room, formerly an extension of the corridor, divided it through the middle. In the open section on his right Vera Avery, his stenographer, was busy at her electric typewriter, her back turned. That was the most Blake saw of Vera—her straight-spined back as she peppered away at her machine, tirelessly turning out letter-perfect work.

Jean Bradley, her desk placed to face the entrance, was talking over the telephone while making a note on her appointment pad. Jean was small, blonde and brown-eyed, prettier than a secretary ought to be if her boss was to keep his mind wholly on his work. She looked up as Blake came in and spontaneously winked at him. His quick smile answered her little gesture of secret intimacy; but at the same time he felt another pinch of guilt.

No, not guilt exactly so much as regret, because his suddenly flattened bankroll would force him to change his plans—which was something that probably hadn't occurred to Todd. Jean was more than a secretary to Blake, immeasurably more—she was the girl he was going to marry. They had both realized this with an instinctive sparkling certainty since the day she had come to work for him on a warm, yellow morning last April. That old bit about love at first sight wasn't strictly true, of course, but a few hours of nearness could start it going.

Being ridiculously sensible about it, they had agreed not to rush into marriage; and although neither knew exactly what more they were waiting to prove, they hadn't yet set a date. They still hadn't become formally engaged, in fact, although they had been looking at new houses for sale. Nothing definite, just looking; but last Sunday they had found one that Jean loved, and Blake had intended to sign up for it after they had gone through a little more sensible discussing. Now, as matters stood, that house or any house would have to be delayed, probably until after Todd had paid up. Blake had had no chance to tell Jean this in advance, but he would explain that postponing a house wasn't at all the same thing as postponing a wedding, and he was sure she would understand and agree that he could not have refused a brother in trouble.

Jean nodded toward the door of his private office. The client who had come in just as he was hurrying out was waiting there. Jean added a little warning shake of her head. She had seen signs that the client might be difficult. He found Valerie Hayward standing at a window, looking toward the bay, nervously expelling cigarette smoke and flicking ashes at random. Her hair was a beautifully styled bouffant, naturally wavy and black with a deep blue sheen. She was less than slender, as skinny as a fashion model—"No appetite," she said; "I'm never hungry"—in a smartly plain linen sheath dress. Her bare shoulders and legs were brown as cocoa and silky-smooth. She was tap-tapping the toe of one spike-heeled shantung pump. When she heard Blake closing the door, she turned quickly and crushed her cigarette in the ash tray on his desk. It was the third stub she had added during his short absence. He noticed a rancorous glitter in her smoky gray eyes, and sensed a suppressed fire in her; and knowing her well, he suspected that she had just come from a long lunch consisting mostly of extra-dry vodka martinis.

"Sit, Val, relax. Tell me what's upsetting you."

"All these fantastic legalities, Blake! I never did learn how to be patient. Isn't there some way you can get this dreadful mess cleared up reasonably soon?"

The "dreadful mess" was her late husband's estate. Mrs. Valerie Palmer Hayward was twenty-six years old and four months a widow. She had asked Blake to act as administrator, and as soon as the court had given him authorization he had begun regretting it.

Alec Hayward had involved himself in a tangle of speculative deals and dubious investments which were now shaping up as all but a total loss. He had only played at business as he had played at everything else, with a buoyant rashness. His supreme folly had been to crash his single-engine Piper into the main span of the Sunshine Skyway while solo stunting over Tampa Bay. It was entirely characteristic of him to die without life insurance, and intestate. Much of the legal and financial shambles he had left behind could have been avoided if he had spent fifteen minutes with a lawyer, dictating a will; but he had been too busy having fun to bother.

"My hands are tied, Val. Settlement has two more months to go and there's no possible short-cut. And eventually, as I've told you before, you'll wind up with very little."

He spread his hands over the open Hayward file folder on his desk, over the sheaf of creditors' claims and receipts for liquidated personal property. He had been bringing this sorry business up to date when Todd's phone call had interrupted.

"Every week, in fact, it looks a little worse."

She stood still, gazing at Blake, judging—not judging him but something else. He had seen her several times in the past few weeks and had begun to sense that something had happened to her recently, something deeply hurtful. A strange change had come over her, a subtle shading toward deviousness, as if she were secretly planning and waiting. Whatever the root of it was, she seemed to be nursing it with a continuing bitterness; but she had kept it to herself.

Was she bringing it to him now? At one moment she seemed about to spill it out—she was given to hair-trigger impulses, and her short temper was made shorter still by too many drinks—but no; she held it in. She was forcing a discreet silence on herself—and discretion was not normally Valerie Hayward's nature.

"Val, how can I help you?"

"I don't know." She went on irritably and cryptically, "Maybe you can't. Maybe I'll have to find ways of my own this time." And without explaining her meaning, she went on brooding.

Outwardly this young woman was excitingly attractive, but Blake could not admire the inner qualities that dominated her. She was extravagant, shallow, willful, petulant, self-pampered and sometimes vengeful. Expressed in action, these traits certainly weren't pretty; yet it was possible to feel sorry for Val because she seemed totally unable to steer clear of disaster. As long as Blake had known her—fifteen years—she had been caught up in a series of disasters, small and large, most of them of her own making.

When she was eleven years old, Valerie Palmer had lost both her parents. Their powerboat had exploded during a sudden thunderstorm—struck by lightning, presumably—in the Gulf off Siesta Key. Val's mother had not survived the blast. Her father, rescued by the Coast Guard, had lived long enough to sign the papers making his old friend Warren Wingate his daughter's testamentary guardian. There had been no relatives to take Val in; without the Wingates' openhearted willingness she would have been lost indeed.

The Wingates had been close friends and neighbors of the Cardens then, and still were. Carden was the circuit judge who had approved the guardianship. Warren's wife Tessa, and their daughter Ruth, now Todd's wife, had tried their generous best to draw Val into the harmony of their family life. Blake remembered her at that time as a pale, bewildered, scared little girl, lonely within herself, too dazed to respond. But shock had passed before long, and then the Wingates' troubles had begun.

Val had become demanding, as if straining to compensate for a heartbreaking loss that could never be recovered, and heedlessly rebellious. Blake could remember five or six episodes during Val's high school and early college years which had plunged the Wingates into despair. For ten rough years they had coped with one escapade after another, all of them wild and preposterous and dangerous, most of them involving men. Blake had often thought how vastly relieved they must have been when Val's twenty-first birthday automatically ended the guardianship.

On that fifth of August five years ago Miss Valerie Palmer had come into full control of the legacy her father had left her—almost a quarter of a million dollars. With that she had really gone into orbit. An expensive apartment all her own, expensively furnished, complete with full-time maid. A Continental convertible, a racy little Mercedes-Benz. A twin-motored cabin cruiser. Flights to Paris for clothes; flights to New York for jewels, furs, the theater; flights to Las Vegas, her appallingly bad luck in the casinos laughed off. Parties, parties and more parties. There was no way of throwing money around that Val had not used lavishly.

Somewhere along the height of these gyrations she had met Alec Hayward, who "had everything"—social position, charm, good looks, manners, vitality, even money—around a hundred thousand, Blake had heard, lately bequeathed him by his mother, the late Mrs. Wainwright Travis of Palm Beach. A wild streak in him to match Val's, a blithe violence about him, a mania for speed. They had lived it up riotously, and when Alec's money was gone, he had merrily helped Val to go on squandering hers. Neither had realized that with an almost uncanny fatality they were in a downhill rush to destroy themselves.

During these past few months Blake had been selling off Alec Hayward's racing cars and speedboats and motorcycles and other expensive toys for little more than the small equity in them. The four-seater plane in which he had killed himself accidentally, with such high-spirited carelessness, had been one quarter paid for; the balance was a lien on the estate. Blake still couldn't believe it possible that two young people could burn up so much money in only five years; but Val and Alec, having a special genius, had done it.

Until now Val had probably never thought her money would someday run out. Not having an abundance of money was a new, bewildering experience for her; she felt helpless, facing a frightening future. She might or might not realize that the only way she could rescue herself was to marry again soon. Unfortunately for her, wealthy bachelors were in very short supply.

During these moments of silence, Blake had been watching a puzzling play of expressions on Val's face. She was in a familiar mood—resentful, spoiling for trouble. She crushed her cigarette again and surprised him with a question that had a sharp point on it.

"Blake, what queered the deal on the house and the boat?"

"I didn't know anything had. Last I heard, the Mannings were planning to sign the contracts and pay you their earnest money this morning."

"They changed their minds. Overnight. I want to know why."

"I can't tell you that, Val. They haven't been in touch with me. Didn't they say?"

"Just that they decided they couldn't quite swing it." Blake gazed at her soberly, sympathizing in her distress. The Hayward home and the yacht *Valec* were exceptional items in the estate: they were paid for, the reason for this oddity being that both had been specially built at a time when the golden tide had not yet begun to ebb noticeably. Moreover, they had been jointly owned properties. Full title had passed to Val; she could dispose of either or both at any time. They were separately in the hands of good, aggressive agents, but even so, considering the high prices on them, she had been lucky to find a buyer so soon. The sale would have put her back on her feet nicely— for a time, at any rate—and she had been counting on it. Plainly the Mannings' sudden reversal was a disheartening blow.

"Did you tell them you would consider selling for less?"

"Of course I did! I'm desperate to get rid of those two white elephants. I need to, Blake! The Mannings wouldn't bargain. Very apologetic, but they'd hardly listen. Blake—" A suspicious animosity had come into her eyes. "There's something behind this. Somebody talked them out of it."

"Why should anyone? They're capable of making up their own minds."

"But they were so delighted at first! Like kids on Christmas Eve— they could hardly wait. Then suddenly they turned so frightfully chilly. Why, why—*why?*" Her voice had lifted to a cry of indignation and pain. She lowered it. "Blake, I know somebody deliberately turned the Mannings against it."

"I can't believe that, Val. The explanation they gave you is probably true—it figures. You've learned from your own experience that the house is much too much for only two people, and maintaining a forty-eight-foot boat is damned costly." For these same reasons, Blake was thinking, Val would probably be a long time finding another likely buyer. "I'm sorry, Val, but Manning hadn't signed, so I'm afraid there's nothing you can do about it."

She sat back, her eyes narrowed and calculating again. "Oh, isn't there," she said with a dangerous quietness. The door opened then. Jean looked in and at Blake's nod came to his desk, bringing a letter. Evidently Vera had just collected the afternoon mail at the post office across the street and this was something Jean thought he should see immediately. She left the page of personal stationery in his hand and went back out while he read the brief message.

Jean was right; this related to Val. Alec Hayward's only surviving blood relatives were an unmarried brother and a married sister living near each other in San Francisco. Blake had written to them suggesting that since the estate was so small they might be willing to relinquish their shares, each one third, to Alec's widow. They were well off, he had learned indirectly, and could easily afford this small compassionate gesture. This reply had been slow in coming. Finally the brother was answering for both: flatly no.

Blake groaned inwardly, commiserating with Val. She was certainly getting the wringer today. It would be an act of kindness, he felt, to hold this extra measure of bad news until later. He laid the letter face down on the desk blotter.

"Thank you, Blake; that's sweet. But I saw the printing. It's from Earl Hayward. And you don't need to tell me what it says."

Val had stiffened to her feet, her face tightening with rage. Blake winced within himself, thinking, *Oh, God, here it comes.*

"Alec hadn't seen either of them in eight years. They didn't write to him. He didn't even like them. They couldn't be bothered to come to his funeral. They don't need this loot, yet they're perfectly willing to grab it off and leave me with one third of practically nothing!"

Blake gave her a regretful look but no other answer. They were within their legal rights, and the original fault had been Alec's; but there was no use reminding her of it.

"What do people expect of me? Do they think I'll sit still and let myself be swindled when I'm already broke? Well, I won't, I won't!" Her voice was rising on a note of fury. "Blake, I'm going to get what's rightfully mine. I promise you I'm damned well going to have what belongs to me, every last cent!" Now she was shrill. "Or I'll pull the roof down!"

He knew what she would do next; he had seen it before. She did it—turned her back, stab-stabbed her spike heels across to the door and banged out.

Blake sat frowning at the door, telling himself that no part of Val's predicament justified such a threat. Alec's brother and sister had taken a selfish position, and possibly a morally weak one, but to accuse them of swindling her was wide of the mark; and in any case she had no recourse. The Mannings had had an honest and permissible change of mind. As for himself, Blake knew that Val trusted him, both personally and as the administrator of her husband's estate. Who, then, was swindling her? Nobody, so far as Blake knew. The more he thought of it, the more pointless Val's outburst seemed, except as an explosive release of unbearable tensions.

No; no, there was more to it than that. Val had come here boiling with resentment, for a specific reason which she had not confided to her attorney. Why hadn't she? . . . Blake shook his head, still wondering what her hidden purpose had been and whether she had accomplished it.

He looked at his desk clock. Val had dropped in without an appointment, and fortunately he had no others. The afternoon was slipping by. He remembered Todd's urgency on the phone, Todd's saying, "I'll try to get home early."

Reaching into the drawer of his desk where he kept his professional stationery, he took up an envelope; then, on second thought, he put it back. He went to the door, swung it open and spoke across the corridor to Jean.

"Do we have a plain envelope, a number ten?"

She looked at him from her desk in a way that struck him as curious, because it wasn't quite like her—embarrassed and a little constrained. She answered quickly, as if protecting him from a hazard he didn't know: "Yes. I'll bring one."

He turned back and she followed him, closing the door. She left the envelope on his blotter and lingered, gazing at him searchingly.

"What did you do to her?"

"Not a damned thing. Val's having a run of bad breaks, and she's looking for somebody to take it out on."

"She screeched, didn't she? Really screeched. We all heard that last. What did she mean, about pulling the roof down? Whose roof?"

"I have no idea. I doubt that she meant anybody's or anything in particular. When Val's temper lets go, she makes meaningless noises. Loud, but meaningless." Closing the Hayward folder, he paused, cocking a surprised glance at Jean. "'We all'? You and Vera and who else? Somebody waiting?"

"A detective. His name's Barcello."

"Lee?" Blake had dealt with Lee Barcello several times professionally, and liked him personally. Those conferences had occurred in the

County Building in St. Pete. Since this was the first time Barcello had sought Blake out, it must be official business. "What does he want?"

"A few questions answered. That's all he'd tell me."

"Ask him to wait another minute or two."

As Jean withdrew, Blake emptied the left-hand pocket of his slacks. He tossed the passbook into a drawer, to be returned to his strongbox later, and found a rubber band to put around the bundle of bank notes. He was stowing them in his slacks again when his caller appeared.

Detective Lieutenant Lee Barcello—the Lee was short for Leopoldo—was assigned to the county prosecutor's office as special investigator. He came in quietly, with a warm and easy smile, a straight, broad-shouldered, tall man with the rich dark coloring of his pure-blooded Spanish ancestors. His eyes were a deep, velvety black-brown. He clasped Blake's hand gently. He said, "Beautiful office, Mr. Carden; beautiful view." A man of disciplined but unaffected formality, he remained standing until Blake invited him to sit.

"What brings you to the beaches, Lee?"

"You're on my list, Mr. Carden." Barcello's soft voice belonged with the rest of him. "That is to say, a list of clients who have done business with Masters-Stowell and Company, in St. Pete. You know them, the stockbrokers?"

"Not as a client. I'm settling the estate of a man named Alec Hayward who was. Is that how I happen to be on your list?"

Barcello nodded pleasantly. "So you probably know George Gibbon. He was a customer's man."

"I dealt directly with Sam Masters. Sam's an old friend of my father's. I never met George Gibbon there, not personally, but I know he handled the Hayward account. Anything irregular about it, Lee?"

"No, no, nothing like that. Mr. Hayward's account is perfectly in order. So are all the other accounts Mr. Gibbon handled." His dark eyes were on Blake's. "Is Mrs. Hayward acquainted with him?"

It occurred to Blake that Barcello must have recognized Val during her dramatic exit. At the time of Alec's death, and also on various social occasions, the *Times* and the *Independent* had printed her picture; and Barcello was known for his photographic memory. If he hadn't stopped her on her way out to ask her his question directly, it was because she obviously hadn't been in a responsive mood.

"She couldn't know anyone at Masters-Stowell. Her husband did the investing, if investing is the name for it. He played with carloads of penny-ante stocks in a way she didn't even try to understand. She has never needed to have any first-hand dealings with a broker. That sort of thing has always been done for her."

"I see. That saves me a little leg work. I won't have to check with her."

Barcello was stirring Blake's curiosity. "You've been speaking of this man Gibbon in the past tense. Is he dead?"

"Just missing, Mr. Carden. He committed a little grand larceny and took off. I'm looking for him."

"So close to home?"

"He's been under cover somewhere along the beaches for most of the past three weeks. A hard man to find. Wherever he's holed in, he's careful about showing himself."

Barcello removed a small photo portrait from his shirt pocket and held it toward Blake. Gibbon's face was square and flat. It seemed to say he was timid, slow-witted, and aware of it. He felt oppressed; the sad look in his eyes was that of a caged animal defeated by his bars. Yet there was a slightly sinister cast to his features, a warning hint that this was a man who might reach a limit of endurance and suddenly break loose—as, evidently, he had.

"Have you seen him, Mr. Carden?"

Blake could say positively, "No, never."

Barcello accepted the answer easily. "Thank you. I won't keep you from your work any longer." He was rising.

"Just a minute, Lee." For the second time within half an hour Blake was puzzled by the motivation of a visit. "So a man named Gibbon stole some money from his employers and skipped. This has no bearing on any of the accounts he'd handled; they're all perfectly okay. Yet you're trying to find a lead to him by looking up his old customers, including Alec Hayward, who is four months dead. I don't get it. Could you fill me in?"

Barcello subsided into the chair, seeming pleased by the opening. "Without going into too many details, I'd like to give you the over-all picture. It might be helpful later. Gibbon is a fairly peculiar case. He was an upright citizen until he tripped—stuffy, even—and since then he hasn't been behaving according to pattern. The amount he stole is small, as loot goes—around fifteen hundred—and he promises to make restitution, provided he'll be forgiven."

Blake sat back, waiting for a logical connection to come up.

"Gibbon simply lifted the cash out of Masters-Stowell's safe. That same night, before anybody in the office had found out about the theft, he packed up and left the cottage in Gulfport where he'd been living with his widowed mother for years. She was asleep when he decamped. He'd never married, he's his mother's only support, and she hasn't seen him since.

"The next morning he cleaned out his small checking account, sixty-odd dollars' worth, and sold his car, a fifty-six Chev. He used most of that money to pay off three time-payment loans he'd been carrying with finance companies, all of them slightly delinquent: total, thirteen hundred. Since he has to have transportation of some kind, he probably bought an older jalopy—of course under an assumed name. He didn't cut and run. We know he's been hiding out somewhere along the Gulf beaches, not far from here, because he's been heard from every few days."

Blake was finding it interesting, but still irrelevant.

"First, he mailed his mother money to live on, along with a note saying please don't worry. The postmark was Madeira Beach. Next he phoned Mr. Masters, a local call, promising to repay what he'd stolen, given a little time. He sounded as if he meant it, and he proved it a few days later by mailing four hundred dollars in cash to Masters-Stowell as part payment. This week he sent his mother more money for running expenses. This time the postmark was Pass-a-Grille."

Without too many details, Barcello had said; but Blake was hearing quite a few. He wondered what lay behind all these particulars. Subtle method?

"Gibbon may be dodging from one motel to another. At any rate, he has had to pay out for rent, wherever he is, and for eating, drinking and miscellaneous. Add it all up—the repaid loans, probably a used car, the cash sent to Mother and Masters-Stowell, plus his own needs—and it amounts to more money than he took away. In addition there's his promise, made very much in earnest, to repay in full in a few more weeks. What this seems to mean is that Gibbon has raised funds from some other source. And not only that, he's expecting to raise considerably more."

"A man on the lam? How could he?"

"One way would be to appeal to the sympathy of some of his old clients, with the idea of getting personal loans from them. His advice on the stock and bond market did make money for most of them, you know. Does this approach strike you as unlikely, Mr. Carden?"

"Unlikely, but not illegal. It does raise a question. If Gibbon is borrowing from some of his old clients in order to reimburse Masters, how will he be able to repay them later?"

Barcello smiled faintly. "I've no idea. It's just a theory. It may not be valid. Still, offhand, I can't account for Gibbon's extra cash in any other way. Some people really are softhearted enough to fall for that sort of pitch. You wouldn't, naturally, but Gibbon is fairly desperate to save his neck, and I thought he might have tried you."

"So that's it. No, Lee, he hasn't. He still might. If he does, I'll let you know."

"I'll appreciate that."

On his way out Barcello paused with the door partly open. "I'm pretty close on his tail, I think. He's been seen in two banks, first in Madeira, ten days ago, then yesterday in the Westcoast, downstairs. Both times he changed a hundred-dollar bill into tens and fives."

"Oh?"

"And that's an interesting thing. The cash he sent to his mother and his boss were also hundred-dollar bills; and none of these came from Masters-Stowell's safe or the used-car buyer. So the question is, Mr. Carden, where did he get them—and how? . . . *Adios.*"

For the second time within half an hour Blake found himself staring at the closed door. Barcello's deft parting shot had jarred him. It could mean only one thing: Barcello had already learned about

Blake's withdrawals, not only today's, but also the first, two weeks ago—which would be the week after Gibbon's disappearance.

Then he thought, *Well, hell, what of it?* It meant nothing. Hundred-dollar bills simply were not rare enough to point a specific finger—not at Todd, or at Blake, or at anyone else. He was still feeling jumpy over nothing, that was all.

No, it wasn't all. The presentiment of evil that had been haunting him was stronger than before.

Chapter 3

Blake had wanted to get home earlier than usual in order to have his talk with Todd as soon as possible, but when he left his office it was ten minutes past six.

Two more important clients had dropped in with problems and questions calling for complex discussion. Afterward he had had to dictate long letters regarding both cases. As soon as he had signed them, Vera had whisked herself out, leaving him alone with Jean. When he was finally ready to go, she was still tidying up their desks after the busy day. Reminding her unnecessarily that he would see her this evening at her apartment, he had given way to temptation and had broken a rule they had made between themselves, never to touch each other during business hours: he had soundly kissed her. She had been a slightly chiding but smiling and willing accomplice, and he had left thinking that a misdemeanor as delightful as that was one he ought to commit more often.

Going to his Thunderbird in the parking lot behind the building, he felt another prickling of guilt, the small guilt of omission. He still hadn't told Jean they might have to put off buying a house. Perhaps this was best; he wasn't entirely sure now that they would need to wait. It depended on Todd's situation, on whether or not some covert connection existed between Todd and the fugitive Gibbon.

This was highly improbable, Blake thought, yet the possibility, thin as it was, had to be explored. As a member of the bar, his position was sensitive; he would be a damned fool to risk involvement in any sort of shady deal, even remotely. Before handing over the three thousand he intended to hear a clear explanation of Todd's reason for needing the money so urgently. In addition to the loan Todd would owe him reassurance; and the question was whether Todd could give it.

He drove southward on Gulf Boulevard between two rows of motels sitting as close together as dominoes. Their varicolored neon signs were already shining, creating a miles-long earthbound rainbow. The sun was a great gilded balloon sinking low over the horizon of the Gulf, and a misty twilight was beginning to cloud westward over the city across the bay. He passed the white-shingled yacht club, resisting an impulse to stop for a cocktail, then turned left over the short hump of the bridge leading onto Zephyr Isle.

It was a man-made island, one of the oldest and largest fills in the bay. Tall Australian pines shaded the inlets. The curving, carefully engineered streets were harmoniously lined with attractive one-family houses with landscaped lawns. The Cardens and the Wingates were old settlers; they had been among the first to build homes here, on the southern point.

Following his long-familiar course, a right turn beyond the bridge, then into the U-shaped bend of Bayvista Drive, Blake came upon the extravaganza of a house that Alec and Valerie Hayward had erected early in their giddy marriage. Beyond it, a private pier jutted into the bay; *Valec* was moored there. The weary old Buick belonging to Val's housekeeper, Amalia Wheeler, was berthed inside the garage, where it remained unmoved for days at a time, and Val's latest Continental convertible sat gleaming in the sun in the driveway. Amalia liked to keep busy and out of Val's way, Blake knew, and he thought that Val probably was still brooding and fueling her unreasonable anger with more vodka martinis, extra-dry, self-made.

Except for a short trip to Nassau following Alec's funeral, and except for Amalia, Val had been living alone here for four bleak months. It was the only two-story structure on the island. Val and Alec had put into it everything they could dream up. Besides the conventional rooms downstairs there was a cocktail lounge in a rumpus room that had seen an almost continual rumpus; a wine cellar; two dressing rooms and a luxuriously tiled, two-tier steam room connecting with the spacious screened-in patio. The free-form swimming pool, heated in winter, and big enough for a motel, featured a cascading fountain. Upstairs there were six bedrooms and six baths. This architectural rhapsody sat on not just one costly water-front lot; it straddled two, the choicest available at the time, priced at $12,000 each. It was Val who had insisted on this location only two doors away from the unpretentious Wingate home, where she had lived for ten years, where for one whole trying decade the Wingates had endeavored to hold her recklessness in check. Blake had suspected from the first that in selecting this site Val was elaborately flaunting her independence with a mocking, nose-thumbing gesture. If so, it was backfiring on her now. She might be years getting this property off her back, and even then she would probably be forced to sell at a heavy loss.

Blake passed the Wingates' home, on the eastern leg of the bend, then swung left into a gravel driveway, and he was home.

The Carden property filled the inside of the U, its gardened lawn following the curve, its front windows looking southward at the bay as it could be seen between the water-front houses across the drive. The four Cardens lived here under an unusual but thoroughly amicable plan. The house had two wings, two rooms and a bath in each, with a common living room and kitchen in between. Todd and his wife Ruth, the Wingates' daughter, had converted the west wing into an apartment; the judge and Blake occupied the other. Ruth cooked and kept house for them all and did it superbly, making them feel well cared for. It was such a mutually agreeable arrangement that none of them had ever thought of changing it, of living separately. Ruth had her own special appreciation of it. The three Wingates had always lived in close rapport, and after marrying Todd three years ago she had had to move no farther from her parents than across the street.

Ruth was evidently at home, Blake saw, and his father too. Her cream-yellow compact and the judge's old black sedan were sitting inside the garage. He was surprised, considering the pressures on

Todd, that his brother hadn't yet shown up, wasn't waiting for him. The third stall, shared by Blake and Todd on a first-come-first-served basis, was empty.

Blake ran his car in. When he opened the door connecting the garage with the kitchen, he heard Ruth speaking in the living room. Her voice was lowered but unsteady, shaking on the verge of tears.

"If Todd would only tell me! I want to help him if I can. But he won't let me, he keeps shutting me out. I don't even know what's wrong—not really, not all of it."

Another familiar voice, a woman's, answered her. This was Tessa Wingate, her mother. Tessa's tone was firm; she was making it plain that she was determined to be calm and sensible about her daughter's upset.

"You just haven't learned how very important a man's work is to him, Ruthie, that's all. When he's having serious business troubles he can become terribly preoccupied. I went through it many times with your father, when you were a little girl. I'm sure you're exaggerating the whole thing, letting it bother you much too much."

Ruth didn't answer. They had heard Blake walking across the kitchen. When he stepped into the living room, their faces were turned toward him—distress in Ruth's, a frown of concern on Tessa's. Then Ruth looked down and Tessa's gaze went back to her daughter—a gaze more worried than her words.

"Would you like me to butt right out again?" Blake asked.

Ruth shook her head, her dark eyelashes wet. "No. It's family."

"I expected to find Todd here."

"He phoned to tell me . . . he'll be late. He and Wally Hawes . . . are in conference with a new client."

Her hesitant answer gave Blake the impression that she was trying to believe this but couldn't quite. She had been setting the dining table. She turned back to it now—including, hopefully, a place for Todd.

Ruth was small, with brown-red hair, clear hazel eyes and an appealingly round and healthy-looking face. She was wearing black flats and a maternity ensemble, a cool green skirt with a matching over-blouse. Her baby was due in mid-October. Her pregnancy had had a charming effect—it had subtracted several years from her twenty-eight and had given her a warm, cuddly look. She could not have been dearer to Blake if she had been his blood sister, and the judge open-heartedly adored her.

"What can I do to help dry those tears, Ruthie?"

"I wish I knew, Blake. Todd's in a bind, a really bad bind, and he just won't open up about it."

Tessa said with an older woman's sympathetic understanding, "Naturally he doesn't want to unload his business troubles on you at a time like this. You just don't realize how extremely concerned a husband can be about his wife when their first child is coming."

Tessa had a catlike love of home and comfort. She was seated snugly in the softest chair in the room. Forty-five now, with a figure inclined to dumpiness, she kept herself in trim by exercising in her swimming pool every day. Ruth was prettier, but Tessa had something as good as beauty—a simplicity of personality and a certain glow of inner peace. She and Win having both come up from cracker poverty, she enjoyed and prized the social position they had won for themselves. She was strongly possession-minded, passionately proud of their material success, and sometimes she let it show too much. If this was a fault, it was easy to overlook, Blake felt, simply because she was so utterly contented with her lot and still truly in love with Win.

"I really think it's very sweet of Todd," she said decidedly, "to show you so much consideration, Ruthie, when he's under such strain and trying so hard to pull the agency out of the red."

"It's more than that, Mother. Todd's business troubles began five months ago. What I'm talking about is something else, something that came up in the past few weeks."

Tessa rose reluctantly. "I have to hurry now to give your father his dinner. Please try to put all this out of your mind."

She kissed Ruth's cheek, hugged her, then hurried out the front door. Ruth shook her head and turned to Blake with a pathetic look that was close to hopelessness.

"I've had time to think about it, but Mother hasn't. I came out with it . . . too much of it . . . all of a sudden."

"Is it really so bad?"

"You'll say it's only little things—but really, it's very bad because it's keeping me from being the kind of wife I want to be to Todd."

He took her arm and led her to the couch. She sat beside him, gazing forlornly out the window at the sky darkening above the bay.

"Go on, Ruthie, tell me."

She clasped her small hands together. "Todd has been so terribly nervous lately. He doesn't sleep well. He gets out of bed in the middle of the night and comes out here and drinks too much. He sits and drinks and thinks for hours."

Tessa would have dismissed it as business troubles. But Blake agreed with Ruth: Todd's worries evidently went deeper.

"One night last week, about nine o'clock," Ruth said, "there was a phone call. Todd seemed in a hurry to answer it. He told me it was Wally—he had to go over to Wally's apartment and talk out a new promotion campaign. About an hour later there was another call from one of the agency's clients. He was at the airport, and his plane was about to leave, so I took the message, then phoned Wally's apartment to tell Todd about it."

"And Todd wasn't there."

"Wally sounded as if I'd caught him off guard. He stammered a little, then gave me that old line, 'He just left.' I waited up . . . and waited. When Todd finally came home it was two o'clock in the morning. He said that after leaving Wally's apartment he'd gone in to the office, then he'd stopped at a bar for a nightcap. But he was upset and trying to hide it . . . and I knew he wasn't telling the truth."

Blake didn't like the sound of it. There was more. Ruth went on unburdening herself as if she couldn't stop.

There had been another night when Todd had left his bed and had gone out of the house wearing his pajamas, robe and slippers. Ruth had heard him coming back in, as stealthy as a thief in the night, just before dawn. The next day she had asked him about it, and he had said he'd gone no farther than the patio. Ruth had dropped it there, although the patio was in back of the house and she was sure she had heard him using the front door. And this Blake liked even less.

Ruth was looking at him intently. "I know what you're asking yourself. Is there another woman? Blake, I'm sure it isn't that. No; it has to be something else."

Ruth lifted her head expectantly. Listening to the sounds of a car turning into the bend of the drive, she was brightened by the hope that it was Todd coming home. The car moved into sight of the windows; and she sagged. Without stopping, the pick-up truck rolled past the house and on.

At the sound of a quiet footstep they turned their heads. Judge Carden had come into the living room from the hallway of the east wing. He was holding his black-rimmed reading glasses in one hand and looking at his watch.

"Let's not wait dinner on Todd, Ruth," he suggested, and as she went into the kitchen, glad to be kept busy, he added, "Blake, I want to talk with you."

They went into the judge's room. It was crowded with a four-poster double bed, bookshelves, file cabinets and an old roll-top desk which he had worked at ever since his early days as a young attorney. He sat in the black leather-upholstered swivel chair facing it, peering up at Blake almost fiercely. Judge Carden was often referred to as the dean of the county's judiciary. He had snow-white hair and a stern, scholarly, slightly bony face that masked an inner kindliness. Since the death of Blake's mother and Todd's he had been a deeply lonely man, but one having the fortitude to endure it. Usually he was quietly tolerant in his manner, or even humorously indulgent. Confronting Blake now, he had a formidable look; he was inwardly fuming.

"Close the door," he said. Blake closed it, not knowing what to expect.

"I'm a sharp-eared old eavesdropper. I overheard every word. How much do you know about this?"

"Next to nothing."

"Blake, you know how highly I think of Ruth. I'm devoted to that girl. Todd's hurting her. I won't stand for it."

Blake couldn't remember when he had seen his father so irate. The normally pale face was flushed with anger.

"And I intend to put a stop to it!"

"How can you?"

"By finding out what Todd's up to."

"But if he won't talk, he won't."

"I know that. Obstinate, even more so than I am. We'll have to watch him—find out where he goes, what he does, who he sees."

"What are you suggesting? A private investigator?"

"Certainly not. But you, Blake—I can rely on you."

"What? Are you asking me to spy on Todd?"

"Call it what you like. Of course the idea is repugnant to you, but, it has to be done. Can you think of a better way of finding out?"

Blake could not. It was true that no one was in a more favorable position than he was to feel his way into Todd's predicament, whatever it might be. No one else's services would be as safe. The judge was so sharply concerned, so firmly determined to right matters, that Blake couldn't refuse. Still, it would be a ticklish assignment.

"Suppose I start tailing Todd around. Suppose I even succeed in finding out what sort of fix he's in. What then? The kid brother advises his big brother to mend his ways? I know how Todd will react to that. He'll laugh in my face."

"He won't laugh in mine," the judge said flatly. "Not if I have the hard facts. The only way I can get them is through you."

"The sooner the better, I take it. I don't know how to be a detective, but I'll do my best." Blake opened the door, then closed it again, a question in mind. "Has Todd borrowed any money from you?"

"Not a cent. He hasn't asked."

Blake left the room frowning over his father's answer. John Carden's position on the bench was even more sensitive than Blake's as an attorney. Todd was fully aware of this. Todd might feel forced to pull his brother onto the fringe of a questionable deal, but he would never go so far as to implicate the judge. To Blake this was the most disturbing turn of all—an almost unmistakable sign that Todd's concealed operations actually were on the dark side.

Charles Willeford

1919-1988

When an interviewer for *Mystery Scene* 10 asked Stephen King for
the names "of some writers you think we ought to be reading but
aren't," King mentioned a few writers, then added, "I would have
said Charles Willeford, but now he is getting the star treatment."
That star treatment came very late in Willeford's career, after
years in the pulp trenches as a writer and editor. When he finally
broke out with a series featuring Miami detective Hoke Moseley
in 1984, the books became hugely popular, spawning six-figure
advances for the author and a successful movie of *Miami Blues*
starring Fred Ward, Jennifer Jason-Leigh, and Alec Baldwin.

Like many writers of the generation that grew up in the Great
Depression, Willeford boasted a variety of occupations and avo-
cations. At a time when most of his contemporaries were still
in elementary school, he rode the rails and called hobo jungles
home. After he had acquired enough wrinkles, he joined the
army, although still only sixteen. His first duty station was the in-
fant Army Air Corps in the Philippines and later he transferred
to the cavalry stateside. When World War II started and the cavalry was abolished, he found himself commanding a tank in General George Patton's European command where he was required
to wear a necktie in combat (at the risk of a fifteen-dollar fine
deducted directly from his pay) and where, by Willeford's own
estimation, every other man was a psychopath. After the war he
began to write—like many classic hard-boiled crime writers—
poetry. His first book was a collection of dark verse called *Prole-
tarian Laughter* (1948).

Willeford's transformation to prose supposedly came by way
of a bet. When an Army barracksmate wagered that he could not
publish a novel, Willeford checked into a San Francisco hotel
one Friday night and worked feverishly until Monday morning to
produce *High Priest of California*. He found a publisher for it in
1953 and received five hundred dollars. Over the next thirty years
he published eleven more novels, only one of which made it into
hardcover. Even though he rarely received more than the stan-

dard five-hundred-dollar advance for any of his works, one of them, *Cockfighter* (1962), became a movie featuring no less a *noir* figure than Warren Oates. Perhaps more importantly, Willeford's work received good, if scant, critical notice. Before the 1980 publication of *Off the Wall,* a true-crime account of the capture of David "Son of Sam" Berkowitz, his only hardcover book was the Florida *noir* classic *The Burnt Orange Heresy* (1971). In addition to the four Hoke Moseley books—*Miami Blues* (1984), *New Hope for the Dead* (1985), *Sideswipe* (1987), and *The Way We Die Now* (1988)—he also finished two volumes of autobiography, *Something about a Soldier* (1986) and *I Was Looking for a Street* (1988).

We offer here the never-before-published opening chapters of a novel that Willeford ultimately abandoned in 1975. Although the work would not have been a detective or mystery novel in the traditional sense, it is a striking example of his distinctively absurdist approach to *noir* fiction. The sharp-edged characterizations, dry wit, and dark humor of this story of plans to create a popular television version of Russian roulette reflect the style readers came to appreciate so well in his paperback years and in the Moseley series. Unfortunately, this fragment is all that Willeford completed.

The First Five in Line

Charles Willeford

"Them that dies'll be the lucky ones."

LONG JOHN SILVER

MEMO: (Confidential)
FROM: Doremus Jessup, Vice-President for Programming, NBN
TO: Russell Haxby, Director of Creative and Special Programs
SUBJECT: "The First Five in Line . . ."
Dear Russ, this is merely an informal memo on the eve of your depar-
ture for Miami to wish you Godspeed, and to mention some other
assorted shit that has been on my mind.

I'm not, for example, satisfied with the program title, even though,
at the present moment, it seems to fit, in an honest way, with the
theme and projected format. The ellipsis following the title implies
that others will eventually join the line, and that this experiment is
only the beginning of a long line of various titillating programs to
attract more jaded viewers, but I'm still not certain whether the ellipsis is a valid addition or not. Do not waver in your thoughts for a better
(exciting?) alternate title. We (the Board and I) are very receptive to
a title change, and you should submit periodic alternates right up
until deadline.

The Board is quite excited about the entire concept. In ancient
Rome it was possible for theatre-goers to see actual fornication on-
stage (including rapes), actual crucifixions and ritual murders (usually with unwilling Xian actors), and it does not seem unlikely to me
that in the not so distant future we shall see planned murders on our
home screens as well as the unplanned, i.e., Ruby shooting Oswald,
the colonel shooting the prisoner in Saigon, the female newscaster's
on-the-air suicide in Sarasota, etc. And NBN may very well start the
trend with our innovative "TFFIL . . ." The design is already apparent,

with from 30 to 35 simulated murders per night on the tube, as if every network were preparing the viewers' minds for the real thing. The latest estimate indicates that the average viewer, by the time he reaches 65, will have seen 400,000 simulated murders and maimings on TV, discounting the murders and maimings he has also seen in movies. I saw the handwriting on the bloody wall as far back as "The Execution of Private Slovik." The huge audience for this show was predicated on the sure knowledge that Slovik would, indeed, be executed before the end of the program. Such knowledge was foreshadowed by the revealing title, even for those viewers unfamiliar with Huie's book. That's one of the reasons I'm not too happy with "The First Five in Line . . ." as a title. In line for what? A viewer may very well ask; so keep thinking about an alternative.

But I also agree with you that real TV murders must be led up to gradually, if we are ever to see them at all. To jump right in with them without prolonged and careful audience preparation, even though the actors—victim and killer—were to sign releases, would still not absolve the network from the many legal problems that would surround such programs, at least initially. When the time is right, we shall have them, of course, and it will always be in keeping for NBN to pioneer in the most dramatic and exciting programming we can provide for our loyal viewers. As a possible title, however, just off the top of my head, for such a show in the distant future, what about "Involuntary Departures"?

But back to "The First Five in Line . . ." The Board concluded that it must run for the full thirteen (13) weeks, not for just the six (6) weeks you and I had planned. This means, Russell, that you're going to have to come up with a good many innovative ideas to stretch out the series, and without the watering down of the entertainment values. Suspense, of course, is the key—but then I don't need to tell you how to do your job. Money is no problem; don't worry about the money. We will have the sponsors, all right; and it will also mean extra money for the five volunteers, even though they are not to know about any money in advance, which would screw up the statistical nature of the selection, as you know. At any rate, the go-go decision for a full 13 weeks puts us right up in there in the Emmy running for a new series,

whereas a six-week mini-series would not. And I think we do have a
No. One Emmy idea.

You will have to handle Harry Thead, the station manager of
WOOZ, with kid gloves—a last minute reminder of this requirement.
The program idea was his in the first place, which is why we have to
originate from Miami instead of St. Louis, even though the latter was
a much better location demographically wise. But Harry Thead had
no objections to you as the overall creative director, just so long as he
could play an active behind-the-scenes part in the production. He
wants the series credits, which he needs and you may tell him that he
will be on the credits, network wide, as "Associate Producer for Miami." The credit is rather meaningless, but it will look good on the
crawl and I think he'll be happy with the title. The main thing is to
keep Harry Thead informed at all times of what you are doing, so that
he'll have the right answers for the WOOZ owners. You could also
use Harry as your coordinator with the Miami office of Baumgarten,
Bates, and Williams, who will handle the national advertising. They
are also very excited about the commercial possibilities.

Harry Thead did not have to come to us with his idea, even though
WOOZ is an affiliate. He could have run the show as a local Miami
show, which would have blown the idea for the network. So we have
a lot to thank Harry Thead for. When he asks questions, answer them;
he's behind us and the new program 110%, and he respects your creative genius.

I wish you had been present when I sold the idea to the Board. I
won't bore you with it, except to say that some of the reactionary
reactions were predictable, ranging as they did from pretended shock
to forced indignation; but we soon settled into the specifics, and your
overall tentative plan (except for the addition of another seven weeks,
which reveals their true enthusiasm) was accepted in toto, without
any major modifications. Mr. Braden, who was in favor of Miami over
St. Louis all along, pointed out that the high crime rate in Miami has
prepared the local audience there for violence better than St. Louis
which is quite religious-oriented, as Mr. Braden mentioned, whereas
Miami has only a few organized religious groups, i.e., Hare Krishna,
Unitarian, and a few other sects. The former isn't taken seriously in

Dade and Broward counties, and the latter discredited itself with Miami businessmen several years ago when they, the Unitarians, protested putting up a cross on the courthouse lawn at Christmastime.

Another update factor, which comes as good news from a statistical standpoint: Unemployment in Miami has increased 3.7% since Harry Thead's original demographic study, which, in turn, increases the predictable volunteers in Miami from 6.9 to 7.1. If I was apprehensive about anything, it was the 6.9 predictability, but the larger range to 7.1 insures the required five volunteers. (The new 7.1 figure includes the overlap into Broward County, as well as Dade County.)

You, your staff, and the five volunteers, when you have them, will all stay at the Los Pinos Motel; the third floor on the wing facing the bay has been reserved, as well as the third floor conference room. The motel is less than three blocks away from the 89th Street Causeway location of WOOZ. Billy Elkhart, the unit manager, is already down there, of course, and he has everything under control, including rental cars. Phone him before you leave Kennedy, and he'll pick you up at the Miami airport.

One last item, and it's not unimportant. Harry Thead is a Free-Mason, with all 32 degrees. Before you leave the city, pick up a blue stone Mason ring (blue is the 4th degree, I think), and wear it while you're down there. Stop by Continuity and ask Jim Preston (I know he's a Mason) to teach you the secret handshake that they use. It will help you gain rapport with Harry Thead (call it insurance), even though he'll be cooperative anyway.

From time to time, send me tape cassettes about your progress, and don't worry about the budget. Simply tell Billy Elkhart what you need, and let him worry about the budget. He has the habit of thrift, anyway, and if he goes over it'll be his ass, not yours. You have enough pressure creative-wise; I don't want you worrying about money.

"The First Five in Line . . ." is undoubtedly the greatest concept of a television series ever to hit the air in modern times, Russell, and we (the Board and I) have every confidence in you as the creative force behind it.

Good luck, and Godspeed!

ls/DJ

Violette Winters

Ms. Violette Winters, 36, had short, slightly bowed legs, a ridiculously wide pelvis, and tiny, narrow hurting feet. She wore size 5 AAA shoes, slit at the big toe with a razor blade to relieve the pressure on her bunions, usually nurse-white with rippled rubber soles, and cotton support hose. So far she did not have varicose veins, but she lived in dread of their purplish emergence, and she hoped that the white cotton support hose would hold them in abeyance for as long as possible; but she was fully aware that varicose veins were the eventual reward of the full-time professional waitress. Violette's broad, blubbery hips and thick thighs, even with her girdle stretched over them, were mushy to the touch, and she bruised easily without healing quickly. Her ankles and calves, however, were trim. In her low-heeled white nurse's shoes, she was five feet four, but appeared to be taller because of her narrow-waisted torso, petite breasts (with inverted nipples), long neck, and the huge mass of curly marmalade hair, which she wore with a rat, piled high on top of her head. When she worked, her hair was covered by a black, cobwebby net, which darkened her curls to an off-shade of dried blood. Her cerulean eyes were deep-set, well-guarded by knobby, bony brows and thick brown eyebrows. Any time a male got within seven feet of her person, her eyes narrowed to oriental dimensions. Her face had been pretty when she was a young girl, and she would have been handsome still if it were not for the harsh frown lines across her broad forehead and the deeply grooved diagonals that ran from the wings of her nose to the corners of her turned down mouth. Her retroussé nose was splattered with tiny pointillistic freckles.

Violette always moved swiftly at her tasks around the restaurants where she worked, rarely made a mistake in addition, and her large white fluttering hands could deftly carry up to six cups of coffee, on saucers, without spilling a drop. A highly skilled waitress, when the time came for her to quit a job, every manager she had ever worked for regretted her departure. By all rights, Violette should have made more money in tips than the other waitresses, if efficiency was a factor, but she was the kind of woman (and men knew this, as if by instinct) who would accept a miserly ten percent tip without making a fuss. Shrewder, middle-aged men, after taking a sharp look at her, left no tip at all. As a consequence, she made much less in tips than the other waitresses.

So far, at this midway point in her life, which frequently—at thirty-six—seems even more than a midway point to women than it does to men, Violette had had three husbands. By her standards, by anyone's standards, they had been losers to a man.

Her first husband, Tommy, was the same boy she went steady with all of the way through junior and senior high in Greenwood, Mississippi. They had moved into Tommy's parents, after getting married upon graduation from high school, but three months later Tommy left Greenwood with a carnival that was passing through town, and no one had ever heard from him again. Two years after Tommy's departure, Violette got a divorce, after giving Tommy notice in the classified section of the Greenwood paper for three weeks in a row.

At the time, in a less than liberal region, it had been embarrassing for a divorced woman to live in Greenwood, so Violette added the extra "te" to her name, and moved to Memphis. She obtained a job as a roller-skating car-hop at the Witch Stand.

After only three months on the job she was hit by a red MG that pulled into the lot at 55 miles per hour. Even then, she would have been able to dodge the MG okay, the manager told the police (Violette was a terrific skater), that she had tried to save a tray full of cheese-burgers, double fries, and two double choc-malts at the same time she tried to make good her escape from the vehicle.

During her stay in the hospital, Violette fell in love with an alco-holic named Bubba Winters, who was recovering from double pneu-monia. Bubba had passed out in a cold rain, down by the levee, and had almost died from exposure before being discovered by an early morning fisherman. They were married two days after their release from the hospital, and Violette went back to work, this time as a waitress at the Blue Goose Café, and still wearing a cast on her left leg. She had to pay off both hospital bills, and support them both, as well, because Bubba's old boss at the Regroovy Tire Center, claimed that Bubba, with his weak chest and all, wasn't strong enough to change tires all day.

To show her love for Bubba, Violette tried to drink with him at night when her work-day was over, but she didn't have the head for it. Bubba, who had learned to drink in the Marines, where he had served three years out of his four-year hitch in Olongapo, on Luzon, had a great capacity for gin. In addition to ugly hangovers, Violette awoke one morning to discover that she had a tattoo on her right forearm, a tattoo she had assented to woozily the night before to show her devotion to Bubba. In addition to a tiny red heart, pierced with a dark blue dagger, there was a stern motto in blue block letters below the heart: DEATH BEFORE DISHONOR. The twin to Violette's tattoo, although it was slightly larger, both heart and lettering, was on Bubba's right forearm, and had been there since his first overnight pass to San Diego from Boot Camp, and somehow, the tattoo looked right on Bubba. But it looked a little funny on Violette's forearm, and because the Blue Goose patrons made remarks about it all the time, she was forced to wear long sleeved blouses to work. She never drank again.

When Bubba's unemployment checks ran out, and Violette was unable to keep him in gin, because of the exorbitant doctor and hospital bills, so did Bubba. When Violette finished paying off her debts, she moved to Jacksonville, Florida. She didn't want to risk the possibility that Bubba might come back to Memphis.

Violette retained Bubba's surname, however, after divorcing her third husband, a civil service warehouseman (G-S 3) in the Jacksonville Naval District, because she had never gotten around to divorcing Bubba Winters before she married him. The warehouseman, Gunter Haas, who didn't drink or smoke, was a compulsive gambler. Every two weeks, when he got paid, he lost his money in the regular warehouse crap game before coming home to Violette. Violette, who worked as a waitress at Smitty's Beef House in downtown Jax, rarely had two dimes to rub together all of the time she was illegally married to warehouseman Haas.

One night, on a pay night, after Haas had lost all of his pay, he brought three of his fellow warehousemen home with him at one A.M. to show them Violette's tattoo. Unbelievers, they had foolishly bet

Haas five bucks apiece that his wife did not have a tattoo on her forearm. She showed them the tattoo, so Haas could collect his winnings, but the next day she left Haas and Jacksonville for Miami on the Greyhound bus. Except for his low I.Q. and penchant for gambling, Haas hadn't been a bad husband, as husbands go, but the insensitivity to her person in bringing three men into her bedroom, and her with just a nighty on, had been too much for her. Besides, as she wrote her married sister back in Greenwood, "we were married in name only. Legally, I'm still married to Mr. Winters, even though I'll never love anyone as much as I loved Tommy."

Three sorry marriages to three sorry losers had made Violette wary of romance. She suspected, wisely, that she could fall in love again, and that she was susceptible to losers. So she solved her problem by staying away from men altogether, except in line of duty as a waitress. Gradually, week by week, Violette was finally building a little nest egg for herself, depositing ten dollars of her tips each week in the First Federal Savings Bank & Trust Company of Miami.

In Miami, Violette had found a job, almost immediately, in the El Quatro Lounge and Restaurant, on the Tamiami Trail (Eighth Street). The El Quatro, because of its peculiar hours (it opened at four A.M., and closed at noon), attracted a unique clientele. The first arrivals, at four A.M., were mostly drunks who came from other bars, or party diehards who had decided to carry on the party elsewhere. By six A.M. another group arrived, mostly hard-working construction workers who liked steak and eggs for breakfast. There were also large breakfast wedding parties two or three mornings a week. By ten-thirty A.M., a good many secretaries arrived, in twos and threes, to eat early lunches. They would be needed to answer the telephones in their offices during the noon hour when their bosses went out for longer and much more leisurely martini lunches. As a consequence, Violette worked hard at the El Quatro, and never quite got accustomed to the hours.

Violette rented a room, with a private bath, from a Cuban family on Second Street. She said very little to the members of the Duarte family because they made it a practice—a dying stab at the preservation of their culture—to only speak Spanish at home. Violette did not sleep very well, that is, for any prolonged stretch at a time. The family was noisy, but that wouldn't have bothered her much; it was the peculiar working hours. Exhausted by the time she arrived home at one P.M., she napped fitfully, off and on, and watched television until it was time to go to work again. She ate two meals at El Quatro, and rarely fixed anything to eat on the hotplate she had in her room. She ate a good deal of candy between meals, mostly Brach's chocolate covered peanut clusters and chocolate covered almonds.

On her day off (Monday) she took the bus to Key Biscayne and rented a cabana at Crandon Park. She would wander around the zoo, sit in the shade of her cabana looking at the muddy sea, and browse idly through the magazines she brought along. Her favorite magazines were *Cosmopolitan* and *Ingenue,* with *Modern Romances* a close third. She also subscribed to *The Enquirer,* but she read that at home. On these lazy, off-days, Violette almost forgot sometimes that she was a waitress, but she always remembered to pick up her clean uniforms for the week on her way home.

Violette hated being a waitress, but she knew there wasn't anything she could do about it because of her astrological sign. She had read it in the *Miami News,* when she checked her daily horoscope on her birthday. "An Aries born on this date will be a good waitress."

And it was true. Violette was a good waitress: she was waiting: and she was an Aries.

Tape Cassette (undated)

Whihh, whihh, wheee! Hello test, hello test. Okay. Note to Engineer. Please make a dub of this cassette for my file, and mail the original to Mr. Doremus Jessup, Veep for Programming, NBN, New York.

Hi, Dory, this is Russell Haxby, and I want you to know first off that the quarters at the Los Pinos are el fino, as they say down here in Miami. Harry Thead and I, you'll be glad to know, are getting along fabulously. In fact, we already have a bond in Quail Roost, and Harry isn't into Scotch like so many TV station-managers. So we drink

Quail Roost, and, thanks to you, the fraternal idea of being Masons together has worked out rather well. Incidentally, Jim Preston, in Continuity, gave me a pretty damned hard time when I asked him to show me the secret handshake. I had to show him your memo ordering him to give it to me before he came across with it. Don't reprimand him, or anything like that, but I hope you'll bear it in mind when cost-of-living time rolls around. No man loyal to the network should put some sort of weird lodge on a level higher than the organization he works for.

Numero uno. The soundproof glass boxes are being built now at the station, according to the specs. We plan to use the narrow parking lot behind WOOZ, which faces Biscayne Bay. This area, ordinarily, is the staff and VIP parking area, but there is plenty of parking space out front, so Harry said to preempt it. A good part of the Miami skyline is in the b.g., so for the interview shows, we can do them outside, putting the skyline in the background when the M.C. talks alone, or goes from booth to booth. We will be able to hear the volunteers, but they won't be able to hear each other. The speaker in each box will pick up the M.C.'s voice, and for control, my mike from the director's booth.

Two. At Harry's suggestion, we are going to lodge the five volunteers, when we have them, but not the staff, in a fairly large two-story houseboat that's moored about fifty feet down the causeway from the studio property. The houseboat belongs to a friend of Harry's, and it will make everything much simpler. No transportation problems, and we can put the psychiatrist in there with them, and station a couple of security men at the gangplank for absolute control. The staff will remain at the Los Pinos. I told Billy Elkhart to work out some kind of fair rent deal with Harry's friend, even though we were offered the houseboat gratis. It's better to lock up a rental contract at a minimum fee, so he doesn't all of a sudden need his goddamned boat back in the middle of things.

Point three. As it turned out, it was a good idea to select the resident psychiatrist down here instead of bringing one down from New York. Not only was it cheaper—twenty applicants from the Miami area answered our ad in *The American Psychiatrist's Journal*—but these Miami doctors are more familiar with Florida mental profiles than New York doctors. Dr. Bernstein, by the way, is enthusiastic as hell about the program. He thinks he'll get a book out of it, poor bastard. A New York doctor would have understood the release he signed, or at least have had his lawyer read it. I didn't tell Bernstein any different; I'll lay that bomb on him after he turns in his pre-and-post program studies. On the release he signed, he won't even be able to retain his notes.

Eliminating the other nineteen psychiatrists was simpler than Harry and I thought it would be. The first five we interviewed had nasal Midwestern accents, so we let them go immediately. Four others hadn't published anything in the last two years, one of our main requirements. As you know, I won't even go to a goddamned dentist if he doesn't write and publish in his field. And three were against the program morally, or said they were, so I let them go. We narrowed down the others on the basis of videotape screen tests, and their publications. Bernstein's recent article in *The Existential Analyst's Journal* was the most objective, and if you want to read it let me know and I'll send you a xerox. He can also fake a fairly good German accent that's still intelligible. He used to imitate and mock his old man, he said, and that's how he learned to do it. He's photogenic, wears a short white goatee, and his crinkly eyes will look kindly—with the right make-up. Also he has a head full of salt-and-pepper hair, and a little below-the-belt melon paunch. If it weren't for his bona fides, he could've been sent over by Central Casting. In fact, he looks so much like a psychiatrist, we're going to have him wear a suit instead of a white doctor's coat when we go on the air.

Problems. A few. And I don't mind suggestions. WOOZ has got six camera operators. Five are women, and one is a fag. Harry says the five women are all good, and he hired them a couple of years back to keep the women's lib people down here off his ass. The same with the fag, who's the secretary/treasurer of the North Miami Gay Lib Group. The women have degrees in Communications, two of them with M.A.'s from Southern Illinois. So there's no way we can fire any of them for cause or incompetence. I talked to them, and none of them object to the program idea. Why should they? They're pros, and they have union cards. But—and here's the problem—these women, being women, and a fag, being a fag, might faint during the operation scenes. They've never seen anything like the stuff we've got coming up, you know. What I wanted, and we discussed this in New York, was some ex-combat Signal Corps cameramen who were used to the sight of blood. These female operators sure as hell wouldn't stand for any stand-by cameramen, either. They want to do a network show, more for the prestige than for the extra money. Anyway, we've still got plenty of time, and if you have any ideas, let me know soonest.

Everything else is on schedule. We're working on the script for the TV spot announcements—to get the volunteers—this afternoon. Dr. Bernstein is a help here, more help than the writer you sent me, Noble Barnes. He can't seem to forget that he's a novelist, and a black novelist at that. He's got to go. I've been around for a long time, Dory, and I've never seen a novelist yet who could do shit with a spot or a screenplay. Noble can't spell, and he leaves the "esses" and "ee dees" off his words as well. On a program as important as this one, I've got to have another writer. "The First Five in Line" isn't "Amos and Andy" for God's sake.

—Sorry, Dory. I know we have to have at least one black on the staff, but if we're lucky enough to get a black volunteer, I'm shipping Noble Barnes' black ass back to Harlem. How, I'll always wonder, did this fucker ever get through C.C.N.Y.?

Tomorrow we meet with the Miami account exec. from Baumgarten, Bates, and Williams, who wants to discuss national accounts at this end. I'll send you a tape or a transcript of the minutes. The WOOZ engineer has rigged up the conference room at the Los Pinos, and we're going to tape everything. It's quite possible that Mr. Williams himself might come to this meeting, according to the account exec. A good sign, don't you think?

Some possible alternate titles from my notes:

"The Five Who Fled"; "The Finalist Quintet"; "The End of the Line"; "Doctor, Lawyer, Indian Chief, Cowboy and Lady"; "Five Fists Full of Dollars."

I'm not crazy about any of these titles, but they're on the record, so you can kick them around.

Ciao, J.D. And that's a ten-four.

John Wheeler Coleman, Col., A.U.S. (Retired)

A good many men in America, if they had to do it at all, would have rather done it John Wheeler Coleman's way than the more conventional method, but Coleman had always felt cheated by the failure of his father to get him into the U.S. Military Academy at West Point, or, failing that, into the Virginia Military Institute where General Marshall had matriculated. In other words, despite Coleman's distinguished military career, he had never managed to become a Regular Army officer.

His failure to become RA had colored his life brown.

Coleman had obtained his commission as a second lieutenant at Fort Benning, at The Infantry School, by attending Officer's Candidate School, and he had served his country well for twenty-four years. He had retired as a lieutenant colonel, with a "gangplank" promotion to full colonel on the day before his retirement, from the A.U.S. (Army of the United States) instead of the U.S.A. (United States Army).

The difference between the A.U.S. and R.A., in Coleman's case, would have made all the difference to his career. As a Reserve officer on active duty—instead of being a Regular Army officer on active duty—Coleman's active duty status was in jeopardy every single day of the full twenty-four years he served. Every Reserve officer on active duty knows this, but Coleman had never been able to adjust to the idea of sudden, peremptory dismissal. There wasn't a day that went by that the possibility of a letter, informing him that he would be "riffed," would land on his desk. The term "riff" is an acronym coined by Louis Johnson, during his tenure as Secretary of Defense, from "R.I.F.," Reduction in Force. Many thousands of officers were able to stay the full distance for twenty years, and retirement, but many more thousands were riffed; and when an officer was riffed there was no way that he could find out the reason, if, indeed, there was a reason other than a further reduction in force.

Coleman often thought bitterly (never voicing it, to be sure) about General Douglas MacArthur's fatuous remark, "There is no security, there is only opportunity."

Sure, a man who was R.A. could say that, and MacArthur had gone to West Point; but if MacArthur had been a Reserve officer, he would have whistled a different tune.

As a combat officer, serving in Korea and Vietnam, Coleman had been decorated with the Distinguished Service Cross; the Silver Star, with one Oak Leaf Cluster; the Bronze Star, with V Device; and two Army Commendation Medals. As a Reserve officer, Coleman had always tried harder than regular officers of the same rank, but the positive knowledge that he could be booted out of the service any day, without a reason, unlike R.A. officers, and without getting a dime in severance pay, either, had affected his decision-making ability. Coleman never hesitated about making a decision, of course (if he had, he never would have lasted the full twenty-four years), but his decisions were always determined by thinking first what kind of decision his immediate superior officer (the officer who made out his bi-annual Effectiveness Report) would have made in the same situation. He had been very successful at this kind of thinking, although the overall pattern of his career, as a consequence, made his record a somewhat eccentric mixture of inconsistencies. A brilliant record, to be true, but a strange one if examined closely, because it reflected the thinking of more than 100 different superior officers. Despite his Superior Effectiveness Reports, with only one Excellent Report to mar his record (the time, when he was a First Lieutenant, and a Supply Officer for Company "A," 19th Infantry, and someone had stolen ten mattress covers from the supply room), Coleman had served under a good many officers who had made dumb decisions. His decisions, under dumb officers, had been equally dumb—but that had been the game he had had to play if he wanted to stay on active duty.

With his daring combat record as a junior officer, Coleman, by all rights, should have been a full colonel with his own regiment at least five years before his retirement, but he had performed so brilliantly in Command and General Staff School, at Fort Leavenworth, he had been marked down for staff work. Without ever getting into command, of at least a battalion, he was doomed to staff work from then on, and no matter how brilliant a staff man happens to be, he is always considered a No. Two man, which means he is passed over for command more often than not.

The key year, for an officer with reserve status on active duty, is his eighteenth year of service. If the officer is allowed to serve for eighteen years, he cannot be riffed (except for a very serious cause) until he has served twenty years and is eligible for retirement. But even when Coleman passed safely through his eighteenth year, and then his twentieth, he was still unable to relax his vigilance. He tried even harder, in fact, feeling now that there was still a chance to make R.A. before his retirement and then stay for thirty years. If he could stay for thirty, or until he became sixty-five, those extra years would make the possibility of becoming a general officer a certainty. But he never made it. He languished as a regimental S-3, and was finally riffed after serving twenty-four years.

One morning, as he had been expecting for all of those years, a letter riffing him from the service, appeared on his desk.

If a man is single, and Coleman had never married, a colonel's retirement is sufficient to live on, providing his needs are simple. He lived frugally in The-Bide-A-While Rec. Center. Once a week he visited the officers club at Homestead Air Force Base, on Bingo Night. The rest of the time, he watched TV, or took long nature walks in the nearby Everglades State Park. He drove a Willy's Jeepster, and sometimes drove to the Keys, just to have somewhere to go. After a few months of this boring retirement, he took a course in Real Estate, like so many other retired officers living in Florida, and passed the examination for Agent. During the long hot days after getting his license, he sat in empty houses for eight hours a day, and sold at least one house a year. His commission was usually $1200 for each house he sold, and he added it to his savings. His savings, more than $100,000 in Gold Certificates, were kept in the Homestead Air Force Base Credit Union, at eight percent. Sitting in empty houses gave him something to do, and he considered the commissions he made as hedges against future inflation.

Coleman had made few friends in the army, and he found it even harder to make friends on the outside. He was a lonely man, and he was ashamed of his military career, which many men would have been proud of—for one reason.

Despite his combat decorations for bravery under fire, Coleman felt as if he had never been tested. Coleman, who had never known any real joy, had never known any real pain, either. He had never been sick a day in his life. He was trim, athletic, and ate with small appetite. Nor had he ever been wounded in combat, or even hurt. He had never known the joy—or pain—of marriage and fatherhood. In short, by normal standards, many men would have considered him to be a lucky bastard all the way 'round. Although he kept his hair in a brush cut, with white sidewalls, he had even retained his hair.

But when a man has never been tested, truly tested to the limits of his endurance, how does he know that he can meet the test? There is only one way, and that is to take the test.

Coleman thought about this a lot, especially during the long days when he watched the soap operas as he sat in empty houses, thinking about the emptiness of his life.

Tape Cassette

Hi Russell, this is D.J. I'll be sending this tape down with Ernie Powell, who'll also bring along some notes, including the comments from Doctor Glass of Bellevue. Ernie's been hired by the unit manager as a production assistant for TFFIL, but he's really a procurer. He has a rep in the trade, in case you haven't heard of him, of being able to get any prop, or anything else for that matter, within twenty minutes. He worked for seventeen years as a stage manager in summer stock, so you know how valuable he is. Ernie's worked with Billy Elkhart before, so I know Ernie'll be glad to have him on the staff.

First, those titles you reeled off were terrible. I'm putting a couple of Columbia grad students on the title. They'll be working free at NBN for two weeks, for two college credits, and they might as well learn something about TV the hard way. It will give them some incentive. I told them that if they came up with a useable title, great, but if they didn't, I wouldn't recommend them for the two college credits.

It's obvious from your last tape that you don't have time to think creatively about an alternative title, and I want your mind to be free for all of the things you have to do.

We're paying Dr. Glass a bundle, and you'll see by his notes that he's finally come up with some valuable stuff, except it's about two months too late. The gist is that the last three weeks in August and the first week in September would be the best time of the year to get volunteers. Our predictions show, as I said in my memo, a possibility ratio of 7.1, counting the new Miami unemployment figures, for volunteers. But in August, plus the first week in September, Glass claims that ninety percent of the Miami analysts, psychologists and psychiatrists, go on their vacations to North Carolina. This means that there are approximately five thousand or more neurotics stumbling around down there without a doctor to turn to for advice. At loose ends, these analysands would undoubtedly boost the probability factor for volunteers. Now, don't think I'm worried, but it's just too bad that Dr. Glass' information was a month late, or as L.B.G. used to say, and "a dollar short."

We also need a black man as a volunteer, or failing that, a Cuban. But Glass said we would never get a black volunteer, never. They're too practical, he said; but at least they won't be able to holler discrimination when we're playing this game straight and we can prove it. So you'll be stuck with Noble Barnes as a writer. At any rate, Glass' figures will be helpful if we get another season out of the show—and next time we'll go to St. Louis where there is a bigger percentage of blacks.

Re the women (and fag) camerapersons. No sweat, here. Hustle their ass over to the emergency ward at Jackson Memorial Hospital and make them watch a few emergency operations from the car wrecks. There will be amputations a plenty, so make them watch a few. If any of them pass out you can replace them before rehearsals begin, and they can't squawk to the union. Anyway, hire at least one ex-Signal Corps cameraman as an advisor only, and have him standby for emergencies during the actual programming. Too bad we decided to do this live, instead of on tape, but we do need the immediacy that a live show engenders.

Are you getting any, Russell? If not, ask Ernie, and he'll have a broad in your room within twenty minutes. It'll be good recreation for you, and you should do it anyway, even if you aren't interested, just to see Ernie work. Here he'll be, with this tape and the notes, right from the airport, and in a strange new city, and I'll bet you a case of Chivas to a case of Quail Roost that he can get a broad in your room within twenty minutes. And a free one, too. It's rather uncanny, when you come to think about it.

I called the Los Angeles office, and it's firm. Warren Oates will be the M.C. We might have to work around his movie schedule, but that'll be Billy Elkhart's problem, not yours. You *will* have Warren Oates as your M.C. Warren used to work a live game show with Jimmy Dean back in the early fifties, and he did a lot of TV work before going into films. He'll be a great M.C., and he has a positive image for this kind of thing. The only snag in his contract is that he gets to wear his dark sunglasses on the show. I had to concede this point, but you may be able to talk him out of it. By the way, when Warren comes out there from Hollywood next week, do not, do not under any circumstances, ask him what he's carrying in that burlap sack he lugs around with him. He's very sensitive about this point. Okay? Okay.

This is D.J., and a ten-four and God Speed.

Leo Zuck (nee Zuckerman), at 82, was a dapper dresser, even by Miami Beach standards, although sartorial standards on Miami Beach are not very high. Leo owned a white gabardine suit and a burnt orange linen suit, which, in various combinations, gave him four different changes. He possessed two white-on-white drip-dry-never-iron shirts, and twenty-five pink neckties. (He had had the neckties made to order out of the same bolt of cloth at a bargain price.) He also owned a red silk dinner jacket, with a ruffled pink shirt and maroon bow-tie to go with it, as well as blue-black tuxedo trousers and the cherry red patent leather pumps to round out the costumes. He did not, unhappily, have any underwear, and he had only two pair of black clock socks left in his wardrobe. The white suede shoes he wore with his suits-sports outfits, although they were clean enough, were very bald.

Leo Zuck, living in very reduced circumstances, was mostly front. Leo had lost his job as the M.C. at the Saturday night pier dance, and he did not know what he was going to do for the little luxuries that extra ten dollars a week had provided him with: a daily cigar, Sen-Sen (for his notoriously bad breath), and an occasional Almond Joy. But now he had to give up these small luxuries.

If Leo had learned or invented some new material each week, he could have, in all probability, kept the M.C. job indefinitely. Abe Ossernan, who ran the weekly dances (Admission 25 cents) and owned the pier concessions on South Beach (as South Miami Beach is called) was not a mean man; and Abe had hinted to Leo more than once that he should brighten up his faded material. But Leo paid no attention to Mr. Ossernan; Leo loved his material, and he had it down ice cold. Leo had purchased his act in 1925 for $150, when $150 *was* $150, and he had sharpened and refined the material to perfection on the Keith-Orpheum Vaudeville circuit for fifteen years. An excellent mimic, with a rubbery, if deeply lined face, Leo did accurate and extremely funny imitations of Charles Ray, George Bancroft, Emil Jannings, and Harry Langdon. He was also able to sing "I'm a Yankee Doodle Dandy" raucously out of the side of his mouth in a near-perfect imitation of George M. Cohan. This act of Leo's had wowed the hicks in the sticks for years, but the material was so old now it baffled even his nostalgic audiences at the pier dance on Saturday nights.

Leo had a large scrapbook filled with yellowed clippings from every large city and from most of the small cities in the United States and Canada, attesting to how good his act was—or had been—and, in Leo's opinion, the act was still as good—if not better than ever. Except for minor alterations in timing, the only addition to Leo's act since 1925 (a socko finish!) was made in 1945. In this cruel year, Leo had had his remaining teeth removed, and was fitted with a full set of upper and lower white plastic choppers. Because of his thick, fairly long nose and pointed, rather long chin, Leo could perform a reasonably accurate imitation of Popeye the Sailor by removing both plates.

Except for elderly persons with very keen memories, however, Popeye the Sailor was the only imitation most audiences recognized.

When vaudeville died out forever, as it had in 1940, Leo had been fortunate enough to get in the U.S. Army Special Services during the war, joining various variety companies as they were put together in New York; and he had entertained troops in the South Pacific, England, and eventually, Italy. Between overseas tours he had made the rounds of stateside Special Service shows, as well. G.I. audiences are not critical, and they had applauded his old gags and imitations of long dead movie stars with cheerful tolerance. They liked especially his introduction:

> M.C. And now, straight from the Great White Way, the famous star from the Keith-Orpheum vaudeville circuit, Leo Zuck!
>
> (Enter Leo Zuck.)
>
> Zuck: Suck what?
>
> *Audience: (Laughter.) And so on. . . .*

When the war and his teeth were finished, Leo obtained summer employment in the Catskills and Poconos at third rate hotels on the Borscht circuit. Social directors did not care greatly for Leo's act, but he was a great success with the old ladies, mostly widows, who sojourned at these cheaper mountain hotels. Leo had never married, and single men were a premium in the mountains.

In his red satin dinner jacket under a pink spot, Leo was distinguished-looking on stage. He knew how to apply make-up for maximum effect, and his full head of blue-white hair reminded many old ladies of Leopold Stokowski. Leo sported a well-trimmed white toothbrush mustache, and it was almost as white (except in the center where it had turned brownish from cigarette tar and nicotine) as his flashing false teeth.

Except for his own act, which was practically engraved on his brain, Leo's memory was not consistent, but no one in the Poconos minded when he put on his reading glasses and introduced the various acts, in his M.C. capacity, by reading the names and remarks off three-by-five inch cards with a flashlight.

In the mid-1960's, however, Leo had been unable to get any more work—even in the Poconos—and he had retired to South Beach to a residential hotel. He drew the minimum in Social Security benefits, of course, because, like many entertainers, he had preferred to be paid in cash for most of his theatrical life, but the minimum had been enough to pay for his room and meals for several years. He had also supplemented his meager income, from time to time, by playing a few dates at parties and social functions. He had been interviewed twice on WKAT radio (for free), and once on a late night talk show on Channel Four. When the host on the Channel Four Talk Show introduced him, Leo said automatically, "Suck what?"

Because of three irate phone calls, Leo wasn't invited back to the TV station, but he was still a kind of celebrity to the retired old people who make up the general population of South Beach. With inflation, Leo's Social Security check was barely enough to cover the rent of his hotel room, and when the rent was raised again—which it soon would be—he would have to find a cheaper room, although there were no rooms cheaper in South Beach than the one he had. After paying the rent, there was no money left over to eat with, and he had to be satisfied with the one free noon meal he got each day at the Jewish Welfare Center. The loss of his M.C. job at the pier, and the tax-free ten dollars that went with it, was a disaster for Leo and, for the first time since 1940, Leo Zuck, the old trouper, began to doubt seriously that vaudeville would ever come back.

Don Tracy

1905-1977

Don Tracy was born in Connecticut in 1905 and over his lifetime
gradually worked his way down the Eastern Seaboard. By the early
1930s he was a reporter in Baltimore. After sojourns in New York
and the army during World War II, he finally arrived in Clear-
water, Florida, where he became, by his own estimation, one of
the few people in the United States to make a full-time living
by freelance writing. He churned out everything from local color
historicals (*Chesapeake Cavalier, Crimson Is the Eastern Shore*)
and crime novels (*The Hated One, The Big Blackout*) to paperback originals under a variety of house pseudonyms and nonfic-
tion books such as *What You Should Know about Alcoholism.*

Tracy's strongest suit as a novelist, and often the best feature
of his writing, is the realistic detail with which he imbues his stories. Take, for example, this passage from his mainstream novel
Bazzaris, a story of Greek divers. The deckhand "who stripped off
Gus's diver's suit, had cried, 'Porrus topos!' This was the term for
the purple skin spot that signaled oxygen in the bloodstream and
a case of the bends unless the proper procedure was followed.
Gus had cursed, remembering that the cigarette the line-tender
had thrust between his lips when the faceplate was unlocked
had been sharp and acid-tasting, a sure sign of trouble. So Gus
donned his diver's gear again and was lowered to thirty fathoms.
There he spent an additional hour for each fathom of lift, until he
finally reached the top again, ravenous, craving tobacco, and with
every muscle aching from the long ordeal."

As a freelance writer, Tracy focused on genres that appeared to
be currently in demand. The novel we offer here, *The Hated One,*
in which a young African-American woman is accused of carrying
on with and murdering the state attorney of the mythical North
Florida county of Tangerine, may appear to have the same story
as Harper Lee's Pulitzer Prize–winning *To Kill a Mockingbird,* but
it also has roots in a famous 1952 murder in which Ruby McCollum, a black woman, was accused of killing a white physician.
Zora Neale Hurston attended the McCollum trial and wrote

about it for the *Pittsburgh Courier,* and William Bradford Huie described the case in *Ruby McCollum, Woman in the Suwanee Jail* (1964). However, Tracy's novel is more than a clever knockoff of either story. Where Harper Lee builds an optimistic novel, with its confidence in the essential goodness of human nature, around an innocent narrator and her idealized attorney father confronting the sexual violence and racism of a fundamentally decent Southern town, Tracy offers a battered, alcoholic narrator whose dark view of human nature seems perfectly suited to the corrupt Florida community to which he returns. Don Tracy's impressive strengths as a novelist—his honest characterization, his realism, his understanding of setting—make *The Hated One* a *noir* classic.

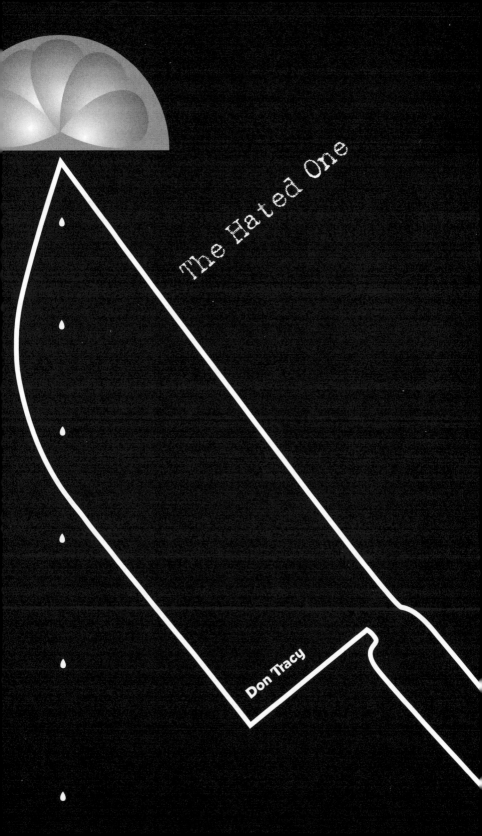

The Hated One

Don Tracy

Chapter 1

I certainly hadn't forgotten that Tangerine County, North Florida, could be hot in September. But until I hit the palmetto and scrub pine stretch that flattened out beyond the Suwannee I didn't remember just how blazing, dizzying, sweat-soaking hot it really was.

I'd been away in the north for eight years and perhaps my blood really had thickened in spite of the doctors' pooh-poohs about such things. Or maybe it was the hangover that made the heat close in on me, smother me, even though I kept the old Ford at sixty-five over the straight, flat county road.

The drinks I'd had that morning had long since faded away. There was the need for another and I called myself a damned fool for not getting a pint at one of the liquor stores clustered close to the Georgia-Florida line, just over the St. Mary's River. After all, what difference did it make whether or not Frank Coombs came back to his old home town half in the bag? I was staying in Lindsley just long enough to get the business over with. What did I expect to do—convince the good people of Lindsley and Tangerine County that here was the new, improved Frank Coombs?

But at the same time, I didn't want to sign the papers in a hand that shook so badly that nobody would be able to read the signature, as had been the case with many of my checks of other years. To exhibit a case of the shakes would be much, much more satisfying to all those dear hearts and gentle people of Lindsley than showing up half stoned. When I got to town I'd head for the club and fortify myself before showing at Bill Carter's. I couldn't do anything about the car I was driving or the face I looked at in the mirror these days, even if I cared enough to want to. But at least I wouldn't shake or get the dry heaves in public if I could help it.

When I got to Lindsley I'd turn off on DeSoto Street and take the back way to the club and once in that cool, cool cavern of a bar I'd order me a—

Then it hit me; I wasn't a member of the club any longer. I probably was the most permanent ex-member the club had ever had. And since Tangerine County was dry except for beer and I was undoubtedly flagged at any speak that might be operating, there was no other place in the county seat where I could get rid of my shakes.

I swore and stomped down hard on the brake pedal. The old Ford wavered and the worn tires squealed as I pulled over to the side of the road, trying to remember how long it had been since I'd passed the sign—ENTERING TANGERINE COUNTY, *Leaving Humphries County.*

I guessed about ten miles and looked at my wristwatch with the sweat-blackened strap. Ten-twenty, and Bill had said to be there at eleven. Well, to hell with Mr. William Sanderson Carter; the party of the second part had to have a drink. At that moment a drink was a lot more important than Bill Carter or the papers I had to sign or even the money I was going to get when I signed the papers.

Of course Bill probably still had that little refrigerator in his office. I could ask him for a drink or two, enough to make me stop shaking, but even Frank Coombs had to draw the line somewhere. I looked at the gas gauge, then peered up and down the heat-shimmered road before I wheeled the Ford in a U-turn.

It was seventeen miles to the Humphries County line and twenty before I hit a place where I could buy a drink, a dilapidated two-story stucco building at a crossroads. It had probably been a general store in its day, but the blunt neon sign—WHISKEY—gave it an aura of gracious charm.

Inside, a couple of old, dried-up woolhats were sitting at one of the half-dozen rickety tables drinking beer. For an awful moment I thought the neon sign out front was an obscene lie and this was just a beer and wine joint, then I turned toward the bar and saw the labels on the bottles behind the bartender. Cheered, I smiled and said good morning to the Crackers and the bartender, a fat man with a red face and a loud sports shirt.

"Hot," I said and he nodded noncommittally. Not a friendly type, this bartender, or perhaps I looked like somebody after a handout.

"Double bourbon, water on the side," I said to the fat bartender and when he turned to pick up the spouted bottle I looked at myself in the scrap of backbar mirror that wasn't covered by headache powder displays, smoked mullet strips, potato chips and the million other goodies for sale.

I didn't look so good. In fact, I looked terrible. I could see that even in the dirty, blurred mirror and the dim light. I'd shaved that morning but not very thoroughly, my shirt looked as though it had been on my back for a hot, dusty week and my hair, which needed cutting, hung dankly over my forehead and ears. There, peering back at me, stood Francis MacWhalen Coombs, onetime attorney-at-law, onetime bright young man, onetime husband of the beautiful Blanche Humphries Coombs, but presently part-time bill collector, part-time gas station attendant, fulltime ginhead.

The fat barkeep put the thick-bottomed shot glass in front of me, drew a glass of water and added one tiny ice cube. "That'll be a dollar-five," he said and he didn't have to add: *Pay when served.* I reached into my hip pocket and brought out my damp, thin wallet and thumbed out one of my four dollar bills. Then I got a quarter out of my pants pocket and put it down on top of the bill.

When he turned to the cash register, I got the double-shot up to my mouth without slopping it over even though I knew the two old men at the table were watching me. The whiskey went down, down, down and took charge, stunning the jumping nerves, sending the first glow of spurious wellbeing through me.

"I'll have another," I said to the man when he gave me back two dimes. "Had a rough night."

It had been rough, all right, one of those things that happen unexpectedly and in spite of a drunk's good intentions. I'd left Baltimore with the quiet resolve to drive to Lindsley with no more than a few beers along the way. I was going to arrive in my beloved old home town sober, if seedy, and if I was going to pitch one with the money I got from Bill Carter I'd wait until I was well out of sight of my beloved former friends and neighbors.

The first night out I'd done pretty good but on the second, the previous night, I hadn't been able to sleep because the air-conditioner in the motel room made so much noise and I'd gotten into the car and gone prowling.

I hit a little joint down a side road, following discreet and promising signs. Oh, we can find those joints if they're to be found. This one was a combination juke and speak-easy, with a crap game in the back room and ladies available in the half-dozen cabins behind the place. I went the whole route—the booze, the crap game and the rather demure little brunette in Cabin Four, please pay when served. That was the reason for my hangover, my blurred face in the backbar mirror, the four (now three) ones in my wallet.

The second double fixed me up. My shakes disappeared and the smothering heat lessened and the shabby little joint became a pleasant place.

"One more and I won't bother you again," I said to the bartender after I'd sipped a half mouthful of my water chaser. He gave me a look but turned to the bottles again. The two Crackers at the table were still eyeing my soaked back with the contemptuous admiration barflies give a lush who can throw down two doubles in the morning, bing-bing, without a gasp or a cough.

I dawdled over my third, sipping it delicately, as a gentleman should. It was horrible bourbon but it was the last for awhile. The fourth buck had to go for gas so I stretched it out as long as I could.

"How many miles is it to Lindsley?" I asked.

The fat man leaned back, his thick arms across his chest. "You mean you forgot, Coombs?"

I looked at him, trying to place him, and finally gave up. "Harry Foyles," he said. "I put on a little weight since I seen you."

I remembered then. I'd defended this man's brother, Charley, a bootlegger like Harry, on a hit-and-run, d.w.i. charge and had talked six good men and true—well, five men and a woman—into finding him not guilty. For some reason, mystifying because I'd always let Miss Elsie keep track of such things in those days, I remembered, too, that Charley Foyles had paid me only three hundred of the thousand he'd promised me if I got him off the hook.

Harry Foyles must have known about that and guessed I remembered. "You had enough for awhile. But stop in on your way back and I'll pop for one."

"I might not stop, coming back," I said.

"You'll stop," he answered and I knew I would. As soon as I got my money from Bill I'd head back for that free drink. For a starter.

Foyles half turned and looked up at the electric clock with the beer ad across its face. "You better get goin'," he said. "And take it easy when you cross the county line. You let one of Henry Taggart's road patrols stop you and you're dead. Henry still don't like you much, from what I hear."

"Sheriff Taggart," I answered, "is an old and valued friend. If we had any misunderstanding it's been cleared up long ago."

"Sure." Foyles grinned. "But just the same don't try to bust no speed records or step outta line any other way, not while you're in Tangerine."

I started to ask this slob who he thought he was to advise *me* and then I remembered the promise of a drink on the house so I nodded. "I guess you're right," I said. "Nice seeing you again, Harry."

I looked at the bottles behind the fat man, then turned away. It wouldn't be so long, not really. I started for the door. I was halfway there when it opened and two men came in.

The first was tall and thin and he wore a wide-brimmed planter's hat but because of the glare from the doorway I didn't recognize him until he spoke. He said: *Morning, Foyles,* and *Morning, boys,* to the two old woolhats at the table. He sounded like he was delivering an important order to the troops so I knew this was my mother's brother, Brigadier-General Edmund Ruffin MacWhalen the Third (Ret.). It followed that the man behind the General must be the guy who was everything I wasn't—the General's son, Edmund the Fourth, Cousin Eddie.

If there were any two people in the world I particularly didn't want to see that morning they were the General and Cousin Eddie. There was a long muster of Tangerine County citizens who had reason to despise me and I guess the General came right behind Blanche for lead-off position.

Besides running Tangerine County politics and owning nearly all the worthwhile property in that part of Florida, he was a Southern Gentleman, God help us all, and if anything was more sacred to him than his own infallibility it was the MacWhalen name. I'd besmirched that noble name a hundred different ways—worst of all by sounding off one time about how I might have been a much different, better man if I'd been born a Smith or a Jones, anything but a distaff-side member of the MacWhalen family.

It took him some time to adjust his eyes to the gloom of Harry Foyles' bar and in those few seconds I tried to get out. I might have made it, too, if the fat man behind the stick hadn't called, "Gen'ral, look who's come back for a visit—your nephew, Frank Coombs."

I goddamned Foyles for the no-good bastard he was. "Hello, General. Hello, Eddie," I said. It sounded more slurred than it should have or maybe those three drinks had hit me harder than I'd suspected.

I watched my uncle's Adam's apple work above the low white collar with its neat bow tie. I saw his nostrils pinch in his tanned face before he said, "You're back." It was as though he were speaking about a malignancy that he'd been assured had been cut out, destroyed, and now it had shown up again.

"Just for a few minutes," I told him. "Got a little business with Bill Carter."

My uncle didn't let on he'd even heard me. His eyes moved over me very slowly, very deliberately, as though he'd never seen a semi-derelict before. I'd thought that the time when I could be embarrassed was long past but I felt embarrassment more than shame or resentment as he carefully, almost reluctantly, moved his eyes from one shabby part of me to the other.

I couldn't take the General's eyes so I switched to Cousin Eddie. Such a handsome man, so clean-cut, so well-dressed, so universally admired, so inevitably bound to take over where his old man left off. Yes, Eddie MacWhalen was quite a man. Looking at him now it was hard to remember what a prick he had been as a kid and even later, at Gainesville.

"Hello, Eddie," I muttered. "How's Laurie?"

"She's fine," he said mechanically. "How you doing, boy?"

"Oh, fine," I said.

He swallowed. "Frank, is there anything—"

"Edmund," the General said. Just one word, spoken quietly, and Cousin Eddie closed his mouth. It had been that way when I'd been around: I saw it still was that way.

"Nice seeing you," I mumbled in thick-tongued idiocy and turned and shambled out of the joint into the heat.

Outside, parked beside my old car, was a beautiful grey Lincoln Continental, the General's car or Eddie's. I'd always wanted a Continental but Blanche had thought Cadillacs were the proper vehicle for a successful young lawyer and his wife. We'd always had two Coupe de Villes in the garage at Spring Bayou and now I had a beat-up Ford that was almost out of gas and falling apart. And Blanche? Well, Blanche probably didn't have much better—if she had a car at all. For a second I wished things had turned out differently so Blanche could have her Cadillac back. Then I said to hell with that might-have-been stuff and I got in my heap and started for Lindsley again.

2

The three doubles got me into town, down Livingston Avenue onto Jefferson and right to the Lawyers Building on the square. I found a parking space and nosed the car into the curb. I found two dimes, two nickels and three pennies in my pockets so I put thirty cents into the meter. I'd be gone in an hour, an hour and a half at the most, but I wasn't taking any chances. If the law was laying for me they could start with a parking ticket and go on from there.

The heat blasted up off the pavement. The sun's glare came right through my dark glasses so I kept my head down as I crossed the sidewalk to the entrance of the Lawyers Building. I went up to the second floor and turned left down the hall to the door marked CARTER, LYNCH & ELEY. Once it had said just CARTER & COOMBS.

Just outside the door all my built-up bitter unconcern with what these people and this town thought of me suddenly deserted me, double shots and all. For a moment I kept my hand hovering above the doorknob, dreading what the next few minutes would bring, a coward afraid to face Miss Elsie or Bill or whoever else might be beyond that door.

I asked myself again why I hadn't transacted this last bit of business by mail? Why had I insisted on coming back to Lindsley to sign over the last piece of property I owned in Tangerine County, the last of an inheritance that once had seemed big enough, rich enough, to last forever? Why hadn't I let Bill Carter handle it and mail me a check? Had it been some last guttering spark of defiance that had made me present the ruin in person? Some need to prove to these people that I still lived, still moved and breathed and drank my drinks in spite of their predictions and their hate?

Or had I subconsciously hoped for the miracle of forgiveness? Had I been driven back by some ridiculous illusion that the love and trust I'd once had and had thrown away could be born again in one man, one woman?

I snorted. If I'd ever thought that, even subconsciously, the General had shown me how stupid I'd been. If I'd managed to stay sober instead of arriving in Lindsley almost drunk, dirty, half-shaved, smelly, there might have been a chance—but I hadn't. What was it that psychiatrist had told me? *The alcoholic insists on punishing himself by getting drunk at the most disastrously inopportune times.*

Nuts; I'd gotten half-fractured because it was hot and I needed a drink to stop my shakes. Who needed Freud or Jung or a fifty dollar an hour headshrinker to make a big, involved thing out of it?

I turned the doorknob and walked into the bliss of air-conditioning. I blinked and looked around. Carter and his new partners had completely redecorated the place. The reception room was a beautiful blend of lemon yellow and grey with Danish furniture and good, unobtrusive prints on the grasscloth walls. The soft lighting came from behind a ledge that circled the room near the ceiling, augmented by mellow-shaded goosenecks on each of the two modern desks facing the entrance.

It was a perfectly designed reception room. Bill and I had often talked about doing something with our offices, bringing them up-to-date, but somehow we never had. They'd stayed just the way they were when our respective fathers and the Judge, my grandfather and Bill's great-uncle, had occupied them.

Nobody was in the outer office. My footsteps made no sound on the thick carpeting so I coughed to let Miss Elsie or whoever was tending store know I was there before I went over to a low coffee table and helped myself to a cigarette from a crystal container. I was just lighting it when a voice as cool as the breeze from the air-conditioner asked, "May I help you?"

I turned and looked at the blonde in the severe blue-grey linen, a very, very pretty blonde with a professionally gracious smile. Her clear, cool eyes looked at my dishevelment, gauged my degree of intoxication and became only a little wary.

"My name's Coombs," I said. "I had an appointment with Bill Carter but I'm late and—"

"Francis!" She stood straight and spare in her dark skirt and white blouse in the doorway, her hair done up in the same bun she'd always worn, her rimless glasses balanced on her narrow nose, her pale, thin-lipped mouth still pinched at the corners.

"Hello, Miss Elsie," I said. Just that: but my heart turned over and my soul retched at sight of this stringy old maid and the thought of what I'd done to her love and trust.

"Oh, Francis," she said, and then she burst into tears. I'd never seen her cry; perhaps I'd thought that a woman as austere and correct as Miss Elsie couldn't, and the sight made me come unglued. My hands started to tremble as I blurted, "Hey, don't do that!"

The tall girl in the blue-grey dress let her formally gracious face collapse into concern. She went over and put an arm around the thin shoulders while she gave me a look that told me to get out, whoever I was, and stop making Miss Elsie cry.

The old lady shrugged out from under the protective arm and came toward me, both hands outstretched. "Oh, Francis," she said. "It's so good to see you!"

She took both my hands in her thin, bony ones and turned her cheek up to be kissed. I held my breath and brushed the side of my mouth along her cheekbone. When I drew back I tried to keep her out of range of my breath. "It's good to see you, too," I said inanely.

She held onto me, looking up, searching out my every sign of failure but with compassion, not the contempt nor the satisfaction I'd seen so often in people's faces. Her eyes were still damp behind the rimless glasses but she managed a wavering smile.

"You look tired, Francis," she said. "Come on in my office and sit a spell." She tried to be sprightly but it didn't quite come off. "Oh, yes, I have my own office these days. They've hidden me so I won't frighten clients away. Come along, you must see it—but you haven't met Miss Williamson, have you?"

"How do you do?" the pretty girl murmured politely. I nodded and gave Miss Judith Williamson an E for Effort in trying not to show she'd heard all about Frank Coombs.

"Miss Williamson is one of our secretaries," Miss Elsie was saying. "Then there's Missus Dwyer but she's at lunch now. Judith, why don't you take your lunch hour now while I talk to Mister Coombs?"

I didn't want to talk to Miss Elsie or to anybody else. I wanted to sign the papers and get my money and get the hell out of town. The banks closed at two o'clock and it was almost one and I had no time to chew the fat with a dried-up old maid even if she was the only person in North Florida who didn't despise me.

"I'd better see Bill, hadn't I, Miss Elsie?" I said. "I mean, I had an eleven o'clock appointment and I'm two hours late. I imagine Bill's about ready to flip, you know how he hates waiting for people."

"You run along, Judith," Miss Elsie said. "You don't mind, do you?"

The blonde smiled and told me she was very glad to have met me, then got her pocketbook out of one of the desks and walked out. She had a splendid figure and a walk that made her hips move enchantingly under the thin cloth of her dress.

"My office is back here," Miss Elsie said. "They've changed everything around. My goodness, they spent a fortune knocking out walls and putting in air-conditioning—"

"I'm sorry," I broke in, "but I've got to see Bill as soon as I can. I've only got a few hours. I'm due back in Baltimore in—"

She looked at me and I let the lie dangle. I was suddenly too tired and sick and hung over to bother. Those double-shot glasses back at Harry Foyles' joint must have had thicker bottoms than I'd suspected. The booze was wearing off and I was on the verge of the shakes again.

Miss Elsie led me into a small office, a little gem of a room with draperies that blended with the carpeting and the furniture. She gestured me toward a chair and I sat down and doubled my fists between my legs to keep them from trembling too obviously.

"Where's Bill?" I asked. "I got to see him."

Instead of answering, Miss Elsie leaned over and brought out a paper sack from the bottom drawer of her desk. The neck of a sealed pint was sticking out of its wrinkled top. She put a paper cup beside the bag. "You'll find water in there," she said, nodding toward a door in the rear wall. "I have to find something in William's office."

That was really something; eight years and still Miss Elsie had a drink ready on the chance I'd need it when I showed up. I started to say thanks, but I kept my mouth shut. Miss Elsie hated drinking and what it did to people, especially me, and it would have made her feel even more guilty if I'd said anything. Even when she'd nursed me through the horrors by judiciously administered belts of straight liquor so I could go into court, Miss Elsie had somehow contrived to make it seem that dirty, smelly, evil *alcohol* was not involved.

So I silently blessed her instead as she went out of her office, shutting the door behind her. I had trouble with the seal of the pint and when I finally got it loose I didn't bother with the paper cup; I put the bottle up to my mouth and gulped. Then, when my stomach started to protest, I went into the little john and drank some water. I had a few more big jolts of bourbon, and I was fine.

I put the sacked bottle back in the drawer and sat down again. The cigarette I'd filched from the free supply in the reception room had gone out and I relit it. I coughed on the first drag and then I sat back, feeling good. The jumps were gone, the need to get out of here and away from Lindsley was gone. I was at peace.

Miss Elsie came back and sat down at her desk without a glance at the drawer. "Now," she said, "William waited for you until eleven-thirty. He had a lunch appointment but he told me to tell you to meet him outside the courtroom a little before two." She looked up at me. "That should give you time for a haircut, Francis."

"I'm not here to win any beauty contests," I answered. "Bill will just have to grit his teeth and bear his shame. He ought to be used to that by now, God knows."

"Don't talk like that, Francis."

"Besides," I said, "I'm broke. I put my last thirty cents in the parking meter. And if I'm not meeting Bill until two, how am I going to cash my check? Do you think Chet Leonard's going to open the bank especially for me?"

She pulled open the center drawer of her desk and took out a long envelope. "William thought of that," she said. "Here's five hundred dollars in cash. William has a check for the balance."

I had to get up to walk over to the desk and if I tilted a little before I caught my balance, Miss Elsie pretended not to notice. I folded the envelope and put it in my hip pocket next to my damp, empty wallet. "Thanks, Miss Elsie," I said. "You think of everything."

Because Bill Carter had never thought about the banks being closed, any more than I'd have thought of it when I'd been like Bill Carter. Well, not exactly like Bill Carter, that fine, upstanding man; let's say a reasonable if basically bleary facsimile.

I ran my hand over my shaggy head. "Thanks for all the rest of it, too. The way you stuck by me, I mean."

"Don't thank me. I didn't do anything."

"You did plenty. I guess I'll never know all you did or tried to do. I only wish—" I broke off. "I'd better get along," I said. "Judge Humphries' court? Is that peanut head still sitting in Part Two, Circuit?"

Miss Elsie clucked her tongue as she nodded, looking down at her hands again.

"I'll be there," I said. "I don't guess I'll see you again, Miss Elsie, so thanks again for everything."

I looked at her and tried to think of something else to say. But what could I say to the person who'd believed in me when everybody else in the world had found me out for a no-good phoney? There was nothing except the feeble word *Thanks*. So I walked out of the office through the reception room and out of the air-conditioning into the heat of the hallway.

The drinks I'd had in Miss Elsie's office and the five hundred dollars in my hip pocket made me feel fine and I wasn't going to let the tears stealing down Miss Elsie's cheeks as I'd left spoil it. I shut that picture out of my mind and thought, instead, of the one I was going to pitch once I'd signed those papers and picked up my check.

Outside the Lawyers Building the sun still blazed. The glare was worse after the soft lights of the office but in a few more minutes I'd be on my way. I looked at the clock on the Baptist Church tower— twenty minutes to two. Unless Lindsley barbershops had changed completely a man couldn't get a haircut in much less than an hour, not with the conversation that went along with it.

I didn't want to take a chance. I walked into the yard beside the courthouse toward the benches under the live oaks.

I hunted through my pockets for cigarettes and remembered I was out and had been for hours. I considered spending some of the money in my hip pocket and decided against it. The closest place was Bentley's Drugstore and one of the lawyers eating at the fountain would be sure to recognize me. Even if nobody spoke, I could imagine the whispering that would scurry around the store. I didn't need a cigarette that much. Bill would have some. I could bum one off him.

I sat there with my thoughts turned inward on my comfortable half-plastered self, then a commotion of loud voices and laughter and commands shook me back into the hot afternoon. A double file of men and women, first a dozen or so whites and then twenty or more colored, was leaving the county jail on the opposite side of the street.

The men wore blue denim uniforms with TANGERINE CO. PRISONER stenciled front and back. The white women wore not unattractive light green dresses with the same message across the shoulders in script. The colored women wore what they had had on when they were arrested.

Herding the group were four male deputies and a matron. The deputies were all young and all handsome in a tanned-faced, white-toothed, loud-voiced way. They wore grey uniforms and wide-brimmed hats, and non-regulation western six-guns at their thighs. I didn't recognize any of them but they were all of a type—young, abounding in good spirits and fiercely proud of their jobs.

I wondered if Henry Taggart had changed much since I'd last seen him. From what Harry Foyles had said I knew he was still sheriff but I'd have known that anyway. Henry Taggart would be sheriff of Tangerine County for as long as he wanted to be—unless he did the fantastically improbable and butted heads with Brigadier-General Edmund Ruffin MacWhalen the Third (Ret.). By looking down his thin, patrician nose and lifting one long, patrician finger the General could ruin even as well-loved a man as Sheriff Henry Taggart. Once he'd been my friend but now Henry Taggart was my enemy and I'd be smart to stay out of his way.

I watched the prisoners pass, bound for arraignment or sentencing. On their way to Circuit Court, Part One, where that old walrus, Judge Thomas R. Thrace, would glare down at them, hating them for taking up his time with their picayune crimes, he who should have been a United States Senator or a member of the United States Supreme Court. As the prisoners passed I silently wished them luck and hoped that this was one of Judge Thrace's rare probation days, not a five-to-ten day.

I didn't recognize any of the white prisoners. I picked out two of the shackled colored men as longtime repeaters, on their way back to Raiford where they'd already spent most of their lives. The second colored girl in line looked vaguely familiar but I couldn't place her. She was a striking figure in her rumpled white maid's uniform, light-skinned with a straight back and with her chin up, her eyes scornfully impenitent.

Don't act that way when you go up before the judge, girl, I told her silently, *Judge Thrace hates an uppity nigra and uppity means anything short of yazzuh boss.*

The double file went up the side steps and into the courthouse. I checked my watch and saw that it was time to go. I got up from the bench and ran my hand over my hair, pulled up my pants and tucked in my damp shirt.

It was nearly over. Five minutes, maybe ten, with Bill Carter and then I'd have my money and it would be good-bye forever to Lindsley, to Tangerine County, to North Florida. I started across the yard toward the side door. Then suddenly behind me I heard someone holler my name.

"Mistuh Frank, suh! 'Fore Gawd in heaven, I *knowed* you'd come. Praise Gawd! I been prayin' and prayin' you'd come back an' he'p us and now you's heah. Now you kin git Coralee off. Now they ain'gonna hang her or put her in the prison house fer somethin' she never done, Mistuh Frank—she never done a-tall!"

3

For a second I thought of saying no, I wasn't Mister Frank, that my name was George Smith and I was in a hurry. But it wouldn't have been any use. The colored prisoner that had looked familiar must have been Coralee, Hattie May's youngest, and it was Hattie May hollering at me.

Once when I was in a Baltimore bar and some stupid loudmouth was sounding off about how he hated niggers, I lost my battle to keep my mouth shut and told him he was entitled to his opinion but to please stop yakking; he was giving me a headache. My accent told him I was from the south and he sneered and said something about he supposed I was raised up by an old nigger mammy down on the old plantation. I forget what I answered before the fight started but I could have said yes, that was right, because I was raised up by Hattie May.

She had come to work for my family when my grandfather, the Judge, was new to the bench and my father was still a young man. My mother, a MacWhalen, had come to the Coombs house as a bride and it had been Hattie May who had taught her how to keep the Coombs menfolks happy, as my mother often admitted. She had had the raising of my brother, Johnny, and me until we were packed off to school, then after I'd married Blanche she had run Spring Bayou, Blanche not being the domestic type.

Nobody knew how old she was, least of all Hattie May. She'd been with the Coombs family for at least sixty years so even if she came to work for my grandfather as a young girl she had to be in her high seventies, more probably her eighties.

Now as I turned around and watched her come toward me I saw she hadn't changed a bit. She was immense and very black and I'd never seen her, even on the hottest day, when she didn't look as though she'd just put on a fresh, starched blue and white polkadot dress. Blanche used to try to get up nerve enough to tell Hattie May to wear a white uniform but she never made it. A blue and white polkadot dress *was* Hattie May's uniform and always had been, why, I never found out.

She descended upon me, a mountain of a woman. She was weeping and if we'd been anywhere but in the center of town she'd have thrown her arms around me and crushed me to her tremendous bosom. As it was, she seized one of my hands in both of hers and all but fell to her knees right there in the courthouse yard.

Imagine, she was glad to see *me*. I was grimy and sweaty and nearly drunk and I needed a haircut. I hadn't written Hattie May a line, not even a Christmas card, since I'd been booted out of Tangerine County eight years before. When I left she must have felt abandoned, cast adrift by the family she'd served so faithfully all those years without so much as a goodbye or thank you. And yet now she was glad to see me, so happy that her black face beamed.

"Thank Gawd, thank Gawd," she kept saying. "Now you'll git my Coralee off. Now you'll show ever'body my Coralee ain' a bad girl, Mistuh Frank."

I said weakly, embarrassed, ashamed. "How are you, Hattie May?"

"Never mind 'bout *me*," she boomed. "Ain' me that's got troubles, it's Coralee." She looked up at the courthouse, a scowl of worry erasing her joy at finding me. "You best hurry, Mistuh Frank. Coralee's goin' up front of Judge Thrace fer the arrangement. He like to be hahd on that po' chile lessen you're theah to set him right."

I knew it was hopeless to try to explain why that was impossible so I asked, "What's Coralee done?"

"Tha's jus' it," she exclaimed. "She ain' done a thing, Mistuh Frank, no mattuh what they say. She tole me she didn't do it and 'at gal never lied to me in her life. She bettuh not. You go on up theah now an' tell

Judge Thrace that. You tell the judge he gotta let her go, Mistuh Frank."

I opened my mouth to say I couldn't, then closed it again without saying a word. It would be so much wasted breath; Hattie May wouldn't listen or if she did she wouldn't believe me.

"You hurry now, heah?" the big black woman said and then, before I could stop her, she raised my hand and kissed it. She dropped my hand before I could snatch it away and turned toward the courthouse entrance. "I be settin' in the gallery to heah you fix it," she said and waddled away. Her head high, her broad shoulders back, she marched off to see her child vindicated.

I should have called her back. Even though it made me late for my appointment with Bill I should have called Hattie May back and patiently explained. I should have talked with her and found out more about the charges against Coralee, perhaps suggested somebody who might go her bond and pull some strings to make sure that the court appointed a capable lawyer for her. But I didn't.

If ever proof were needed that the ginhead's way of reasoning is totally unpredictable, there it was. I hadn't given much of a damn about admitting failure, criminal neglect, even treachery to men and women who'd been enraged and heartbroken by my activities. But I couldn't bring myself to tell Hattie May that I wasn't the man she'd raised me up to be.

I watched her go through the door. I'd see Bill, get my check and blow and what difference did it make if Hattie May sat in the gallery and waited in vain? I'd cut myself free from all the Hattie Mays of my life and what could her final disillusionment mean to me? I'd ask Bill Carter if he wouldn't take Coralee's case as a last favor. He did a lot of free work for nigras and Judge Thrace approved of him. The judge would take it easy on Coralee if Bill represented her.

I felt quite pleased with myself as I walked into the courthouse and turned down the hall toward Judge Humphries' civil court. I'd leave Lindsley for good with one last act of kindness. When Hattie May got over her first disappointment, she'd be grateful to me for arranging for Bill Carter to take over. Good old Frank Coombs, friend of the poor and the oppressed.

I rounded a corner of the corridor and saw Bill beside the courtroom doors, attaché case in hand, an annoyed frown on his face. Bill
had put on a little weight but nothing like Harry Foyles; he was still
trim in the middle, still square of shoulder, still the picture of integrity, ambition and purpose that he'd always been. The newly acquired
touch of grey at the temples added to his dignity. Just looking at him
from a distance, bleary as I was getting to be, I could tell his election
to the bench was only a question of time and General MacWhalen's
pleasure.

He spotted me and the shadow that lay across his face passed
quickly into a smile. His hand came out to meet mine and by his grip
I might still have been an old and valued friend, a respected colleague, instead of the unkempt wreck who'd once nearly wrecked his
career merely by being his law partner.

"Well, Frank," he said. "How are you, boy?"

"Like a million," I said. "Got those things you want me to sign?"

He walked over to the window ledge across the corridor.

"Hate to make this such a hurry-up thing," he apologized. "Hoped
we could have had lunch together but you were late so I made another
appointment."

"I had a little trouble with my car," I lied. I watched him as he laid
the case on the broad windowsill and unsnapped the locks. "Sorry if
I'm making you late for court."

"No, they're still winding up arguments in there—ran longer than
they expected." He pulled out some papers. "Here they are. Do you
want to read them over or will you take my word for it that they're in
order?"

"I'll take your word for it," I said. "Just show me where to sign. Like
a dope I left my glasses in the car." Actually, the drinks made it hard
for me to read.

Bill put his finger on signature lines and I scribbled my name in an
admirably free-flowing hand. He said that did it and handed me the
check for the balance and asked if Miss Elsie had given me the envelope.

"She did and I thank you, William," I said. I took the check out of
its envelope and glanced at it. The writing and the perforated figures

wavered so I just nodded and put it back, folded the envelope and stuck it in my hip pocket. "I know you're busy so I'll be running along."

He put out his hand again and there was no smile this time. "Good luck, Frank," he said. "I hope things will straighten out for you. I really do."

"Sure," I said. I knew my voice was slurring badly but it didn't matter. "Someday I'm going to get my feet on the ground and put my shoulder to the wheel and you're going to be proud of me, William."

I started off but as I turned a small, thin colored woman in a black dress walked by, obviously lost, and she reminded me that I had one last gesture to make. I swung around and said, "By the way, I met Hattie May outside and she told me her daughter Coralee is coming up for arraignment today before Judge Thrace."

Bill nodded, eyeing me carefully. "Well, you know Hattie May," I went on. "She ordered me to get right in there and straighten out the judge. I was wondering if you'd take on Coralee's case, Bill, or at least see that Thrace doesn't appoint someone like Ham Rogers, or that Hawkins guy."

I expected him to say sure, he'd take care of it, but he shook his head. "What do you mean?" I asked when it sank in that he was saying no.

"I'm sorry, Frank, you can't ask me to touch that case," he answered. "Nobody will, not even Hawkins or Rogers, unless Judge Thrace appoints them."

"What's the charge, for God's sake?" I asked. His thick eyebrows went up. "Didn't you know?" When I shook my head he said, "Murder."

"What happened, a cutting at the *Purple Rose?*"

He shook his head again. "No, she killed a white man. I thought surely you must have heard about it. They spread it all over the papers before we had a chance to hush it up. She killed Jack Taggart."

That shook me almost sober. Jack Taggart was Henry Taggart's nephew. The Henry Taggarts had three girls and Jack had been more like a son than a nephew to the sheriff. Henry thought the sun rose and set on Jack and with some reason. I should have been his worst enemy, but in my soberer moments I'd have to admit that Jack was one of the finest, most decent young men in Tangerine County.

And Coralee had murdered him. And by killing him made a widow of Blanche Humphries Coombs Taggart, my ex-wife.

Chapter 2

I couldn't speak for perhaps five seconds. When I finally found my voice I asked, "What happened, Bill?"

He looked mad, sickened, as he fussed with the snaps of his attaché case. "A dirty, lousy mess," he said in a low voice. "Fine man like Jack going crazy over—" He looked up at me. "To put it bluntly, they found him shot to death in the girl's house. She was passed-out with the gun on the floor beside her. Her gun. I understand she admits that even though she denies everything else."

I shook my head, trying to clear it. "Jack Taggart?" I said. "What was he doing there?"

Bill grimaced. "Pretty obvious what he was doing there, isn't it?" he muttered savagely. "At first I hoped—we all hoped—it was somehow connected with his office—oh, a real bastard of a mess." He fell silent, scowling.

"What office?" I asked. Bill seemed impatiently annoyed by my question so I added, "It's been eight years, you know."

"Yes, but it was in all the papers. It even made the New York and Chicago papers."

"I don't read anything but the race results," I said. "What office did Jack hold?"

"State's Attorney. General MacWhalen picked him as a candidate and he won the primary by such a big vote that we didn't even have a runoff. First time in history. And now look."

I pushed back a lock of hair that had slid down over my forehead. Hattie May's Coralee had fixed herself up right. "She's going to need a change of venue," I said automatically. "She doesn't stand a chance in this county."

"She doesn't stand a chance anywhere," Bill said, flatly. "Jack's staff all loved him and they're good men. They don't need any orders from the top to nail that girl down for keeps. As far as your change of venue is concerned, not a prayer. Judge Thrace thought a lot of Jack Taggart, too."

"But he'll more or less have to grant a change of venue, won't he?" I protested. "Her lawyer could claim prejudicial—"

"Sure," Bill broke in. "Her lawyer would stand a good chance of getting a new trial order from the appellate court at Lakeland—if he appealed. But can you imagine the attorney Thrace appoints carrying it to the Court of Appeals? And staying on here in Tangerine County?"

"He'd be crazy," I admitted. "Poor Hattie May."

"Uh-huh," Bill agreed, "poor Hattie May. Poor Jack Taggart, too, the poor mixed-up sonofabitch, and poor Blanche, poor Henry and everybody else." He shook his head. "I still can't understand how a man like Jack could let himself get mixed up with—" He broke off, helplessly.

I shook my head, too, and started to turn away again. "I'd better be going."

In another couple of seconds I'd have been gone. But just then, from behind me, came the remembered growl of Sheriff Henry Taggart. "Coombs, that woman's mother is telling every nigra in the gallery that you're going to defend her. So I'm giving you just five minutes to get out of Tangerine County. Five minutes, Coombs, or so help me God I'll fix you so's you'll wish you never got up the likker-courage to set foot down here again."

I didn't have to turn around to know that eight years had done nothing to change Sheriff Henry Taggart. His voice told me that. Even before I looked at him I knew he still carried his giant's body as erect as a man of forty and that he still had a full, thick crop of white curly hair under his wide-brimmed Stetson; that the perpetual flush of his bronzed skin still warned of the high blood pressure that would kill him some day—perhaps when he was a hundred—and about which he refused to do anything.

When I turned, his eyes were hard as polished blue stones and his wide mouth was fixed in an ugly twist, his big body rigid with anger and hate. Looking at him, it was hard to remember the time when I'd called him Uncle Henry.

Gone now that friendship, gone with the friendship of a thousand other people who'd liked and trusted me. Down the drain, washed down by a flood of booze and the ink I'd used on bad checks when I was on the sauce, a walking zombie, a thief and a forger, when, as the old ladies of Tangerine County liked to say, I "was not myself."

"You hear me, Coombs?" the sheriff demanded. "Do I make myself clear?"

"Frank was just leaving, Sheriff," Bill Carter said quickly. "He was just this minute saying goodbye. Whatever Hattie May is telling her folks in the gallery didn't come from him."

Henry gave Bill only a flick of a glance. "Maybe I'd better make sure he's leaving," he growled. "Where's your car or did you hitch-hike into town?"

I was sick and shaky from the booze, both what I'd had and what I now needed, and from what Bill had told me about Jack Taggart. I had my money and I wanted nothing more than to get out of there, away from trouble, to someplace where I wasn't known and there were no memories or old guilts. And yet there was still enough of Crazy Frank Coombs left in me to refuse to be pushed around.

"I'll leave when I'm ready to leave, Sheriff," I said, "and not before."

His flush deepened. "You still don't know trouble when you're looking at it, do you?" he said. "You ain't learned a thing."

"Now, now," Bill said. "Let's take it easy. Frank, you'd better go now."

I would have, too, if the sheriff hadn't said, "Before I slam the door on you for drunk and disorderly. You haven't got your family to get you out of it now."

I turned back and this simple action infuriated the big man in the wide-brimmed hat. "Drunk! Disgrace to a good name. A shame to your family. Look at you, a lousy bum, no good to yourself or anybody else—"

"Why do you hate me this much, Henry? Sure, I did you dirt along with everybody else but that was a long time ago."

"Fixing to defend that woman," Taggart muttered. "Just like you. You'd enjoy that, wouldn't you? Smearing Jack's name, spreading it out in the open when decent people want to keep it quiet."

"I told you he wasn't planning to defend her," Bill said. "Hattie May just jumped to conclusions, that's all. Frank's got too much sense to try anything like that, Henry." He waved a hand in my direction. "Look at him—does he look like a man who's fixing to get up in front of Judge Thrace? The shape he's in?"

Perhaps it was the liquor or the first symptoms of a personal pride I thought I'd buried deep a long while back. "Was I permanently disbarred or was the Bar satisfied with a one year's suspension?"

Bill looked at me, his mouth dropping open. "Why—your friends managed to hold it to a suspension but it was with the understanding, promise, really, that you'd never come back here to practice."

"Technically, I'm qualified to plead a case in Florida, then?"

"I suppose so," he said. "But you're not going to do anything crazy, are you? Frank, you can't!"

"He will, though," Henry Taggart muttered. "Whatever he told you was a goddam lie, Bill. The only reason he came back here was to stir up trouble, to get back at all of us. But he ain't going to get away with it."

Henry took a step toward me, his big hand out. "Go ahead," I said, "throw me in jail on a drunk and disorderly. Just do that, Henry, and I promise you every northern do-gooder in the country, every crackpot rabble-rouser, will know about it. Bill said the murder got in the papers, well, you haven't seen anything 'til you see what they'll print when they hear the sheriff of Tangerine County threw the defendant's counsel in jail to keep him from seeing that she got justice!"

"Damn you," Taggart said. His eyes burned me and he said something I couldn't catch before he whirled and paced to the stairway.

There was a silence and then Bill said, "I hope you're proud of yourself, Frank."

"No," I said carefully. "No, I don't guess I'll ever be proud of myself again."

"You've said your piece. You backed Henry down. Now, will you get out of town before you do any more harm?"

I shook my head. "Not yet," I said. I should have known better; I should have known that neither Bill Carter nor anybody else who'd been close to me in the old days would believe me. But I had to explain something. "Bill, you said the reason for Jack Taggart's being in Coralee's shack was obvious. Well, I've been away a long time and I won't buy that. Not Jack Taggart. Something stinks here, Bill. If Jack was State's Attorney he must've made a lot of enemies and maybe somebody framed him—"

"Look, Frank," Bill broke in. "You don't know anything about it so just stay out of it. You're trying to justify a stupid, vicious revenge motive. You've been drinking—you're half plastered right now—and this looks like a good chance to get even. Don't pose as a seeker after justice with me, my friend. I know you too well. You've lost everything and you figure there's nothing much ahead for you so why not wind up with one last big explosion? Splatter everybody in Tangerine County with mud, that will show the world you were right and we were all wrong!"

"You're not addressing a jury, counsellor," I said.

He gave me one last look of loathing. Then he turned his back on me and pushed open the door to the courtroom.

So I was left alone and the courage I'd dredged up from some unsuspected source drained out of me, leaving me a sick lush again. My stomach churned, my throat and chest ached, my head swam, my knees felt as though they wanted to bend inward, my hands trembled.

Why don't you crawl off someplace and die? Henry Taggart had asked. *Does he look like a man who's fixing to get up in front of Judge Thrace,* Bill Carter had said.

I stood there for a couple of seconds before I turned and went back along the corridor. People stared at me as I walked up the stairs into Circuit Court, Part One, the criminal court ruled over by my old, enormous enemy, Judge Thomas R. Thrace.

The suicide urge? Mere drunken stubbornness? Don't ask me.

I got no further than one foot inside the door before the uniformed court attendant put a hand on my shoulder, spun me deftly and pushed me outside. "Nobody allowed inside without a coat," he said and then saw who I was. "My God, Frank Coombs!"

He tried to be kind, I guess. "You better take a walk somewhere. The judge, he ain't in a very good mood today. You don't want to tangle with him the way you are."

"Got to represent my client," I said with all the dignity a sick drunk could muster. I pushed back the strand of hair that kept falling over my forehead, hitched at my belt. "Client depending on me."

"I bet," he said humorlessly. "You better go along now, Mister Coombs. Come back tomorrow, huh?"

I didn't argue with him. Even in my muddled state I realized that without a coat I was asking for a contempt citation. Thrace was a stickler for coats in his court.

"How far are they along with the arraignments?" I asked.

"Haven't started yet," the attendant said. "The last case ran over the noon hour and the judge just got back from lunch." He laughed. "Don't look like it agreed with him, neither."

I had time, then. I wobbled out of the courthouse into the terrible heat. I'd mislaid my sunglasses somewhere, probably on the window ledge outside Judge Humphries' court. I squinted up and down the street, trying to get oriented, and finally located Jackson's Men's Store. Good old Cramer Jackson; we'd gone to Lindsley High and Gainesville together and he'd been an usher at my wedding.

On the way, I passed a new addition to the Lindsley business community, a billiard parlor that advertised beer on tap. I wavered and then told myself I'd stop there on my way back to the courthouse after I got myself a jacket. Three steps past the joint I regretted my decision but it was too late then. I was afraid to turn back lest I lose sight of my objective, swimming in the heat ahead of me.

I was panting by the time I made Jackson's but the cool of the store revived me. I walked to the rear, past all the counters of shirts and underclothes and racks of neckties.

I didn't recognize the salesman who came up gingerly—I'd have had trouble recognizing Cramer Jackson himself at that point—but I got his message of general disapproval. Maybe he recognized who I was or maybe he just thought he had an objectionable drunk on his hands; in either case his tone was cold when he asked if he could help me.

"Want a dark coat," I said. "Got to have a dark coat to wear to court." I sensed his doubts and reached into my hip pocket for the envelope Miss Elsie had given me. I ripped open the flap to show him the money inside.

Finally I was able to buy a dark blue wash-and-wear jacket with too-short sleeves. That enormous undertaking completed, I bought a white shirt and a navy blue tie. I used one of the dressing booths to put on the clean shirt and when I looked at myself in the three-way glass I appeared a little less disreputable but still pretty much of a mess. But at least I had a coat and a clean shirt and a tie and the attendant at the door of Judge Thrace's courtroom would have to let me in.

I gave the clerk a fifty-dollar bill, stuffed the change into the pocket of my wrinkled pants and headed for the door. Just as I was pulling at the brass handle Cramer Jackson appeared beside me.

"Don't come back in here, Frank," he said. His voice contained a nasty undertone. "I was out to lunch or you'd never have got in."

Good old Cramer.

"George," he called to the clerk who had waited on me, "this man didn't pay by check, did he?"

I heard the clerk answer that it was a cash transaction as I pulled at the door handle and went back into the heat. I squinted at the courthouse dome and started down the street, my new shirt soaked before I'd gone a block.

Perhaps I was staggering by that time, I don't remember. I know only that I was driven through a hell of heat and faceless humans by some strange compulsion, back to Judge Thrace's courtroom. The next time I was able to focus I was sitting in the courtroom as the stubby, bald-headed bailiff called: "Coralee Preston!"

I looked around. The place was packed; how I'd found a seat I'll never know. I craned my neck and peered up at the gallery. It was solid with black faces. I turned back in time to see Coralee leave the railed enclosure where the few remaining colored prisoners waited. The girl wavered in my vision and then showed through the mist—head raised, a fatal look of defiance plain on her handsome, light-skinned face.

"Looks like she owns the place," I heard a man behind me say. "Just as good as anybody here."

The girl stopped in front of the high bench and stood there with her hands folded behind her, straight as a pine, utterly unflinching. A lanky man with heavy horn-rimmed glasses—the Assistant State's Attorney—shuffled some papers in his hand and then spoke into the mike in front of him. "Your name is Coralee Eunice Preston?"

The girl's nod was almost lofty.

"Coralee Eunice Preston," the Assistant S.A. repeated and his voice went into a low-pitched singsong as he recited the charge, "you are charged with feloniously causing the death of John Blair Taggart on or about the afternoon or early evening of. . . ."

If I was going through with it I'd have to make my move now. If I could stand up. The courtroom was cool and restful. I could just lean back and close my eyes and everything would go away—my mistreated body, the impossible task of standing, walking, talking, all of Lindsley and Tangerine County, the whole world.

I'd never done anything like that before but now I said: *Help me, God, because I've got to.*

No flash of light, no bells ringing or trumpets sounding. I reached out and grasped the back of the bench in front of me and pulled myself erect. I pushed past the knees between me and the aisle and walked down to the gate in the railed enclosure where Coralee and the Assistant S.A. stood in front of Judge Thrace. I walked and I didn't stagger. The hand that pushed open the gate was steady even though the muscles that moved it were twitching. And the look I gave the bailiff wasn't the look of a drunken bum.

The Assistant State's Attorney's voice faltered, paused, then spurted again. Behind me I was dimly conscious of a mounting rumble. Then came the flat, commanding crack of the gavel and the sounds were cut off.

I pushed back a strand of hair and walked to the side of the colored girl in the wrinkled white maid's uniform. They had not let her bathe in jail and her smell came strong and lemon-bitter. She half turned to look at me and as though through a faulty windowpane I saw her scowl and edge away. She didn't welcome the sight of me, she didn't want me there, but what had I expected, that she'd melt into tears of gratitude?

The prosecutor finished his recitation and there was a silence, then Judge Thrace's piping voice came down over the edge of the high bench. "How do you plead?" he asked. "The plea of guilty admits the charge, the plea of not guilty denies the charge. How do you plead?"

Coralee gave me another indignant, bewildered look and started to speak. I beat her to it.

"My client pleads not guilty, Your Honor," I said, and my voice rolled out, strong and sure.

There was a silence that stretched over the courtroom like a taut canvas, the silence of many people straining to listen, holding their breath for fear their breathing might keep them from hearing what would happen to Frank Coombs who dared affront all decency like this.

I heard the faint creak of Judge Thrace's high-backed leather chair as he shifted his vast bulk forward to put his arms on the bench and peer down at me. I stared back at him, meeting his small, pouched eyes, keeping myself from turning away.

"Well, well," he piped. "Mister Francis MacWhalen Coombs is back with us, I see. Good afternoon, Counsellor."

There was a little rosebud mouth set in that jowled, sagging white face and he pursed it into a smile that any lawyer who'd ever appeared before him knew was more dangerous than a scowl. It was the sneer of a pitiless man of power who had only contempt for the weakling and the wrongdoer and if there had ever been compassion around that little mouth, the years had rubbed it off.

I had to answer. "Good afternoon, sir."

He folded his dimple-knuckled hands on the bench and said, "This court hasn't had the honor of your presence for some time, has it, Mister Coombs?"

"No, sir," I said. Beside me, I could hear Coralee shift uneasily; she could feel the contempt that was directed at the two of us.

Judge Thrace's laugh was a titter. "To tell you the truth, Mister Coombs, I hardly expected to see you again—in the role of counsellor, that is. I must say it's a surprise."

Before I could think of anything to say to that he turned his domed, almost hairless head toward the Assistant State's Attorney. "Mister Briley," he piped, "do you know if this man is eligible to practice in this state?"

Briley looked at me, swallowed and said he wasn't sure but he'd find out if the judge wanted him to.

"May I answer that, Judge Thrace?" I asked. The judge looked at me but he neither nodded nor shook his head. "My former law partner, William Carter, tells me I'm fully qualified to practice in the State of Florida."

"Well, we all have a great respect for *Mister Carter,*" Judge Thrace said, "and so we'll assume that you're in good standing. Somehow. You plead not guilty for your—client?"

"Yes, Your Honor," I said. "And may it please the court, I only arrived in Lindsley a few hours ago. I haven't even had a chance to talk to my client so I respectfully request at least a month to—"

"Trial on the twenty-second," the judge purred. I tried to remember the date. I heard Coralee mutter, "Dear Gawd, this the fifteenth already."

"Your Honor," I cried. "That's only a week from today. I couldn't possibly—"

"The twenty-second," he broke in again. He looked at mummified Jimmy Nicholson, his clerk, and asked, "You have that down? Ten o'clock, the morning of the twenty-second."

"Your Honor," I said. My vision was beginning to clear again and my voice sounded far away. "Your Honor, I beg the court to give me more time to prepare my case. In the interests of justice, I ask that—"

"The twenty-second, Mister Coombs," Judge Thrace piped. "Defendant has been in custody at least three weeks. She's had ample time to arrange for counsel. This court doesn't intend to be delayed by defendant's indifference, Mister Coombs."

I couldn't see more than the outline of the judge's head and shoulders because of the shifting mists of alcohol and nausea. My voice came back into range, though, and it sounded steady enough, unless my ears were playing tricks on me. "Your Honor, unless I'm given more time to prepare my case, I feel that in justice to my client I must file a motion for transfer of venue to another judicial district."

I couldn't see the old man's face but I knew he was quirking his mouth in that bitter, hateful smile. "It will be denied, Mister Coombs, I can promise you that right now. Call the next case, Bailiff."

"Your Honor," I said, but of course it was no use. One of the deputies had his hand on Coralee's arm, pulling her away from in front of the bench. I'd had my say in court and what sober common sense would have told me would happen, had happened.

I stumbled after Coralee and the deputy who was leading her out into the hallway where the colored prisoners were being shackled again for the return trip to jail.

"I'll be around to talk to you, Coralee," I said. "Just you try to remember all the facts and tell me the truth and don't worry."

The other prisoners were silent, uneasy, rolling their eyes at us, wanting to be free of this girl who had killed the State's Attorney and this unshaven white man who was going to stand up for her.

Coralee turned her brown eyes on me in a cold stare. "Mistuh," she said, "I din't ask fer you to be my lawyuh. I din't know nothin' about it twell you jus' gotten up there in front of the jedge."

"Your mother asked me to represent you, Coralee," I said.

The deputy in charge of the prisoners was a large young man with freckles and a turned-up nose. "If you don't want Coombs for your lawyer, if you want somebody else, all you have to do is say so, girl. The court will appoint you a lawyer. A *real* lawyer that'd stand a chance to do you some good, not him."

The girl turned her brown eyes toward the deputy. The dangerous unafraid scorn was visible in them. "I never did take no advice from no po-lice, thank you," she said quietly. "Iffen my mama say fer this gemmun to represent me, tha's what I do."

She looked back at me. "I 'spects you, then," she continued loftily. "Bring some cigarettes with you accounten that no-good Gibby done stole mine. An' I smokes filters, too."

2

Waking up without a drink was the worst part of the whole nightmare. My watch showed me it was only a few minutes past midnight but in Lindsley there was no place to buy even a glass of beer after eleven. I got up off the damp bed and groped my way through the darkness to the window.

I sat in the old upholstered chair in my shorts, lit one of the cigarettes I'd gotten out of the machine downstairs and got ready to sweat it out. It was a good night for it; the temperature must have been at least eighty-five and the humidity was even worse. There was a tiny fan mounted on a wall bracket and it made a loud noise but no difference in the sticky heat of the fourth floor room.

I was in the Princess Hotel, down by the Seaboard station. It had been the drummers' hotel when I was a kid, a place known for the meals served in its tall, narrow dining room with its slow-moving ceiling fans. But that had been almost forty years ago and now the Princess was only a step above a flophouse—four dollars double, fireproof, excellent cuisine, if you believed the signs.

I'd come to the Princess after the air-conditioned General Lindsley and the Floridian had regretted that all their rooms were occupied, booked solid for as far ahead as the eye could see. The motels on the outskirts of town had expressed like regrets. It's probable that I'd have gotten the same story at the Princess if I hadn't put a fifty-dollar bill on the desk when I asked for a room.

The owner and manager was an old man named Theron Charles, whom my father had defended several times on a variety of charges, all unsavory. He'd looked hungrily at the fifty and his need had obviously overcome his sense of civic duty. The word was out to turn Frank Coombs away but when I said I'd need a room for a few days and here was fifty on account, old Theron snatched up the bill and revolved the old-fashioned register.

I'd intended to nap for an hour or so to get my strength back, then I'd take a bath and shave and drive to Harry Foyles' place to get some liquor—even further, to Ocala if necessary, in case Foyles had gotten the word to shut me off. After that I'd get some food, scrambled eggs or a bowl of soup. The last thing I'd had to eat had been a barbeque sandwich some time the day before.

I'd intended to do all these things, but when a diesel freight's droning horn woke me it was pitch dark and I stripped off my sodden, smelly clothes and went back to sleep.

Now I faced those terrible hours when every place a man can get a transfusion of life-giving alcohol is closed; when clocks tick thunderously as their hands stand still; when all the devils in Hell romp through a man's guts and along every nerve of his body there crawls a nonexistent bug. These are the hours when some drunks scream and sob and sometimes throw themselves out of windows. Others sit for a few seconds on one chair before moving to another while we shiver and take a few puffs off a cigarette before grinding it out and lighting another, searching for the one that will bring the miracle of peace. We shudder and our hearts pound and we know we're going to die and we don't care—anything, *anything,* to escape. And then eventually dawn comes to most of us and ages after dawn some bar or liquor store opens and we can begin a new day.

I don't know what purpose would be served by describing those hours from a couple of minutes past midnight until the eight o'clock sun began blazing hot and vicious off the tin roof of the Seaboard freight depot below my window. Suffice it to say that it was rough, and what made it worse was the gradually shattering realization that when morning finally did arrive no bar or liquor store would open in Lindsley; I wouldn't be able to get the drink or the bottle that would take me off the rack until I somehow got over the county line.

Then as the hours passed came a new, frightening thought. Even if I did drive miles and find a saloon or a package store, I still couldn't drink. Not without surrendering my last hope of someday being able to look back and say: *This one thing was good.*

I'd gotten myself involved in the messy case of Coralee Preston by a trusting old woman who had aroused a wild hallucination in my boozy mind. I'd staggered into a situation that any sane man would have fled from. Now I was committed to go through with it against hopeless odds or run to some safe hole from which I could never emerge. Worst of all, if I ran I'd leave nothing for anybody to remember about Francis MacWhalen Coombs except this one last laughable failure, this final drunken posturing.

At some time during those early morning hours I irrevocably saddled myself with the responsibility of staying alive and sober enough to do my poor best to help my client, Hattie May's daughter, the scowling, impenitent Coralee, who'd told me to be sure to bring her filter cigarettes.

When it was light enough for me to dare to move about my room without blundering into deep shadows full of frightful menace, I went into the bathroom and showered. The cold needle spray poured over me as I shuddered under the physical discomfort of water on my skin. I felt some better then and I was able to stand the shrill whine of my electric razor after I rested awhile in the damp upholstered chair by the window. Shaving took a long time; my razor slid over my beard and I had to mop my face with a towel constantly but eventually I got a cleaner shave than I'd given myself the morning before.

I looked at my clothes lying beside the bed where I'd shucked them in the middle of the night. All I had in my bag was some beat-up underwear and one wash-and-wear shirt that had seen better days. I went to the phone and asked for a bellboy.

Somebody with a whine said, "He kain't get you no likker, Mistuh Coombs. Anything else, I'd be glad to, breakfast or a bromo, mebbe, but no likker."

"I don't want any liquor. Send up a boy." The bellboy was a middle-aged Negro in a green uniform older than he was. He smiled at me, glad to see me up and showered, shaved, combed and dressed and not a hotel hole-up drunk, after all. "G'mawnin', Mistuh Coombs," he said. "Nice t'see you ag'in, suh."

"Do I know you?" I asked.

"I don' 'spect you remembuh me but I'm Johnbert Allison, Mauney-Joe's boy, used to work for your family."

I remembered Mauney-Joe, all right. He was the yard-man who'd bossed around my father and my grandfather, the Judge, when they tried to tell him where they wanted certain things planted and certain others not planted. It had been Mauney-Joe who one summer encircled the big house at Spring Bayou with pungent pepper plants that made our guests sneeze all the time they were visiting, especially on humid evenings.

When my father had ordered Mauney-Joe to root up the damned things, he wasn't running a pepper farm, the old yardman had promised he would as soon as the plants stopped bearing, since it was a sin to tear up a bearing plant. As peppers bore year-round, or at least Mauney-Joe's did, there was always enough fruit on the vines to save the plants until one day my father blew his stack and personally hoed up the beds—phlox, zinnias, chrysanthemums and all the rest along with the peppers.

I laughed, remembering, and asked, "Johnbert, can you drive a car?"

His muddy eyes regarded me warily but he nodded. "I need somebody to drive me around," I said. "I've got a case of nerves and I have to go several places before I'll be feeling up to driving. Do you think Mister Theron would let you drive me?"

"I reckon he will, Mistuh Coombs, iffen you hires me out. We ain' too busy at the Princess right about now."

I got one of the long butts out of an ash tray and lit it, not trying to hide the tremor in my hands. Johnbert probably knew I was drunk when I checked in; there wasn't any use trying to fool an old colored bellhop. I inhaled and coughed. "I'd better get some breakfast up here first," I said. "A pack of cigarettes, too."

"Yessuh. What you like fo' breakfus'?" He was beaming now. "How 'bout some nice milk toast, Mistuh Coombs? A lot of coffee, some milk toast and mebbe a poached aig?"

It had been eight years since I'd been in Lindsley and I didn't remember Johnbert Allison ever having waited on me. In the old days when I faced the fact that I had to eat it had always been milk toast and a poached egg. I had no doubt that Johnbert Allison knew a great deal about Frank Coombs.

"Good idea," I said. He started out, then hesitated, reached under the green jacket and came out with an unlabelled half pint. He put it on the straight-backed chair beside the door and looked at me, half apologetically. "Gemmun sometimes needs somethin' to brighten his eye," he murmured. "Jus' so long he don' overdo it." His look was pleading. "We knows 'bout you 'presentin' Hattie May's littlest an' a gemmun what's sick to death kain't do much. But we's sorta hopin' . . ." His voice trailed off and he looked down at the bottle on the chair. "It's medicine, you use it right." Then he turned and walked out.

I went over to the half pint and wrenched the cap off. The fumes came up, raw and strong, and I knew this had been dripped out of some bootlegger's still and ran at least a hundred and twenty proof. I put it to my lips and sipped a mouthful, then swallowed, letting it burn its way down.

I wanted to finish the half pint right there. I wanted to more than I wanted to do anything else on God's green earth. O *Jesus*, I whispered, *why do I have to do this?*

My fingers shook so badly that I couldn't get the cap back on so I put it beside the bottle and went over and sat down. By that time the alcohol had reached the raw and aching nerve tendrils and soothed them, bidding me to take hope. My hands steadied, my brain cleared, and I was able to walk back to the chair, take another sip and cap the half pint.

When Johnbert came up with breakfast he took one look at the bottle and widened his smile. "Mistuh Theron, he say it'll be all right fo' me to drive you, Mistuh Coombs. He say ten dolluhs but you don' have to pay me iffen it's too much."

"You'll get paid, Johnbert," I said, and choked down my breakfast, every last mouthful of it. I drank three cups of coffee and another sip of corn and then Johnbert brought the old Ford around.

I had him drive me to Bargo, a little town in Humphries County northwest of Lindsley, where I got a haircut and a hundred and twenty-seven dollars' worth of new clothes. Bargo was no style center but the slacks and shorts I got there would do and the two white linen coats would be acceptable in any courtroom. The slacks were already cuffed and fitted well enough so I could change from the skin out in the small dressing room of the Regent Dept. Store.

I resorted to Johnbert's half pint three times that morning when the shakes came back but by the time we stopped at a drive-in at noon I found myself hungry. I had two hamburgers and a milkshake while Johnbert went around back to the colored window and got what he wanted.

A torrent of rain came just after we left the drive-in and I told Johnbert to pull over to the side of the road and park until it was over or he could see more than twenty feet of the narrow county road ahead. I reached over the back of the front seat—oh, yes, I'd been sitting in the back seat with my knees under my chin because that's what a white man did when a colored man was driving him in that part of North Florida—and offered Johnbert a cigarette but he shook his head.

I turned so I could stretch my legs out and dragged on my cigarette, dulling with smoke my stomach's uneasy protestations over that too-ambitious lunch. "What do you know about Coralee and the trouble she's in?" I asked.

Johnbert shook his head. "Nothin', suh," he said automatically.

I was a bit surprised. It was the field hand's answer to the White Man Boss and somehow I'd expected something different. "You think she killed him then?"

Stolidly he answered, "Ain' a white pusson in Tangerine County don' think she didn't."

"All right," I said and pulled at my cigarette. "What do you people think?"

He waited a long time, his eyes on the streaming windshield. "What we thinks is whoever tries to show she din't is a brave man, Mistuh Coombs." He hesitated a moment and then added, "Mebbe even bein' brave ain't enough—mebbe *nothin's* enough."

"But do you think she's guilty?"

"No, suh, she ain' guilty no mattuh what kine of talk went aroun', Mistuh Coombs. But somebody fix it so she kain't prove she *din't*. With ever'body what has any say thinkin' she done it, what chance she got?"

"By everybody who has any say you mean the sheriff?"

Johnbert paused a second and then nodded. "Yes, suh, him most of all, I reckon. But Gen'ral MacWhalen, too, and the Gen'ral's Committee. They says Coralee done it and nobody says nothin' against The Committee, not if they knows anything they don't."

"What's this Committee thing?" I asked.

"Mistuh Coombs, suh, all I kin tell you is The Committee hates us cullud folks. I dunno what they want us to do but it ain't like we been doin' fer as long as I can remember. Hit's somethin' diff'rent but I dunno what they 'spects—" He broke it off and looked straight ahead, his heavy lower lip thrust out.

I tried to figure it out. Since I'd been gone had somebody come up with a White Supremacy Council to take the place of the old Klan that Henry Taggart had run out of Tangerine County? Then why hadn't Henry taken care of this new bunch? Crackpot organizations have flourished and disappeared from time to time in our part of Florida, headed by fanatics or smart promoters and nourished by dues extracted from grove workers who hate Negroes because their mental and social level is slightly inferior and they wanted to keep it that way.

Then I remembered that Johnbert had mentioned the General's name. If Edmund Ruffin MacWhalen the Third was big in this new Committee, how could Henry Taggart run it out of Tangerine?

"You mean this Committee has been bearing down on you folks?" I asked. "You probably know I never got along very well with the General but I always thought he gave you people a pretty good deal."

Johnbert didn't say anything.

"I mean, he paid going wages in his groves, didn't he?"

And what else? I was stuck.

Johnbert waited awhile and then said, "Rain's lettin' up."

I knew there was no use trying to get any more information out of him. "Drive me down to the county jail. Then you can take the car around to the hotel and leave this stuff I bought in my room."

He drove the car back onto the rain-slicked blacktop and started for town. "It be all right iffen I leave you off on Pierce Street, suh? 'At way, I won' have to make no left-hand turn."

That way he wouldn't be seen by whoever might be looking out the jail office window, either. He let me off half a block from the corner and I gave him twenty dollars, ten for Theron Charles and ten for himself.

It was still sprinkling here in Lindsley but I kept close to the buildings so I didn't get wet. I went up the steps to the thickly barred grill that stretched inside the jail's front entrance. The deputy at the admittance desk looked me over and pressed the release. There was a high-pitched buzz as the lock disengaged and I pushed the door open.

"I'd like to see Coralee Preston," I said to the deputy at the desk.

He was an older man with glasses and a mean, long-nosed face whose name was Bradbury, but he looked at me as though he'd never seen me before in his life. Then he went through a small index file and pulled out a card which he studied intently. "She's here on a murder charge," he said. "Only allowed to see one close relative on visitin' days, Sundays and Thursdays, them and her attorney." He made a production of putting the card back in the file and giggled. "You ain't a close relative so you must be her lawyer, huh?"

Don't let them get you sore, that's what they're hoping for.

Bradbury leaned back in his chair and hooked his thumbs into his wide belt. "I heard you was back in town, Coombs. Didn't hardly believe it at first. Come back here to defend that girl, huh? Gettin' paid big money by them northern niggers, I bet."

"Look, Bradbury," I said, "do I see my client or don't I?"

"That's up to the Cap'n," he said pleasantly. "A murder defendant, maximum security. You got to see the Cap'n."

"Is Pret Newbern still Chief Deputy?" I asked.

He nodded and I said, "Well you tell him I want to see Coralee."

He grinned at me, showing long, strong teeth. "Why don't you have a seat, Counsellor?" he suggested. "The Cap'n, he's a busy man but he might be able to see you if you want to wait."

I knew it was what Bradbury wanted but I couldn't help it; I planted both hands on his desk and leaned toward him. "Call Pret Newbern, or tell me I can't see my client. Either one, but don't play big shot with this sit and wait stuff."

He straightened in his chair, smirking with satisfaction. "You're real tough, huh, Coombs?" He waited for my reply to that and when

I didn't make one he said, "We get a lot of real tough ones in here. Mostly they're drunks that tell us we can't keep their old buddy in the can. You know what happens to them, Coombs?" He waited again. "Usually they land right in with their old buddy and sometimes they get banged around, fallin' over things or walking into a door like."

"In other words, I can't see Coralee Preston?"

"I didn't say that," he protested. "I just said you'd have to see the Cap'n about talkin' to a maximum security prisoner, is all I said. If you want to get tough about it, why go ahead. All I got to do is put my finger on this little button here and we'll see how tough you really are."

"I'll bet there's a button," I said. I don't know what would have happened next if at that moment Pret Newbern hadn't come out of his office. He was a tall, dark man with a big nose and a strong chin whom I'd known since he was a kid. Before I left Lindsley I'd watched him come up through the sheriff's office until now he was second in command, a serious, humorless, dedicated law enforcement officer who was going to be Tangerine County's next sheriff. That is after Henry Taggart retired or his blood pressure caught up with him.

Pret glanced at me and came over. "Hello, Frank," he said. "I suppose you want to see that woman." His voice was hardly friendly but it did not contain the sneer that Bradbury's had.

"Coralee Preston." I nodded. "I'm handling her defense."

He nodded gravely and brought his hand up to rub his chin. "I guess you can see her, all right," he said. "She's under maximum security so a deputy will have to be there while you're talking to her."

"Unh-unh." I shook my head. "No deputy listening in, Pret."

"It's a new regulation," he said. "Sheriff Taggart just issued the order. All maximum security prisoners have to have a deputy with them when they're talking to visitors."

"You know as well as I do that this would be a violation of the girl's rights." I kept my voice down, though I wanted to yell. "Do you think she's going to tell me anything with one of your boys leaning over us?"

"I can't help it, Frank," Newbern said earnestly. "I get my orders, that's all. If you've got a beef you can take it up with the sheriff. He might—"

"I just bet he might," I broke in. It had been a long time since I'd had a sip of Johnbert's corn and my nerves were starting to act up. "Who's running the county now, Pret, the Klan?"

His long face tightened and he flushed under the dark skin. "That's a hell of a thing to say, Frank."

"It's a hell of a thing that's going on here," I answered. "I don't care what this girl's charged with or how much you people hate me—this is still the United States of America. I want to see Coralee Preston right now and with no big-eared deputy sitting in, either. If I don't, by God, I'll phone the Attorney-General at Tallahassee. And if he won't do anything about it I'll call Washington!"

"Oh, you'll raise pure hell, won't you?" Sheriff Taggart asked from behind me.

I turned and let Henry's eyes rake me. I thanked God I'd gotten a haircut and that I hadn't finished Johnbert's whiskey in a couple of gulps. "Sheriff," I said, "you know you can't deny me the right to speak to my client in private. You know the law better than that."

He loomed over me in his crisp uniform and wide-brimmed hat. He grunted, either in plain contempt or because he was disappointed that I was too sober to lock up. "And if I don't you're going to call down the northern crackpots on our heads, huh?"

"I'm going to do everything I have to do to protect my client's rights," I said.

I think that if Taggart had been anywhere but in his own jail he'd have spat on the floor in disgust. "Judge Coombs' grandson," he muttered and turned away. He spoke over his shoulder to Pret Newbern. "Let him see her alone, Cap'n. Oh, God, yes, let's make sure we don't violate that slut's civil rights, whatever we do!"

I called "Thanks, Sheriff," after him as he went out through the front gate, but if he heard me he gave no sign.

Pret took me behind the white cellblocks, back to the old jail, *circa* 1916, where the Negro prisoners were kept. There was a sort of makeshift air-conditioning there, at least up in the front part, but the big fans and the white-washing and the floor-scrubbings with creosote couldn't do away with the smell or the bugs.

As we walked down the corridor to the rear cell where Coralee was lodged, four-inch flying cockroaches—palm beetles if you're trying to sell an old house to a northerner—scuttled out of our way and my ankles told me that the fleas were still doing business at the old stand.

Coralee lay on her bunk in a six-by-ten cell with a barred window high up on the outside wall. There was a covered slop bucket in one corner and a battered three-legged metal stool chained to the wall—and that was it. The white maid's uniform Coralee had worn to court the previous day was folded under her head for a pillow and her shoes were under her bunk. Her pink-soled feet, crossed at the ankles, greeted us as we walked in.

She was wearing a white rayon slip and as she sat up, wakened by the rattle of the lock, I saw the top edge of a violently pink brassiere under the slip. For some reason that struck me funny.

The black turnkey who had brought us was an old rascal named Gibby, first or last name unknown. He was a tyrant in his domain and he had to show that he was boss back here. "Cap'n and yore law-yuhman heah, 'ooman," he growled. "Git decent 'stead of layin' round half nekkid, you that's killed Mistuh Jack Taggart."

"All right, Gibby, that's enough," Pret said. "Put your dress on, girl. You've got fifteen minutes to talk to Mister Coombs."

Coralee ignored me. Instead, she started an indignant complaint addressed to Pret Newbern. "When I get a chance at them showuhs?" she demanded. "When I get them clean clo'es my mama sent heah fo' me? He—" With a rigid forefinger she pointed at Gibby "—he don' lemme go to the showuhs like the law say. The clo'es, liken he taken 'em like he taken the vittles and cigarettes and everything else he lay hand onto."

"No sech thing," Gibby bawled. "I never seed no clo'es ner no food, neither. You ain't allowed in the showuhs with the othuhs, not no murderer."

Coralee whirled on Newbern, her pink-brassiered breasts swelling

with indignation. "You heah that?" she cried. "Huhcome I ain' allowed no showuhbath, Cap'n, suh? Huhcome this ole man—"

"Shut up," Pret Newbern said dispassionately. "Get your dress on."

"But why don' he—"

"I'll see you get what's coming to you," I broke in before she could
make things any worse. "Get your dress on, Coralee. I've got to talk to
you."

She wanted to argue some more but either my headshake or Pret's
cold stare stopped her and she leaned over to pick up the uniform
she'd been using as a pillow. The old turnkey stumped off muttering
about uppity girls that never had no bringing up as Pret and I walked
outside the cell.

"How about her using the showers?"

"She gets a wash basin every morning," Newbern said. "That's all
she's allowed, a maximum security prisoner. I can't give her the run of
the place even if she is your client, Frank."

"Is that another of Henry's new regulations?" I asked. "One wash
basin a day. Not much from those fans gets back this far—it must be
a hundred in that cell. Give her a break, Pret. Her clothes, too. You
know Hattie May, she must have sent Coralee clean clothes."

Pret looked down at the stone floor and absently kicked at a cock-
roach that ran past. "I'll see," he muttered. "That Gibby's getting too
big for his britches. I'll see she gets her clothes and—well, she could
go to the showers late at night when the other women couldn't get at
her."

"Get at her?" He glanced over his shoulder and lowered his voice.
"D'you think she's some kind of a heroine, Frank? There are nigras in
here who'd beat her to death for what she did. She's made it tough on
all of them, every Tangerine County nigra in or out of jail. You should
have heard some of them cussing her out when we brought her in."

I knew this section of Florida and I thought I knew Negroes but
Pret's murmured explanation shocked me. For some reason I'd taken
it for granted that all the colored people of Lindsley and the county
were on Coralee's side. But what Pret said must be true; if Coralee
had done what she was accused of doing she was a traitor to her color

and her people. She'd be hated by every nigra except those who believed in her innocence—Hattie May, Johnbert, who else?

"I'm ready, Mistuh Coombs," Coralee said. She had a peculiarly irritating tone of voice when she spoke to me, as though she were doing me a favor.

"Where can we talk?" I asked Pret. He jerked his head toward the cell where Coralee stood waiting. "Right in there. I'll be back in fifteen minutes."

I think Coralee wanted to say something about not being taken to an interrogation room, away from this hot cell where she'd been so many days—how long had Judge Thrace said she'd had to have gotten a lawyer, three weeks? But I shook my head again and the girl subsided sulkily. She went back to her bunk and sat down. She'd put her shoes on but now she slipped them off again; no sense in torturing her feet if she wasn't going anywhere.

I went inside the cell and sat down on the stool, trying to ignore the heat and the smell. Coralee kept her eyes on her hands in her lap and when she spoke it was in an ungracious mutter. "Huhcome you ain' got no briefcase?" she asked. "Lawyuhman always ca'ies a briefcase with a lot of papuhs in it, don't he?"

My acid retort was stopped by the fact that she had a point there. I had nothing at all, not even the back of an old envelope or the stub of a pencil with which to take notes. I'd been so concerned with making myself presentable that now I found I'd have to depend on my memory if anything came out of this first consultation.

Which was a laugh. My memory had always been at best an average one, perhaps better than average, but that time was not now. Now I wrote things down and forgot where I put them and couldn't see them when I looked right at them.

"Plenty of time for briefcases and papers, Coralee," I said. "First, we've got to get some facts straight, get to know each other. You must have been a little girl when I left Lindsley eight years ago."

She pushed out her lower lip. "Not so little," she muttered. "I goin' on twenny-five. I remembuhs you." She darted a glance up at me before she returned her eyes to her hands, a look that said she *sure* remembered me. "I wukked fo' Mizz Blanche a little, he'pin' Mama with the house-cleanin,' befo' Mizz Blanche got the dee-vorce—I mean befo' you went away."

Blanche had always been Mizz Blanche, never Missus Coombs, to the help.

"That's right," I said with phoney friendliness. "Now I do remember seeing you around the house with Hattie May." I pulled out a pack of cigarettes, took one and gave Coralee the pack. "I forgot to bring you your filters." I lit my cigarette and handed her my cheap lighter. "Might as well keep that, too. I've got another one."

For a second I actually thought she was going to give me a hard time about forgetting the filters but she mumbled something that might have been thank you. She dragged hard and hungrily at her cigarette.

"I'll send you in a carton of filters," I said. "What brand do you smoke?"

She looked up at me, her eyes faintly narrowed. "Why you doin' this fo' me?" she demanded. "Representin' me in court, buyin' me cigarettes—huhcome out of ever'body in the world you come along and do this fo' me?"

"Your mother asked me to," I said. "Hattie May practically raised me."

"That the oney reason? You ain' been put up to it by nobody else?"

I shook my head, trying to tell myself that behind this suspicious, ungrateful exterior this girl must be terrified, that her hostility was a front behind which she was trying to hide from panic.

She dragged at her cigarette again, her eyes on me. "Well, all right," she said finally. "But they's so *many* things been done to me I don' rightly know what to think no mo', hahdly."

"One thing I want you to understand," I said. "I'm going to do the best I can for you but you've got to be on the level with me. Not even a little lie, Coralee, no matter how bad you think it may make you look to tell the truth. If you killed Mister Jack Taggart, tell me so—"

"I din't kill Mistuh Jack Taggart, I sweah to Jesus," Coralee interrupted. Her voice was quiet, almost pensive. "I don' know who killed him or why they put it on me but I din't kill him. Nobody'll b'lieve me but I din't."

I wanted to believe her but somehow her denial sounded empty. Of all the nigras I'd represented in my day as a practicing attorney not one of them had "done" the thing they were charged with. Not at first. Only after the whole story finally came out, most of them had done almost exactly what they were charged with having done.

I was no sociologist able to expound on the North Florida Negro's instinctive need to lie when accused by a white man but I could understand it. For Coralee to have admitted the killing under any circumstances would have seemed to her a stark act of suicide. Later, when she learned to trust me—if she could in the scant week we had before the trial—she might tell me the true story.

"All right, Coralee," I said. "We've got that much straight. Now, was Mister Jack Taggart friendly with you? Especially friendly, I mean?"

She stared at me, round-eyed. "You mean was he messin' 'round with me? Mistuh Jack *Taggart?*" I was right there, at least; Jack hadn't been messing around with Coralee Preston.

"Then why was he in your house?"

She shook her head numbly. "'Fore Gawd, I don' know," she whispered. "What he want with me? How he even know whar I live, 'way down in the bottom, end of nowhere?"

"Did he speak to you on the street, ever? Tell you he wanted to talk to you?"

"What he want to talk t'me about, Mistuh Coombs?"

"Well, he was State's Attorney—did you know about some case he was investigating?"

The girl shrugged and shook her head. "I don' know nothin' 'bout no case," she muttered. "How'd I know anything 'bout any case, a paht-time maid never been outta this town, hahdly?"

How, indeed? Yet my spirits rose a little at her rejection of my suggestion. Coralee wasn't stupid and yet she'd refused even to examine the possibilities. So maybe she was telling the truth. Maybe she really hadn't killed Jack Taggart.

I looked at my wristwatch. I hadn't noticed the time when Pret Newbern had left us but there couldn't be too many minutes left for consultation. "Coralee, will you tell me exactly what happened?" I asked. "Tell me what happened that day in as few words as you can."

Instead of answering she spent precious seconds holding the smoked-down butt of her cigarette between thumb and forefinger as she walked across the cell, lifted the lid of the slop bucket and dropped it in. She took her time coming back to the bunk and sitting down again, returning her eyes to the contemplation of her hands in her lap.

"Cap'n Newbern will be back in a minute," I said. I couldn't keep still any longer. "If you won't talk to me there's no use in my coming to see you again."

The words spilled out then in a tumbling torrent that lapsed into the slurred and half-worded gullah talk that nigras use among themselves, a dialect unintelligible to many whites. It's no code, no secret language, but merely the elimination of syllables not needed if the listener is tuned in on the same wavelength.

I remembered enough gullah talk to get the gist of what Coralee was saying. She'd worked half a day at Miss Elsie Dillon's. That was *my* Miss Elsie and I recalled that Hattie May's daughters, four or five of them besides Coralee, had done for Miss Elsie as they grew up, one after the other.

Coralee worked for Mizz Elsie on Mondays, Wednesdays, and Fridays, eight to one thirty, she said. I could ask Mizz Elsie about her being there because that was the day Mizz Elsie came home for lunch although she usually stayed downtown. She'd come home at noon and Coralee had fixed her some scrambled aigs and toastes and cawfee and Mizz Elsie had given her some dress material she'd been going to make a dress out of but had decided was too young-looking for her.

"Mizz Elsie, she tole me to finish up a half hour early so's she c'ld drive me back downtown," Coralee said. "I was 'bout thoo anyhow accounten I come early that day. I was so early that when I got there Mizz Elsie hadn' even left. Mos' times she already gone to the office time I comes but this mawnin' I was so—"

"All right," I broke in impatiently. "Miss Elsie drove you back downtown. Where did you go from there?"

"Nowheres. I toted my dress material straight on home. I was fixin' on gettin' Leola lives the top of my street to he'p me cut it out. I reckoned I was to git stahted on it right away I mebbe c'ld weah it Sat'dy night. Leola raat handy at sewin'—"

"What time did you get there?" I cut in again. I hoped I could remember some of this long enough to put it in the notebook I'd buy when I left the jail.

Coralee hunched her shoulders. "My clock busted," she told me. "Sometime around ha'pas' one, I reckon, accounten Mizz Elsie was fussin' she had to be back at her office at one o'clock. The clock striken one befo' we got downtown. You know it ain' far to the Ridge from where she wuhks, fi'-ten minutes. Even if I live 'way down in the bottom it don' take more'n fifteen minutes from the Centuh."

The Ridge was the colored community that lay southwest of town, distinct from the Grove which lay to the southeast. It was funny—I suppose in a pathetic way—but the Ridge people considered themselves of higher quality than those who lived in the Grove, and vice versa. But no white could see any difference in the shacks, the million kids, the dirty-white and brown hound dogs, the waterpipe tripods with their huge castiron cauldrons in which the old laundresses still boiled their clothes over fat-pine fires, quarter-in-the-slot laundromats notwithstanding.

"So when you got home what did you do?" I asked. I was trying to impress Coralee with the idea that I had to know everything so that in some miraculous way known only to lawyermen I could get Judge Thrace to set her free.

She took another cigarette from the pack I'd given her and although I ached for a smoke I knew better than to borrow one back. She used my gift lighter, thumbing it several times before it caught. "This the hahd paht," she said. She sounded sullen.

"What do you mean, the hard part?" She shook her head and dragged at her cigarette. Down the corridor I could hear Pret Newbern talking to old Gibby, the turnkey, giving him hell in a low, biting voice. "Here comes the cap'n," I warned. "You'd better tell me fast, Coralee."

"You won' b'lieve me."

"Try me," I said. "But make it fast."

"Mistuh Coombs, so he'p me Gawd, I walked into my place with my yahd goods and a little sack with some cottage cheese and cole chicken Mizz Elsie give me. An' raat there on top of the radio was two pints of Old Mistuh Oxford bourbon whiskey. Jus' settin' there 'thout even the seals broke. Jus' settin' there."

She took her cigarette out of her mouth and looked at me. "I tole you you wouldn' b'lieve me."

"Go ahead," I said. "What did you do?"

"Do?" She sounded as though I'd asked her whether she was male or female, black or white. "Do? Why, I set down my bundles and I walk over and open up one of the bottles and had myse'f a big ole drink of whiskey. Then I got me some water and taken off my shoes and got in the easy chair and had me some mo' drinks, twell I fell asleep."

"And when you woke up, there was Mister Jack Taggart dead on the floor with your gun beside him?" I asked bitterly.

She nodded. "With all my clo'es off," she said. "Mistuh She'iff Henry Taggart was there hisse'f, shakin' me and callin' me bad names. But I didn't kill Mistuh Jack Taggart, I sweah. I got drunk, yessuh. Mebbe I got me a bad name with some accounten my drinkin'. Mebbe they's some that's got it in fer me accounten what happened. But no mattuh what, I din't kill Mistuh Jack Taggart."

Just then Pret Newbern came down the corridor to the door of the cell. "Time's up," he announced.

"Give me a couple of minutes more," I begged. "It couldn't have been fifteen minutes."

"It's been closer to twenty-five. Come on, Frank. You can see her tomorrow."

I got up off the little stool and walked to the door. I turned back to Coralee. "I'll be back tomorrow. I'll send in some cigarettes and if you don't get them, let me know."

"I've got that all straightened out with Gibby," Pret said. "He had the wrong idea about maximum security, that's all."

"And the showers?" I asked. He nodded somberly. "Gibby will take her to the shower room late tonight after the others get locked in."

"An' he'll stand there lookin' while I got my clo'es off," Coralee grumbled from the bunk.

"He better hadn't," Pret said. He turned and let his voice ring down the corridor. "Gibby, I hear of you bothering this girl while she takes her shower and you'll have the sheriff on your neck, understand?"

From somewhere toward the front of the jail came Gibby's respectful voice. "Not me, suh. Not ole Gibby."

"Let'm look," Coralee muttered. "So long's I kin git me a showuh, let'm look. Oney way a ole man has any fun."

"I'll see you tomorrow," I said again. "Goodbye, Coralee."

She might have said goodbye or she might merely have grunted her dismissal of this lawyerman who didn't even carry a briefcase. When I last saw her she was sitting on the bunk, smoking and wriggling her toes, frowning over all the things she hadn't told me.

3

Walking down the corridor, Pret said, "You've got a real bad girl there. She's never once acted like she was sorry."

I started to ask him why Coralee should act sorry about something she didn't do but I let it go. At the iron grill that separated the old jail from the new, Gibby waited to get his old-fashioned ring of keys back from Newbern.

"I'm going to send some things in to Coralee Preston," I told the old villain. "I want you to be sure she gets them."

He looked at me and started to raise a corner of his upper lip as though to ask me what right I had to give him orders. Then Pret's long arm shot out and his hand caught the old man's blue denim shirt between the second and third buttons. Pret didn't even bunch the cloth; it was almost as though he were examining its texture and his tone was thoughtful. "You better listen to what Mister Coombs says, Gibby. That girl gets everything sent in to her. And when she takes her bath I don't want you bothering her."

Gibby sputtered injured assurances as we walked into the cooler corridor of the new jail. I said thanks to Pret and went on down through the lobby and past Bradbury without looking at him. I let the people stare at me and mutter asides while I bought the things I needed in Bentley's but when I tried to get them to deliver a carton of filters to Coralee at the jail the clerk said delivery service was only for regular customers.

Back out on the street, I tried to get a couple of colored boys to deliver the carton for a half a buck tip but they shook their heads silently. Finally I had to go back to the jail myself. I knew I ought to give Gibby a buck to insure delivery but I was damned if I would. Without Pret there, the old man was just short of insulting.

That chore done, I went to my room at the Princess to write in my new notebook before I forgot too much of what Coralee had told me. I nodded to the desk clerk, an old man I didn't know, and went over to the elevator. A skinny colored boy with popeyes and a slack mouth took me up to the fourth floor. By the way he twitched his shoulder, I got the impression he wanted to talk but was afraid to, so I asked him his name.

"Norman, suh," he all but whispered.

"Do you know Coralee Preston?"

"Nossuh. Leastwise I don' know nothin' about it." He hurled open the elevator gate with a clash. "Fo'th floor, suh."

I got out of the rickety contraption and walked the threadbare hall carpet to my door. I put the key in the old-fashioned lock, juggling my bundles, but before I could turn the knob the door swung open.

I started back, dropping a couple of my parcels, but a hand reached out for me and grabbed my shoulder, a hand as big as a catcher's mitt and strong as a bear trap. It flung me into the room and while I was still off balance, trying to keep hold of my silly little bundles, somebody let me have it on the side of the head like a club.

I sagged over sideways but the grip on my shoulder pulled me back upright. I let my parcels spill and tried to shield my head. I had my guard half up when somebody clouted me across the back of the skull and at the same time another one looped a long, hard-knuckled punch to my mouth.

They did all this silently except for impulsive grunts when the punches connected. There were five of them, all of a size and shape, taller than average, narrow-shouldered but young, strong, whip-muscled. I had no more than a blurred impression of their faces before another blow on the chin sent me down but it was enough to tell me who they were. Not by name, because it had been eight years since I'd seen any of this breed and even when I'd lived in Tangerine County and saw them every week I'd had trouble separating one from the other.

They didn't need names. They were Crackers from the back-county sandpatches and bayous, men who performed back-breaking labor all their lives for a cash income of something like four hundred dollars a year. They lived where the mosquitoes were so thick they clogged an outsider's nostrils and puffed his face blind in an hour, yet they were never bitten, and they hunted barefoot through palmetto that no one else would dare walk into without snake boots, but if they were killed by rattlers nobody ever heard of it. Not that anybody bothered to keep track of their health or even their increase or decrease. They wouldn't have any truck with doctors—a healing preacher, maybe, or a hoodoo woman but not a doctor. Doctors were for rich men.

On Saturdays they came to Lindsley and to the other county seats like it in incredibly decrepit cars—along with their stringy-haired, gap-toothed women and their healthy, dirty kids—to buy the few things they couldn't make or catch or grow or do without. They were a mannerly, silent people, except for the children, and almost never got into any trouble save on rare occasions when one of them mixed store-bought beer with homemade whiskey. Mostly, they just walked up and down the main streets, looking in shop windows at the marvels that rich people could own.

When a colored man or woman, even a colored child, saw them coming he or she went down an alley or crossed the street. If it was too late for that, they stepped off the curb between two parked cars and waited until the danger had passed. For these people hated nigras. There was no reason for it; it was just that they always had, as had their daddies and grand-daddies before them. Their children and their children's children would, too, if they were brought up right and made to understand that unless a nigger was kept in his place there'd be trouble.

What kind of trouble? They didn't know. If anybody had ever explained the calamity that would befall them all if they stopped hating people with black skin, it had been a long time ago.

So now they were giving me a beating. They would probably kill me because I, a white man, was defending a colored woman accused of murdering a white man. Five of them had come out of the hammock to my room at the Princess Hotel on a day that wasn't their regular town day, Saturday, to punish me because I didn't hate niggers, too.

They didn't come here on their own, I told myself, *somebody sent for them.*

I rolled out of the way of a heel that came down in a savage stomp and managed to scramble to my feet. I got in one, overhand left, a pretty good one for a man in my physical condition, and then somebody connected with my jaw at the same time that a fist sank into my gut. I went down and this time I figured it was no use getting up. I was deathly sick to my stomach; I felt the nausea more than I did the pain. And a man who's sick to his stomach just wants to lie where he is.

You stupid bastards, after you get me killed you'll have the F.B.I. and the civil rights crowd knocking at your door, for sure. Lindsley and Tangerine County will stink forever after those professional bleeding hearts up north get through with you.

Maybe it was my anger at the stupidity of whatever fellow Floridian had bolluxed this up that made me get off the floor again. I made it to my feet with the help of the straight-backed chair that had been kicked across the room and when I was upright I picked it up and turned to heave it through the window. My room overlooked the Seaboard freight station but there was a chance that somebody down there would investigate if a chair came sailing out of a fourth floor window.

I don't know whether or not I could have, weak and wobbly as I was. I didn't have to find out because at that moment my five visitors all stopped what they were doing and turned toward the door. I followed their eyes to the giant in the wide-brimmed hat in the doorway.

It was Sheriff Henry Taggart, his gold star as big as a dishpan on his chest, his wide leather belt and holster gleaming even in this shabby, sunless hotel room. He didn't move a hand to his gun: he didn't need to. He was the sheriff and these Crackers knew it. They respected him, trusted him, came out of the boondocks every primary day to vote for him and for no other candidate.

"You can put that chair down, Coombs," he said. "You won't be needing it."

I lowered the chair to the floor and sat down in it. I raised a hand to my mouth and when I brought it away there was blood on it. I twisted in the chair and got a handkerchief out of my hip pocket. The shock of the punches I'd taken wore off all at once and I hurt all over—face, ribs, belly, the back of my neck and my groin.

I sat there, watching the sheriff and the five Crackers over my stained handkerchief. Henry looked at me, his face a blank, and then spoke quietly, barely moving his lips. "Get out."

I blinked in surprise and then realized he wasn't talking to me.

"Get on out of town," he said once more to the five young Crackers. "Get out and stay out. If I see you in Lindsley again this side of a month you'll wish I hadn't."

One of the men said softly, "She'iff, we jes'—"

"Get out," Taggart said, and his voice went up a notch. "In about three seconds I'm going to change my mind and run you in."

The five moved smoothly out of the room. The last to leave closed the door behind him gently, as though he were afraid of waking a sleeping baby. The sheriff kept his eyes fixed on me, his wide mouth thin, his big frame stiff. His voice was almost a whisper. "Goddam knotheads," he said.

Suddenly my belly heaved and I headed for the john. I just made it and after I was sick I washed my face in cold water and soaked my nose. I felt some better. I made it back to the upholstered chair by the window and fell into it.

The sheriff came over and stood by the foot of the bed. "I can't say you didn't ask for something like this, Coombs," he said, "but I want you to know I didn't know anything about it 'til somebody here at the hotel called my office a few minutes ago. I may hate your guts but I wouldn't let anything like this happen in my county."

I took the towel down from my nose and grinned at him. "To tell you the truth, I thought you sicced them on me."

"I don't send anybody to do my job for me." He grunted. "You ought to know me better than that."

"I *knew* you better than that eight years ago," I said. "But from what I've seen, everything's changed since then. I thought maybe you had, too."

He looked at me, dead-pan, not asking what I meant. Which might have meant that he knew things had changed, too, or it might merely mean he didn't want to talk to me.

"If you didn't send them, who did?" I asked. "I know for damn sure they didn't come to town on their own. Somebody called them in and told them who I was and where to find me."

He kept on looking at me, his eyes still hard. "Who gave them the word?" I persisted. "The Klan back in business?"

He shook his head. "You know the Klan's dead in Tangerine. It'll stay dead as long as I'm sheriff."

"Then it must have been this new Committee I've heard about," I said. "My sainted uncle has a new thing going for him, hasn't he?"

Henry Taggart's lips barely parted. "The nigras are full of talk about some kind of committee," he said. "Just talk. There was a sort of vigilante committee awhile back but that broke up." He found himself explaining things to Frank Coombs, the drunk, and broke it off.

"I'd better get you to a hospital." The words came out grudgingly, forced by duty, not consideration.

I shook my head. "Not me. I've got a case coming up in court next week, remember? I don't want some cooperative doctor keeping me in the observation ward ten days to make sure I haven't got any internal injuries. Or was that the idea? To beat me up and stow me away in the hospital 'til Coralee's on her way to the chair?"

"If it was, I didn't have anything to do with it," he answered tonelessly. "Personally, I think some of the good people wanted to show you you'd be smart to leave town while you're able. I may not approve of their methods but I sure-God agree with what they're trying to do."

"The good people," I said. "There was a time when the good people were men like my father and Uncle Alex and you, Henry. None of you would have dreamed of using five ignorant Crackers to do their dirty work, to take care of somebody you didn't agree with. Now this happens. What's happened to this place, anyway? What's happened to you?"

He gave me a searching look. "You happened to me, Frank. First you, and then Jack."

"Okay, so I drunked out on you," I said. "But Jack—"

"Don't say anything about Jack," he burst out. "You don't know anything about it so don't say anything. I don't want to hear it. Just get out of town, Frank. You keep on with what you're doing and it'll get even worse than it is now. What're you trying to do, get people so stirred up that there'll be a race riot? Is that what you're aiming to do, Frank? Settle your score with us?"

There didn't seem to be much point in trying to explain but I shook my head. "No, Henry. What I'm trying to do is get a fair shake for Hattie May's daughter. And the best way—the only way—I can do that is by proving Jack Taggart wasn't the kind of man all you people seem ready to believe he was. Even you, Henry. I'd never have believed you could think that of Jack."

The big man looked at me and then away before he turned and headed for the door. He stalked out of the room, banging the door behind him, and I could hear his heavy tread receding down the hallway. I knew there was no use chasing him; he was through talking to me.

If he'd still been the man I called Uncle Henry I'd have somehow made him tell me how he who had much more reason to trust Jack Taggart's integrity and basic decency than I could believe that Jack had died the way it appeared he had.

If Henry Taggart really did believe this. Which I doubted.

Chapter 3

After I showered and cleaned up as best I could, I stuffed the blood-soaked shirt in the wastebasket and got into some of the new clothes I'd bought. Then I called Room Service and asked them to send me up something to eat. Old Theron Charles appeared with the waiter who delivered the tray—bowl of rich vegetable soup; done-to-death roast beef, mashed potatoes, black-eyed peas and turnip greens; a small mountain of thick-sliced bread with only one small pat of butter; a pot of lukewarm coffee.

I tipped the waiter big, a buck—I'd have made it fifty cents, I think, if Charles hadn't come—and when he left I waved the hotel proprietor to the easy chair by the window. "I'd ask you to have a cup of coffee with me, Mister Charles, but there's only one cup."

He was a man in his late seventies, stooped with arthritis and bald except for his thick black eyebrows. He had a simian face, deeply lined, and so ugly that it was almost shocking to a stranger.

No, he said, he'd had his dinner early. It was the night clerk's night off and he had to take care of things, at least until the eleven-oh-eight came down from Pensacola and Tallahassee. After that, he could sleep in the little room behind the desk. If anyone came late they could ring the bell on the desk.

"Not that there'll be anybody on the eleven-oh-eight," he added gloomily when he finished his explanation of why he didn't want a cup of coffee.

I tried the soup and congratulated him on it. He nodded, but morosely. I figured he was trying to get up the nerve to tell me I'd have to get out of the Princess.

"I'm sorry about those men coming up," he said finally. "I didn't know about it 'til Norman, the boy on the elevator, got up nerve enough to tell me. I called the sheriff right away."

I nodded. "No damage done except to my face and that was pretty beat-up to start with. They didn't break any furniture but I'm afraid I ruined a hand towel bleeding on it."

He turned to look at the towel lying on the bathroom floor under the washbasin. He sighed and looked at me out of pale grey eyes. "I'll have to charge you," he said mournfully.

"You just do that."

He squinted at me, trying to figure out whether or not I was being sarcastic. He decided I was and sighed again. "I don't suppose you'd take it very kindly if I told you I had to have your room, would you?"

I finished the soup and reached for the blueplate dinner. "No."

"I don't want any more trouble here," he said. "Times are bad enough without that."

"The sheriff told those five Crackers to stay out of town for a month," I answered. "I'll be long gone before then, I hope."

"There'll be others. They're not quitting that easy, sheriff or no sheriff." He paused, watching me eat my dinner. "Frank," he said suddenly, "why don't you give up the whole idea? I mean, I ain't like some who say you're just doing this to get back at Lindsley. I'm your friend, Frank, if you want one. Your father helped me out of a couple of bad scrapes and I always thought highly of you, no matter how bad you looked."

"Thanks," I said. I didn't mean to sneer. For all I knew, Theron Charles actually may have been on my side when the roof was coming down on my head. I wouldn't have known, I was too drunk.

The bald-headed old man shifted in the easy chair and his voice was injured. "I was, Frank, honest I was. Of course I couldn't do much, not against all the people was determined on running you out of town—the General, the Humphries family and the rest of them—but I *wanted* to. I even—well, I don't guess you remember it but I phoned you and told you you could stay here 'til you got back on your feet."

I used the whole pat of butter on one, inch-thick slab of bread. "And what did I say to that?"

He shrugged his stooped shoulders. "You wasn't yourself," he answered. "You said something about damned if you were down so low you'd hole up in the Princess. But I knew you was—uh—hitting it pretty hard and was half crazy the way things were going."

"It's a little late but I thank you, Mister Charles," I said. "I thank you very much."

"Oh, that's all right." He was embarrassed by the trend of the conversation and covered it by getting his cigarettes out of his pants pocket, a painful and difficult task. He scraped a match with his twisted fingers and blew smoke out through the screened window.

"That girl, that Coralee, you ain't got a Chinaman's chance getting her off, Frank," he said quietly. "You ought to know that."

"She says she didn't do it. I believe her."

He sighed. "What'd you expect her to do, admit it? She done it, all right. She was there, passed-out drunk on the bed and nekkid as a jaybird. Her gun was there, had her fingerprints all over it."

I nodded. One of the first things I was going to do was raise a big question about that gun. Since when were Tangerine County nigras allowed to buy pistols and if Coralee hadn't bought it, where had she gotten it? A knife, a razor, even a shotgun, and I wouldn't have a point. But a pistol was a strange weapon for a colored girl in Tangerine County to own.

I considered asking Theron Charles about that and decided against it. Instead I said, "Let me ask you one big question, Mister Charles. You've lived here all your life, you know everybody in Tangerine County. Do you think Jack Taggart was the sort of man who'd mess around with a girl like Coralee Preston?"

Theron pulled at his cigarette, his brows down. "There was some talk about it, some time before the shooting."

That jolted me. "I don't believe it. Jack just wasn't like that."

Theron Charles looked at his cigarette ash. "Who knows what a man's really like? Anybody'd say no, of course not, not Jack Taggart. Not with a lovely wife like Blanche Humphries." He looked up at me quickly. "Excuse me, Frank. I didn't think."

I was still groggy and he went on hurriedly. "Young Taggart, with a career like he had in front of him, everything going for him, you'd say it was just gossip. But like I said, you never really know."

"I hadn't heard about any stories," I said. "But I watched Coralee's reaction when I asked her about Jack Taggart. She was really shocked that I'd even think such a thing."

He shrugged. Then he got out of his chair with a groan and started for the door. "You're going to keep on with it, then?" he asked sadly.

I nodded and went back to my dinner, even though my appetite was gone.

"I don't suppose I can stop you, Frank," he said, still mournfully, "but you want to be awful careful. This place ain't what it was when your grand-daddy was sitting on the bench and your father was practicing law. It ain't like when you was a little old boy and used to sit on a couple of big history books in the dining room so's you could see over the edge of the table, back when we had seven-eight girls waiting table and every train used to bring—"

He broke off with the longest, deepest sigh.

"Everything was fine back then, wasn't it?" I asked. "What happened to change it? Why is everything so different now? Why does Tangerine County need some kind of goddam Committee nowadays to scare nigras? I thought we were finished with all that kind of stuff when Henry Taggart ran the Klan out of business."

Theron moved his misshapen hand over his hairless skull. "Well, the Klan was different," he said, loyal to some memory. "A lot of fine people belonged to the Klan—at first, before the chiselers got in. But this Committee, it ain't nothing like the Klan, Frank. Used to be you knew where you stood with the Klan. There's no telling with this Committee."

"From what I hear, all you have to do is ask the General where you stand. He runs the Committee, doesn't he?"

"I don't know for sure, Frank, and that's the God's truth," he said. "I never had any dealings with it. Even if they asked me, I wouldn't join unless I had to."

"Had to?"

"Well, they say there's some businessmen, chain stores with lunch counters, mostly, got told they'd better join or they'd have a lot of trouble. I don't know for sure, they never bothered me none. Why should they? I've been here so long they ought to know where I stand."

"Just where do you stand, Theron?" I asked.

"I always got along with nigras," he said defensively. "You ask any nigra that ever worked for me if I didn't treat him right."

"I know that," I said and I meant it. The whole county had always treated its Negroes right, according to the only available mores. In the past, whenever any Tangerine County Negro had needed help against white cruelty or exploitation or injustice, that help had been forthcoming from men like Henry Taggart and my grandfather, the judge, and, yes, my own father, too. But now it seemed all this had changed.

"What happened that this Committee had to be formed?" I asked. "Did the militant integration people move in? Was there some trouble I haven't heard about?"

The old man shook his head, then looked around the room as though making sure nobody was listening. "No, it didn't start that way. It started—well, about five years ago Henry Taggart had a heart attack. I don't know what happened, the General must've figured wrong, but, anyway, we had a pretty sorry bunch of county commissioners and the city commission was third rate. Well, Henry was in the hospital and Pret Newbern tried hard to fill Henry's shoes but he was younger then and he didn't know as much as he knows now. A bad lot moved into Tangerine—bolita, whores, bootleg, even this here marijuana and worse. Looked for a time like they was going to make this the worst county in Florida. There was Henry laying in the hospital, not able to do much about it, so finally some of the people—they always said the General got them going but I swear I don't know for sure—decided they'd do something about it. So they formed this vigilante committee. All they called it was The Committee and the best people belonged, I guess. I wasn't asked to join, too old."

Poor Theron; he never had been asked to join things. "The Committee did a good job," he went on. "Maybe they stepped over the line a few times, smashing up joints, beating up those outsiders, those hoodlums. There weren't any arrests, you understand. The Committee just took the law into its own hands for a spell. I heard a couple of those crooks were in bad shape when they went back to wherever they came from."

"Oh, swell," I said.

"Well, the folks thought they had to. They were good people, Frank, pillars of the church and like that. They did what they set out to do. By the time Henry Taggart was able to be up and around again the crooks and hoods and dope-peddlers had pulled out of Tangerine. The Committee was supposed to break up then, go out of existence."

"But it didn't," I said. "The General and his fine, up-standing pillars of society got a taste of what it was like to run things without having to bother with any foolishness like due process of law. So they're still in business, only now it's Tangerine County nigras they got it in for, is that it?"

He shook his head. "I keep out of such things but—well, maybe these days you've got to have something like The Committee. These freedom riders. These Black Mohammedans you read about. How else are you going to handle it when the Supreme Court and everybody else in Washington says they're right and we're wrong?"

Oh, Theron, not you, too.

"Besides, The Committee don't bother anybody behaves himself. They always give a warning first. But when they go right ahead anyway? There was two nigra shacks burned out and a couple of uppity equal-rights nigras beat up and I heard one boy, a bad nigra from Tampa, just dropped out of sight after he shot off his mouth about how he wasn't scared of The Committee. Nobody's seen him since. Then they beat up a trashy white boy—beat him up bad and threw him in the river and he nearly drowned—because he was supposed to be fooling around with colored gals and making no secret of it. The boy and his family left town right after that."

Theron shrugged again. He walked to the door. At the threshold he said over his shoulder, "I see they forgot your dessert. I'll have the boy bring you up a piece of pie, if there's any left. Ella makes real good pie."

"And another pot of coffee," I said. Waiting for the pie and coffee, I lit a cigarette and held out my hand. It trembled only slightly. I was coming out of it faster than I'd expected. Maybe Johnbert's bootleg corn had medicinal qualities; or was a beating-up by five deep-county Crackers my longsought quick cure for a hangover?

I knew I was safe for at least a week, perhaps longer. My appetite was back, my cigarettes were starting to taste good, my sweat no longer smelled like antifreeze, I didn't even itch. When this was over—but why look ahead that far? As some stupid sage must have said at least once: *Tomorrow Never Comes.* But if I did live through this, there was a drink on the house at Harry Foyles' dump waiting for me.

The telephone rang and I answered it, thinking it was Theron telling me there was no more pie.

"Yeah?" I said into the mouthpiece of the old-fashioned phone.

There was a moment's silence and then Blanche Humphries Coombs Taggart said, "Frank, if you can spare the time from your precious client, I think you owe it to me to come out here and have a little talk."

2

Eight years—closer to nine—was a long time to have gone without hearing Blanche's voice. I had trouble speaking. "Blanche?"

"Yes, Frank."

Cold was not the exact word for her voice, nor angry, either; rather it was wearily exasperated. As though this was a hell of a thing I was doing, defending her husband's murderer, but what could be expected from her lush of an ex-husband? "Yes, it's Blanche."

"Well," I said. I swallowed. "How are you?" She didn't answer.

"I'm sorry," I blurted. "I mean about Jack and—"

"Yes," she said. "I've heard you say that before, that you were sorry. I want you to come out here right away, Frank. Believe me, it's important or I wouldn't call you."

"Sure. But where's out there? I've been away. I don't know where you live."

She hesitated before she went on. "The same place. Spring Bayou. I thought surely you knew."

Spring Bayou had been the Coombs Place before there was a Lindsley, before there was a Tangerine County, and yet it had gone down the drain with everything else. "How come?" I asked. "Did Jack buy the place back as a wedding present?"

There was a long silence and I said, "I'm sorry again, Blanche. I keep forgetting he's dead. Okay, I'll be out as soon as I can. But on one condition. If His Honor, Uncle Earl, or the General or any other of our sanctimonious kinfolk are there, I'm coming back to town."

Her voice was cold now. "I'm quite alone. Please try to be sober enough to talk sense. If you're drunk, I won't let you in."

With that she hung up. Some reunion for two hearts that had once beat as one. Eight years, going on nine, and we couldn't even talk over a telephone without snapping at each other.

I was shrugging into one of my new white linen coats when there was a knock at the door. It was my pie and coffee. I gave the boy a half a buck and told him to take it back, I'd changed my mind. I left him gawking at the door.

I went out the side door to the parking lot next door. My old Ford caught after a lot of groaning and I wheeled out and up Jackson Street, then over on Harrison to County 55, the old Spring Bayou Road.

I'd often bragged that I could drive that narrow, twisting road blindfolded and I'd driven it at eighty miles an hour blind with booze more times than I cared to remember. But now I had to sort of grope my way along. The turns didn't come back to me; the road seemed narrower than I'd remembered it. Once, when I came to a fork, I slanted off onto the side road and went a quarter of a mile before I realized I'd gone wrong.

For some reason this shook me up worse than most of the things that had happened to me since I'd come back. The idea that I couldn't remember the road I'd traveled ever since I was a kid hit me with a true realization of how far I'd slipped. Lost weekend? Hell, I'd had a lost decade.

I told myself I ought to stop somewhere and get a drink, or maybe a half-pint, just enough to sharpen my wits. Then it would all come back to me. I laughed at myself. A few hours earlier I'd called myself safe for a week at least.

The white cement pillars on which I'd scraped so many fenders in my day still flanked the drive to Spring Bayou. As I drove toward the house my headlights showed that the lawn was well-kept and fresh gravel had recently been laid down on the stretches that were first to wash out in the rainy season. Had Blanche been able to supervise the yardmen in spite of her grief or did the place run itself these days or had ordering the gravel, keeping the grounds up, been one of Jack Taggart's last acts as a good husband and responsible freeholder?

As I drove further up the lane I saw that none of the live oaks hanging over the drive was festooned with Spanish moss. That was more proof that Jack Taggert had made a hell of a sight better husband for Blanche than I ever was. When I had lived here with Blanche and when we had still been in communication with each other, she'd always been after me to have the moss taken down: she hated the stuff and claimed it killed the trees, regardless of what the experts said. I don't know why I didn't give in to her about that Spanish moss; it would have been easy enough to have gotten a crew in to clean up the live oaks, but I never had. I'd argued that those trees had been draped with moss for as long as I could remember and it hadn't hurt them, it wouldn't look like the Coombs Place without moss on the trees, it would be a waste of money because the moss would be back in a month, because, because, because. And to that night when I drove up the lane and saw the trees had been cleaned I couldn't honestly say why I hadn't given her this little thing.

But I had denied her so much that the business about the Spanish moss was a little silly to think about now. I'd denied her security and consideration and the respect a man should earn in his wife's regard. And in the end I'd denied her love, spiritual and physical love, because I was ashamed to talk to her, much less touch her.

I drove the Ford under the porte cochere where once slaves had held horses' heads while Coombses swung into their saddles or helped their ladies into barouches.

The front light was on and as I walked up the steps the tall front door opened. At first glance it seemed that Blanche hadn't changed a bit. She was still tall and sweetly shaped and lovely and she wore her dark hair as always in the same neat coiffure that had outlasted a dozen style changes.

She watched me for a moment to see if I teetered and I could swear I saw her nostrils widen a little as she sniffed the night air. It was only after she was sure that I wasn't falling-down drunk that she said, "Hello, Frank."

I said hello and saw her eyes go to the bruises on my face. Her expression may have changed a little but not much. "What happened to you?" she asked. "Did you fall down?"

I put a hand to my cheek, trying to think of something smart to say. I touched one of the lumps and it hurt like hell. "I was pushed." I grinned. "Somebody sent a couple of the boys around to reason with me. Since I've been back everybody seems to want to reason with me. I guess you want to reason with me, too, huh?"

Thunder sounded in the southeast as I stood there waiting to be let inside the house where I was born, the house where I'd brought this woman as a bride. The rumble seemed to startle Blanche; she raised her head and looked off in the direction of the storm. Blanche had been born and brought up here where thunderstorms came almost every day, from June until early October. Why was she standing there in the doorway listening as if she was hearing the sound of gunfire instead of an ordinary September shower?

I cleared my throat. "Sounds as though we're going to get some rain."

She came back from wherever she'd been and nodded as she turned and walked inside. I followed her down the hallway toward the little parlor and as I looked around I noticed a few strange pieces of furniture. But most were still old Coombs pieces with a scattering of Humphries heirlooms, some valuable but many junk to anybody but a Coombs or a Humphries.

I didn't ask Blanche how this furniture, which had all been sold at auction, had reappeared. The answer obviously was that Jack Taggart, the solid, thoughtful man I never was, had somehow bought it all back as a gift of love to Blanche, the woman he'd always loved and once had lost to me.

The little parlor—there was another, bigger one across the hall used only on state occasions—was the same, save for a couple of good new lamps, as it had been when I'd been lord of this manor, technically, at least.

I crossed over to the old loveseat under the curtained window and sat down as Blanche moved toward the desk my father had had made into a liquor cabinet. "Still bourbon, I suppose," she said over her shoulder. "Or would you prefer scotch or gin?"

"Do you want the sun to rise in the west tomorrow?" I asked. "Still bourbon and water, Blanche."

I suppose I could have said I didn't want anything but somehow I knew that would have sounded pretty phoney. Blanche probably knew how stiff I'd been when I'd shown up at the courthouse; to pose as a teetotaler now would be rather ridiculous. So I got up and took the squat tumbler of bourbon and water and went back to the loveseat.

I watched her pour a scotch and water that was almost as dark as my bourbon. Blanche had never let my drinking stop her from having a cocktail or a highball when she wanted one but the drink she poured now was more than a social gesture. It was too strong and the way she took her first sip before she turned away from the desk and sat down in a wing chair showed she'd wanted that drink badly.

I noticed other things when she sat in the full light of a lamp; her mouth was pinched, her eyes tired, and she smoked her cigarette too rapidly.

I asked myself what I expected from a woman whose husband had been murdered under such circumstances. First the years with Francis MacWhalen Coombs, practicing alcoholic, and then when she finally found a decent man he wound up dead. No wonder she was making her drinks stronger these days.

"Frank," Blanche said after a brief silence, "I swore a long time ago I'd never ask you for another thing, but now I have to. Stop what you're doing. Leave town. Now. Tonight."

"Why don't I go back where I came from, you mean?" I jeered. "Hell, Blanche, you could have asked me that over the phone and saved me the gas." I looked around the room. "It's nice, though, to see the place again. It's still the same, almost as though I never left it."

It was as though I hadn't said a word. "How much would it take to—pay you for your trouble?" she asked and sipped her dark scotch.

I doubt that my shock showed. "Beg pardon?"

She made a short, savage gesture with the hand holding her cigarette. "Stop trying to be cute," she said. "A down and out drunk can't afford the luxury of settling grudges if it costs him—say, five thousand dollars?"

Five thousand bucks. Just to drop a hopeless case and leave a place where I wasn't wanted. The offer was tempting. Why not? If I wanted to keep my shining armor bright I could give Hattie May half to hire some big shot crusader for justice and I'd still be twenty-five hundred ahead.

I leaned back in my chair. "I don't want to seem nosey but how come you can afford to hand over five thousand dollars? Did Jack leave you a fortune in insurance or are you the pay-off girl for the MacWhalen-Humphries-Taggart syndicate?"

It was pretty crude but Blanche Humphries Coombs Taggart was tough enough to face plain language. I'd found that out. Under that soft, beautiful exterior there was a soul of steel. I should know; I'd forged it.

"What difference does it make who's putting up the money? It'll still buy a whole lot of whiskey, won't it?"

"It would indeed but there's a question of ethics."

"Ethics!"

"Yes, darling. An attorney has to be very careful not to breach the code of ethics. Now, if my relatives and friends got together, say, and were to decide that they'd been unduly harsh with me, that they'd found there'd been something like five thousand dollars more in my final settlement—"

"Oh, stop it," she broke in. "You make me physically ill. Will you take the money we've gotten together and leave town?"

"Ah, you said *we've gotten together.*" I smiled. "That answers my question. It is a group effort. Who heads up the list of subscribers to the *Get Frank Coombs Out of Town Fund,* Brigadier-General Edmund Ruffin MacWhalen the Third, Retired?"

She hesitated and then nodded. "It was his idea," she said. "I had the same thought but the General actually raised the money." She paused. "I told him five thousand was too much—that you'd probably be glad to get five hundred."

"A wife, even an ex-wife, is often the last to realize a man's true worth," I said.

"Oh, for God's sake stop trying to be funny," she said with irritation. "Will you leave town tonight—tomorrow morning at the latest? The check will have to be post-dated. We're none of us naïve enough to give you the chance to cash it here and then thumb your nose at us."

I shook my head. "I'm sorry, Blanche," I said. "Give the General and the others back their money."

She didn't seem too surprised although her mouth went bitter. "You mean you intend to go through with it?" she asked. "You want revenge that badly?"

"I don't want revenge on anybody. I'm not carrying a grudge against a single soul. I love you all, even Judge Thrace and Cramer Jackson."

"What has Cramer to do—"

"Nothing," I broke in. "Blanche, I don't expect you to believe this but maybe I'm the one drunk in the world who hasn't ended up blaming everybody for what happened to him. So I fouled up; okay, I paid for it. I lost all those precious things because I didn't take care of them when I had them. It's as simple as that."

I waited for her to say something and when she didn't I went on, "I'm not doing what I'm doing because I hate anybody or want to get back at anybody. Just the opposite. Can you believe that?"

"What do you mean just the opposite?"

"I don't know how much you know about it but I got mixed up in this because of Hattie May."

"I know about that," she said. "But when Bill Carter told you what had happened you could have done the decent thing. Bill said you would have, too, if Uncle Henry Taggart hadn't made you so mad."

I started to say something but she kept on. "I guess that when you sobered up enough to see what you had you really congratulated yourself. Made to order, wasn't it? By posing as the defender of this poor, downtrodden nigra you could get even with all the decent people who despised you. But most of all—Jack Taggart and Blanche Humphries."

She finished her drink while I sat there, trying to think of something to say.

She sounded strangely spiteful when she said, "I suppose you know I loved Jack all the time I was married to you?"

"Well, no," I said carefully. "I didn't know that. I may have suspected that you had your regrets—"

She gave me one quick look and got up out of the wing chair and went to the bar. She looked back over her shoulder and saw that my drink hadn't been touched, then busied herself building another scotch and water.

I spoke to her straight, slender back, the gently rounded shoulders, the nape of her neck where the tiny tendrils of hair curled sweetly. "Blanche, if I didn't believe Jack Taggart deserved something better than you people are giving him, I'd be halfway back to Baltimore by now—"

She turned and came back to the wing chair, carrying her drink in both hands, eyeing me curiously.

"What's happened to this place? What's happened to all you people?" I asked. "Am I the only friend Jack Taggart had in Tangerine County who knows he couldn't have been killed that way?"

Her face had gone blank but as she raised her glass I saw a faint tremble in her hand.

"Okay, so I stumbled into this thing by bad luck," I went on when I saw she wasn't going to answer. "Maybe I wish to God that Hattie May hadn't seen me sitting on that bench but she did. Perhaps if Henry Taggart hadn't piled into me the way he did I still would've gotten out, I don't know. But he did and I got involved. I'm going through with this because I'm damned if I can walk away and let everybody believe Jack was killed by a colored girl he was—he was playing around with."

Her lips barely parted. "She killed him, Frank."

"She says she didn't," I said stubbornly.

Her voice was very low. "Did you think she'd admit killing him?"

"I don't know about that but I do know she couldn't have faked her shocked amazement when I asked her if she'd been messing around with Jack. Not Coralee. She's essentially a simple girl, almost stupid at times. I've known nigras all my life. If she'd tried to lie about Jack I'd have known it. She didn't."

Her glass went up to her mouth again before she answered. "You've been away too long. You've lost your keen insight into the ways of Tangerine nigras if you think Coralee's stupid or even simple."

Her head came up with her chin set. "I tell you this only because I hope to God you're not lying to me. We're only trying to be kind to Uncle Henry—and Jack's memory, too, I suppose—by hushing this up, as you put it." She hesitated, swallowed and then said, "Jack was carrying on with Coralee, if that's what you can call it. I know."

Her fine eyes were tortured. "Now will you stop this? Now will you go away and leave us alone?"

There was a long silence as thunder bumped softly in the far distance. The grandfather clock in the hallway had never ticked louder, even during those endless nights when I'd fought off the horrors in this room.

"Are you sure?" I asked feebly. "About Jack, I mean?"

Her voice was flat again, totally without emotion. "If you mean did I ever catch them together, no. I didn't try to. You left me with a little pride, Frank. Not much but a little."

"Enough to keep you from ever asking Jack if the rumors your dear friends were spreading were true?" I asked.

She started to make a reply, then held herself back. She shook her head before she sipped from her scotch and water again. "I don't intend to waste any more time talking to you. In spite of all you've said I still think you're a liar. You're doing this to hurt us again, one last time."

"Blanche, I don't want to hurt anybody. All I want to do is clear Jack's name by proving—"

"You can't," she broke in. "It happened the way they say. Do you think I'd say that if it didn't? Do you think I'd sit here and admit I lost the man I loved because he preferred a—"

She bit it off and her head dropped as she stared down at her drink. "Go away," she whispered. "Go away before you spoil even the little that's left."

Then her head came up sharply and her voice roughened. "Or was that why you came back to Tangerine, really? Did your new northern friends send you down here to start something that would set the Black Mohammedans on us?"

She came out of her chair and stalked past me out into the hall and down toward the front door. I trailed her, suddenly wanting to be out of there. Was this Blanche Humphries who claimed her dead husband was guilty of betraying her, who spoke wildly and with such deep, ugly hate of Black Mohammedans?

She flung open the heavy outer door and stood aside to let me pass. Thunder sounded again, still a long way off; the storm was passing by Spring Bayou far to the south.

"Goodnight," she said. "I hope they stop you before you do this thing, Frank Coombs. God forgive me, I hope they stop you their way because we've tried to do it decently and you spit on us. The General said you would but I hoped—"

Then before I could say anything, she slammed the door. I heard her slide home the bolt that never in all the years I'd lived there had been used.

3

Back in Lindsley, I drove straight to the Ridge, the colored section where Hattie May lived. Unless she had a live-in job now, and she was getting pretty old for that, she would be there. It was impossible that she'd moved since I'd last been in Lindsley; Ridge people never moved.

Don't ask me about Tangerine County colored people because I couldn't give you an answer without reverting to the old worn-out generalities with which we whites have covered our ignorance down through the years. Even when I was a practicing North Floridian, I'd winced inwardly at hearing one of my fellows boast about knowing exactly how nigras reasoned and reacted. Of course the boast was never phrased so precisely; usually the blabbermouth bragged, "Ain't a nigra livin' that can fool me."

The day doubtless was coming when education and the breakdown of all the economic, sociological, and philosophical differences would give some future generation of Tangerine County colored boys and girls thought processes that would more nearly parallel the whites. But at the time I drove in from Spring Bayou and headed for the Ridge there was a void between the two ways of thinking and I knew it. I couldn't hope to understand these people any more than they could understand me. But I could try to make one or two of them trust me and my best bet at the moment was Hattie May.

The city's new amber street lamps gave way to widely scattered old naked-bulb lights when I hit the dividing line between the white community and the Ridge. The paving got worse and eventually disappeared into a sand and shell road, dusty in dry spells, slick as grease in wet weather. Little shacks, some neat and tidy and others filthy, lined the narrow street.

On the porch of every one sat the black people of Lindsley. Their talk and laughter, their checker games and gittar playing, stopped as they watched me drive past slowly, slowing to let an occasional hound dog irritably raise himself from his dust puddle and meander out of range of my headlights. Children quit the mysterious games they played with cardboard cartons and old tires and stared round-eyed at me from the yards, their voices choked off like their elders. They knew who I was, every one of them, and perhaps they'd been expecting me but nobody called *Evenin' Mistuh Coombs* as I drove past.

The Ridge had one main street stretching its length, with seven or eight side roads wandering off it back into the palmetto on each side. It was down one of these side streets that Hattie May had had her shack since the Year One.

I passed the white clapboard church with its crazy homemade steeple and my memory astonishingly returned to tell me to turn left at the next corner. I drove down a narrower, deep-rutted road until I reached the fifth shack on the right. A big woman got up out of a rocking chair on the porch. Even at that distance my lights picked out Hattie May's polkadots so I cut the motor and shut off the lights.

Two or three deep-throated dogs set up a clamor the minute my foot hit the sand. Hattie May shouted *hesh up* and they fell silent, sniffing at me as I opened the sagging gate and walked the shell path to the screened porch.

"I been 'spectin' you, Mistuh Frank," Hattie May said quietly. "Set down. Whut kin I offuh you?"

"Not a thing, thanks," I said. I picked a chair and sat down gingerly, found it firm enough and relaxed. I still had on my white jacket though the night was close with the warm pressure of an approaching thunderstorm. A procession of heavy thunder showers followed each other across Tangerine County nearly every night at this time of year. But I left my coat on. *Status symbol,* I jeered inwardly and lit a cigarette.

"I seed Coralee right aftuh you was there, Mistuh Frank," Hattie May said. "You already made it a lot easier fo' me to see 'at guhl. 'At Gibby, he was almos' polite fer a change. I knowed you'd fix things."

"It was Cap'n Newbern who really fixed things, I guess," I said.

I leaned back in the chair and closed my eyes, then opened them again, and fast. I'd had quite a day, without much sleep the night before, and it was catching up with me all of a sudden. Sitting there on Hattie May's front porch with the night-blooming jasmine spreading its overpowering fragrance, I could have dropped off to sleep in a second if I'd kept them shut.

"You're taard," Hattie May said. "Man oughtn't tuh wuhk so hahd in this heat. I'm sorry I put you to it, Mistuh Frank."

"It's good for me," I murmured. I had a thousand things to ask her but it was peaceful sitting there smoking my cigarette and I hated to get started.

"Did they huht you much?" Hattie May asked gently.

"Not much," I said. "The sheriff came just in time. I was lucky."

"You calls it lucky," she grumbled. "Lucky where a gemmun tryin' to do right gits beat on by the likes of them? Huh. Whyn't Mistuh She'iff Taggart git there *befo'* you got beat on?"

"Now, Hattie May," I said. "He came as soon as he heard about it."
I heard her grunt again as I inhaled. "I just came from Spring Bayou.
Miss Blanche called me up at the hotel and asked me to come out
there. I didn't know Mister Jack Taggart bought the place back for
her. It was a surprise."

Apparently she didn't know what to say to that so she kept quiet. I
figured that she was on a spot. She probably loved Blanche almost as
much as she'd once loved me. She'd been a Coombs servant and
Spring Bayou had been her home for fifty years. When I lost the place
she'd wept more bitterly than anyone else, and then Jack Taggart had
recovered the homestead and moved Miss Blanche back in as his
bride. He'd slept in my bed, taken the rightful place of Francis Mac-
Whalen Coombs. Poor Hattie May; it must have been hard for her to
get things straight in her mind.

I went on with an effort. "Hattie May, you know I'm your friend,
don't you?"

"The best frien' a pusson ever had, Mistuh Frank."

"Then you know I've got to ask you questions you won't like. I've
got to tell you what other people are saying. I'll probably have to hurt
your feelings, even make you mad. But it'll be because I'm trying to
help Coralee. You know that, too, don't you?"

"Uh-huh, I s'pose you'll have to do all them things. But what othuh
folks say, hit ain't right, Mistuh Frank. Coralee never done nothin'."

"I haven't told you what they've been saying so how can you say
they're wrong?" I asked. "Don't jump the gun on me, Hattie May."

Her chair squeaked as she shifted her vast bulk uneasily. "What
Mizz Blanche say about 'at po' chile, Mistuh Frank?"

It was then I realized that I'd been banking on the impossible in
hoping that Hattie May would trust me enough to give me the straight
story about Coralee. It wouldn't be a matter of trust anyway, it would
be a case of maternal protective instinct at its most basic level. Love
me she might, but Hattie May would lie her last breath away before
she'd admit that her littlest, Coralee, had ever been anything but a
saint. My only hope of gaining anything from this session, then, was
in finding something in the old woman's flood of protestation that she

wouldn't intend to let me know. Like most of her kind, Hattie May was apt to overdo her indignant refutals.

"Sometimes I think Mizz Blanche never like Coralee too much," Hattie May prodded. "No mattuh how hahd she try to please Mizz Blanche, she don' exactly suit. What Mizz Blanche say, Mistuh Frank?"

When I'd been a practicing attorney I'd been pretty rough on witnesses. Give me a timid person or an arrogant witness to cross-examine and I could get him or her mad and flustered in a few words. But now I hesitated to come out with the words that I had to say sooner or later.

So I hedged, I stalled, as I tried to think of some way to get the answer without asking the question. I had to know for sure. Coralee might actually be far more clever an actress than I'd imagined but Hattie May was no actress at all. Her reaction to Blanche's accusation would be genuinely painful or her denial riddled with shame.

Finally I blurted out, "Hattie May, Miss Blanche told me that Mister Jack and Coralee were—"

"No!" The cry was wrung from the depths of Hattie May's old and weary soul. It was spiked by grief but at the same time it bore a note of stricken anger. She had spent her life in uncomplaining love and loyal service and now when she so desperately needed help they had turned on her. Hattie May believed it to be a lie, no matter that the whole world might believe differently.

I balanced Coralee's and Hattie May's denials. If the two had been anybody except a colored mother and daughter in Tangerine County I'd have considered the possibility that Coralee had hidden her sins from Hattie May. But I knew this was impossible. There may be more closely knit social groups than the Negro families of Tangerine but if there are I've never known one. In that part of North Florida, at least, there exists a matriarchy. The oldest woman of the colored family is revered with a sort of loving dread and not even the most insignificant misdeed of the most distant member of the tribe goes unreported, nor unreproved by her. For Coralee to have "carried on" with Jack Taggart without somebody among her multitude of brothers and sisters, aunts, uncles and cousins finding out and getting the word to Hattie May was unthinkable.

"Why she say 'at?" The big woman in the polkadot dress was keening softly. "Why Mizz Blanche say sech a thing?"

"You know she wouldn't have unless she believed it."

"But how kin she b'lieve it, Mistuh Frank? How kin she b'lieve all 'at duhty talk when all she'd have to do was ask me? Why did anybody ever staht sech a lie in the fust place?"

Why, indeed? First make Jack Taggart the philandering husband and then frame his colored mistress, had that been somebody's deliberate scheme? Fantastic, but what other explanation was there if I believed Hattie May and Coralee?

Fantastic? That was mild compared to what Judge Thrace and a jury would call it if I tried it out in court.

Above the creak-creak of the rocking chair, Hattie May asked quietly, "You fixin' to tell me there ain' no use you tryin' any more, Mistuh Frank?" She waited a moment and when I didn't answer she went on in a dead voice, "I don't guess nobody c'ld blame you iffen you quits. Mizz Blanche b'lieves that lie then the whole world b'lieves it, I reckon."

"I don't believe the lie, Hattie May," I said. I tried to laugh. "But seeing we're about the only two who don't, you better start praying."

There was a trace of returning warmth and strength in her voice. "What I says 'bout you quittin,' I din't really 'spect you to. Not you. Gawd bless you, Mistuh Frank."

"Maybe I'm just doing it to get back at them, like they say."

"Not you. You doin' this 'cause it's the right thing. Like your daddy and your grand-daddy befo' you, you jus' kain't he'p but do what's right."

"Hold it, Hattie May. You may not think I'm such a wonderful guy when I get through asking you my questions."

"You ask away," she said ponderously. "I answers 'em all. But you got to remembuh, I'm Coralee's mama."

I nodded in the darkness. "If we're going to help her you're going to have to tell me the whole truth, Hattie May, good or bad. Coralee's a drinking woman, isn't she?"

There was a long, rigid silence. "Do you think a man who's drunk away as much as I have could damn Coralee for that?"

"It's diff'runt, though," she said wretchedly. She heaved another sigh that was half groan. "But all right, yessuh, she drinken too much. I kep' tryin' to git her to stop but she won'."

"Did she get in much trouble with her drinking? I mean, did a lot of people know she hit the bottle?"

"Well, she never got in no bad trouble. But as fer folks knowin' she drinken too much, can't keep that a secret long aroun' heah."

"I mean white folks," I said. "Did they know she drank?" Another long pause and Hattie May said, "I reckon they did. Coralee, she jus' couldn' stop he'pin' herse'f to the likker where she wuhked. Got so's she couldn' keep a job 'ceptin' at places where there ain' no likker, like Mizz Elsie's."

So whoever had planted the two pints of Old Mister Oxford in Coralee's shack had known what would happen. "How about Coralee having her own house in the bottom?" I asked. "Did you have to put her out of here on account of her drinking, Hattie May?"

"No, *suh!* Coralee, she live heah with me ontwell the day she got ma'ied."

"I didn't know Coralee was married. How long ago was that?"

"Fo' years, about. She ma'ied a man name Guturez, John Guturez but he call hisse'f Who-awn. Coralee was the bes' guhl you'd want to see twell she took up with him. He stahted her drinkin' and all. Huh, serve him right what happen to him."

"What did happen to him?" I asked. A shutter closed; a door slammed. "I don' know, an' 'at's the troof, Mistuh Frank."

"Juan Guturez?" I asked. "Where did he come from with a name like that, for God's sake?"

"Coralee, she went on a 'scursion one time down to a cullud beach near Tampa. She met him there. I—well, I reckon I made 'em git ma'ied when I found out she was doin' wrong with him. Spanish, he calls hisse'f, but he's nothin' but trash with a big mouf and fancy clo'es."

Casually, indifferently, I asked, "Where can I get hold of this Juan Guturez, Hattie May?"

"I done tole you, I don' know what happen to him," she said. "He lef' Coralee after they don' live togethuh more'n six months." She took a deep breath. "I taken Coralee to Mistuh William Cartuh an' he got her a reg'lar dee-vorce, writ down in the book an' all. They never was no chile, praise Gawd, and so far's Coralee's concerned she never met that trashy nigguh with the big mouf."

Now that she was confident she'd gotten safely past the subject of Juan Guturez, I slipped the question in over her lowered guard. "This man Coralee married, is he the one who disappeared after he shot off his mouth about The Committee?"

I heard her grunt as though she'd been hit. There was a long pause and when she spoke she sounded almost sulky. "I don' know nothin' 'bout him 'ceptin' he was no-count."

"Hattie May," I said reproachfully.

"Well, nobody know fer sure," she said desperately. "Could be he up an' went back to Tampa. Nobody never know fer sure. Man like 'at, no tellin' where he might take it into his haid to go. He was always down-talkin' us, callin' us Uncle Toms and 'Lizas 'caus we don' rare aroun' and make trouble. Mebbe he jus' lit out fer someplace where they do 'em things. Nobody knows fer sure."

"Did the sheriff or the city police look for him?"

It was hard going for her. "I don' rightly know," she said, then she leveled with me. "Well, yessuh, Mistuh She'iff Henry Taggart, he come aroun' to Coralee's place and axed her some questions. She couldn' tell him nothin' accounten she din't know nothin'."

I tried it again. "Now, Hattie May." She flung out her massive arms in a gesture that was both a protest and an appeal. "'Fo' Gawd, Mistuh Frank, how you 'spect me to tell *anybody* things like 'at?"

A sepulchral voice spoke mournfully out of the blackness of the window at my elbow. "You tell 'im, Mama," a male voice said from inside the dark room. "You tell 'im about The Committee and what the Gen'ral tell Coralee. You don' tell 'im, I will."

4

The voice tolling out of the pitch-black silence knotted my abused nerves for a moment. I came up out of my chair, then cursed myself for being so twitchy. What had I expected, that we'd have privacy on the front porch of a Negro shack?

I'd been away from Tangerine County too long; I should have remembered that no shanty on the Ridge was permitted to waste space, least of all the home of the matriarch. While I'd been talking to Hattie May there'd been a dozen or more of her family inside, kids and grownups, rolling their eyes at each other in the darkness, straining to catch every syllable.

I should have expected that but not the demand from a son that his mother tell something she wanted to keep quiet. That was a breach of all the rules and the big woman opposite me on the porch reacted indignantly.

"You hesh up, Hubbard!" she yelled. "What call you got buttin' in like that, anyhow?"

I couldn't remember which of Hattie May's brood Hubbard was but he must have been the youngest; the older ones would hardly have kept on coming. Mournfully, stubbornly, he said, "Mistuh Frank gotta right to know, Mama. You heerd him say he gotta know the troof kin he he'p Coralee."

I leaned over to peer in the window. Barely discernible were several darker shadows, but I couldn't pick out Hubbard from the others so I spoke to them all. "What did the General tell Coralee, Hubbard?"

"You set down and don' lissen to him," Hattie May commanded. "Iffen you gotta know, I tells you, not Hubbard. He git it all wrong."

"Yes'm," the bass voice said humbly and was stilled. I sat down again.

"Two-three days after Who-awn Guturez lef' Coralee, the Gen'ral, he come aroun' to Coralee's place one evenin' an' he say—" Hattie May broke off and struggled with herself. "Mistuh Frank, you *sure* you gotta know all this? 'Cause I promised I won't never tell *nobody.*"

"I've got to know," I said gravely.

"Well—well, he was right nice about it, almost polite, Coralee say. He say it's too bad a nice guhl like her mixen up with a no-count trashy nigguh like Who-awn Guturez, an' Gawd knows *that's* the troof. Ever'body likes her, he say, all the white folks, an they don' want her to git in no more trouble. He say iffen she smaht she won' do a lotta talkin' like Who-awn Guturez was always doin'.

"Coralee, she come runnin' to me, skeered mos' to death, Mistuh Frank. She cryin' and carryin' on. She so skeered they gonna do with her like they done with Who-awn Guturez. She *tole* him to hesh his big talk befo' they come after him."

"Is that what happened?" I asked sharply. "Did The Committee do away with Coralee's husband?"

"I sweah to Gawd, Mistuh Frank, I don' know—like I tole you. Coralee say he tole her he gonna meet somebody sommers an' git a lotta money an' when he come back they's bofe gonna go to New Yawk. 'At's what he tole Coralee, Mistuh Frank. He went out an' tha's the las' she ever seed of him."

"Did Coralee tell Sheriff Taggart about this?" I asked. She didn't answer except with a shake of her head.

I didn't dare hope that some pieces might be starting to fall into place, that this was anything I could use in the defense of Coralee Preston. All I had was the fact that Coralee's alien husband had been a lippy nigra and The Committee apparently had disposed of him and then had told Coralee to keep her mouth shut. That had been four years ago and it had been kept secret until now. How could it have anything to do with the murder of Jack Taggart?

I yawned and got up out of the chair. "Mistuh Frank, you ain' fixin' to tell ever'body what I said about the Gen'ral, is you?" Hattie May asked. "'Cause iffen it gits back to him it's likely to go hahd on a lot of folks. Not jus' me and Coralee but a whole lot of cullud folks got nothin' to do with this 'ceptin' they's cullud."

Well, there was that to consider, too. If I could possibly use this four-year-old information would it be worth bringing the General and his goddam Committee down on every Negro?

"Don't worry about it," I told Hattie May. It was the best I could offer her.

I would have driven back to the Princess then and rolled into bed if I hadn't seen Reverend Gail sitting on the steps of his church when I turned the corner. There he was, thin as a rail and straight as a pole, alone and sitting down, his wide-brimmed straw hat on the stair beside him. His white hair gleamed above his black face.

My first thought was: *Oh, no!* But I had to stop. I left the Ford in the middle of the road, and walked around the car to the church steps. I said good evening and his mellow voice returned the greeting gravely, with dignity.

"Evenin,' Mister Coombs. Heerd tell you'd come back to town for a visit. I'm afraid you mus' find it pretty warm after the no'thern climate."

I'd never particularly liked Gail—not many white people in Lindsley did. No white man called across the street to him as they did to the pastor of the Grove church, "Father" Gracie, who wore a cassock and delivered the Grove votes to the primary candidates who contributed the most to his "fund for the poor." A million laughs, Father Gracie, always involved in some petty swindle and giggling with no guilt at all on his round face when he was accused of sticking the dough in his own pocket.

"De Lawd he'ps them 'at he'ps demselves," he'd say in his exaggerated Uncle Tom accent to the white folks he was hitting for a handout. The Grove churchgoers certainly must have known they were getting the worst of it—money for "repairing the steeple" had been collected four times over and not a dime spent on the spire—but so far as I'd ever heard there'd never been the first move to kick the old fraud out of his pulpit.

Reverend Gail was nothing like that. He was spare, seldom-smiling, soft-spoken, austere. He was civil enough to the whites he had to deal with but he never fawned like Father Gracie and he never asked for a dollar from anyone except his own people. Even before I'd left Lindsley there had been mutterings that Gail was an equal rights man beneath his silence.

The Supreme Court decision hadn't come down then and the

N.A.A.C.P. wasn't active, at least not in Tangerine County, but I'd heard that Gail had told his parishioners that something had to be done about the colored schools—if only from a health and fire hazard standpoint. I remember that when the indignant report was relayed to me I'd agreed with the old boy, much as I disliked having to. Negro schools in Tangerine were no more than stinking firetraps run by barely literate teachers. Not that I'd gotten up on any soap boxes to do anything about it; I was too busy staying drunk.

But what was Gail, friend or enemy? I'd been told often enough that everything had changed in Lindsley and Tangerine County and now for all I knew Gail was the big messiah, a man turned militant by the years of seeing nothing done to improve his people's lot. Or he might have finally sold out, to make it easier on himself in his declining years.

"It's hot, all right," I said. "I guess I'd forgotten how hot it can get in Lindsley in September."

"Very enervating," he agreed. He was as fond of big words as Father Gracie but Gail usually put them in the right places.

I noticed that up and down the street the porch talk had stopped again. I decided that Reverend Gail hadn't been waiting for me to talk about the weather and that if I stalled around I'd be at a disadvantage, so I opened the proceedings. I kept my voice down.

"I've just been talking to Hattie May," I said needlessly and he nodded. "Reverend Gail, do you know about Coralee's husband, the man who called himself Guturez?"

"Yes," he said gravely. "We all do, Mister Coombs. I wouldn't wonder that at least sixty-five percent of the citizens of Tangerine County know what happened to Juan Guturez. Colored and white."

I wondered why he'd picked sixty-five percent as a figure instead of the more traditional ninety-eight. "You mean they know he dropped out of sight, is that it?"

Calmly, deliberately, Reverend Gail said, "They know he was killed by The Committee, Mister Coombs. That's what I meant when I said they know what happened to Juan Guturez."

He didn't sound particularly bitter about it. It was more the voice of a person speaking about war or a hurricane or a long drought; it was a terrible thing but it happened every so often and man hadn't yet found a way to keep it from happening. But there was no tone of defeat. Resignation was there but behind the acceptance of the deplorable fact was a solid strength. Although this thing had been done and there was no preventive or redress at hand, it would not be so always.

"If you people knew this why didn't you go to the proper authorities?"

I looked into his eyes, shining in the light from the street and felt like a fool. Just what were "the proper authorities" supposed to do when the man who got those "proper authorities" elected—Brigadier-General Edmund Ruffin MacWhalen the Third (Ret.)—also ran The Committee?

"Sheriff Taggart wouldn't have let that stop him," I said, angry, at what I wasn't sure. "Sheriff Taggart would throw The—would throw anybody in jail who had it coming, no matter who he was."

"You think so, Mister Coombs?" he asked quietly.

"I know it. Henry Taggart's a good man. He's been a good man to you people, Reverend Gail."

"You mean because Tangerine County hasn't had a lynching during his incumbency, Mister Coombs? Does that make him good to my people?"

If these people didn't have any faith in Henry Taggart I'd been wrong about them all these years. Either that, or Henry had changed, along with so many other things in Tangerine County.

"Matter of fact, She'iff Taggart did conduct an investigation," the preacher said after a pause. His voice was non-committal. "Doubtless the she'iff department's records will show there was no evidence of foul play."

"Because you didn't tell him what he tried to find out," I muttered. "Hattie May just admitted that Coralee wouldn't cooperate."

"Cooperate," Gail murmured softly. "A word of many interpretations, isn't it, Mister Coombs? A word that's used so easily when you tell us cullud folks what we're expected to do."

"Reverend, I'm tired. If you don't mind, let's skip the N.A.A.C.P. lecture, shall we?"

He chuckled deep in his throat. "I'm not qualified to deliver that kind of a lecture, Mister Coombs," he said and in spite of the chuckle there was a trace of sadness. "Maybe once, when I was a young man, but not now. I'm too old—old enough to take my refuge in Old Testament doctrine if I'm not careful." He saw I didn't understand and went on. "It's a whole lot easier for us to lay everything that happens to God's will, you know, picture him as an angry, jealous, punishin' God. A sort of great big white-man boss."

I walked up the church steps and sat down beside Reverend Gail. I had a cigarette in my mouth and my lighter ready before I asked, "D'you mind, Reverend?"

It seemed a natural thing to ask: this was his church. He shook his head. When I got my cigarette going I asked, "Did Coralee come to your church, Reverend Gail?"

"Not very often, I'm afraid," he said. "She was married here and sometimes her good mother brought her to services. But I wouldn't call her a steady churchgoer, Mister Coombs." He ran a long hand over his white hair. "She's a strange young woman, Mister Coombs, rebellious, withdrawn from the rest of us most of the time. Her drinking—it's easy enough to blame everything on her drinking but even before that she was different. Unhappy. Ever since—since she was a young girl."

I'd caught his quick oblique glance as he hesitated. "Since when, Reverend. What happened to make her so unhappy?"

He thought over my question for what seemed a long time and then shook his head slowly. "I'm afraid that's not for me to say, Mister Coombs. It would be a violation of an ecclesiastical confidence."

"Look, Reverend," I said harshly, "don't give me that ecclesiastical confidence crap. You don't have the confessional in your church. This girl's damn likely to be the first woman ever electrocuted at Raiford unless I get something to work with. I can't even start building a case for her if you people go around keeping your precious nigra secrets to yourselves."

He didn't get angry although perhaps he had that right. If he had I'd have blown the whole thing. Getting Reverend Gail down on me would have made it about unanimous in Tangerine County.

"No, Mister Coombs," he said gently, "you're wrong. These secrets ain't precious to us—they're the mark of fear, they're leftovers from our slave days. There was such a long time when we didn't know for sure how you folks would take what we said out loud. There were so many times when something we thought was all right to say turned out to be all wrong. We decided it was best not to say anything except amongst ourselves. Do you think we wouldn't love to speak out, knowing we'd be understood or if we weren't you'd ask us to explain? Brother, brother, it would be a bigger victory than anything about schools or lunch counters or riding up front in a bus!"

"I'll understand anything you tell me," I said. "I grew up here and my daddy and grand-daddy before me. We've always tried to—"

He was nodding as though he meant it. "I reckon you would understand," he said thoughtfully, "but it's not my right to tell you, honestly. Get Coralee to tell you. She's the only person who can. I don't believe even her mother knows."

"At least give me an idea of what to ask," I begged. "How old was she when this thing happened?"

He thought that over and finally answered reluctantly. "'Bout thirteen or fourteen, I reckon. But I can't tell you more, Mister Coombs. I'm sorry."

I dragged on my cigarette, trying to whip my brain into remembering back ten years. That would have been about two years before I'd left Lindsley and, hell, there'd been things vital to my existence going on about me then. I'd never even known they happened, not Frank Coombs in his cups. How could I remember anything about Coralee Preston, a little colored girl?

"I'll ask Coralee," I said. My voice sounded distant in my own ears. I'd better get in the car and make it back to the Princess or I'd fall asleep at the wheel and give them a fine excuse for throwing me in jail.

"I reckon you've been told a lot about the terrible blood-lettin' that's coming when the Black Mohammedans are turned loose on Tangerine County, haven't you, Mister Coombs?"

That was almost the last thing Blanche had said—*Did your new northern friends send you down here to start something that would set the Black Mohammedans on us?* "I've heard mention of it," I said. "Who are they?"

"They're nobody," he answered promptly. "At least not in Tangerine County. Mebbe somewhere else but not here. They're the great big boogy man that's going to do something terrible to every white woman in Tangerine County if that woman's husband or brother or daddy don't let General MacWhalen and his Committee protect them. The General's own way, of course."

I knew the General ran The Committee and God knows I never had any love for Edmund Ruffin MacWhalen the Third, but hearing a nigra speak with such dispassionate—almost contemptuous—sarcasm about the man who had run Tangerine County for so long shook me up. Things certainly had changed when any colored person, even the stand-offish minister of the Ridge church, could speak so of the General, much less even obliquely mention the subject of violence against a white woman. One taboo had been almost as strong as the other when I'd been around Tangerine.

The General owned the biggest of Lindsley's three banks, although he let Chet Leonard run it for him, and he had a voice in what the other two banks did. He owned outright or held mortgages on more than half the Negro shacks in the Grove and the Ridge. The packing company was his and so was the concentrate plant, the lumberyard, the concrete block factory. Nearly every colored wage-earner in Tangerine County worked directly or indirectly for the General and that went for those few who worked for the county or the city. The General had both in his pocket. If a Negro was able to borrow money at all it was from a small loan company which the General controlled.

That was the way things were and yet Reverend Gail's words shocked me. Which, I suppose, would have been significant to anybody trying to analyze the character of Frank Coombs. I hated everything the General and his Committee stood for, and yet when a colored preacher made an irreverent observation about MacWhalen I was jolted and disturbed.

It wasn't the way things had always been done in Tangerine County. Negroes didn't speak out against a white man in talking to another white man. And if Reverend Gail, an intelligent, deliberate-minded Negro, could risk this, what might not the younger, rebellious, tired-of-waiting Negroes dare say? Or do?

"The person who mentioned Black Mohammedans wasn't a person to be frightened by a boogy man," I said stiffly. I noticed his quick recognition of my change. "I've read about some pretty militant Negro underground organization—"

"Why, so have I," Reverend Gail broke in. "It looks like the General has, too. But there're none here in Lindsley or anywhere in Tangerine County, Mister Coombs."

"Maybe your people just haven't told you about them," I said.

He chuckled softly as he shook his head. "You said awhile back that we don't have the confessional in my church and mebbe we don't, not with the box and all. But there isn't anything—anything, Mister Coombs—that goes on in this town or this county or even over in Humphries among the cullud folks that they don't tell me about. And I don't mean just those in my own flock. Folks in the Grove, folks that belong to Zion A.M.E. out in the county, and Bethel and Pillar of Fire Tabernacle—they all get the word, the true word, to me."

He reached for the straw hat beside him on the step, a gesture that indicated that this talk was about ended. "You see, Mister Coombs, it's not that I'm so wise or so good that makes them come to me. For a long, long time I've been about the one person in Tangerine County they could come to and know that what they told or asked me wouldn't go any further, wouldn't get back to—to anybody who'd make trouble for them."

He stood up and placed the hat carefully on his white thatch. "And 'til this very night," he said, "I never have repeated anything, not even so much as the little I've told you."

"Then why have you talked to me?" I asked. His eyes searched mine in the light from the nearby street lamp. "I don't know for sure," he said slowly, "except I got the idea mebbe you were the one sent to help us, Mister Coombs."

His teeth showed in one of his rare smiles. "I've always been sure *somebody* was comin' *sometime,* even when things looked worst," he said gently. "I never expected it to be Mister Frank Coombs but now I'm like the rest of my people—I've got a lot of hope that you're the one."

Chapter 4

I woke up the next morning to the jangling of the old-fashioned phone beside the bed. As I came awake I heard hell's own bedlam of shunting freight cars from the freight depot below. I'd been sounder asleep than I ever remembered having been in years without a handful of pills to knock me out and I woke up hungry and clear-headed.

I picked up the receiver. A strange voice asked, "Mister Frank Coombs? You don't know me, Mister Coombs. My name's Young, Emmert Young, and I'm from Miami. I'd like to talk to you a minute if I may, about the Preston case."

"What time is it?" I asked.

"Quarter past nine. Sorry to bother you so early but I just got into town. I hoped to see you before you left the hotel."

"Exactly what did you want to see me about?"

"I'd rather talk to you personally," he said, still brisk, almost officious. "It's something I don't think you'd care to discuss over the phone."

I started to say sorry, I was busy, and then I reminded myself: *You'd better look for any break that comes along, boy. Maybe this guy has something.*

"Okay, meet me in the dining room in half an hour."

"I could come up to your room," he suggested. "I'd prefer to—"

"And I'd prefer the dining room, Mister Young," I said briskly. "I'll be down in half an hour."

Mr. Emmert Young was easy enough to find; the dining room was empty except for a man at a table in a corner by the windows reading a Tallahassee paper. He raised his eyes as I walked in and then stood up, folding his paper and smiling—sleek, confident, on the con or very close to it. Walking toward him and saying good morning to the colored girl who came out of the kitchen with the menu, I decided I didn't like Mr. Emmert Young at first sight.

He held out a manicured hand that went with the plastered-back dark hair and the rich grey silk suit. "Good morning, Mister Coombs," he said. "Very glad to know you, Sir."

I said good morning, took the menu and ordered.

"You eaten?" I asked. He nodded but gestured at his half-empty cup of coffee and said he'd have another.

I lit a cigarette. "What did you want to talk to me about?"

"I understand you're representing Coralee Preston," he said.

"I happened to be in court when she was arraigned," I said.

I let him wait for me to say something more and when I didn't he leaned back in his chair with a small frown. "You sound as though that was it," he said. "Do you mean you're not going any further as her attorney?"

"I didn't say that," I countered.

"But you didn't say you intend to carry the case through, either."

"Look, Mister Young," I said. "I don't know who you are or what your interest is in this case. I seldom give anybody information unless I know whom I'm talking to."

"Very commendable," he said. "Especially in this situation, eh? I've heard you've had a lot of pressure put on you since you came into the case. If you'll pardon me, the bruises on your face show the expression was a little more than a figure of speech."

The waitress came with our coffee. He said, "Thank you, Mary Jane," and the colored girl sniffed. I wondered what her name really was and if he thought he was insuring himself good service with such talk. When the girl left he took some time getting his cigarette lit.

"You said you were from Miami," I prompted.

He nodded. "I have an office there. Actually, I make New York my headquarters."

"I figured you for a New Yorker," I said. I didn't make it sound like a compliment, though I didn't have anything against New Yorkers that I knew of. "And what's your line of work, Mister Young?"

"I'm an attorney," he explained. "That's why I'm here, of course, to offer our services if you think you could use some help." He smiled and added, "Financial and otherwise."

The waitress came with my order. I waited until she left, then swallowed my tomato juice and began forking in purely delicious food. I swallowed some coffee and said, "By our services I take it you represent some legal defense organization? Civil Liberties Union?"

He shook his head, his smile registering faint disdain. "No, I'm with the Organization for Relief of Suppressed Minorities. The O.R.S.M."

"Never heard of it," I said bluntly.

"You will," he answered. "Everybody will. We intend to take up where the others leave off because of their fear or their inherent underlying doctrine of compromise." He laughed. "Or, most frequently, the under the table pay-off. Ours is a militant organization, Mister Coombs. We intend to make the Preston case our opening salvo, so to speak."

"I see."

"The set-up is perfect." He leaned across the table and lowered his voice. "Better than Georgia, better than Mississippi. North Florida, a few miles from Miami, Palm Beach, Hialeah, places that every northerner can identify with. And here we have a Negress—beautiful woman, too, I understand—persecuted by the very prototype of all the nigger-hating Simon Legrees that ever lived. We've got a venal, tobacco-chawing sheriff and an ignorant old judge who deplores the fact that the slave block and the overseer's whip are out of style. And a tawdry little sun-baked county seat run by the Ku Klux Klan. We've got—"

"You've also got yourself the wrong boy," I said.

His eyes narrowed as he looked across the table, "What do you mean?"

"I mean I don't want your help," I said. "Any organization that would call a colored girl a Negress is off on the wrong foot at the start. Anyway, I don't like the way you talk about my friends and my home town. Besides being insulting, you're a hundred percent wrong. The sheriff isn't venal and he smokes cigarettes or a cigar once in awhile. Judge Thrace isn't ignorant—and if you think he is, try stepping one inch over the line on a point of law. Lindsley may look tawdry to a stranger but the Klan doesn't run the place and hasn't since Reconstruction days. That venal, tobacco-chawing sheriff made the Klan the laughingstock of Tangerine County a few years back."

Young leaned back in his chair and squinted at me. "What is this?" he asked slowly. "You mean you're one of these Crackers, yourself?"

"It just goes to show you," I said, as pleasantly as I could. "You should never make a pitch without finding out all about whom you're talking to. I was born just outside of town. My family moved in while the Spanish were still moving out."

"But—" he spluttered, and swallowed. "If you're one of them, why do they treat you like this?"

"Let me ask a couple of questions," I said. "What would you gain out of bringing your bunch in here? What's in it for you? You're no do-gooder, Young, you're no wild-eyed liberal. Where does the dough come from, how much is there and what does it buy?"

He eyed me carefully, speculatively. "The money interests you, eh?"

"I'm always interested in money," I said. "Who isn't?"

He gave a nasty laugh. "So that's it. You've got the Preston girl sewed up but for the right consideration you'd be willing to forget all the impolite things I said about your home town and your dear friends. You'd make a deal so we could move in, is that it?"

"You're doing the talking." He eyed me some more and finally his smile came back. "No deal," he announced. "We'll come in whether you like it or not. If you try to turn your back on us we'll crucify you. We'll show you up as the straw man set up by the State to prove that Miss Preston was represented by counsel, that her civil rights were not violated."

"You sound like a very tough gang," I said.

"We are," he said, and his smile disappeared when he said it. "When we have to we swing a lot of weight in various places. Like to know what we could do?"

"Don't bother," I said. "I wouldn't be half as much afraid of your crucifying me as having you and your crowd on my side. That would be murder in Tangerine. You know why? You don't give a damn about Coralee Preston or the suppressed minorities. All you care about are those big headlines you can clip out and send to Moscow to prove you're earning your fee. For God's sake, get out, Young. You're spoiling my breakfast. Go talk to The Committee. You're their type."

"Committee? What Committee?"

"The Committee for the Liquidation of Everybody the General Doesn't Approve of."

He looked at me as though he was wondering what the hell I was talking about. He stopped behind my chair and his voice was low and vicious. "You needn't think you're getting me out of this case, Coombs. I'll be back."

"Hooray for General MacArthur," I said. "Now drag it out of here before I complain to the management about peddlers in the dining room."

He muttered something I didn't catch and left. I went on with my breakfast and relished every mouthful of it. When I finished I asked for my check and saw that two coffees had been added to my bill and then crossed off.

"Mistuh Charles, he say not to chahge you fo' what 'at gemmun had, Mistuh Coombs," the waitress said. "He listenin' and he say what you tole 'at gemmun, it give him a deal of pleasuh to pay fo' the cawfee."

I laughed. "Then why didn't he pick up the whole check and have himself a ball?" I asked. The girl looked bewildered. "Never mind, and thank Mister Charles for me."

"I sho will," she promised, and then scowled at the dining room doorway. "Callin' me Mary Jane."

2

Walking up the street from the Princess to the Bank of Lindsley I amused myself by trying to hold the eyes that glanced at me and then slid away. It didn't work; people couldn't help looking at me but that didn't mean they had to nod, smile or speak. I met several men and women I'd known very well during my life in Lindsley, including Reverend D. Holloway Hurtt, assistant rector of the Episcopal church my family had helped found. Hurtt did no better than the others, although I have to admit his neck reddened a little over the clerical collar he wore with his grey summer bib or whatever they call that dickey Episcopal clergymen wear.

The colored people I recognized gave me the same treatment. Was it fear or just possibly because somebody (Gail?) had told them I had a tough enough row to hoe without them publicly hailing me as their champion? Whatever the reason, most of the Negroes I met didn't even risk a glance. They kept their eyes on the sidewalk as they passed.

The clock outside the bank showed ten-forty as I went in. Once I'd been a director of that bank, a job I inherited from my grandfather and my father and one which I'd been permitted to hold despite the General's disapproval. Now I was half afraid to walk inside and ask Chet Leonard if I could deposit my check for the property sale.

I felt my breast pocket to make sure I had Carter's check and took a deep breath before I pushed open the door. It was mostly imagination, of course, but it seemed that every typewriter, every adding machine, every other piece of business equipment, stopped the second I set foot in the place. I walked across the room toward the railed enclosure where Chet sat, talking to an old man in a starched white collarless shirt and a black felt hat.

I'd never noticed before that Chet had a round, fat face with a prissy mouth. He was wearing rimless glasses instead of the hornrims I remembered. If he'd made the change to give himself more dignity, he'd missed; all he'd accomplished was to make himself look mean and sanctimonious.

Chet's glasses reflected the overhead lights and the little mouth stayed half open when he saw me coming toward him. I bet myself that old Chet was wishing for the days when a bank president didn't have to sit right out in the open, when he'd have had an office and could have sent word out that he was too busy to see me for another year or so. But he was game enough. After that first double-take he said something to his customer and got up from his desk and walked over to the railing.

"Hello, Chet," I said. "I came in to see if I could open an account." He didn't say hello. Instead, he began fumbling around in his mind for reasons why he couldn't let me open an account. Those new glasses didn't do a thing for him when it came to hiding what he was thinking.

"Yes or no, Chet?" I asked. "You don't have to explain. Your real estate department handled the deal so you know it's Carter's check."

He rubbed his chin. "Oh, that," he murmured. "Well, I'll tell you, Frank. Uh. I'd have to take it up with the board before I could let you open a straight checking account. Personally, I'd—"

Taking it up with the board meant asking the General. "Never mind," I said and turned to walk out.

"No, wait," he said. "You don't have to get sore. I said I'd take it up with the board, didn't I? How much is the check for?"

I took it out of my pocket and unfolded it. Three thousand eight hundred and sixty-two dollars and fourteen cents. The detachable voucher listed all the deductions, commissions, stamps and whatnots that had gnawed away at the full sale price until it had shrunk to its present enfeebled state. There it was, my patrimony, the estate I'd built for my heirs and assigns, a grand total of three thousand eight hundred and sixty-two dollars and fourteen cents plus about two hundred and fifty bucks left from the five hundred Miss Elsie had advanced me.

"You realize, of course, that your creditors could slap an attachment on this as soon as you deposited it?" Chet said.

"I don't have any creditors. Bill tells me everybody's been paid."

"But there might be somebody Bill missed," Leonard insisted.

"Not Bill," I said. "He dug up some characters I never heard of. But at the time I was acquiring all these creditors I wasn't very good at remembering names and faces."

"How about now, Frank?" he asked me. "I mean, are you through with that stuff?"

"If you mean am I through with liquor, the answer is no," I said. "I haven't joined A.A. But I don't intend getting stinking and writing any bum checks on your bank. I promise to be good until I get out of town, which will be the minute I get through with this case." He looked distressed, as though I'd said a disgustingly dirty word.

"Jack Taggart was one of my best friends," he said stiffly.

"Then maybe you can tell me how Jack bought Spring Bayou for Blanche. Where did he get the dough? When I left here Jack was doing all right but he wasn't in the big money—matter of fact, he was always complaining about the tights. He bought all the furniture that was sold at auction, too. It must have taken a lot of dough, where did he get it?"

"I can't discuss our depositors' affairs," Chet said primly.

Suddenly I found myself getting a boot out of making him suffer. "Of course I could always subpoena you," I said.

"Why don't you ask Bill?" he said. "Bill knows all about it. Ask him."

"You mean you discuss your depositors' affairs with Bill Carter?" I asked. "He isn't on the board, is he?"

"No—no, he's not but he knows about it. He took care of the auction sale, didn't he?"

I was afraid that he'd bolt in another minute so I let him off the hook. "I'll do that," I said. "Now, how about the checking account?"

He reached in a hip pocket and brought out a folded handkerchief to polish his glasses. Without them he looked weak-eyed, meaner than ever. "To be blunt, I think you'd have trouble cashing a check around here, one of your own."

"I'll worry about that," I said but the warning was valid. Who in Lindsley or all Tangerine County, for that matter, would cash one of my checks? "Okay, then, how about cashing Bill's check and I'll put the money in Theron Charles' safe?"

He nodded, put his glasses back on and reached for the check. He jotted his initials neatly under Bill Carter's signature.

"Thanks."

"You're welcome," he said formally, the bank president again. He hesitated. "I understand you went out to see Blanche last night."

"Did I?" He pursed his little mouth. "There are a lot of people in this county who wouldn't like the idea of you bothering Blanche. She's suffered enough, Frank."

"The General knows why I went out there, Chet," I said. "Before you start throwing your weight around you'd better check with Big Brother."

He started to say something, changed his mind and turned his back on me to walk back to the desk where the old Cracker in the black hat was waiting.

There was a line at every teller's window. I chose the shortest and of course I got behind a guy who must have operated a thousand coin machines around town. He kept hauling rolls of nickels, dimes and quarters out of a satchel and stacking them on the counter for the teller to count.

Eventually I got to the window and pushed the check under the grill. The teller looked at it and then at me. He turned around and I had a good view of his narrow shoulders under his alpaca coat as he nodded to somebody. Immediately a large man in a wide-brimmed hat got up from a chair next to the corridor that led to the safety deposit boxes.

I recognized the large man—Fred Mosely, Deputy Sheriff of Tangerine County—and I knew what was coming.

3

"I've changed my mind. Give me back my check," I said quickly.

The teller had gone deaf on me. He turned slowly, watching Mosely's approach. The deputy sheriff ranged up beside me and although he knew damn well who I was asked, "Frank Coombs?"

"You sonofabitch," I said to the teller.

"Mister Coombs," Mosely said, still very formal about the whole thing, "I got here a writ of attachment issued to Mister Edmund MacWhalen and I hereby—"

"Who?" I cried. "You mean the General?"

"No, I mean Edmund MacWhalen, junior, of six-four-oh Calypso Drive, Riviera Estates, County of Tangerine."

"Edmund the Fourth, not junior," I corrected. "Are you one of the General's errand boys now, Fred, or are you just doing a favor for Henry Taggart?"

"You talk like that to me and I'll push the rest of your face in, you nigger-lovin' rumdum," Mosely said softly. He waited for me to swing and when I didn't he turned to the teller. "You got to keep hold of the check 'til the hearin'."

"I'll take it to Mister Leonard right away," the teller whispered. He darted a look at me and I could read the shamed apology in his eyes. "If you'll go to Mister Leonard's desk with the deputy I'm sure he can explain, Mister Coombs."

"I don't need to have it explained," I said. "I'd better not, if I get within swinging distance I might sock him and then this ape with the badge would have an excuse to lock me up."

"You're askin' for it real nice," the deputy murmured. "Just keep talkin',' Coombs."

"Now, now, gentlemen," that idiot of a teller kept saying, "I'm sure this can all be straightened out."

"For Christ's sake shut up and go back to counting your pennies," I said. "You did fine. The General will maybe even give you a two-dollar raise. Come out of your cage and I'll give you something else, you fink."

"You want to make a complaint, Andy?" Mosely asked eagerly. "Threatened with violence?"

"No, no, I don't want to get mixed up in it."

"You'd better bring a charge," I said. "The Committee might come around to your bedroom window some night and go boo."

Childish, sure, but I was sore, mostly at myself for being such a chump. Later I'd call myself a nitwit for not catching the warning Chet Leonard had tried to flash me about possible creditors, real or imagined. Since then, I've about convinced myself that Chet was leveling, hoping I'd get my cash and stick it in my pocket where the General's busy little workers couldn't touch it.

I turned and headed for the door, every eye in the place on me. I leaned into the door and flung myself out into the hot, damp day, then started for the Lawyers Building and the newly decorated offices of CARTER, LYNCH & ELEY.

I was still burning as I walked into the reception room and marched across the thick-piled carpet to the desk where Judith Williamson sat in her cool mauve linen. She looked into my bruised and scowling face. "Good morning, Mister Coombs."

"G'morning," I grunted. "I want to see Bill Carter."

"He has someone with him right now. Can I help you?"

"Not unless you're carrying the thirty-eight hundred bucks I just had stolen off me because of Bill's slight oversight," I said. "Tell him I want to see him right away."

She reached for one of the three phones on her desk. "Just a moment, Mister Coombs," she said and gave me another smile. She dialed two digits. "Mister Coombs is here, Miss Elsie."

"I want to see Bill, not Miss Elsie," I said. She blinked her eyes at me, half-nodding, and widened her smile. "Miss Dillon will be right out."

I didn't say whatever I'd started to. Miss Elsie would be as good as Bill Carter to explain this damned attachment and I wouldn't lose my temper with her and maybe make even more trouble for myself. "Thanks," I said.

"You're welcome, Mister Coombs," she said. "Won't you sit down?"

In spite of my burn I admired her poise and her pleasant efficiency, her fine skin and the way she fitted into the mauve linen dress. I turned as somebody came down the corridor from the offices. It was Miss Elsie, hurried and worried. She looked at my face and gave a little cry. "Oh, Francis, what did those awful men do to you?" She examined my lumps and blotches with anxious eyes. "They should go to Raiford for this," she said furiously. "I told Henry Taggart those men ought to get ten years for beating a poor, defenseless—"

"Hold it," I broke in. "I'm a great big thirty-eight-year-old boy now and besides I was dumb enough to walk into it. What I'm interested in right now is Eddie MacWhalen and a note Bill forgot to take care of."

She nodded and pinched her mouth. "Chet Leonard just called William. I think it's a horrid thing to do and I told William as much."

"Well, that's a big help," I said. "What's the idea of telling me everybody's been paid and then having this happen so conveniently. Or is Bill counsel for The Committee these days?"

"Francis," Miss Elsie said. "How can you say such a thing?"

I saw that Miss Williamson was glaring at me because I was upsetting Miss Elsie. "I'm sorry," I answered. "I just got a kick in the teeth and I'm still shook up. But how could Bill—can you get me in there to talk to him, just for a minute?"

She shook her head sadly. "He—I'm sorry, Francis, but William doesn't want to see you." She looked at Judith Williamson and put her hand on my arm. "Let's go back to my office and see what we can do about this."

I went along meekly. After she closed her office door she brought out the paper sack and started to leave, but I said never mind, I didn't feel like a drink, thanks. She turned back, her thin face beaming. "Oh, Francis, I'm so glad," she said. "I knew that some day you'd see what that terrible whiskey was doing to you!"

I started to tell her not to make any bets that I wouldn't be drunk before nightfall if many more surprises like Cousin Eddie Mac-Whalen's attachment came along. Poor Miss Elsie; let her enjoy the dream she'd always clung to no matter how rough the going got, the vision of Francis seeing the light, taking the pledge, going off the sauce.

"What's this about Bill not wanting to see me?" I asked as she straightened up from stowing the jug.

She shook her head dolefully. "I can't understand it. I thought William would be the last one to stop being your friend but he says— oh, Francis, you've got to understand that all his friends, all his clients, are—well—"

"Members of the General's hate club," I finished for her. "Good old William. What have I done for him lately, huh?"

Which was unfair. Hell, Bill Carter had to live in this county and make a living here. Why should he be expected to go up against the General to help out a onetime partner who was playing Sir Galahad with a busted spear?

"I didn't mean that last," I said. "I can see Bill's point. I guess. What about Eddie's attachment?"

Another sad headshake. "Francis, how much do you remember of the two years or so before—before everything happened?"

"Not much," I admitted. "You ought to know, you sat in on the wake before I gave Bill the okay to handle everything and blew town."

She nodded. "Yes, but I thought that perhaps—well, I've read of cases where the memory came back as time passed. I hoped that since you've been gone you might have filled in some of the gaps."

"I haven't tried," I said. "Once in awhile I remember something I'd forgotten but it's an involuntary action. Nothing I remembered was very pleasant."

"How about the Sundown Club?"

Sure, I remembered the joint, all right. It was an ultraexclusive place up the river in Humphries County and it had started out to be an expensive restaurant and cocktail lounge. It had lost money until the promoters had opened a backroom for a little friendly gambling that had gotten less and less friendly. Finally it became a regular joint—craps and roulette, blackjack, poker and birdcage. But although they closed the kitchen, the Sundown Club kept the bar open twenty-four hours a day, seven days a week, so guess where a person could most likely find that promising young attorney, Frank Coombs, in those days?

I'd found out since I left Lindsley that I was a lousy gambler but nothing could convince me of that in those days. Cards, dice or the wheel, when I was drunk I bucked them all with the conviction that I was a shrewd operator with a temporary run of bad luck. I was usually drunk. The jokers who ran the club saw to that.

When the crash came, Bill Carter had been handed a wad of Sundown Club I.O.U.'s along with the rest of the bad news but he'd told me to forget them. The heel-dragging law of Humphries County had closed up the joint just before I left town and while breaking up the equipment they'd found that there wasn't an honest card or pair of dice or unwired wheel in the place. So I didn't have to be a little gentleman and make good my gambling debts, even if the I.O.U.'s had been collectible in court, which they weren't.

"What about the Sundown?" I asked Miss Elsie. "I understood from Bill that those I.O.U.'s—"

"This hasn't anything to do with I.O.U.'s," Miss Elsie broke in. "It's a personal note you signed—Francis, try to think back. Do you remember where that awful place was?"

"Sure, just over the line in Humphries County."

"And on what used to be part of the original MacWhalen plantation," Miss Elsie said. "The General still owns that property. He built the club building and he held the mortgage."

"So?"

"As I understand it, once when a large payment was due the proprietors of the club were short and they offered a sight draft given them by one of their customers. It was your note, Francis, and the General told Edmund to accept it—young Edmund is titleholder of record—because he didn't want gamblers to be holding the paper of any member of the MacWhalen family, even you."

"Then why didn't he file his claim when all the others did?" I cried. "My God, didn't the General engineer the whole debacle? I should think he'd have been first in line."

Miss Elsie bit her lip. "Perhaps I shouldn't tell you this," she said reluctantly. "Technically, your paper belonged to young Eddie and he thought you were having a hard enough time without the note being presented. He said no when his father told him to collect."

"Eddie MacWhalen?" I cried. "I can just see him saying no to anything his old man told him to do."

"I know, but—well, Laurie undoubtedly had something to do with Eddie's remarkable stand against his father, Francis. I don't think I have to tell you that Laurie MacWhalen has always—"

She didn't have to go on. Laurie had been Laurie Taggart, Jack's sister, before she became Mrs. Edmund Ruffin MacWhalen the Fourth and she had been my girl, too. Then Blanche had come home from school one summer, suddenly a beautiful woman.

"Laurie persuaded Edmund to oppose the General and hold out that note eight years ago. But now—well, Jack was Laurie's brother, Francis, and you can understand how she must feel." She stopped talking again, sighed, and said, "Oh, dear."

I couldn't blame Laurie. How big a torch was the poor kid expected to carry? "How come Bill didn't warn me that the note was still out?" I asked miserably.

"William and I—everybody who knew you were coming to Lindsley—expected you to leave right away. William had no idea you'd cash that check here."

But I had and right now the question was how to get money

enough to keep going. Who was going to finance me? Emmett Young's Organization for Relief of Suppressed Minorities, perhaps? I'd be damned.

"What burns me is that if I'd gone through bankruptcy, that note wouldn't be worth a nickel," I muttered.

"And I blame myself for not insisting," Miss Elsie said. "I tried, if you remember, but you said no, you'd sell everything rather than have a Coombs go bankrupt. Do you remember William and I trying to persuade you to change your mind, Francis?"

I didn't but I nodded. Hell, I remembered almost nothing about that time but it sure sounded like me—drunk, broke but oh so proud. "So what do we do now?"

She waited for what seemed a long time before she answered. "We could contest it," she said, "but we wouldn't stand a chance. You couldn't find a sympathetic jury in this county right now and—and Judge Earl Humphries is sitting in the civil section of Circuit Court."

I'd forgotten but when Miss Elsie reminded me I knew my money was down the drain. Judge Thrace hated me and I sure didn't love him but I respected his knowledge of law; Judge Earl Humphries was an ignorant, bigoted stump-knocker who also happened to be Blanche's uncle. Long before I'd proved my general unworthiness, even as far back as when I was courting Blanche, her uncle had despised me.

Sure, I could fight Edmund Ruffin MacWhalen the Fourth but I stood no chance at all before Humphries without a jury and less than that with any jury that would be chosen from among the veniremen available in this judicial district.

"Wait a minute," I said. I reached back into my memory of law for an out. "That check they grabbed was for thirty-eight hundred dollars. That's less than five thousand. Wouldn't that put the case in the Court of Record?"

Miss Elsie shook her head mournfully. "The note is for six thousand, Francis."

Hoo boy, this was one of those days. "So what do you suggest I do?"

Miss Elsie hesitated. "I never thought I'd advise anyone to do a thing like this, least of all you, Francis, but I have to," she said slowly. "I hate to say this, Francis, but you—you've been hurt enough, your face and the Good Lord only knows what they'll do to you next. Francis, give up this thing. Whatever reason you might think you had to get mixed up in this terrible affair, let it go!"

"We were talking about my check," I said.

She nodded and looked down at her hands. "I've no authority to promise anything," she said carefully, "but if you could see your way clear to leaving Lindsley, I'm pretty sure William could prevail on Edmund and his father to drop the action."

I thought that over. "Maybe The Committee will give William a gold star for his fine work, too," I said.

She looked mad. "You've no right to say that," she snapped. "If you had any idea of how hard William worked to clear up your affairs—"

"Okay, okay," I said. "I'm sorry. Sure, Bill did a lot for me and I'm grateful. But that was eight years ago and everything around here has changed. Whose side is Bill on now?"

"Your side," she said stoutly. "As much as I am."

"And so he won't even speak to me," I said.

"He's provoked right now but he'll get over it. He thinks you're being bull-headed and he's afraid you'll hurt a lot of people, including yourself."

"And if I quit, Bill Carter speaks to me again, huh?" I asked. "But that would be a little tough on Coralee, wouldn't it?"

"Coralee," Miss Elsie snorted.

"Uh-huh, Coralee. Let's not forget Coralee. What happens to her is a lot more important than what happens to me when you come right down to it."

"How can you say such a thing?" she cried. "A no-count nigra girl. You're a Coombs!"

"A lush," I corrected. "A lush who's had it. Coralee—well, maybe Coralee's not much, either, but she's young, she's healthy, she's full of life. She deserves more than what somebody framed her for, for some reason."

There was a silence and then Miss Elsie asked, "Do you really believe she's innocent, Francis? Or is all this just your chance to strike back at all the people who hurt you?"

I'd always had to be honest with Miss Elsie. "I don't know, for sure," I said after awhile. "But I can't see Jack Taggart messing around like that even though the rest of you don't seem to have had any trouble believing it."

Miss Elsie was an old maid, after all, and her face showed her embarrassment. "It didn't come easy, believing that of Jack Taggart. Of all the young men I ever knew he was one of the last I'd believe it of. But it happened, Francis. We were all horrified but—"

"How is everybody so sure it happened? Did somebody catch them at it?" I asked bluntly.

Her face went rigid with repugnance and she twisted uncomfortably in her chair. "I don't know," she murmured, "Ask some of his friends, they'll tell you. How would I know such a thing?"

"Well, how about Coralee?" I asked. "Does she fit the picture any more than Jack?"

Her mouth pinched again. "Coralee's always been in trouble with her drinking," she said. "Aside from that, she's always been a—a discontented sort of girl. Yes, I'd say she fits the picture. And it was her gun. How can you remove that from the picture, Francis?"

"What about that gun?" I asked. "Did the police know she had a gun, a colored girl with a drinking record?"

"No, of course they didn't know. The idea."

"And still she admitted it was hers? That's funny."

"Well, they found her fingerprints all over it. Besides, she didn't actually say it was hers. She said that man she was married to, that worthless Tampa nigra, owned the gun to begin with."

"The mysteriously missing Juan Guturez," I said.

She looked surprised. "You know about him?"

"Only that he dropped out of sight one night. Did anybody ever find out what happened to him?"

Miss Elsie sniffed. "What do you suppose happened? He got tired of Coralee's carrying-on and he just walked out on her, most probably. You know how they are, always leaving their wives or husbands and then getting married again without bothering to get a divorce. Disgraceful. And they say we should treat them as though they were as good as—" She broke it off. "When you talked to her, did she tell you that ridiculous story about finding a bottle of whiskey somebody'd left her, just sitting there waiting to get her so drunk she wouldn't know anything that happened?"

I nodded. "Maybe that story's a little too crazy to be a lie, have you ever thought of that?"

"Regardless of what it is, how will it sound to a jury?" Miss Elsie asked. "Do you think you could make a hostile jury believe it?"

I could just imagine myself trying. It would be murder. I could see the jury—every man and woman hating me and lying in their teeth about not having formed an opinion so they could show me how much they hated me by voting guilty on the first ballot. I could hear Judge Thrace tittering from the bench. And Coralee being led off to spend the rest of her life in prison, very possibly to become the first woman hanged in Florida.

"Maybe something will come up." I sighed and got up from my chair. Halfway to the door I remembered Chet Leonard's advice that I ask Bill Carter something I wanted to know.

"Just for my information," I asked, "where did Jack get the money to buy back Spring Bayou and all the furnishings that were sold at auction?"

Her face never had too much color; now it went white. She licked her lips and looked around the office as though trying to find inspiration. I slowly walked back to her desk, starting to get the idea.

"He didn't," I said softly. "Blanche bought it back herself, didn't she?"

Miss Elsie looked miserably at her hands on the top of the desk.

"Was there ever an auction?" I asked. "I wondered why Bill rushed me out of town a couple of days before the sale. Were all those bum checks and forged documents and the other crimes I committed when I was plastered all part of a nightmare, too?"

"Oh, Francis, Francis," she cried softly. "You mustn't. William and I didn't let you know about it because we agreed that it would only make you feel worse."

"What happened?" I asked harshly. "Was there an auction?"

She nodded. "Yes, but not the way we'd planned. You remember we'd advertised that everything was to be sold and then, the night before the auction, Blanche came to William and said she had the money to pay off your obligations. She said her family had gotten together and raised the money—all the Humphries in these parts—to keep her from losing her home."

"*My* home," I said.

"Yes, of course. When Blanche burst this bombshell William said she couldn't do it, that the sale was advertised. The auctioneer wouldn't permit it, there were strict laws about such things."

"But that wouldn't stop Blanche," I muttered.

"No, it didn't. She got everybody, Judge Humphries and the General and Judge Thrace, too, I guess, everybody who was a friend of the Humphries or owed the General a favor, and they found loopholes enough to make the auction cover just a few items." Tears showed in her eyes. "Most of the things that were auctioned were yours, Francis, your guns and fishpoles—"

"Rods," I said idiotically.

"Rods, then, and—and things like that. William and I were there, of course, but I made William take me home. I couldn't bear it."

"Oh, come, come," I said. "You admire clever people and Blanche was very clever. She wanted Spring Bayou and she got it. Of course she had to live with me a few years and that wasn't easy. You might even say she earned it. She bided her time and watched me get drunker and drunker—even helped me get drunker and drunker—and when everything caught up with me and I had to blow she was right there with her piggy bank. Why, I think what Blanche did was very, very clever."

Miss Elsie said evenly, "Maybe she deserves that, Francis, but you left out one thing. Blanche loves Spring Bayou, yes, but she loved you, too, until you—until you drank her love away."

One thing about an alcoholic; he can blame everybody and everything for what happens to him. He can rationalize and twist and turn and squirm and wriggle to avoid the truth, but when it's given to him as Miss Elsie gave it to me, it's branded on what's left of his soul. All his shouting that it didn't happen that way at all, it was altogether different, can't dim the realization that it *is* the truth, nor ease the pain one bit.

4

When I came out of Miss Elsie's office I was wrung out, empty, ready to quit. But when I walked through the reception room I heard the soft voice of Judith Williamson call my name.

There was a woman in one of the Danish easy chairs waiting to see somebody so she got up from behind her desk and walked over to where I'd stopped near the door. She was taller than I remembered, flat-backed, full-breasted, and she smelled good when she came close.

"Mister Coombs," she said in a low voice, "perhaps this is out of place but I just wanted you to know that I—I have a great deal of admiration for what you're doing."

I guess I goggled at her, if a man with one slightly puffed eye and an assortment of bruises can goggle.

She was embarrassed. "I just want to wish you luck," she said.

Luck, I needed a whole lot of luck to get through the next hour sober. But this girl had brought it. "Miss Williamson, you're a wonderful thing for a man like me to have happen to him at a time like this. I thank you."

"Why, you're welcome," she said.

"And I assume you know Lindsley well enough to confine your good wishes to here and now. I wouldn't want you to get your feelings hurt by spreading this admiration around and about."

I saw now that her eyes had a touch of violet. They may have sparked a little with defiance or it may have been my imagination. "I'm not afraid to tell anybody where I stand on anything," she said, a bit louder than before.

"That's a good way to be. But not in Tangerine County when it's a matter of taking a stand with Frank Coombs. Where are you from, Miss Williamson?"

"What difference—"

"Maybe I'm just curious," I said. "I know you're not a native of Lindsley. I would have noticed a girl like you around Lindsley even if you were six years old and wore braces on your teeth when I left. But you're not from the north, are you?"

She shook her head, her eyes amused. "I'll make a guess then. Miami?"

She shook her head. "I'm from Dunedin. It's—"

"Oh, I know Dunedin," I broke in. "I've played golf there on the P.G.A. course. I've always liked Dunedin. Knowing you're from there, I shall ever hold it dear in my memory. I really do thank you for your good wishes and I—"

"Oh, Judith, dear," Miss Elsie called from the mouth of the corridor to her office. "Can you take some dictation from Mister Carter, please?"

Judith Williamson was all cool, efficient business. "Of course, Miss Elsie," she said and bid me goodbye. I left the office with a light step that was almost macabre, all things considered, and headed for the State's Attorney's office, even though I knew that it was a waste of time.

The usual procedure, when a lawyer takes a case late, was for the S.A.'s office to furnish him with a list of the State's witnesses and the police file on the case plus any other information that might help the defense get its case in shape.

It was strictly a matter of courtesy; under the law all the state had to do was give the defense the list of witnesses it intended to call. Ordinarily, though, a Lindsley lawyer in good standing could get almost everything he asked for, up to and sometimes including a transcript of the grand jury proceedings against his client.

I expected little cooperation from the men and women who'd worked under Jack Taggart but I owed it to Coralee to make the try. I guess I owed it to myself, too, to walk into that courthouse and face those people if only to prove I wasn't kidding myself, that my cause was right and I was willing to face anything.

Hooray for Frank Coombs.

I got a lot of hard looks and no greeting from the crowd around the coffee and coke stand run by old Jake Benefield, the blind veteran from World War One, as I went up the steps to the State's Attorney's office on the second floor. The perennial State's Attorney's secretary, Mabel Kershaw, was still at her desk just inside the counter, older than God and twice as fearsome.

"What do *you* want?" she asked acidly.

"Hello, Miss Mabel." She stared at me as though a cottonmouth moccasin had tipped its hat to her. "I'd like to see somebody about the Coralee Preston case," I said. "Briley handled the arraignment so I suppose he's the one—"

"They're all busy," she snapped. The telephone rang and she grabbed it. It wasn't for her but she made a production of informing whoever it was that the party they wanted was away on vacation. When she'd strung this out as long as she could, Miss Mabel finally hung up and went back to her papers. I waited awhile.

"Miss Mabel, pardon me all to hell for daring to thrust myself into your hallowed presence this way but I've got to have some information about the Coralee Preston case. If everybody's as busy as you say you'd better get that list of witnesses out of the file yourself because I'm not about to be pushed around."

It was quite a mouthful. It left me out of breath and Mabel Kershaw stunned speechless. While she gaped at me I went on, "I don't think Judge Thrace would like it if a trial in his court was scrubbed out at Lakeland because the State's Attorney's secretary refused to follow proper legal procedure and kept witnesses' names from me."

She glared at me, then snorted and got up and flounced into an inner office. She slammed the door behind her and I could hear her, shrill with indignation, telling somebody what I'd dared say to her. I waited, wondering what was going to happen next.

There was quite a wait and I was beginning to wonder what I'd do if everybody in the State's Attorney's office simply stayed out of sight and left me standing there. I could lift the flap in the counter and go inside and start banging on those closed doors, demanding to be heard, but wouldn't that constitute trespass if this bunch wanted to make it trespass, or even breaking and entering?

They finally sent out ancient Jimmy Nicholson, the clerk of Judge Thrace's court. Jimmy had never been a big man and age had withered him until now he was a bent-over midget. But he was full of fire when he came stumping out with a sheet of yellow legal pad paper in his hand. He threw it at me and snarled, "There you are, you—you *Yankee!* Now get out of here."

"Why, Jimmy," I said, "I always stand up when they play "Dixie" and tears come to my eyes whenever anybody even mentions the name of Robert E. Lee. How come you're calling me a Yankee?"

"Get out, you damn nigger-lover," the old man shouted. "Stinkin' Communist, that's what you are."

I'd called Emmert Young a Commie and he'd laughed at me but I couldn't laugh at poor old Jimmy. Instead, I leaned over the counter. "If you weren't so old and a half-pint halfwit to begin with, I'd come in there and slap the meanness out of you, old man."

I turned around and walked out of there, disgusted with myself. Threatening little Jimmy Nicholson—big hero.

Outside, in the corridor, I looked over the list. Most of the names were those of sheriff's deputies and city cops who'd been there when they found Jack Taggart. Then, next to last, was a name that surprised me some. MacWhalen, Edmund R., IV. No address but I'd already been told that by Fred Mosely, Something-something, Some-thing Drive, Riviera Estates, County of Tangerine.

I wondered just what kind of evidence the General was having Cousin Eddie offer in the case of Coralee Preston. I decided that it might be worth-while to go out there, wherever it was, and find out if I could. If I could get Cousin Eddie alone, without his old man there to tell him what to say and do, there was a slim chance I could make him tell me things. Growing up together he'd always been afraid of me and later, as young men, I'd had the Indian sign on him.

It was a thousand to one shot. And if I made any attempt to talk him out of grabbing my precious check it might wind up with me taking a swing at him and being tossed in the white section of the same jail that held my client, Coralee Preston. But I confess that at that moment I didn't much care.

I checked my watch and saw it was too close to lunch time to visit the jail. And Henry Taggart's office probably would give me the same treatment I'd gotten at the State's Attorney's. Lunchtime was the worst time to try the sheriff's office; some junior subordinate who'd welcome the chance to get tough with me was almost certain to be in charge. I told myself I might as well drive out to Cousin Eddie's.

If he wasn't home, maybe I could see Laurie. Somehow, knowing

Laurie, I depended on her to be different from all the others even though I was defending the girl accused of murdering her brother. Tangerine County may have changed completely in the past eight years but for some reason I believed that Laurie would still be the same Laurie.

I walked down to Bentley's Drugstore for a sandwich but one look at the crowd at the fountain convinced me that I wasn't quite that brave yet.

I bought a pack of cigarettes instead and when Charley Inglis slid them across the counter to me, frozen-faced, I asked, "Charley, where's Riviera Estates? It's a new one on me."

He looked at me as though I were a tourist in shorts with no shirt and with a Confederate flag and a SEE ROCK CITY sticker on my car.

"We sell maps of Lindsley and Tangerine County, twenty-five cents, or you can get a free one at the Chamber of Commerce right down the street." He paused a second. "Or maybe you'd rather trade at The Leader."

The Leader was Lindsley's colored general store on the edge of the Grove. I swallowed what I wanted to say and gave Charley a quarter and a penny tax for a map of the town and county the Coombs family founded. Walking out of Bentley's I came face to face with the beautiful Miss Williamson.

"Hello," she said. "I was just going to have lunch." She looked at the packed counter in Bentley's and then back at me. Her chin started to come up, her eyes began to take on that defiant look again. "I wonder if you'd like to—"

"I'm sorry, I've eaten," I lied quickly. "What are you trying to do, lose friends and antagonize people, for God's sake?"

"No, I just don't think it's right that they should treat you like this because you're trying to help that girl."

"There's more to it than that," I said. "Believe me, these people think they have every right to hate me and perhaps they have. I certainly worked hard enough at it."

She looked at me for a moment out of those clear, beautiful, faintly violet eyes. "When are you going to stop beating yourself over the head with a club?" she asked coolly. "So you made a mess of things a hundred years ago. Okay, as far as I can see, you've paid for it about sixteen times over. Why don't you give yourself a break and stop hating yourself so dramatically?"

"Thank you, Anne Landers." I bowed. Her lovely mouth tightened and she started to say something, changed her mind, and marched inside without a backward look. I went down the street toward the Princess. All the spring in my step I'd had earlier was long gone.

Johnbert Allison stopped me in the lobby when I came in. His big-lipped mouth was dragged down and his eyes were woeful. "I got some bad news fo' you, Mistuh Coombs."

"What have they done now?"

"I dunno who done it but somebody done slash yo' taars, all fo' of 'em. Besides which they tore out all the wirin' they could reach." He shook his head. "Firs' time 'at ever happen in the pahkin' lot, suh. Mistuh Chahles, he mighty opset about it."

We went out to the parking lot beside the hotel to look at my car, Johnbert and I. The tires weren't just slashed, they were shredded, and when I raised up the hood the wiring looked like spaghetti. I hoped Charles was insured.

"No," he said when we came back in. "Who'd ever think a man would need to be insured against vandalism right next to the hotel? We've been parking cars there since the place was built and this is the first time anything like this ever happened. Why, we've had people leave their valuables in unlocked cars and nothing was ever so much as touched."

"The Committee works in a juvenile delinquent's ways, its wonders to perform," I said bitterly. I looked at my old heap. If I bought four new tires, even retreads, it would make an awful hole in what was left of my bankroll.

"God damn them," I said. "Those five Crackers who beat me up at least had the guts to show their faces. They didn't sneak around at night and slash my tires like a dog-poisoner."

"I called Henry Taggart and told him what happened," Charles said.

"Goody," I said. "I'll bet that will be a big help. He probably busted his britches laughing."

"Don't say that, Frank. You're on opposite sides now and, sure, you're getting a raw deal. But Henry Taggart is still the best sheriff Tangerine ever had."

"God help our forefathers who had to put up with the worst, then," I muttered. I reached for my handkerchief to wipe the sweat off my forehead and felt the two-bit map I'd bought at Bentley's. I'd planned on having some lunch before I drove out to see Eddie MacWhalen but I sure didn't have any appetite now.

"Theron, how about lending me your car for a couple of hours until I can get mine fixed?"

He started to mumble something about his car heating up, something wrong with the water pump, but I cut him off. "My car was wrecked while it was on your parking lot," I reminded him. "It's the least you can do."

"I had a sign that said you park at your own risk," the old man said, "but it blew down and I forgot to put it back up. I'm not legally responsible, so long as it's not under my roof, you know."

"Mistuh Coombs, y'kin use my cah," Johnbert said suddenly. "Ain' much but you wekkum to it."

That hurt Charles' conscience or his sense of what was fitting or something and he said no need to do that. I could drive his car, the blue Olds, but take it easy on account of the water pump.

"Where's Riviera Estates?" I asked. "I never heard of it."

He gave me a look, his face twisted into a curious expression. "Riviera Estates? Guess they started that after you left town, come to think of it. It's—well, to tell you the truth, they made Riviera Estates out of your Uncle Alex's old place down by the river. Most stylish address anywhere around here now. They say they got three hundred dollars a front foot for the river lots." He gave me another took. "Shame you couldn't have hung onto it, Frank."

I said dully, "Yeah, it's too bad." Uncle Alex's place, Wide Run, the beautiful rolling acres that came down to the river in a sweep that made the big house one of the showplaces of that part of Florida. The empty house had burned down about three years before I had everything close in on me but I'd always told Blanche—well, not always; at first when I was a new husband—that Wide Run would sell for enough to send our kids through college and their kids, too, even if we had a dozen of them and each one of them gave us a passel of grandchildren.

Well, there hadn't been kid One, of course, and before the roof fell in I'd sold off the Alexander Coombs property, trying to keep my head above water.

I felt anger again but not for long.

"Gen'ral MacWhalen and his boy made a lot of money off it," Theron Charles was saying. "Developing Riviera Estates, I mean. Those people you sold it to were acting for the General and when you left he turned it over to Eddie and a big shot developer from the East Coast. They cleaned up on it."

I didn't say anything. What was the use? But I told myself that seeing that the General and his gang had made so much money off of my thirst it was a wonder they couldn't be a little kinder to me now.

5

I found that the MacWhalens and the big shot developer from the East Coast had transformed Uncle Alex's old place into a beautiful residential community. Whoever had been in charge of the landscaping had done a good job and he couldn't have been a Floridian because he'd left most of the big live oaks and pin oaks and gum trees standing instead of bulldozing everything flat. The shore of the river where I'd hunted ducks and caught big bass in my youth had been cleaned up some but not too much; the place retained the flavor of what it once had been, a sugar plantation before Union raiders in a gunboat burned the mill and after that a gentleman's ranch that never met expenses but made possible one of the best tables in the State. My Uncle Alex, a bachelor, had been a locally famous eater and drinker right up to the day he was killed in a hunting accident.

I didn't have any trouble finding Cousin Eddie's new home. I turned up a circular gravel drive and parked the Olds in front of a tall, brass-knockered front door. A colored butler I'd never seen before answered the door. When I asked him if Mr. MacWhalen was in he said he'd see, would I step in, sir, and what was the name, please? I gave him my name and wondered where this Negro was from; every colored person in Tangerine must know who I was by this time. I also wondered how any Negro could work for Eddie MacWhalen whose old man ran an outfit dedicated to keeping Negroes in the "place" the General thought proper for them. Then I laughed at myself: for five bucks a week over scale almost anybody would work for almost anybody else.

I followed the butler into a perfectly decorated, deliciously cool room with a glass wall on the river side. When the butler departed noiselessly, I went over to the window and looked out at the river, remembering a lot of things.

I stood there quite awhile before I heard Laurie MacWhalen's musical laugh behind me. "Well, hel-*lo*, Frank. Long time no see and all other suitable cliches. Welcome to Sleepy Hollow Heights. What can I fix you?"

I turned and there was little Laurie in stretch pants that moulded her perfect legs and a sweater that proudly exhibited every line of her, firm, small-breasted, incredibly young. A whole flock of years had passed since the days when she was at Rollins and I was at Gainesville and we'd been so sure there'd never been a love like ours nor ever would be again. Physically, at least, Laurie was still the same girl— slender, vibrant, pretty in a gamin sort of way.

I knew I'd hurt her when I'd fallen so completely for Blanche Humphries even though she'd refused to show it. Soon after, to my surprise and the horror of the Humphries family, Eddie MacWhalen and Laurie eloped. That was fourteen years ago, more or less, and from the size of this house, plus other considerations, it looked as though Eddie and Laurie had made a pretty good thing of it.

I watched her move across the big room toward a long, low cabinet against the wall.

"I suppose you're still a bourbon and branch man, aren't you, Frank?" she asked. She pressed a button and the lid came up to reveal a row of bottles, glasses, mixers, everything a thirsty person could need.

"How 'bout that?" Laurie crowed over her shoulder. "I'm always expecting the damn thing to shoot off skyrockets and play 'Dixie' every time I press the button. Like those baseball scoreboards when some-body hits a home run."

She reached for a heavy crystal decanter and picked up a squat, thick tumbler.

"Pour yourself one, Laurie, but skip me this round," I said.

She looked at me over her shoulder, her eyebrows up. "Good God, don't tell me," she said after a pause. "Since when?"

"Since a couple of days ago. I found out that for some reason alcohol was raising hell with my sobriety. Must be my advanced years."

"Or the things they keep shooting off over at Cape Canaveral," Laurie added seriously. She put the bourbon decanter back and picked out another. "You don't mind if I stun my reflexes a little, do you?"

"Drink hearty," I said mechanically and watched her pour a man-sized dollop of gin into a glass and add a couple of lumps of ice.

"Sit down, Frank," she said over the rim of her glass. She dropped into the nearest chair and crossed her pretty legs in the skin-tight chartreuse pants. "You're really raising hell, aren't you?"

I sat down in a chair across the room from her. "Do you want me to try to explain why I'm doing what I'm doing?" I asked. "Or would I be wasting my time?"

"You don't have to tell me," she said briskly, almost cheerfully. "You don't think the wench killed Jack so you're defending her. Simple as that."

I couldn't detect a trace of bitterness or sarcasm in her voice. As much as Laurie must have loved her brother, she didn't apparently hate me for going to bat for Coralee.

Her next words shook me though. Still in that brisk voice she said, "I think you're crazy in the head but I love you for having the guts to stand up against His Exalted Highness, General MacWhalen. Let's talk about something else. How long's it been since we've seen each other?"

"Too long," I managed and cleared my throat. "You're looking fine, Laurie." I tried to remember whether she and Eddie had one kid or two or even three. "How are the kids?"

She squinched up her nose and laughed. "The *kid* is fine. She left for boarding school last week. She's quite the young lady."

She raised her glass and finished the gin, then got out of her chair with a characteristic scramble and headed for the bar.

I thought I heard a noise at the hall door and looked out there but nobody was in sight. "Is Eddie around?" I asked Laurie's straight back and round bottom. "I've got to see him. I haven't much time."

"Not enough time to talk to good ole Laurie?" she asked. The decanter clinked against her glass and the gin gurgled. "Why, when Andrew told me who'd come calling I said to myself, hot dog, we'll spend a pleasant afternoon talking over old times—the house-party at Captiva, the time we went up to Jacksonville for the Georgia game. Or at least *we started* for Jacksonville but on the way we decided there were better things to do than watch an ole football game. Remember?"

She turned from the bar and looked at my beat-up face. "Sorry, Franky. Well below the belt, huh? You caught me at a bad time. I was sitting around feeling sorry for myself when the doorbell rang."

She made a sweeping gesture with her free hand and encompassed the magnificent room with all its costly furnishings. "I'm as crazy as you are, Franky," she said. "Everything a woman could want—my God, I hear *that* often enough—beautiful home, wonderful daughter, a husband everybody admires, more clothes than I can wear, cars, and here I sit, weeping into my beer over poor little ole Laurie."

She looked at me again over the rim of her glass. "You know something?" she said. "If you hadn't jilted me, I wouldn't be the way I am and you wouldn't be the way you are. Did you ever think of that, Frank? Did you ever wonder what we could have done together if—"

"Cut it out!"

She squeezed her eyes tight shut and her face was wrinkled in a grimace of pain for a second, then when she opened them she was the old Laurie again. "What did you want to see Eddie about?" she asked pertly. "To ask him to have his sainted father call off the strongarm boys? Won't do you any good, Franky. Eddie wouldn't dare ask the General and the General wouldn't listen if he did."

"I wasn't going to ask him that," I said. "It was about that old sight draft everybody'd forgotten about until they hit me with it at the bank this morning."

"Sight draft? What's a sight draft?"

"A note that's payable on demand," I said. "Didn't you know about it?"

"How would I know about it? They don't tell me anything. But I listen—oh, I'm a good listener, Frank. I didn't know anything about any sight draft but I knew they were going to hit you with *something*. The two of them were mumbling around here 'til all hours the night you came to town."

"Laurie," I said softly. "This guy was your brother Jack. You of all people should know that this girl couldn't have killed him because he never—"

She had her head bent and she spoke rapidly, addressing the glass she held tightly with both hands. "I know, I know," she said. "Everything everybody whispered about Jack was a goddam lie. I keep telling myself that, Frank. I told you I was crazy—otherwise I wouldn't have such hard job believing in Jack."

She raised her head, her chin set, her eyes bright with unshed tears. "Okay, I'm with you, Franky. Just tell me how I can help and I'll be there. I'd like nothing better." She laughed in a way that chilled me. "Imagine the General when I get up on the witness stand and say this woman didn't do it because—well, because at that very minute she was eating with me at the lunch counter in the bus station."

"Laurie, for God's sake!"

She dabbed at her eyes. "I'm not very funny, am I?" she asked. "Don't mind me. Don't go away mad. Stay there and I'll buy you a Coke or a ginger ale or something. Or a beer—you can have a bottle of beer, can't you? Real fine imported beer, Frank?"

But I wanted out. I wanted to be away from this girl who looked just like the Laurie Taggart I'd known a long time ago but who now called herself crazy and talked as though she really were. I stood up. "I'm sorry, but I've got to—"

She was out of her chair again, her glass left behind on the end table, and across the room in one frantic bound. She grabbed both my arms and pressed herself against me so fiercely that I felt the twin pressures of her hard little breasts. "Don't leave me, Franky," she said in a low, intense voice. "You can't. For Christ's sake have a heart. You told me once you loved me, don't walk out on me now. I'm afraid of what I might do, Frank. Honest, I'm scared."

What can a man say to a woman in a situation like that? I'd come here hoping to get me my money back, and now this girl I'd once loved was begging me to help her, protect her—from what? Had Jack's murder really unhinged Laurie mentally or was the simpler explanation that she'd spent too much time at that ornate bar.

"Take it easy, Laurie," I said gently. "There's nothing to be afraid of. Not for you, of all people. Not the General's daughter-in-law."

She uttered a short, ugly word I'd never have believed her capable of saying. "Listen, Frank. You need money, don't you, to—to fight them? All the people who beat you down, the General, the Humphries, all the rest. I've got money. A whole lot of money. Let me give you what you need. I don't care if she did it—beating them is all I care about now. Just so somebody shows them that they can be hurt, too." She looked up at me and her eyes pleaded. "Please take the money, Frank."

I shook my head. "You don't mean that. You and Eddie had a fight about something and—"

"Oh, my God." She dropped her hands from my arms and turned away. "Eddie and I had a fight, he says. Don't you know he's afraid even to get in a fight with me, his own wife? I wish he would. I wish he'd blow his top, beat me up, anything but giving me that soft, silly, whimpering smile that says he's sorry. Sorry I'm such a bitch. Sorry he can't do anything—not one single god-damned thing—unless the General tells him it's all right."

She spread her hands. "This house, the cars, the horses, the money, do you think any of it's Eddie's? Or mine? Do you think his life belongs to him? Do you think he dares do anything on his own, even be a man? Why he doesn't even dare make love to me without—without my starting it!"

"Laurie."

"I'd feel sorry for him if he didn't try to justify it," she went on. "You ought to hear him, Frank. He chatters about this damned Committee of his father's being necessary because the Black Mohammedans will rape us all unless those poor ignorant Crackers follow orders and terrorize poor, helpless nigras—nigras that were our friends until the General turned senile and began to be afraid of them."

"The General afraid of nigras?"

She nodded vigorously. "Scared to death of them. I guess he imagines they're out to get him for all the things he's done to them over the years. The Black Mohammedans seem real enough to him. But Eddie—Eddie knows they're not real and he's afraid to say so. He's afraid of what that old man might do to him if he had the *balls* to say the whole business was a hallucination."

She walked over to an end table and picked up a cigarette from a crystal container. She snapped a lighter and puffed nervously before she swung around again. "The General has to be beaten, Frank, or else he'll lead all of us straight to hell. I wish you had something different to fight him with, something besides the girl who killed my own brother, but—"

"Laurie, you've got to believe me," I cut in. "Coralee didn't kill Jack. Regardless of the stories you heard, Jack wasn't messing around with her. My God, Laurie, you knew Jack better than that!"

"Did I?" she asked. Her voice was suddenly flat. "What do I know about any of you, even my own brother, when it comes to a thing like that?"

"What in hell are you talking about?"

"Why, nothing except that I thought I knew Eddie MacWhalen pretty well when I married him. I thought that if anything Eddie was a little too prissy about women but he showed me differently. If it hadn't been for Little Laurie, I'd have walked out. I should have anyway, I suppose, but the General talked me out of it. Think of the family name. It was regrettable but it was nothing that hadn't been done before by Southern Gentlemen." Her mouth went up at one corner. "I think it's called changing your luck, isn't it?"

"Eddie?" I said. "Eddie MacWhalen?"

"Eddie MacWhalen." She nodded. "Some—some *child* he got into his car somehow and took out the Bargo Road. The county patrol—oh, my God, it was so sordid and cruel, to the little colored girl, to me—"

She was crying at last, the tears running out the corners of her eyes and wetting her cheeks.

"Go away," she choked. "I don't want you to see me like this. Oh, Frank, why couldn't you have kept on loving me forever and forever the way you promised you would?"

Before I could say anything she whirled and ran out of the room, head down, her shoulders shaking under the tight sweater.

As I let myself out of that big, expensive house I asked myself the same question that Laurie had asked. But then I reminded myself that they'd still have been bottling eight-year-old bourbon even if I'd married Laurie Taggart. She might have gone by a different road, but she'd probably have eventually arrived at the same desperation she faced now.

Just before I got into Theron Charles' Olds I looked back at the face of the big house. A curtain at a second-floor window fell back into place as whoever had been holding it aside let go. That didn't necessarily mean that Eddie MacWhalen had been home all the time listening to his wife tell me what he really was. It could have been one of the servants peering out at this strange white man who opposed his own kind to fight for one of theirs.

I hoped it hadn't been Eddie. No matter what he was, no matter what his terror of his old man made him do—no man deserved hearing his wife tell another that kind of truth.

Chapter 5

It was during the drive back to Lindsley that the idea started gnawing at me, an idea that was crazy from the word go but which still persisted.

It was this: Laurie's disillusionment with her husband seemed to date back to the night when Edmund Ruffin MacWhalen the Fourth had been caught tampering with a female Negro minor by the county patrol.

Laurie had told me that this had happened when Little Laurie, who was away at school now, was a baby. Now the daughter was "quite the young lady." How old, twelve to fourteen?

Reverend Gail had mentioned that whatever had happened to Coralee Preston had occurred when she was thirteen or fourteen, roughly ten years ago. Could Eddie MacWhalen have been responsible for what had happened to Coralee?

I told myself, no. I didn't have anything else to go on so I was taking a sketchy coincidence in dates and trying to fit it to my own needs.

It was ridiculous—hell, wouldn't Hattie May have come crying to me if anything like that had happened to her precious Coralee? Of course Hattie May would have told me. Or had she and I'd been so drunk that it hadn't registered?

Or suppose the General's intervention had scared the child so badly that she hadn't even told her mother? Reverend Gail had said that he doubted Hattie May knew about the thing he'd refused to tell me. Could a little girl be frightened that badly? Not impossible if she'd been born with a black skin.

Now, wait a minute, I told myself. *You're building a story on nothing and even if it proves out, how could you use it? Suppose it was Coralee in Eddie's car when the county patrol flashed their spotlight on it, what difference does that make? Are you going to plead that the experience gave Coralee some kind of trauma that excuses her murder of Jack Taggart?*

I'd be serving no other purpose than inflaming the violent among the whites and possibly giving the more rebellious young Negroes an excuse to rise up and make the General's bogeyman a reality. Not probable, this last, but possible even in Tangerine County. There must be men on the Ridge and in the Grove who'd heard and read about the real Black Mohammedans.

For the old colored-white relationship which I had known (and my father and grandfather before me) was gone, swept away by outside forces after it had been warped and subverted by selfish men like the General. The white people of the Tangerine County I'd always known hadn't been cruel to or contemptuous of the colored. For more than two centuries the blacks and whites of that area had lived together in peace and friendship—always excluding the back-county Crackers such as the five who'd jumped me. Sure, nigras lived in shacks and worked for peanuts and their kids didn't get the right kind of schooling. And a nigra landed in jail when he got less drunk than a Tangerine County white man who might be driven home in a patrol car. White customers were waited on first in stores, even if colored patrons had been waiting far longer—yes, all these things were wrong in my day but they were the tired, tattered, soiled remnants of a system founded on inhumanity by men long dead. It was handed down to us and we didn't ask for it or want it, and it was up to us to try to modify, improve, remedy, as best we could.

I'm no apologist. I admit most of the charges leveled against my homeland by the intellectuals from New York and Chicago and all those other places that have solved this same problem in such an inspiring spirit of love. But I have to say in fairness that there was in Tangerine County, before The Committee, an understanding and a dependence of one group upon the other, which no one who never lived here—perhaps no one who wasn't born and raised here—could ever possibly understand.

I find myself falling back upon the threadbare thesis that unless you're a Southerner you can't *understand*. And I had such high hopes of making it all clear.

End of lecture.

As I came into town there was a crowd of people milling around the bus station on Tyler Street and half a dozen police cars, their blinkers flashing. I'd been stopped by a red light at the corner of Livingston and Tyler where two city cops, one straddling his motorcycle, were detouring traffic away from the bus station. Not that I wanted to go down there; I had an idea of what was going on.

Brother Emmett Young, he of the pearly teeth, had told me that his Organization for Relief of Suppressed Minorities wasn't going to stay out of the Coralee Preston case just because I'd told him to get lost. It looked like they'd come. But why the bus station? Had Young sent his advance skirmishers in as Freedom Riders?

The light changed then and the cops blew their whistles and waved savagely, trying to get the gawking, craning drivers on their way again. I knew it was the worst possible time to pay a visit to Henry Taggart but I didn't have the time to pick my spots.

I drove to the county jail. When I stopped at the barred gate I thought for a second that Bradbury wasn't going to buzz me through but he did.

"Thought you'd be down at the bus station with your niggers," he said in greeting. "Or do you just order them in to get pushed around while you keep outta sight?"

There was no use trying to change Bradbury's opinion of me so I said, "You'd better go on sick call quick. They might be Black Moham-medans."

"I sure wish they were," he grunted. "Time we stopped treatin' the black bastards with kid gloves." He grinned at me. "Some nigger-lovin' whites, too."

"You've got the badge and gun to do it, too," I said. I looked over at the open door of Henry Taggart's office. "Sheriff's down at the bus station, I suppose."

Bradbury nodded, still trying to come up with an answer to my last crack.

"How about Pret Newbern?"

"He's there, too. Why don't you go down there if you want to see 'em? Some people usta be friends of yours are in that crowd. They'd be right glad to give you a home-comin,' y'might say."

"How would you know who's in the crowd?" I asked. "The *Standard-Sentinel* hasn't come out with the story yet, has it?"

"Look, Coombs, I done my share of police work before I got my bad back," he blustered. "I ain't always been settin' here. And I can still handle a shyster lawyer if he tries to get wise with me. Don't you ferget that, neither."

While the big-mouth was sounding off I got out the list Jimmy Nicholson had thrown at me. I went down the column of names and picked a deputy who'd been at Coralee's house when she was arrested, a man named White, Thos. E. I didn't remember any White among Henry's deputies when I'd been in Lindsley.

"Deputy White around?" I asked.

Bradbury hated to admit it but he finally said he guessed White was around somewhere. He flipped a switch on the desk intercom and the P.A. system sent the name of Tom White echoing through the corridors. Pretty soon a slender kid with a short-cropped head of red hair and freckles came up the corridor and asked who wanted him.

Bradbury jerked a thumb at me. "He does," he grunted. "Gawd's gift to the N.A.A.C.P. He's the lawyer for that girl that killed Jack Taggart. He brought them niggers to the bus station, most likely."

The kid scowled at me and started to turn away. "I don't know nothin' about it," he said. "See the cap'n."

"Aren't you Fatso White's boy?" I asked before he could get away. He turned back, eyeing me curiously. "Yeah. You knew my father?"

"I used to know him pretty well," I said. I'd gotten old Fatso off a pretty bad hook one time when I had the charge reduced from second-degree murder to involuntary manslaughter. He was a nice old guy, Fatso, but Raiford was too much for him.

"Oh, hell, yes," Bradbury said. "He knows everybody in Tangerine County, Coombs does. Thing is, nobody wants to know him."

The boy gave Bradbury a glance and then turned back to me. "Coombs?" he asked. "You must be the lawyer that got me in Boys Ranch after—" His expression changed. "What did you want to see me about?"

"He prob'ly wants to sign you up in the N.A.A.C.P.," Bradbury said.

I'd had it up to here. I'd sworn I wouldn't let Bradbury get to me but he had. "Look, loudmouth, you'd better push that button of yours because I'm telling you either come out from behind that desk and get the hell kicked out of you or keep your goddam mouth shut."

Bradbury's hand flew up to his glasses in an instinctive gesture. Young White stepped between me and the desk. "You don't want no trouble with the corporal, Mister Coombs," he said. "We can talk in here."

He put his hand on my arm and led me into a little file room off the main lobby. He shut the door and leaned back against it, one hand hooked in his wide belt. "What did you want to see me about?"

"Did the sheriff's office analyze the whiskey they found in Coralee Preston's shack to see if it had been mickeyed?"

He shook his head. "Wasn't no likker. She claimed somebody gave her a jug but we couldn't find none. A few empties out back, three-four cans of beer in the icebox but no likker."

"What brand were the empties?"

He hunched his shoulders under the gabardine shirt. "You know what they drink, bootleg."

"But she said somebody gave her some good whiskey, didn't she?"

"She didn't make much sense, to tell you the truth," he replied. "She was awful drunk and when she saw Mister Taggart layin' there on the floor she started hollerin'. But she did tell the sheriff somebody gave her a jug. A brand new pint—two pints, she told him, as a matter of fact. But she didn't know who gave it to her and we sure didn't find no bottles around."

"You mean she got so drunk she passed out and there wasn't a bottle in the room when you got there?"

"Nossir, nary a bottle." The kid saw what was missing from the picture and raised a hand to scratch his head. "I reckon she must've threw the jug out the window or somethin', huh?"

"Could be," I agreed. "And somebody happened by who wanted an empty jug for some reason."

"Uh-huh," he nodded, but uncertainly.

"How did the alarm come through?"

Another shrug. "Somebody called the switchboard. They said there'd been a killin' at the girl's shack and a white man was involved, then hung up. Prob'ly some nigra who was scared of gettin' mixed up in it."

"Were you present when the sheriff questioned Coralee later?" I asked.

He gave me a funny look. "There wasn't much questionin,' Mister Coombs. The sheriff or nobody else."

"You mean to say—" I began.

"What the hell," he broke in, "would you have questioned her if you'd been Jack Taggart's uncle? Or maybe a fella that worked in the State's Attorney's office and liked him as much as they-all did? What was there to find out? It was all there, wasn't it? What's the sense in gettin' the whole lousy story? Mister Taggart—well, he made a bad mistake, is all, and he sure-gawd paid for it. No sense in getting all the dirty details."

"You mean everybody assumed the worst, right from the start? There weren't any questions raised about what Jack might have been doing there?"

Deputy White looked miserable, wanting to get away from me. "It wasn't—I mean a guy hears things sometimes. You don't believe the first guy that tells you and you call him a goddam liar. But then you hear it again and again and then all of a sudden—" He shrugged and swallowed hard. "And then you feel like the world's a big ole dirty sonofabitch and you don't know who or what to believe—"

He was through talking; he'd said too much already and he was sorry he'd spilled. "That's all I know about it," he said. "I gotta get back to duty."

He left me standing there in worse shape than ever. I'd been told by a lot of people why Jack Taggart was in Coralee's shack that day but for some reason it was this kid deputy's words that shook my faith the most. I told myself I could be wrong, all wrong. If Jack had changed that much, if there had been an open scandal that had made everybody accept Jack Taggart's murder out of consideration of those Jack left behind, I sure didn't belong here. In that case, I deserved to be hated.

2

But I had to keep going until I knew *for sure*. If I was on a wrong kick, I'd crawl out of Tangerine and never bother anybody again but I had to know. I had to get at the truth and I meant to get it out of Coralee Preston by any means.

I went back to Bradbury's desk and told him I wanted to see my client. He started to say no but before he had a chance there was a commotion at the entrance to the jail as they began bringing in the bus station demonstrators, a dozen of them. About half were colored and half white.

Sheriff Taggart led the way to the booking desk, his face old and sort of greyish when it should have been bright red with anger. He left the booking to Pret Newbern when he saw me and came over to Bradbury's desk. His voice was flat, dispirited. "Does it give you any pride to see these kids in trouble like this, Frank? Does it prove something to that ginhead of yours?"

He waved a hand toward the crowd in front of the booking desk. None of the prisoners could have been over twenty-one and most of them wore a glow of triumph. One of the white girls and a colored boy had cuts on their faces and several of the others sported visible lumps.

"Where'd you get 'em?" the sheriff asked. "God knows they're none of 'em from around here. The white kids talk like Yankees and these nigras ain't Tangerine nigras. How'd you get 'em here so fast?"

"I didn't bring them here, Sheriff," I said. "The last thing in the world I want right now is anything like this."

"It'll help your appeal, won't it? Impossible for you to get a fair trial if there's a riot going on outside the courtroom," he said scornfully.

The prisoners started singing, something about burying Jim Crow and don't fear the Gestapo. The words were set to an old football fight song I'd once grown sick of while being trampled into the turf at Gainesville and other stadia on our schedule, goddaming the rooters who urged us to give our all against clubs that could have beaten the New York Giants when Charley Connerly was young and quick.

The girls threw their lank, disordered hair back from their thin, intense faces and screamed the song; the young nigras sang defiantly, belligerently, as though expecting a club across the backs of their heads at any moment. Only two of the white youths seemed uncertain about what they were doing. They looked almost apologetic, as though they didn't really want to be doing this but they had to or be called chicken by the others.

"Listen to 'em," Taggart growled. "We just had to beat the hell out of four-five good, upstanding citizens to get these kids away in one piece and they're singing about us being Gestapos. I'd Gestapo 'em if they belonged to me—right across the seat of their pants."

He left me and walked to the window, looked out and came back, scowling more deeply. "Y'might know," he said, as though to himself, and tipped the switch on Bradbury's intercom. "White, Freeze, Lisles," he barked. "Get over to the square and break up that crowd. Tell 'em to go on home, the show's over."

Henry straightened up and shook his big-hatted head. "Not that it'll do any good. They'll just get together again around the corner and those city police . . ." He glared toward the desk. "Haven't you got those people booked yet, Captain?" he bellowed.

"Right away," Pret called back. "Finishing up the last one."

I took a deep breath. "Henry," I said, "I have to talk to you."

"Well, I don't have to talk to you," he answered. "You here to see that woman? Well, go see her. Me, I've got more important things to do than talk to you. I've got to try to keep down the real trouble you've brought this town."

Before I could say anything he turned to Bradbury. "Give this man an hour with that woman, no more. And have the switchboard get me city police headquarters on the phone."

He stalked into his office and banged shut the door before I could say another word.

I heard Bradbury snicker. Just then one of the white girls broke loose from the line and scurried across the room toward me. She thrust her young, pretty face up at mine and bawled, "Justice for Laura Lee, you lousy cop!"

A deputy was right behind her and he grabbed her by the arm and pulled her back to the desk, her feet dragging. Bradbury gave a horse laugh. "Laura Lee—that's a hot one. Whyn't you at least give 'em the right name when you hired 'em?"

"I picked them for weight, mostly," I snapped. "I figured she'd be just about the right size for you to give a real working over."

He opened his mouth to make rebuttal and I said quickly: "Where's the visitors' book for me to sign? You heard the sheriff."

He shoved it over, grumbling about what he'd like to do to me.

3

Gibby led me out of the coolness back to the stifling cell where Coralee was kept. She was lying on her bunk in a clean blue dress and her perfume was dizzying in the airless cell. She'd fixed her hair and daubed on lipstick and I made a mental note to make sure she didn't have any on when she went to court.

There were three unopened cartons of cigarettes under Coralee's bunk and an opened one beside her. In spite of the clean clothes, the cigarettes, the lipstick, the hairdo and the shower she must have been allowed, my client was no more gracious than she'd been the day before.

"I 'spects you this mawnin'," she said peevishly. "I waited all mawnin' and you never come aroun'."

"I was busy. Are they treating you all right?"

"I reckon so," she sniffed.

"'At ole Gibby, he peeken at me in the showuh but I tole him I'd tell the cap'n and he go way." She touched her hair, found a compact somewhere and inspected her makeup, grimacing into the mirror. "You reckon you could git me a reg'lar lookin' glass and a 'lectric fan?"

"No," I said. "I want to ask you some questions, Coralee, and I want straight answers."

She touched her hair, her eyes on the compact. "Mo' questions," she murmured. "I already tole you everything I know." She snapped the compact shut and blew out through her painted lips. "Sho is hot in heah. Sho wisht I c'ld have me a 'lectric fan."

"You'd better get used to it," I said. "They don't have any electric fans up at Raiford, either. Only a big electric chair."

That jarred her. Her head came up and she stared at me, her eyes big, her mouth open. "What you mean, Mistuh Coombs?"

"I mean I'm tired of you acting so high and mighty, as though you were doing me a favor letting me talk to you. There's a whole county outside there wanting to see you put in that electric chair."

She glanced toward the high barred window in sudden terror.

"And they might see it happen, too, unless you tell me the truth, Coralee."

"Mistuh Coombs, I sweah to Jesus—"

"Never mind swearing to Jesus," I cut in. "Just tell me the truth. No matter how bad it is, understand?"

She nodded mutely, her eyes fixed on me. For the first time since I'd gotten into this mess, Coralee was really scared.

"I tell you everything you want to know, I sweah—"

I sat down on the stool and lowered my voice so that Gibby or some other big-eared character couldn't possibly hear what I said. "Coralee, when you were a little girl about fourteen or fifteen years old you had a big trouble."

Her eyes lost their immediate panic and in its stead there came a look of wary dread. The penitentiary and its execution chamber were terrible to contemplate but they were abstract horrors. What was reflected in Coralee's eyes now was something closer to home, something already experienced.

She wet her lips with her tongue, pale pink against the crimson of her lipstick. "Ain' never happen to me, Mistuh Coombs," she croaked. "Nossuh, ain' me. Mus' been somebody else."

I got up off the stool and took a couple of steps toward the door. "If you won't talk to me, there's no use in my staying."

For a minute I thought she was going to let me go. I got to the door and wondered what my next move could be. If Coralee refused to talk, if she considered her old secret even more dangerous than the threat of Raiford's electric chair, I was finished.

I ached to have her speak, say anything, even repeat her denials, but the cell behind me was silent except for her hoarse breathing. I wanted to turn around, plead with her to talk, but I knew that wouldn't work. I'd lose her completely.

"Gibby!" I called down the corridor. "You, Gibby!"

There was the shuffle of Gibby's feet off down the long corridor. I dreaded his approach; once he let me out of this cell there'd be no place to go.

Then came Coralee's hoarse whisper. "Oh, my Gawd, Mistuh Frank, don' go 'way and leave me without *nothin'!* I tell you anything you want to know, I don' care what. But please-Gawd, don' go 'way and leave me all alone!"

She'd surrendered, finally, and I could get the truth out of her. I sagged against the bars with the strange joy that surged through me and then I straightened just as Gibby came around the corner. "Never mind," I called to the turnkey. "I've changed my mind."

He wanted to grumble out loud but he didn't dare. He had to content himself with showing his contempt in a grunt as he turned and shuffled off. I went back to the stool and sat down. Coralee was crouched on the edge of her bunk, looking down at her hands twisting in her lap.

"Now, what happened, Coralee?" I asked softly.

She hesitated a moment but not from reluctance, rather to give herself time to choose her words. "Ain' easy to talk about, Mistuh Coombs," she said. "Ain' even easy to *think* about."

"It was a long time ago," I prompted. "You were a little girl. Nobody could blame you."

She shook her head, glistening with hair dressing. "Ain' what they tole me," she murmured. "They tole me I c'ld—I c'ld git locked up in the bad house twell I was twenny-one. Is what they said."

"Who said, Coralee?"

There was agony in her eyes as she looked up at me. "She'iff Taggart," she whispered. "Him and Gen'ral MacWhalen, bofe."

I had expected, almost hoped, that the General had been involved but when Coralee mentioned Henry Taggart's name I felt sick. *A big ole dirty sonofabitch of a world,* the White kid had said, *and you don't know who or what to believe in.* Henry Taggart, the man I'd once called Uncle Henry, had frightened a mistreated little colored girl into silence to protect the man he should have jailed.

"Tell me what happened," I said. "Take it slow. Don't worry, nobody's going to hurt you for telling me."

She was looking at her pink-palmed hands again, examining them carefully. "Well, I was a litty ole guhl, like you says, and one night Mama, she say I kain't go to a pahty over on the Ridge so I snuck out. I was comin' home late, pas' midnight, and this gemmun in this cah, he pass me and then he stop and when I come alongside he—he ast kin he drive me home. A white gemmun and I was skeered 'cause I know it ain' right so I said no thank you, suh, but he say git in, git in, he wasn't gonna huht me and I seed who it was. It was—" She broke off and looked up at me. "Is I gotta tell you who it was, Mistuh Coombs?"

"I think I know," I said. "It was young Eddie MacWhalen, wasn't it?"

She nodded dumbly and looked down at her hands again. "So fin'lly I got in and—and he din't drive me home. 'Stead of that, he druv out in the country and he stopped the cah and I was so skeered I couldn' do nothin' and—and—" She put her hands up to her face and made an animal sound that chilled my blood.

"Never mind the rest," I said huskily. "I know about it, how the county patrol picked you up. Did they bring you here to jail, Coralee?"

She took her hands down to show her face, strangely swollen in that one brief, wretched moment. "Nossuh, they taken me, us to the she'iff's house, where he lives at. The po-liceman, he taken me 'round to the side doah and they set me in a lil room with a deer haid on the wall and the she'iff, he talk with Mistuh Eddie MacWhalen a long time and—"

She sniffed and dabbed at her nose with a knuckle.

"Then the she'iff he come back with Gen'ral MacWhalen and they bofe treated me mighty hahd, Mistuh Coombs, so hahd I liken to die I was so skeered. They tole me iffen I tole *anybody* what happened, even Mama, they gonna find out and put me in the bad house twell I'm twenny-one, it's the law."

She probed the pocket of the blue dress until she found a handkerchief, stained with crimson lipstick. She blew her nose and replaced the handkerchief before she went on.

"So I never tole Mama, even when she licked me fer stayin' out so late. I never tole nobody 'ceptin' Rev'rend Gail." Her mouth curved cynically in recollection, "Time they had the big tent meetin' revival 'at time. I thought I gotten the sperrit, and I tole Rev'rend Gail. He said he wouldn't never tell nobody but it looks like he did."

"No, he didn't, Coralee. He told me you had trouble but he wouldn't say what it was even though he knew it might help you. He said he'd given his word not to."

She examined me and nodded, satisfied that she hadn't been betrayed. "So that's all they was," she said. "They wasn't no—I mean nothin' happened on account of it. I din't fergit it but the she'iff he never bothuhed me none about it or nothin'."

"Until your husband disappeared."

I caught the flash of terror in her eyes again as her head jerked up. I met her stare and she looked down at her lap again. "Look like you know ever'thing," she muttered. "Why you gotta ast me things when you know, Mistuh Coombs?"

"Because there's a lot I don't know. Where did your husband go the night he disappeared, Coralee?"

This wasn't much easier for her than telling the story of the night Eddie MacWhalen picked her up. She made a couple of false starts before she murmured, "I don' reckon he never was no good, Who-awn wasn't, but I loved 'at man. I don' reckon he'd even ma'ied me iffen Mama hadn' caught us and made him, sort of. But he was fun, Mistuh Coombs. He was the *bes'* dancer and he could always make me laugh. But he was mean, too, when he wanted to be."

"How did he find out about Mister Eddie MacWhalen?" I asked.

"We was drinkin' one time and I reckon I tole him when I din't hahdly know what I was doin'. Leastwise the next day he tole me what I said and he ast me a miyyun questions about it and Mistuh Eddie MacWhalen. I din't know what he was gonna do, Mistuh Coombs, I sweah to Jesus I din't, not at first."

Her face twisted and I thought she was going to cry again. "I *tole* him he'd git us in bad trouble but he did it anyway. He went to Mistuh Eddie MacWhalen and he come back with a lot of money. He got it fer promising not to tell nobody what happened."

Poor spineless Cousin Eddie. Whom did he think Juan Guturez would tell? Who would have listened to a lippy Tampa nigra's story of an old crime that actually was not so evil according to most Tangerine County standards, unless its principals had been reversed?

Coralee had fallen silent so I had to prompt her again. "What happened then?"

"I knows I oughtn't to but—Mistuh Coombs, you don' know what it's like to have a lot of money when you never had none. And Who-awn, he say that nex' time he gonna get enough so's we kin go to New Yawk and live there. So I holt my tongue." She considered her error gravely and added, "The likkuh, it he'p."

"Yes," I said, as gravely, "it does, doesn't it? And so Juan went to Mister Eddie MacWhalen for more money and this time he didn't come back, is that it?"

She nodded and then looked up suddenly, her fear replaced by a fierce need to make me believe her. "'At gun they found 'side of Mistuh Jack Taggart," she said. "Who-awn he taken 'at gun with him the night he went to c'lect the money f'm Mistuh Eddie MacWhalen. I sweah to Jesus he did."

So there it was, or most of it. I should have felt satisfied, even happy. I'd won something even if it was torn to pieces, trampled in the dirt, thrown out as ridiculous when I took it into court. I knew now that I hadn't let booze betray me into one last outrage against my relatives and friends of Tangerine County.

I should have been happy but I felt old and tired and sick. Maybe I'd saved Coralee from the electric chair but the price was too high. I felt a sudden anger at this girl's long silence.

"For God's sake, why didn't you tell somebody all this before?" I asked. "Why did you wait 'til now to tell the truth? If you'd told somebody, Mister Jack Taggart wouldn't have had to investigate on his own and be killed for it."

"Who could I tell twell now, Mistuh Coombs?" she asked. Her voice was low and infinitely sad. "Who gonna listen to Coralee say

bad things about Mistuh She'iff Taggart and Mistuh Gen'ral Mac-
Whalen?"

4

When I got back to the front of the jail there was all hell busting loose,
inside the building, outside and overhead. A late afternoon thunderstorm was cracking and rumbling and the rain was sluicing down with
that hissing roar peculiar to Florida line squall showers. It was audible even though the windows were closed and the air-conditioning
was humming. And in spite of the loud talking all around me.

The talking had to do with the people who were back in the courthouse yard across the street. I went to a front window for a quick look
at the crowd and saw the men who could be expected to be there, the
woolhats brought out of the hammock by some summons, sent or
mysteriously sensed, to loose their vengeance on the Yankee nigger-
lovers and the uppity nigras who'd come into town to start trouble.
There they stood, the lightning flashing on their glistening faces,
oblivious to the near-cloudburst that plastered their shirts to their
lean, sun-scorched bodies and turned their sleazy khaki pants dark
with wet, filled their cheap, run-over quarter-boots. They didn't talk
among themselves, they didn't move around much, they simply gathered under the live oaks or out in the open when the sheltered places
grew too crowded and waited.

For what? They weren't sure. Some of them had driven twenty
miles or more to be there without knowing more than that somebody
was trying to start something that would encourage nigras to make
free with white folks.

I turned back from the window to face Pret Newbern, ten feet tall
and somber as an archangel. "Did you have anything to do with this,
Frank?" he asked. He jerked his head back toward the cell block
where the white members of Emmert Young's little band were quar-
tered. "Is Henry right about you calling in these people?"

"You know better than that, Pret," I said. "Henry Taggart does, too."

The chief deputy considered this and finally nodded. "I didn't
figure you for that kind," he acknowledged, "but Bradbury said one of

the kids knew you. He said she spoke to you while they were being booked."

"No," I answered, "I don't know them. Never saw any of them before in my life, so far as I know. But I do know who brought them into town. A fellow named Young, Emmert Young, called on me at the hotel this morning and offered to help out with Coralee's case. He said he represented some bunch called the Organization for Relief of Suppressed Minorities."

Newbern nodded again. "That's what these kids were hollering, something like that. You know where I can find this Young?"

"No, he said he'd be around even though I told him I didn't want any part of him. I knew I'd be dead if I went into Judge Thrace's court with a Yankee integration lawyer beside me."

Pret gave me a long hard look.

The phone operator, an old civilian with a gimpy leg I remembered dimly as Tippy Somebody, came hobbling across the room with his earphones still on his head, the jack dangling down his front. "Cap'n," he said to Pret breathlessly, "Joe in Six-oh called in. A busload of whites and colored comin' in on County 83, headed this way."

Pret glanced at the sheriff's closed office door and the old man said, "I gave him the report and he told me to give it to you to handle. Joe wants to know what to do, stop 'em?"

Newbern looked at Henry's door again, frowning. "Tell him to pull 'em over and stall the driver with a license and safety regulations check 'til I can get there. Get all the units in that area over there. Tell Joe I'll be right out."

Tippy hippety-hopped away and Pret shook his head solemnly. "That crowd across the street hears about that bus and we've got a mess on our hands."

A mounting hum of voices came from across the street, just audible above the rain. I didn't have to go to the window to know what was happening; the boys had found out about the bus coming in on County 83. Pret cursed under his breath and hurried off, beckoning three or four deputies along with him. I went back to the window and watched the crowd in the courthouse yard dissolve.

The Crackers were heading for their old heaps, not running but walking swiftly with their easy, graceful, sloping stride, splashing through the puddles, stopping the few cars squashing up the street by simply crossing in front of them, ignoring the squawking horns. As the ancient convertibles and pickup trucks got going they swung into line in a ragged parade and went through the red light at Livingston Avenue. I saw the slickered city cop at the intersection fumble his whistle out and raise it to his mouth, then drop it, exactly as I'd have done.

I turned back and looked over at the door of Henry Taggart's office. I wondered how I was going to say what I had to say to the old man who'd been so close to me when I was growing up. Henry had stayed with me four or five days at his river shack after one disastrous drunk and when I was able to get around he'd toted me to A.A. meetings in towns thirty and even fifty miles away trying to find somebody someplace who could convince me I ought to join. He'd sent me to a Miami psychiatrist who was highly recommended as a drunk-curer, then arranged for me to talk to a young Methodist minister 'way to hell and gone up in Virginia who'd had good luck with only-the-best-bourbon lushes like me.

Henry had been the last real friend I'd had, except Miss Elsie, and when I lost him the final collapse had rushed at me like a trailer truck highballing out of a fog.

And now I had to face him with what I'd found out. Or, I didn't have to, not really. I could walk out of there into the rain and drive Theron Charles' Olds back to the hotel. I could get four retreads and have the wiring fixed on my old Ford and drive out of Lindsley and Tangerine County, leaving Coralee in her jail cell and the General and his Committee in full charge. Even the destruction they were bringing might not be as bad as the pain of one old man's broken heart.

I rapped on Henry Taggart's door and before he could ask who it was I turned the knob and walked in. Henry sat at his desk, his massive pearl-handled gun on the green blotter in front of him. He raised eyes that were deadened by failure and remorse and looked at me.

"I've been expecting you, Frank," he said. His voice was as dead as his dull blue eyes. "You see, I had that woman's cell bugged while she was taking a shower."

He turned his head in the big Stetson and looked across the office at the small table where a pair of earphones lay and then turned back to me. He held my eyes in a long, flat stare and then looked down at the gun in front of him.

"Funny how things turn out, ain't it?" he said. "I remember the night Eddie got caught with that little nigra girl I came damn near telling the General he could have my star. And then I said to myself what the hell, Eddie MacWhalen deserved a break and the girl probably got banged plenty, a big-built kid like her. And so I started something that ended up with Jack being murdered. Jack, the boy I thought as much of as I would my own son, and I got him killed."

His hand went out to touch the gun's bright barrel, the gleaming butt. "I guess the only answer is right here, huh?" he asked me. "Or do you hold with the preachers and the doctors, who never had a bellyache or felt a minute's sorrow, that only a coward would do a thing like that?"

5

"You don't want to do anything like that, Uncle Henry."

He considered this erudite statement only briefly before he nodded, slowly, carefully. "Oh, yes I do, Frank," he said seriously, "but not before I make sure the others are going to hell with me—the General and that pretty-boy son of his. I may have set it up for them but they killed Jack Taggart and I can't leave them behind laughing at me."

"You can't just shoot everything right again, Uncle Henry! That's not the way to do it. The law—"

He broke in on me. "I've been the law in Tangerine County all these years and you see what's happened. The law's as rotten as I am, Frank. You can't depend on the law any more. It's old-fashioned, out of date. We twisted it and turned it around to suit ourselves, the General and I, until it got its back broken."

I struggled to find words while he went on, speaking in that softly savage voice. "I just got through calling the General. He was at Eddie's house, the big house they built with the money we all helped cheat you out of, Frank. I told him what I'd heard on the bug I put in that woman's cell. I told him I knew he'd killed Jack because he was getting too close to the murder of that nigra that tried to blackmail Eddie. I said the three of us was one as guilty as the other—maybe me most of all because I really knew what happened and I made myself close my eyes to it. I made myself believe those stinking lies they'd spread around town about Jack and that girl. I was even willing to believe that, Frank, rather than face up to what I'd done."

"I guess if I'd stayed here I'd have believed those stories, too."

He shook his head. "No, you wouldn't. Hell, you didn't believe them when everybody in Tangerine County was telling you they were true. Not even when it gave you an easy out of a lot of trouble, maybe getting your head busted in, you wouldn't believe them."

"Well, I—"

"So I told the General to come in here with Eddie," the sheriff went on steadily. "I told him to come in or I was comin' out there after them."

"Uncle Henry," I said weakly, "you can't do a thing like that. Let me work on Eddie a few minutes. I bet I can get him to admit everything and then we've got them. You don't have to kill them."

He shook his head. "It wouldn't work," he said grimly. "Jack tried it the legal way and look what happened to him. He wanted to break the General and he thought he had him with this Tampa nigra thing and—oh, Jesus."

His wide face crumpled into a million wrinkles and he raised his hands to cover his eyes. "He wouldn't listen, he wouldn't listen," he said, his words muffled. "I tried to tell him to lay off but he wouldn't listen."

He brought his hands down and I saw he was dry-eyed. "Jack must've known I was in with them. He must have known I didn't more than go through the motions of looking into that nigra's disappearance. He as good as told me he knew I was covering up for the Mac-Whalens the last time he talked to me, the last time I saw him alive."

His hand touched the big gun again. "I had my chance to do it the decent way then, Frank. Jack was fairly begging me to say yes I knew the MacWhalens had killed that nigra or had him killed. But I wanted to keep this damned star and I was afraid the General would—"

The intercom box on the desk began scratching and mumbling and then a voice said, "Cap'n Newbern calling you Sheriff."

Then Pret's voice: "Sheriff?"

Henry looked at the wire-mesh face of the box and shook his head slightly. He got up from his chair and for a moment I thought he was going to walk away, turn his back on the duty he'd honored for thirty years. I opened my mouth to say something but he shook his head again, this time as though a gnat were bothering him, and reached out a big hand to the switch. "Go ahead, Pret."

"Sheriff, we got a pretty bad thing out here. Besides this busload of Freedom Riders or whatever the hell they are there's two cars full of reporters and a truck with a teevee camera. We got them all pulled off to the side of the road and so far we've kept the mob off about a hundred yards down the road to the south and maybe seventy yards up the road to the north. They cut around and tried to hit us from the rear. Over."

The intercom whistled and crackled a moment and then Henry pressed the switch down. "How many men you got, Pret?" he asked. "Over."

"Five patrol units besides the four deputies I brought with me. Fifteen of us, counting me."

"You need more?"

"Not so far but we're going to have to move this damn bus somewhere sooner or later. We can't wait it out forever. Some of these Crackers are getting likkered up and that teevee camera has them half crazy to get at it. There's not much light now and there's no way we can keep them from—uh—infiltrating us, I guess you'd call it, once it gets dark."

The box rasped and buzzed while Henry Taggart stood there studying it with a slight frown. I saw him half-nod and reach for the transmitter switch. "Those people inside the bus, still?"

"Yessir, they're trying to sing like the bunch we run in earlier but they look pretty scared, most of them, especially the nigras. They got a right to."

"Where they from, did you find out?"

"The bus has Maryland plates besides the I.C.C. plate but the colored driver says they're from Washington. He's got Maryland and Dee Cee bus driver's licenses."

"Think you can get the bus through with nobody hurt, Pret? Give it to me straight, now. If you think there's a chance of anybody getting hurt I can call the State Road Patrol."

Unless a person were well acquainted with Tangerine County cops he'd never know what that last meant. Ever since the State Road Patrol was started it had been the county's boast that the sheriff department could take care of any trouble without any help from the state troopers. So that explained the surprised indignation in Newbern's voice.

"What do we need with them?" he asked. "You come out here and tell these Crackers to go home. They'll listen to you, Sheriff."

"Not me," Henry Taggart said in a low voice. But he'd neglected to press the transmitting switch so the box just hummed and crackled.

I decided it was time I said something. "You've got to," I said. "Otherwise there'll be all hell to pay out there and when those reporters and teevee people get through with it, Tangerine County will be worse than Little Rock."

He swung toward me, his face showing crimson anger for the first time. "It is anyway, ain't it?" he demanded. His strident voice jeered at me. "Why are you so anxious to keep the world from knowing what Tangerine County is like?"

"Come in, Sheriff," the box squawked. "Over."

"Look, Uncle Henry," I said. "I was born here. I grew up here. Just because I turned into a drunk and got myself run out doesn't mean I don't belong here."

Tangerine County Patrol Car One-one calling Sheriff Taggert do you read me Sheriff over.

"And the people?" Henry asked. "You love all your dear friends and sweet relatives who stripped you clean while you were drunk?

Blanche Humphries who robbed your joint account of enough to buy Spring Bayou for herself? Or Miss Elsie who copied your drunken signature on all those pieces of paper that nearly sent you to Raiford and ten to one forged your name on that damn note they attached your check with? Those are the people you love and want to protect? Or maybe me who knew all these things were going on and looked the other way because I thought it served you right for not listening to me?"

I tried to speak and found I couldn't. "Miss Elsie?" I said finally. "For God's sake, why Miss Elsie?"

Tangerine County Patrol Car One-one calling . . .

"Money," Henry said. "Why else? She handled your bookkeeping, didn't she? When you made out a couple of checks and then admitted you didn't remember writing them, she saw a chance to steal you bad. Later, I think she went in with Blanche on a bigger scale and maybe Bill Carter was in on it, too, I don't know. You still want to keep everybody from knowing what kind of cesspool Tangerine's gotten to be?"

Tangerine County Patrol Car One-one calling headquarters do you read me over.

This is headquarters One-one we read you okay over.

I can't raise the sheriff. Get the sheriff to the switchboard, Tippy. I don't read him at all. Get him quick. Over.

Will do, One-one. Stand by.

"Well?" Henry Taggart asked. I nodded.

"Yes, I do. If what you tell me is true, I figure you owe me, Henry." He stared at me. "Owe you?"

"If you don't go out there and stop what's about to happen, everybody'll blame me. I don't care what happens afterward, the only thing anybody will remember is that when they had that riot out on County 83—the time it got in all the papers and on the teevee and maybe even the government had to send in troops like they did in Little Rock—that nigger-lovin' sonofabitch, Frank Coombs, was to blame."

Someone knocked on the door. "Sheriff? You having trouble talkin' to the captain?"

"I'll tell 'em what really happened, Frank. That's the least I can do—"

"I'm asking this one thing—go out there and straighten things out, Uncle Henry. For old times' sake, when we were good friends. Do this for me."

"Sheriff?" Tippy hollered.

"But I've got the MacWhalens coming in."

"They'll still be here after you fix things out on County 83," I said. "You didn't think they were going to run away, did you? Fix this for me and you can have the General and Eddie to do with what you like. But do this first."

Tippy dared open the door and stuck his head inside. "Sheriff, Cap'n Newbern needs you in a hurry. You best come to the switchboard—your extension must be busted."

The Sheriff kept his eyes fixed on me as though he hadn't heard.

"Go ahead, Uncle Henry. Talk to Pret. Tell him."

He stretched out his hand and depressed the transmitter switch, his eyes still on me. "Be right out, Pret. Tell the boys I'm on my way. Got it? Over."

"Got it," Pret Newbern said jubilantly. "Over and out."

The jangled squawk of the intercom was shut off abruptly, leaving a peculiarly empty silence. Henry reached down and picked up the big pearl-handled thirty-eight and slipped it into the holster on his thigh. "Okay, I'm going out there and shoo those Crackers off so the beatniks and their colored friends can ride into Lindsley." He settled the hat on his head and started for the door.

"You'd better come with me, Frank," he said as he opened it. "I don't know what the General could do if he found you here but he might think of something." He hesitated. "Besides, I want people to see me taking my last ride as sheriff with a friend of mine. It'll make it easier afterwards."

6

Henry didn't talk on the way out and I didn't have anything to say. I sat there beside him and although I thought about the wrongs that the people I'd loved had done me it was only for a few minutes. Maybe because I'd lost them all so long ago—all except Miss Elsie—what Henry had told me didn't pain me as much as it probably should have. As for Miss Elsie—well, she might be harder to forgive than the others because she'd pretended to love me long after they had turned their backs on me. But I found I couldn't even hate her.

"Looks like we're here," Henry grumbled beside me and I looked through the windshield at the crowd gathered in the road ahead. They let Henry slide his big car into their midst, no blinker flashing, no siren growling, no spotlight on, nothing except the bulk of Sheriff Henry Taggart behind the wheel.

The mob welcomed him, grinning, and a couple of them raising their wet hands in greeting. They ganged around and when Henry rolled down the window to let a sweep of hot, sticky air into the air-conditioned sedan, the first man to look in set up a howl of glee.

"You bring him with you, huh, She'iff? You brought the nigger-lovin'—"

"Hold it, Walt," Henry cut in. "This boy's all right. We had him wrong."

Walt, whoever he was, had a long face coated with a heavy bristle that held the raindrops. He opened his mouth in either a snarl or a laugh and showed a wide gap in his upper teeth. "Why, f'crissake, She'iff, he's the sonofabitch that—"

"We had him wrong, I tell you. I'll explain later. Now, let me out of here so we can see what all this is about."

He surged out of the car and stood immense among the rain-soaked mob that crowded around him, all talking at once, ignoring me whom they doubtless would have dragged out of the car and stomped into the mud if Henry hadn't guaranteed my safety. It was enough that the sheriff had said I was okay.

So they forgot me and clamored their complaints at Henry about the goddam nigger-lovers and the N.A.A.C.P. who were fixin' to come in and run the schools and the churches and pretty soon they'd run the whole county if somebody didn't do somethin' about it. They were fixin' to burn the bus, tar and feather the occupants, take down the sonsabitches' pants and geld them right there on the road and let the goddam teevee take a pitcher of that for them Yankee bastards—liken it would make the next ones think twice before they started down to Tangerine County to make trouble.

Henry listened to them all, grave-faced, nodding now and then, never interrupting or trying to hush a single one until they'd all had their say and were reduced to aimless curses. Then he pushed his hat back on his forehead.

"What you boys fixin' to do, get everybody laughin' at us?" His voice was their voice, his drawl theirs, without the least exaggeration to show that he didn't always talk that way.

There was an outraged babel. What did he mean? By God, let any goddam Communist laugh at them and they'd find out quick. Who'd laugh? What was there to laugh about?

The big sheriff turned slowly, lazily, toward the stranded bus with its load of scared black and white boys and girls, and gestured at it. "If I was a north'n do-gooder and I heard practically the whole damn County of Tangerine turned out in the pourin' rain to defend theirselves against a busload of teenagers, I'd laugh. I'd laugh good and loud and I'd say, by jeezus, it don't take much to scare a Tangerine man, does it?"

They'd get the kids out then and burn up the goddam bus is what they'd do and the goddam teevee camera along with it—that'd show 'em.

"It sure would," Henry agreed. "It'd show that crowd in Washington that maybe they'd better send in the army like they did in Little Rock. Busload of kids come through here on their way to Miami, behavin' theirselves even if they come from places where they don't draw the color line like we do, and five hundred full-grown men burn up their bus and beat up on the boys when they try to show their girlfriends they ain't chicken."

Miami? This bus was going through to Miami?

"Well, I don't know for sure," the sheriff acknowledged. "I ain't talked to the driver yet but it looks that way to me. If they weren't, howcome they got this far, howcome they weren't stopped in Humphries County or anyplace else they passed through to get here?" He paused and stroked his chin. "Unless some of them other counties passed 'em through just to dump trouble on us. Kinda hard to b'lieve, though."

It wasn't hard for these Crackers to believe. The enmity of one North Florida county for another has always been a phenomenon. So when Henry Taggart slid in the suggestion that Tangerine's oldtime enemies, them chigger-bitten bastards in Humphries or them sneaky still squealers in Pohachalaxee, could have let these Freedom Riders through just to make trouble for honest Tangerine County folks, it gave them pause.

There was a silence, then the same Walt who had spotted me asked, "You reckon that's what them Humphries County people done to us, She'iff?"

"I don't rightly know *for sure*," Taggart answered. "I only know if we let ourselves get in a mess over this here busload of teenagers it ain't goin' to make 'em unhappy over there."

From somewhere back in the crowd a man, drunker than the rest, shouted, "You sure you ain't turnin' into a nigger-lover yourself, She'iff, liken your neph—"

That was as far as he got. The men standing around him struck quickly, silently, savagely and he was still. Another silence and Walt called: "What you want we should do, She'iff?"

The sheriff stood there, rubbing his chin, pondering the question while the Crackers strained to hear.

"I tell you," he said finally. "Just so's we won't be givin' anybody a chance to have the laugh on us and so's those teevee people won't have no pictures to take, I'd just get in my car and run along home. Teevee people can't take no pictures of County 83 in the rain if there's nobody standin' along the ditch shakin' their fist or nothin'." He pushed his hat a little further back, letting the rain stream down his broad face. "'Course, if you do that, you'll have to trust me to handle it for you. You'd have to leave it up to me to handle the way I see fit. Maybe you boys don't trust me that far?"

These boys had let Henry Taggart handle things for them for more than thirty years and he'd never done them wrong yet. Sure, they'd leave it to him to straighten this thing out. Within a matter of a few minutes the old heaps and their dripping owners rattled off and the road was clear.

Henry started for the bus and I got out of the big car in the rain and followed him. Pret Newbern and a couple of the deputies gave me startled looks, surprised at seeing me there, but I was with the sheriff so it must be okay. When I got to the bus, Henry was standing on the step, talking to the kids very quietly, almost paternally. He told them that if they insisted, they had every legal right to keep on into Lindsley. Once they got there, though, they'd be under the protection of the Lindsley city police force.

"They've got maybe a dozen officers on the force," he said to the emissaries of the Organization for Relief of Suppressed Minorities. "Most of them are pretty good traffic cops but not much else. They've never had any experience with a riot, for instance."

He let that sink in. "I just asked that crowd out there to trust me and they did. They went home. You don't know me but I'm asking the same of you. I promise you people that the thing that started all this trouble, the murder charge against Coralee Preston, is going to be cleared up within the next few hours and that girl is going to go free."

I heard Pret grunt behind me. Inside the bus there was a splatter of young voices and some girl squealed, "We won!"

"So if you go on in to Lindsley," Henry said, "and there's trouble and some of you get hurt—maybe worse—you won't be helping the girl one little bit, you'll likely be hurting her bad. If you turn around and go back, if you'll wait and see if what I've told you isn't the straight story, then you can claim anything you want to. You can say you got that girl out of jail or you can go on the teevee and make speeches and call us Gestapos or anything at all, just so long as you do it someplace else. Now, which is it going to be?"

There was some more talk while a couple of the kids tried to make up for having been so scared by asking jeering questions and making flip remarks about Henry's answers. But all those kids knew from the start what they were going to do. Henry kept his temper although I saw him bite down hard a couple of times and finally a girl in a thick, loose sweater asked for a vote. It was four to one to turn back. The deputies used their powerful hand torches to help the almost tear-fully relieved bus driver turn around without skidding into a ditch.

Just before the bus took off, the kids started singing about never fearing the Gestapo as one of the teevee crew, a tall, heavy-set man with thick glasses who was wearing an honest-to-God foreign corre-spondent trenchcoat, came up to Henry. "That was a fine piece of work, Sheriff. How about a shot of you shaking hands with one of the colored riders? We could set up some lights—"

"No," Taggart said flatly.

"Why not? Nationwide coverage. It would prove that all the sher-iffs down here aren't hard-shell reactionaries."

"Look, mister," Henry said, low and gritty. "Just because I tried to save that crowd from getting hurt or maybe killed don't mean I like 'em well enough to shake hands with 'em. Like 'em? By God, I hate 'em and everything they stand for."

He turned his back on the amazed man in the trenchcoat and strode through the rain toward Pret Newbern's patrol car with the big 11 on its side. He hauled open the door and picking up the radio phone from its cradle he shoved over the butterfly switch with his thumb. "Taggart calling headquarters."

"Come in, Sheriff."

"Has General MacWhalen shown up, Tippy, and is he still there?"

There was a moment's wait. "Nobody's seen him around here, Sheriff."

Henry slammed the phone back into its holder and hunched his shoulders against the rain as he sloshed back toward his car with me trailing him. "We'll go along to Eddie's house," he said. "It's only three-four miles from here. If they're not there we start hunting for 'em."

"They haven't run," I told him. "Not the General."

"They can run as far and as fast as they like but I'll still get 'em," Henry Taggart said grimly.

But Henry Taggart didn't have to chase Brigadier-General Ed-mund Ruffin MacWhalen or his son, Eddie, for at that moment the short-wave radio on the dashboard, the special-channel set, notified the sheriff that a call had just come through from Eddie Mac-

Whalen's home. A nigra servant named Andrew had just phoned that the General was dead, shot through the head with a bullet from a deer rifle, and that young Eddie was bad hurt, and that Missus MacWhalen was upstairs in her bedroom, dead, too, by the same rifle she'd used to kill her father-in-law and nearly kill her husband.

"God damn me," Henry cried. "The phone extension! I thought there was somebody listening in when I told the General everything I knew about his killing Jack Taggart, Laurie's brother!"

Chapter 6

Three days later, after Judge Thrace got through agreeing to the Assistant State's Attorney's motion that the charges against Coralee Preston be dismissed, he called me up to the bench. He peered down over the edge at me out of his pouched eyes for a moment.

"I talked with Henry Taggart yesterday," he said in his squeaky voice. "We talked a long time and he told me everything. A terrible thing."

I didn't say anything.

His jowls flapped as he shook his domed head. "I guess we all had you wrong, eh, Mister Coombs? I guess we all owe you an apology, all of us."

"I don't want any apologies, Your Honor."

He pinched his rosebud mouth between thumb and forefinger. "Well, now, I hope you're planning to stay on here, Mister Coombs. Your family has always stood mighty high in Tangerine County and I'd hoped you'd want to help us—well, repair the damage."

"No, sir," I said. "I'm leaving for Maryland today. The new State's Attorney tells me he won't need me for the trial if Eddie MacWhalen lives and I've refused to bring charges against Miss Elsie or the others. I don't want to stay here a minute longer than I have to."

"Well, now," he said reproachfully. He looked into my eyes and read there what I thought of him and his court and the insults he enjoyed using on the weak and the sinful and he looked away.

Don Tracy

"Next case, Mister Clerk," he squeaked. "Next case."

Bill Carter was waiting outside the courtroom. He tried to say something about blaming himself for not having seen what Miss Elsie was doing but I cut him off with something about my knowing he was as pure as the driven snow and walked away. Chet Leonard was waiting down the corridor with my check and a rather frantic plea that I didn't think for a minute that he'd suspected anything like forgery, did I? I said I didn't care one way or the other, it didn't matter, and then I walked away from him, too.

I went down to the first floor and walked through a lot of hello's and hi's without answering. Outside the courthouse, Hattie May collared me and I had to wait until she got through weeping and blessing me. I finally broke loose from her and started walking down to the Princess.

Judith Williamson was waiting for me on the street just beyond the Lawyers Building. She wore a deep pink dress and it suited her better than any of the others I'd seen her in. I stopped and she studied me for awhile, neither of us saying anything. Finally she asked, "What happens now?"

"I don't know."

"You've got a whole lot of new things to be sorry for yourself about," she said. "Nobody would blame you if you never drew another sober breath. That poor girl, you can think yourself into feeling guilty about that. And of course you can never trust another human being. The people you loved did this to you—how can you ever fall for that old gag about there being true love somewhere in this life for every man and woman?"

"Maybe Laurie was my true love and I didn't see it," I said.

"Maybe," she said gravely. "Right now you must think so but did you ever think it in all the years before this happened?"

"No."

She held out her hand and I felt a folded slip of paper between my thumb and forefinger. "I'm going home," she said, "back to Dunedin. I couldn't stay here, not after this. My address is written down there." One corner of her lovely mouth smiled. "My telephone number, too. I'm quite shameless."

I tucked the slip of paper in my breast pocket. "I'll write you or phone you when I—when I decide," I said.

"I hope you do," she answered earnestly. "I hope you'll make another try at happiness." Her mouth quirked again. "No obligation, of course."

"Of course not," I said. I looked into her eyes with the faint violet tinge. "I'm not making any promises, remember. I just said I'd call you."

She nodded matter-of-factly, then leaned over and lightly kissed me on the mouth, right there on the street for anybody to see. "Goodbye, Frank," she said softly. "Good luck."

"Goodbye, Judith," I said and went on down to the Princess to pack.

Theron Charles had had my car's ignition fixed and four recaps put on in place of the slashed tires. He charged me for them, but he took my check and while I was packing he went to the bank and cashed it for me.

"I wish you'd stay, Frank," he said when I checked out. "After what's happened, this place needs men like you to pick up the pieces. If Tangerine's ever going to be anything again it'll be men like you that'll get us back to where we can look one another in the face."

"No, thanks," I told him. "I've got to get back to Baltimore and take care of my interests there."

My interests—a part-time filling station job and the bill-collecting profession. Some interests.

I shook hands with Theron Charles and Johnbert Allison and carried my bag out to the Ford and took off. I wanted to drive around to say goodbye to Henry Taggart but he'd told me over the phone that he'd rather I wouldn't. He'd handed over his star to Pret pending whatever action the Governor or the grand jury might take and while he was waiting for things to happen he thought he'd go down to the river shack and do a little fishing. Goodbye, take care of yourself, he said and then he'd hung up.

Driving up Jefferson I was conscious of everybody looking at me and a couple of people raised a hand but I kept my eyes straight ahead. I drove slowly, carefully, until I reached the city limits and then I put the Ford up to sixty-five and got the hell out of Tangerine County.

When I crossed the Humphries County line I began looking for Harry Foyles' place. He owed me a drink. I'd been without a drop for a long time and a lot had happened and I could use a drink or three or nine. I had money and all the time in the world; I owed it to myself to collect that drink on the house.

He was alone in his little dump and when he saw me he put on a sort of a smile, not much but I guess it was the best he could do.

"Hi, Frank," he said. "I heard all about it. You sure raised hell back there in Lindsley, didn't you? Did me out of a landlord, too, the old bastard. That's why he was in here that day you stopped in, come to c'lect his ninety bucks. Ninety bucks a month f'r this goddam—"

"You promised me a drink on the house when I was here last," I said.

"Sure, sure." He grinned. He turned and brought down a bottle of Jack Daniels, the best he had, and poured a double shot with a flourish. "Drink up, Frank."

I looked at the booze glowing in the shot glass and I felt its warmth in my belly, the wonderful calm and courage and promise spreading through my body. And then I remembered the night I'd spent in the sweat-soaked easy chair beside the window overlooking the Seaboard freight station. And I remembered the touch of Judith Williamson's mouth on mine.

I shook my head and turned around and walked out.

"What the hell?" Harry Foyles called after me. I didn't answer because I didn't know what the hell any more than he did.

I got in the car and started out again. I kept telling myself that this didn't prove a thing. I spoke aloud and I told Judith not to put any importance to this. I might stop at the next neon sign that said WHIS-KEY or I might keep on past that one and stop at the next or the next after the next. There were never any guarantees.

But as I drove on I forgot about the drink twinkling in the shot glass on Harry Foyles' bar and I remembered the last thing Coralee had said to me. Judge Thrace had just finished telling her that she was free, she could go home, that she wouldn't end her life in Raiford or in a big ugly chair, straining at the straps the electric current had thrown her against, when I felt her tugging at my sleeve.

"You tell the jedge 'at Gibby he stole four packs of filters often me this mawnin' when I went to the showuh," she whispered. "You tell him 'at."

Remembering, I burst out laughing. I was still laughing as I drove on up the road away from Lindsley and Tangerine County.